Runes

BRIANNA MARSING

Order this book online at www.trafford.com
or email orders@trafford.com

Most Trafford titles are also available at major online book retailers.

Printed in the United States of America.

ISBN: 978-1-4269-9679-5 (sc)
ISBN: 978-1-4269-9680-1 (e)

Library of Congress Control Number: 2011917275

Trafford rev. 10/05/2011

 www.trafford.com

North America & international
toll-free: 1 888 232 4444 (USA & Canada)
phone: 250 383 6864 ✦ fax: 812 355 4082

Chapter 1

Have you ever had a dream? A fantastical dream that you so wished would be true? I've always dreamed of dragons, unicorns, faeries, everything that most in this world would tell you to be fairytales, make believe, untrue. I believe otherwise. I know otherwise. I've been to a place where I saw these things, touched them with my own two hands. They're not fairytales, they're real. And they're here, thanks to my cousin and I. It all started about a year ago, with a peculiar bracelet.

My cousin Shaelynn and I sat outside of the mall, sipping cappuccinos while we looked through our shopping bags and enjoyed the cool autumn air. It was one of the few days we had alone. Usually we were busy with different activities, different families, different lives. Even at church twice a week, we did not often get time to spend with just each other. So on a free weekend, I had come to Albuquerque with Shaelynn, and her mom had dropped us off at the mall for a few hours while she went shopping elsewhere.

I looked through the three contents of my bag; two of them were from a gift store, and one of them I had bought at an accessories shop. It wasn't much in the first place as I wasn't much of a shopper, but it really didn't look like much compared to Shaelynn's stuffed bag containing a few shirts, some new earrings and scarves, and a poster or two.

I looked at the box my new dragon statue was carefully stuffed in and wanted to take another peek at it, but I knew that if I took out the packaging I probably wouldn't be able to put it back in the right way, and it would end up getting broken, with my luck. Instead, I took out my bracelet I had bought at the accessories store. Shaelynn looked up from examining her new shirt.

"When did you get that, Liz?" she asked me. "I didn't see you buy it."

"Oh," I answered, "I bought it when you were looking at the necklaces at the back of the store. I saw it at the counter lying there, so I bought it. It was only like three bucks."

"Let me see?" she asked, leaning over the table to take it out of my hand. "Wow," she mumbled to herself, looking at the tiny, ancient-looking runes on every bead. Then, seeing the tag attached to it, she squinted at the odd writing above the price.

"Read that, Liz, I can't make it out." She handed it back to me, brushing a lock of short blonde hair behind her ear. I swiped my long dark blonde hair out of my face; it was down for once, and it was bothering me with the breeze.

I looked at the tiny letters, and my eyes could easily make them out. I read aloud:

"On the full moon shining
Dreams shall take flight.
Back to a place of old,
Wonders shall be seen.
Restore a lost land to return home.
One may be lost, many will fall
Hardships will come, friendships tried.
Defeat the evil one, to close the gap
And a lost land will be restored anew."

"Well, what's that supposed to mean?" Shaelynn asked.

"I don't know," I replied, shaking my head and frowning. "I have absolutely no idea." We both looked down at the bracelet again, and for an instant I could have sworn that the runes flickered with light. I looked up at Shaelynn, but neither of us said anything.

Our examining finished, we went inside a book store and took the escalator up to the second story, where the books for young adults were. I looked over some fantasy novels while Shaelynn glanced around for a minute and then went to find some CDs. I picked up a book that looked good and found a comfy chair and sat down to read.

The next week, on Friday, I met Shaelynn in front of her class when the last bell rang, hauling my change of clothes that I had picked up from my dad's office at the front of the school. We walked out the front door and met her mom, Teri, who picked us up in her car. Teri's short blonde curls bounced back and forth as she moved her head from side to side to talk to Shaelynn in the front and me, in the back seat.

When we got to Shaelynn's house we went straight to her room and dumped our stuff on the bed and took our jackets off. Just when I had moved my bag off of Shaelynn's bed and to the floor in a corner I heard yelling coming up the hallway, and her little brother Caden ran into the room screaming, "Sissy, Sissy!" Shaelynn scooped him up as he blabbered on and on about what he did that day, not even having noticed me.

When he stopped for a breath I put in a small, "Hey, Bubba."

He looked at me for a long moment, and then whispered to Shaelynn, "Liz is here, Sissy." It was not often that I came to her house, and he was surprised to see me there.

"You wanna give me a kiss, Bubba?" I asked him. Shaelynn set him on the floor and I squatted down while he gave me a sloppy, wet kiss on the cheek—then he turned and ran down the hallway, yelling for Teri, saying, "Liz is here, Liz is here!"

Shaelynn grinned in a silent laugh, then turned to her small entertainment center/dresser and popped in a CD. We sat on her bed and started talking about friends and boys and some who were both. Caden ran in again and jumped on the bed, then started bugging Shaelynn, his favorite pastime. Teri called down the hallway for us to come and get a snack, and we got up from the bed and went to the kitchen.

That night we watched a movie with Caden, but halfway through it he fell asleep and Teri put him to bed. While she was busy doing that Shaelynn and I put the movie up and left the TV on for Teri so she could watch the news, then grabbed our jackets and went outside in the cool air. It was just cold enough that we could see wisps of air from our breath issuing from our mouths when we breathed.

It was a full moon tonight, and it lit up Teri's backyard as if the sun were still out. We tried to be quiet coming out the door, but the dog heard us anyway and came running up to the fence of her pen to greet us. We went in the gate and Shaelynn's new hunting dog, Annie, jumped up and down like a pogo stick. She was only a puppy, but she was growing fast. She put her paws on my chest and nearly knocked me over.

"Annie, down!" I said, and Annie got off my chest, but she still followed me around and sneaked licks at my hand. I looked up the moon, slipping the rune bracelet out of my hoodie's pocket, the tag still attached.

"Why'd you bring that?" Shaelynn asked.

"I don't know," I said. "I kind of wanted to show Teri, but I forgot it was in my pocket, and I felt it just now."

"Hmm," Shaelynn said to herself, sitting down, almost to have Annie jump all over her. She quickly got up and we left Annie's pen and returned to the backyard, sitting on a bench.

We sat in silence for a moment, thinking. I stared at the moon then glanced at my cousin. Shaelynn took a deep breath.

"You know what would be really cool?" she asked without looking at me.

"Huh?" I was only half-paying attention to her, looking up at the night sky.

"If all those creatures you read about in books and stuff were real. Like centaurs, unicorns, winged horses, dragons, faeries, stuff like that."

"Yeah," I laughed. "Imagine having a pet dragon in your backyard and a unicorn up the street and you rode a magic carpet to work. But, the winged horse thing would be cool, or the centaur part." I laughed at myself, and Shaelynn smiled. She knew how completely obsessed I was with horses and had ridden my horse a few times before.

"Yeah," she said, laughing, "the centaur part would be neat—but only if he was hot." I glanced at her, and we both burst out laughing.

"You better make sure the faeries don't steal him first, Shaelynn," I told her, and we laughed even more.

Teri opened the back door and popped her head out, trying to keep any moths from getting in. "You kids better get inside before you freeze," she said, then went back inside. We followed a few minutes later. We had a bowl of ice cream, then Teri went to bed and Shaelynn and I went in her room and shut the door.

"Hey Liz," Shaelynn said, sitting on the edge of her bed after putting another CD into her player.

"What?" I asked, sitting cross-legged on her bed.

"What does your bracelet tag say again? Maybe I can make sense of it." I read the small writing at the top of the tag. As soon as I was done Shaelynn was about to say something, but she stopped, staring at the bracelet. I looked down at it while Shaelynn grabbed one of the beads. The runes on the bracelet had started to glow, brighter and brighter, and it nearly filled the room. Then the light in the room started to get brighter, but it wasn't from the bracelet. I looked at the window and saw the full moon through the blinds, and it seemed to get bigger and bigger and brighter and brighter.

Both of us were still clutching the bracelet, staring at the huge full moon. It seemed to pull us in, then there was a blinding flash of light, and Shaelynn and I plummeted and crashed to the ground, rolling end over end down a steep hill until a large bush caught us both.

Unbelievably, I still had the bracelet in my hand. I slipped it on, tag and all, to make sure I didn't lose it. I looked at the bush we were in and the ground under my folded legs. Where were we? I wondered. I looked up at Shaelynn, only to see her staring, wide-eyed, at something just above my right ear. I whipped my upper half of my body around and saw a giant serpent coming straight at us up the slope at an angle. I saw the yellow stripe going down its back before I saw its ugly yellow eyes.

Shaelynn was still staring wide-eyed at it, and I knew she was gawking at its vivid yellow eyes as I had. Her mouth opened to say something. Hurriedly I clamped a hand over her mouth before she could say anything.

I mouthed to her, "Don't make a sound. Shh!" I took the hand away from her mouth as she nodded, and we sat silently together inside the bush, barely breathing.

At the angle the serpent was going, it was not over three feet away from us when it was closest to us, straight up the hill from our bush. It stopped suddenly, looking around up the hill, sucking in air as it tried to catch our scent. It turned its head up the way we had tumbled down the hill and followed our path, disappearing over the top of the hill, and then it was gone.

I waited another minute to be sure it wouldn't come back, then crawled out of the bush, Shaelynn right behind me, and helped her to her feet. We kept on our way down the hill until we reached its base and then walked straight into the forest that awaited us at the bottom.

It wasn't a very thick forest, but it was thick enough that we couldn't see for very far around us. We found a narrow dirt track that wound through the forest, then turned in the general direction the serpent had come from, thinking that if it had already been that way, it would have no interest in going that way again and would continue on in the other direction.

We walked for hours on end, until the sun sank to the horizon ahead of us and then disappeared, leaving darkness in its absence. For fear of losing the path, we stopped in a grassy field not too far from the left side of the trail. Shaelynn and I pulled off our jackets and lay down in the grass just as the moon rose above the trees behind us, a crescent moon as I had never seen before. Its thinnest edge went almost all the way around, more than the usual half-circle I always saw out of my front yard. There was a star to its right, just where the thin edge disappeared. Settling down for sleep, I put my jacket over myself as a sort of blanket and fell into a light sleep.

The next morning, after waking countless times in the night, and I knew Shaelynn did too, I woke with the sun as it peeked over the trees and its light pierced through the branches to settle on my cousin and I. I looked at Shaelynn; she was still sleeping. I quietly got up and slipped my hoodie on.

I took my bracelet off and examined the runes. The rock-like beads seemed clearer and less rubbed-down looking than when I had bought it, as if it were younger and less weathered. I saw one that caught my eye, a spiral with the stick figure of a man in the center silhouetted from the rest. I knew that symbol; I recognized it a Native American symbol for journey. I found another one I barely remembered. It was of a hand with a spiral in the palm—friendship, or companionship.

I didn't recognize any of the others, though one of them looked like two beasts twisted around each other. One of them looked like a dragon from its wings and ropy tail, but the other one I couldn't make out.

I heard a noise behind me and whipped around, but it was just Shaelynn. She blinked from the glare of the sun and then looked around wildly for me. She saw me standing at the edge of the trees, leaning against a trunk. I didn't even remember how I had gotten there. I guess I had wandered when I was looking at the runes, headed for the forest, then had whipped around at Shaelynn and leaned against a trunk. But why was I headed into the forest? I wondered, and then answered myself, I was just wandering, and that was the direction I happened to take.

No matter. I walked over to Shaelynn, who was putting her jacket on. She tried to straighten out her stiff back at the same moment I did; we looked at each other, and then laughed.

"We must be cousins or something," I joked.

"Yeah, or something, huh?" she laughed back, and we continued on our way.

We didn't get very far before there was a sharp cry above and ahead of us, then something blocked the glare of the sun for an instant. What now? I looked up to see what it was, but by the time my eyes found the sun it was gone and I stumbled, half-blind, and I saw Shaelynn do the same beside me.

I stopped trying to find it in the sun and watched its shadow on the ground when my vision cleared, and saw wide wings, a body, four legs, and a tail that tapered down to a tuft at the end. Its shadow was huge, and I realized it must be close. I grabbed Shaelynn's hand and dragged her toward the edge of the forest on my right. I didn't have to drag her very far before she ran on her own; she had realized the same thing at almost the same instant I did.

I saw the creature's shadow off to my side get bigger and bigger, looming over mine and Shaelynn's, and then its shadow overpowered ours. At the same instant I felt talon-like claws reach into my shoulder, piercing through my sweater and scratching my shoulder. The front claws of the talon hooked on my collarbone, and Shaelynn and I were lifted from the ground. I screamed out in pain and helplessness as I saw the ground start to sink away from me as whatever the creature was started to beat its wings harder and harder, trying to get altitude.

Then I saw a flash of tan and black as something leaped out of the trees at us. My first thought was, oh great—now we're going to be fought over for food. I heard Shaelynn shriek as the thing grabbed onto her and pulled her out of our attacker's grasp. Twisting around to see what had happened to Shaelynn, I saw that the thing was a centaur, buckskin in color, the human part male and with black curly hair. No way, I thought.

The creature that still had me suddenly dropped to the ground as it realized that the centaur had stolen one of its meals. I was almost smashed under the weight of its talon as it pushed off from the ground again, releasing its hold on me to take flight over the centaur and Shaelynn.

Forgetting the wound in my shoulder, I stood up and saw the fight about twenty feet to my right. The creature was a griffin, half eagle and half lion, the eagle's part being the front end. It had an eagle's oversized head, talons, and wings, feathers and all. The lion's end started where the feathers ended, about just behind the shoulders and the bases of the wings. It was larger than a normal lion, but had the same tawny color and tuft of fur at the end of the tail, along with the powerful hindquarters. A centaur, and a griffin. This day was getting better and better.

The centaur had just pushed Shaelynn toward the forest when the griffin started its first dive at them. The griffin lunged at the centaur, who reared high and kicked out at the griffin's head with a fore hoof. The griffin's head came back to avoid the blow, and a talon swiped out at the centaur's head. The centaur blocked it with a forearm; he was still badly scratched, although the move did save his head.

Wincing, the centaur lunged forward at the griffin, beating its soft belly with his front hooves. The griffin cried out, then quickly backed off, pumping its wings. It saw Shaelynn and me at the edge of the forest, where I had run to her, and it flew towards us, but the centaur stopped it with a few more kicks. Wounded and beaten, the griffin flew off the way it had come.

The centaur looked at his forearm for a moment and then looked over at us, huddled together. We both whimpered softly at the same instant when he started towards us, but the centaur lowered his head and shoulders and held his hands out, palms up, keeping his horse tail close to his hind legs and his feet low when he took a step. Reading his signs of peace, I straightened up from next to Shaelynn, and then lowered my head as well, accepting his gesture and allowing him to come to us.

He came to my shoulder, a horse's gesture of friendship. We both looked each other over for a second. I saw his amber eyes and jet black hair, the stockings on his legs, his muscled chests (both human and horse), the black line that ran from his withers down his rump to his tail, and his powerful hindquarters.

I glanced out of the corner of my eye and saw Shaelynn gawking at his face, stunned by his body, but most of all, transfixed by his eyes. I made a casual swipe of my hair, swinging my arm in front of her face, snapping her out of it. She blinked, and then stood next to me.

"Thanks," Shaelynn said shyly, trying to meet his eyes. I blushed at my love-struck cousin, but repeated the thank you. I had never really been the one to fall for cute boys, but Shaelynn was. She was constantly going on about this boy or that, and always staring at boys she thought were hot.

"You're welcome," the centaur answered in a rumbling deep voice; Shaelynn just sighed happily, but I was surprised he had answered.

"Since I'm the one who has my head on straight," I started, looking at Shaelynn, then looking at the centaur, "my name is Liz. This is my cousin, Shaelynn."

"I'm Geoff," he answered. Shaelynn sighed again and then collapsed to the ground in a faint, but I caught her halfway and eased her to the ground. Geoff looked at her, and then scooped her up off the ground and put her on his back, with some of my help. He told me to climb on behind her, to make sure she wouldn't fall off. I got on uneasily, then asked if I could move her up so I could sit up further, where I was more comfortable. He warned me not to rub very many of his hairs the wrong way, and I tried not to.

It was odd, not having any reins or a piece of mane to hang on to, but having a bare back in front of me. I gripped his horse stomach with my legs to make sure I wouldn't slip, then put one hand on Shaelynn to hold her, but wondered where to put the other one. Geoff sensed my discomfort, and guessing what I wanted, took my hand and wrapped it around his human middle. I blushed horribly, but I knew he couldn't see me.

"You often ride horses, then?" Geoff asked.

"Yeah," I said, out of breath as he took off at a trot and settled to a canter. His motion was smoother than any horse I had ridden, even at the usually bone-jarring trot.

"I noticed how you sit and grip me with your legs. You have a very good seat, if I must say so. Your back is straight, your hands steady, and your hips moving with my motion." I blushed even harder at the compliments, but silently thanked one of my other cousins, who had taught me to ride when I was nine.

"Geoff?" I asked. He tilted his head to the side to tell me he had heard. "Where are we?"

"Partaenia."

"Where?"

"Partaenia. You are not familiar with it?"

"No, I've never heard of it before."

"Oh, I see." He remained silent, and I looked down at Shaelynn. She was starting to come to, but still wasn't completely awake. Turning my gaze from her, I looked around at where we were going, as if I might recognize something, even though I knew I wouldn't.

"Hey Geoff?" I asked, and he cocked his head for an instant in acknowledgement. I went on, "Where are we going, anyway?"

"To my grove," he answered.

"Your what?"

"My grove—my home. Where I live."

"Oh," I fell silent, looking around as we went, knowing my mind was storing little landmarks in my memory so I could know where I was the next time we went here.

Just as Geoff started to slow, Shaelynn snapped awake, and it took a lot for me to not let her fall. I helped her to straddle Geoff as she looked around her, and then her eyes came to rest on the back of Geoff's head.

I tugged her ear to snap her out of her daze, and pointed ahead when she turned toward me, scowling. She looked in the direction I was pointing and her jaw dropped in amazement, seeing Geoff's grove.

And what a grove it was. Everywhere there were fruit trees in blossom, even though back at home it was starting to turn to winter. The bright blossoms made the whole grove seem alive, as if it were more than just trees. The pink petals that softly fell caressed us for as long as they could before they had to continue on their way downward to the ground, as if they were actually alive. They all fell only on Geoff at first, and then slowly more and more of them fell on Shaelynn and me, as if they were unsure about us, but decided we were all right if we were with Geoff.

In the center of the grove was a little shack with smoke coming out of the chimney. The door was much too small for Geoff, and I wondered what else was here. He let us off at the door and then went around to the side of the house, motioning for us to go inside before he disappeared around the corner of the shack. I looked at Shaelynn, and then pushed the door open.

I heard bustling around inside, and it sounded like it was coming from a small kitchen. I saw a flash of pale skin and white fabric, then whatever it was moved out of the way. I heard another noise, and then heard Geoff's voice.

"Tayna, I'm back," Geoff said, and I heard one of his hooves strike wood as he stepped on the floor of the shack. Wondering how he had gotten inside, I went to the doorway of the kitchen, Shaelynn close behind.

Geoff was halfway through a wide doorway, facing a tall woman with snow-white hair, an off-white shirt, and light tan pants, with tan shoes. There was a quiver full of arrows strapped to her back, with a curved bow over one shoulder lying alongside the quiver, and a horn tied to her waist. She wore her long hair half up, half down, tied with a small silver string. Geoff gestured to us silently, and the elf woman turned toward us, her hand reaching behind her back for her bow until she realized it was only Shaelynn and I.

"Welcome, humans, to the grove!" she greeted us warmly, her arms opened wide. Shaelynn was the first to run into her embrace, accepting the gesture gratefully. I followed, and Tayna's long, graceful arm was wrapped around my shoulders. Warmth and happiness spread through me like a building cloud, and I looked and saw that Shaelynn was experiencing the same sensation.

Tayna looked first at Shaelynn, then at me, a smile on her face. She gave us one last squeeze, and then let us go. I looked at Geoff, and saw that he was smiling with satisfaction. He must have known what Tayna had done. Whatever it was, I felt a hundred percent better. I looked down at my shoulder, but the blood on my shirt was gone. There were no marks on my shoulder where the griffin had grazed my skin with its talons.

Shaelynn, for once, wasn't gawking at Geoff, but was looking around the small shack. She fingered a delicate and beautiful plate, picked up and examined a few small handmade figurines, and explored all the cabinets.

I followed her for a few minutes, then stopped when she returned to the kitchen and then went past it to a bedroom. I looked to Geoff, who had been watching her, and he met my gaze. He sucked in a breath and looked at me in a way that told me he was about to ask me something, but Tayna interrupted him, whether or not on purpose I do not know.

"Geoff, would you go and get some water from the stream, so I can make tea?" She was about to hand him a bucket when I jumped in and took it. She looked at me funny, and I stuttered out a quick response.

"I—I'll go with him, if you or he doesn't mind." I paused, waiting for her answer, and then she smiled and nodded her head. I followed Geoff out the door.

When we were out of Tayna's extraordinary hearing, Geoff looked at me quizzically. I nodded my head, allowing him to ask his question.

"How did you end up here?" he asked, turning left into the blossoming apple trees. I took a quick look at him, knowing he still noticed it anyway. The way he said it; he knew Shaelynn and I didn't belong here. I wasn't sure if he knew whether or not we were from a different time altogether, or if we were from some distant land.

I decided that if he saved our lives, he deserved to know who we were. I told him about how I had come across the bracelet, reading the words on the tag on a full moon, how we wound up here, the giant snake (turns out it was a basilisk), spending the night in the forest, and about the griffin, until Geoff had showed up.

All the time he stood quietly next to the small stream that curved through the outer edge of the grove, listening intently. He nodded his head every once in a while, or his eyes would dart to the side and glance quickly at something, but his eyes would always return to my face, seemingly searching it as he watched me talk.

When I was finished he was silent, still looking at my face, his eyes darting around, taking in every feature. He continued until I pushed my eyebrows together and cocked my head to the side, asking him what he was doing. He shook his head, smiling, then looked all around.

"That's quite a story," he said.

"Yeah," I said, looking down. "I kind of have an idea of how to get home but I'm really not sure."

"How's that?" he asked, looking at me. I was about to read the tag myself again, pulling it out of my pocket, but I thought the better of it and gave it to him to read. He went through it quickly and then asked, "Where did you say you got this?" His voice was low, and it gave me the chills. I told him, and he looked at it again.

"Zathos," he whispered quietly.

"What?" I asked, confused.

"Zathos." He turned to me. "The sorcerer king. The worst thing that ever happened to our land. He must want you here, so he sent the bracelet with the spell on the paper, so you would end up here."

I thought about that for a moment, then answered, "What I'm wondering is if we were sent back in time, or to a different world. Because everyone knows about centaurs and elves, and basilisks and stuff, but we have no proof that any of you ever existed."

"Really?" he asked. "Why?"

"I don't know. Ancient peoples have carvings and old, old stories about centaurs, goblins, unicorns, dwarves, elves, basilisks, dragons, and all sorts of creatures, but no one has been able to prove that any of them ever existed. Everyone thinks they're not real; even I kind of did, until now."

"You did not think we existed?" he asked incredulously.

"I knew there had to be a reason every culture in the world had some kind of creature that resembled other creatures on opposite sides of the world, and how we knew so much about them, but no, I didn't think any of them were real."

"What kinds of creatures did the different cultures have in common?" he asked.

"Well, it was usually dragons, but the Romans and Greeks had all kinds of carvings about centaurs, fauns, and giant animals of some kind, and a lot of cultures believed that some kind of sprites and faeries existed."

"They do. We have wood sprites here in the grove, but they seldom come out. Tayna can get them to come out, and I can too sometimes, but I do better with water sprites."

"Really?" I asked. "Can you get some of them to come out now?"

"Well, I don't know about wood sprites, but I can try the water ones." He watched as I nodded my head quickly, and then stepped closer when he gestured for me to. I leaned on his shoulder and peeked around the front of his chest as he began to sing.

It was a song with no words, or really even a beat. It just flowed together, different pitches, ranging from soft to semi-loud, to soft again, and from a higher pitch to a low, deep one, back up to somewhere in the middle. It sounded almost eerie, but beautiful. It reminded me of a small stream gently rolling down a hillside, with a few rough spots here and there.

My eyes were drawn to a spot in the stream in front of me, where a patch of light was collecting, some of the spots apart from the rest. Then, one by one, little heads stuck up out of the surface of the water. I gasped at the sight of them, and most of them ducked under the water again. I looked to Geoff, who nodded his head, still singing the song.

I stayed quiet as more heads poked up, then a few came up out of the water, slowly flapping small wings that still dripped water. They were a really light blue in color and almost transparent, seemingly having lines of light dancing around their edges, like water. Their hands were webbed and their feet looked like flippers.

Geoff held out a hand, letting one rest on the end of his finger, then another landed on his forearm, another in the crook of his arm, another on his shoulder, and more and more until they started to cautiously land on me too, once I held out a shaking finger. One of them landed on my head, lying on its stomach to peer over my forehead at my face.

The sprite sitting on Geoff's finger had turned to look at me, as most of them had. He sang the same kind of song to Geoff, and it sounded like a rushing creek babbling over the rocks. Geoff answered in the same song, making it sound like a gentle pool of water in a slow moving river.

Then all of them joined in Geoff's song in their own pitches, making beautiful chords throughout the song until one by one, they all came to land on me until I was covered with them, then as one they pushed off gently and flowed back into the water, disappearing beneath the surface.

The song stayed in my head as Geoff and I walked silently back to the shack to give the water to Tayna. When we were in sight of the shack, I looked at Geoff, who was walking easily and relaxed through the blossoming trees that whispered to us.

"Geoff," I started, and he turned to me, telling me I had his attention. "You can tell Tayna our story, if my cousin hasn't already. She deserves to know who she has staying in her house."

"She already knows, more than likely. She would have heard it from the trees."

"The trees?" I asked, taken aback.

"Aye. The trees near the stream love to gossip, and they would have sent your story to her through the rest of the trees by now. That's how she gets most of her information, is from the trees, especially from the ones by the stream. And she doesn't just get information from the trees in the grove, either. She can get messages from trees almost anywhere, except for the places where Zathos has turned them to his side."

I shook my head, confused. He sighed and smiled, knowing that I really hadn't understood all he had said.

"Can you hear the trees whispering to us now?" I nodded. "Listen for a moment and see if you can't make them out." He stopped, watching me while I did what he said. It grew very quiet for a moment, and then the trees started up for us again.

A human, in the grove! Welcome, but we must wonder why you were sent here. Why does Zathos want you here? It must not be good. But you are with Geoff, and Tayna. They consider you trustworthy to have you here. Watch yourself, for only bad things happen when Zathos is involved with good people. Oh, the things he does! He . . .

Geoff waved a hand, murmuring for them to hush, and then he looked at me. I had heard the trees talking almost a mile a minute, sounding like a bunch of old ladies at a tea party. I nodded, telling him I had heard them.

"That's how Tayna gets her information, and how she probably knows your story by now. The trees pass it from one to another; that's how she can get news from trees hundreds of miles away. But Zathos has turned entire forests to his side, and the trees have turned dark. If he wants you here for a reason, it cannot be good, like the trees said. So you and your cousin had better do as they say and watch your back, or he'll find a way to get you.

"But you don't have to worry here. The trees on the edge of the grove don't let anything evil in, so you are safe as long as you are here."

He turned and walked to the other side of the shack to give the water to Tayna. A part of me wanted to stay here because of Geoff and Tayna and how beautiful it was here, but another part of wanted to stay here simply because Geoff had said it was safe and we couldn't be harmed. Before the trees could start talking to me in the silence again, I opened the front door and went inside.

Shaelynn was lying on her stomach on the floor, an old book carefully opened. She was flipping through its pages, skimming through the words. It seemed to be like a history book, full of pictures of odd creatures that I had never even imagined before, with lots of text. Here and there I saw dates and pictures of kings.

She looked up from the floor as I heard a hoof strike wood and Geoff's voice. It was answered by Tayna's exasperated voice, wondering where we had been. Then her voice dropped, and I knew she was talking to him about where we had come from.

"Liz, you have to see this book," Shaelynn said, taking me out of my thoughts. "It's the history of this world, starting with the first king. It doesn't say whether or not this is Earth, but we're not in our present time. This book was published in 9879 AM—After Man—and Tayna said it's still like a hundred and twenty years old. That means we're in 9999 AM."

"So?" I asked. "We're here 9,999 years after man appeared. Yeah, we're a long time, but we still don't know if this is some other planet that we reach in the future, and we went forward."

"Or, this is Earth," she retorted, "and we're a long ways back in time, before even the countdown in B.C. started."

I stuck my tongue out at her, and she stuck hers out at me too. We both cracked up laughing at the same time, causing Tayna and Geoff to peek around the corner of the kitchen curiously. I sat down cross-legged next to her and we looked through the book together.

Chapter 2

WE SPENT ABOUT A MONTH or so with Tayna and Geoff exploring the grove, helping Tayna and Geoff, and learning from them. Tayna taught us some elfish dishes that we could make at home if we wanted to, and Geoff taught us different things here and there, like skinning a rabbit, cooking meat, catching fish in a net, and fixing things up around the shack.

When the leaves had just started to change color Tayna and Geoff led us out of the grove, now full of fruit on the trees, into the forest to a small clearing.

While Tayna had us turned away from Geoff and facing the woods, I heard Geoff quietly walking around behind us, then he approached. Tayna turned us around, and Geoff held out two quivers for Shaelynn and I, full of arrows, and two beautiful bows. We took them, astonished at the gift.

Tayna had moved away while we were looking at our new bows and returned, holding two lumps of cloth in both hands; both of them were tied with a string, but one was tied with a strong strip of leather, and the other with a silver string not unlike Tayna's that she used to tie her hair. She gave one to me and the one with the silver string to Shaelynn. I opened mine after Shaelynn, and found a new pair of pants, a blouse, and a pair of shoes, all of them in grayish blue colors. I looked at Shaelynn's, hers different shades of light brown.

Simultaneously, Shaelynn and I ran to Tayna and gave her a hug, then gave one to Geoff also. They smiled as we thanked them, looking at each other. Tayna silently took our new clothes while Geoff helped us put our quivers on.

"Now," Tayna said, returning from setting our clothes down on a rock, "we'll teach you how to shoot." She pulled her own bow out of her quiver that she wore everywhere, and I saw that it was milk white, decorated with silver carvings.

For almost three hours we spent the rest of the evening learning to quickly shoot, pulling the bow and one arrow from the quiver, nocking the bow, and in one movement pulling it up, drawing the string back, aiming, and firing, and of course, hitting our target. For today we used blunt arrows that didn't have the tips sharpened yet so we wouldn't ruin good arrows by hitting something too solid.

Shaelynn turned out to be a better shot than me, and easily learned how to shoot almost as good as Tayna, in my opinion. As for me, I had a harder time of it just getting the arrow to fly. Time and time again it would either stick to my fingers or simply fall off the bow. I was finally hitting my target at a good enough range by the time it was getting dark.

The next day Geoff went outside with me to help me shoot while Shaelynn stayed inside with Tayna, learning how to cook different things. We went to the same clearing again, and spent half the day learning how to shoot better.

Back at the shack, Tayna was cooking dinner for everybody, and at the same time, teaching Shaelynn. They made roast rabbit cooked with apples and mint leaves, cooked a special spiced root, and made a soup of potatoes, celery, more roots, and water with a stone in it for flavoring, Tayna said.

When everything was cooking and they could take a breath, Tayna took Shaelynn outside for some fresh air. They walked a ways into the grove where an old shed was, and Shaelynn helped Tayna look for something.

"It looks like an old rusted pot, but it's very useful," Tayna said, digging through a wooden chest.

"Like this?" Shaelynn asked, leaning over a bucket full of odds and ends. When Tayna turned to look, Shaelynn picked it up by its handle, using only one hand. It was rusty, all right, and full of dirt and cobwebs.

"Tayna, we're not going to use this to cook, are we?" Shaelynn asked, uneasy. Tayna laughed.

"No, darling. You are! It is my gift to you, when you are on the road. Come here, let me show you." Tayna walked past Shaelynn, who was still holding it by its one handle. Tayna stopped and turned around, looking at Shaelynn.

"It's not going to bite you. Come now, and I'll show you how it works." Tayna walked off and Shaelynn followed at a trot, though she still held the pot a good distance away from her.

They went on until they found the stream, where Tayna quickly dipped it in. She picked it back up, full of water, and handed to Shaelynn.

"Watch," she said.

Shaelynn studied the contents as they began to swirl, slowly at first and then faster and faster. All of the rust from inside the pot leapt up and settled to the ground, then the dirt rose up from it, and then small particles that Shaelynn guessed were from the water. In under two minutes, she held a gleaming pot full of clear, clean water.

"Drink it," Tayna said, still watching Shaelynn. Shaelynn hesitated, then tipped the edge of the pot to her mouth and drank the water inside. It was the best tasting water she had ever had, and it seemed to rejuvenate her. She drank another mouthful and another, then passed it to Tayna, who also drank from it.

Tayna started toward the house again, and Shaelynn followed her, wanting an explanation, but she didn't get one until she asked.

"Tayna?" Shaelynn asked. Tayna cocked her head to the side for an instant, just long enough that Shaelynn noticed. She went on, "What was that about? I mean, what just happened?"

"The pot has a gift—to make anything that goes into it clean. It must like you, though. Normally it will clean the inside for cleanliness, but it will usually be stubborn and leave the outside of it as dirty as it ever was. But it cleaned itself for you, so it must like you. Like I said, it is my gift to you—use it well."

"Now," she said as they neared the door of the shack, "I can smell that rabbit, so what do you say we check up on it?"

Meanwhile, I was finishing up with Geoff. I could certainly shoot better; the arrow flew every time now, and I was getting closer and closer to the target, though I still had a stray shot every once in a while. The sun had already started towards the horizon, but we still had almost an hour before it was dark.

Geoff stopped me when I finally hit the target, closer to the center than I had ever been. As I put everything back into the quiver on my back, Geoff went to the rock where he had put his own bow. I watched as he stooped behind the rock, and pulled out two wooden swords.

He turned, sensing me watching him, and suddenly threw one of the swords through the air to me. Out of instinct, my hand reached up to grab it—I snatched it out of the air, by its handle, right side up. I started at my hand as Geoff smiled.

"Take your quiver and bow off; let's see how you are." I slowly took my quiver off my back and set it on the ground next to me, then lited my bow over my head and laid it in the dirt, watching him the whole while. As soon as I had straightened, he advanced on me, swinging his wooden sword wide. I met it halfway and pushed it away from me, using my own sword.

"Very good!" he said. "Have you ever fought with a sword?"

"No!" I said, surprised at my own self. He tried the other side, going wide again, and I blocked it again, then advanced on him. He stumbled backward, but blocked it all the same.

"Well, I must say," he said, going straight in. I thought for a split second, then blocked it and pushed it to the side, weakening his grip for an instant. I took that moment to go at him, but he quickly recovered his grip and easily knocked my sword out of the way.

"You're a natural," he said, out of breath.

"Thanks," I said, also out of breath. I went at it again, and gave some trouble, but to no effect. As soon as he had blocked my blow he brought his sword in, pushing it up against my neck, gripping my hand that held my sword.

He smiled, then backed off. He let me recover for a minute and then said, "Don't think of the sword as a tool but as an extra length of your arm. It is a part of you, not separate from you."

He took a step forward and slowly brought his sword toward me again. I retaliated quickly, fiercely knocking it away. He shook his head, then slowly brought his sword in again.

I also brought my sword in again, and it turned into a slow series of strike, block, strike, block, and so on. He'd bring his sword in, I'd block it, then bring mine in on him. We went back and forth like that for some time, until the sun finally started to sink below the horizon.

Geoff hid the wooden swords behind the rock again, then picked everything up and let me up on his back for a ride home (one thing to remember, only get on a centaur's back when he gives you permission to).

By the time we reached the shack and had gone inside, my arm was already starting to get sore, and I knew Geoff would want me to practice tomorrow. I didn't say anything through dinner, though it wasn't hard not to. The food was so good that nobody talked until they started getting full.

Geoff leaned back, resting his elbows on his wide horse back. He sighed, then watched us finish our meal one by one. When everyone was leaning back in their own chairs, the conversations started.

Tayna turned toward me at almost the same instant the Geoff asked Shaelynn what they had used in the stew. When she started to talk about some root and a stone or something, I looked to Tayna.

"How did your practice go today?" she asked me.

"It went well—my arrow flies now," I said, and we both laughed. I caught my breath, then went on, "It hits the target as well, and almost on the bull's-eye."

She nodded in approval, and was silent for a moment. I heard Shaelynn telling Geoff about something that had happened at the stream.

"Did Geoff teach you anything else new?" Tayna asked, and we both smiled, knowing she had heard it from the trees.

"Yeah, he started teaching me how to fight with a sword, though they were just little wooden ones."

"I heard that even he considered you talented. A natural, even."

"Yeah, he did. He said I was good, even though he's a lot better than me." We laughed, and I rubbed my shoulder.

"Are you sore?" she asked, and I nodded. "Well, that will be better. After everything is done this evening, come in my room and I'll give you something that might help." I nodded, and we sat for a moment, listening to the murmur of Geoff's and Shaelynn's voices, not trying to make out the words.

"I'd like to practice with you sometime, if you'd like," she said.

"You can swordfight?" I asked.

"Yes. Archery and cooking aren't the only things I'm talented at. Geoff and I practice all the time, or we used to. Back at my village, I used to battle the boys—and win."

"Your village?" I asked.

"Yes, my elfish village. I haven't lived here with Geoff all my life, you know." She stopped, remembering a time far away, a lifetime for humans. "It was in a valley in the mountains, steep hills on both sides, but with a river running in the bottom and trees next to the river.

"I lived by the river, with my father. He was a great man, known for some battle he had fought before I was born. Then men moved from their low valleys in the flats into the mountains, bringing with them rage and death. My village survived, but most of the elves were killed, the rest scattered.

"My nanny took me out of the village two days before it happened; I didn't want to go. My father was staying behind to fight. I was only a hundred thirty-seven. I didn't understand.

"My nanny and I traveled for some time with another elf who escaped with us. He made me my bow, and taught me how to use it well, as well as how to fight, with swords or fists, and how to survive on my own. Then my nanny died, and he and I traveled into these forests. I found Geoff, during a small battle that occurred in a human town; the elf died. Geoff and I retreated into the forests and found the grove, already with the small shack and protective spells."

All this time she had been staring blankly into space, and Geoff and Shaelynn had stopped talking to listen. When she was done she snapped out of her trance, looking around at all of us watching her. She blushed and looked down at her lap.

"Well, it's time to get ready for sleep, ladies," Geoff said, leaning forward and picking up plates to start clearing the table. We all grabbed something and headed for the kitchen, putting the dishes in a wooden tub they used for a sink.

I watched Tayna as she warmed water over a fire outside to put in the tub for washing the dishes. She stared into the flames, still thinking about her past. I thought about what she had said. "I was only a hundred thirty-seven . . ." I wondered how she figured that, going through everything I knew about elves.

Then I remembered something I had read in a book: elves took forever to age. Old for them was at least a thousand years, maybe more.

A dying age was around two thousand years. To me she looked only thirty, maybe younger, but in elf years she was probably four hundred or so years old.

She looked up from the flames, sensing me watching her. She smiled a little and gestured for me to sit down next to her, and I did so. She picked up a stick and poked the fire, seeking something to do. After a bit of thought she put it down again, quickly blowing air out her nose, making a sound like she was trying to convince herself of something.

"Remember the elf I said traveled with my nanny and I and took care of me after she died?" I nodded. She sighed again, then went on, "I was with him when he died. It wasn't really a small battle. We were ambushed—by Zathos and his men." I gasped, and she ignored it.

"We were in a forest; it was dark. We were going to stop soon, but we couldn't find a tree to sleep in. Zathos was just starting to rebel against the king and had gathered followers. He knew that elves supported the king—and saw us as open targets.

"We were walking when he—Barg, the elf—just dropped to the ground, right next to me, an arrow protruding from his chest. Right through his heart." Her voice grew cold, her face hard. She started stonily into the flames.

"They all came from the trees, shrieking and yelling. I was on the ground next to Barg, but he was gone. The look in his eyes—I still see it in my sleep. They grabbed me, bound my wrists in front of me, gagged me. I screamed, and they hit me. They ripped my clothes from me, and took my weapons.

"Barg they strung up, by his ankles. They tossed the rope over a tree branch, and lit his body on fire. I watched him burn and heard their laughter. Then they turned on me. I screamed again, and Zathos, young then, slashed out at me with his knife; I still have the scar. That was when the centaur came. He was young, but he did his best." She sniffed, remembering.

"He created enough of a distraction that I ran, and got away. They found me gone and turned on the centaur, saying that he would replace the fun they would have had with me. They bound his wrists behind his back and knocked him unconscious, then lit a fire.

"Zathos shackled his legs together, then they waited till he woke. He tricked them in his own way and did not move till he was fully awake, then lunged to his feet, kicking some of them away with his hooves, even though they were shackled.

"I was standing behind a tree, watching, when Zathos picked up my bow and nocked it, then let it fly. It struck the centaur in his middle, on his left side. He staggered backward as another one struck his stomach. Then he turned, and he saw me behind the tree. The look on his face—it was the same as Barg's.

"Then Zathos—the centaur had paused in his walk backwards, standing on his hind legs. Zathos grabbed one of the other men's spears, and—" Tayna choked, shaking her head, tears streaming down her cheeks.

"It's okay," I said, reaching for her shoulder. She leaned away, sobbing.

"He plunged it into his horse chest, through his heart," she choked out. "He . . . he trapped the centaur's spirit here. He was never able to find rest for what he did for me." She sobbed harder, leaning into me. I cradled her, not knowing what to do. I was never good at these things, Shaelynn was. She should be the one here, not me. I had no idea what to do to comfort her. We sat together for a long time, until eventually she stopped crying.

"Well, this water is warm enough." Tayna got up and lifted the skin of water from over the fire and went inside, wiping her eyes and sniffling. I sat outside for a moment, listening to the sounds of work inside, then got up and joined everyone else.

That night, I told Shaelynn what Tayna had told me by the fire. We were in the sitting room on the floor, where we slept every night in blankets that Tayna and Geoff had loaned us.

We had been far from sleep as soon as we had laid down, so we had rolled over on our stomachs and talked. She listened to Tayna's story quietly and without interrupting, then sat and thought for a moment after I was finished.

"That's really sad," she said, looking down at her hands.

"Yeah," I said, sighing.

"But why would Zathos trap the centaur's spirit here, instead of just killing him?" she asked.

"I don't know," I said. "Maybe just because the centaur had caused her to escape. Maybe it's just Zathos. Maybe . . . I don't know. You could go on forever." I rolled to my side and pretended to be asleep, the same questions racing through my mind, all of them unanswered. Shaelynn stared at my back for a moment, then rolled to her side too. Briefly I remembered that Tayna was going to give me something for my aching shoulder. Oh well.

We woke one morning another several weeks later before it was even light, Tayna shaking us both awake. She was muttering to herself about something, but I could only hear snatches of the trees, and something coming.

"Pack your things, hurry!" She said once she had our attention. I jumped out of my sheets, Shaelynn right behind me, and we started to gather everything we had, which wasn't much; most of it was the things Geoff and Tayna had made for us. Tayna had gone to hers and Geoff's bedroom; I heard him mumble something to her as she woke him up too.

Tayna half trotted out of their room and down the hall, then disappeared into the kitchen when she saw we were doing as she asked. I heard her drop something and curse as it shattered, then Geoff was going into the kitchen to help once he, too, saw that we were packing. They spoke quietly for a moment, but low enough that we couldn't hear.

Geoff came into the sitting room again and gathered our weapons for us.

"Are you warm enough at night?" he asked. We both hummed our agreement, still looking for things that were lying around.

"Take the blankets then. You'll need them. Shaelynn, when you're done, go into the kitchen. Tayna needs your help." She quickly rolled her blankets and tied them on top of her pack, then went into the kitchen.

I was just finishing rolling my blankets too, when Geoff quietly cleared his throat. He had gone to his bedroom and back and was holding a belt, a sword and sheath attached to it. I gasped, taking it in my hands. The handle was a plain black and the sheath and belt made of simple leather, but the blade was sharpened and gleaming from the small light from the kitchen.

"It should fit you; use it well, and never out of anger. Remember that. Patience, never anger."

"You do stupid things when you are mad," I said with him, and he smiled. "I know, Geoff. You taught me well." He pulled me into a tight hug just as Shaelynn and Tayna came out of the kitchen. She saw the sword in my hands and gasped, and I looked inquiringly at the pot she held in her own hands.

Tayna pulled a folded piece of old parchment from a pocket, then spread it out on the floor for Shaelynn and I to see. It was a map of the land, with the forest and the grove at the very bottom left corner.

"According to your spell," Tayna said, moving her finger over the map, "you need to find Zathos. Go here." Her finger landed on a spot at almost the opposite end of the map. "I don't know what exactly you're supposed to do, but you're bound to find out along the way. Liz?"

"Hmm?" I asked, still looking at the map.

"Geoff's told you about dark parts of the forest. Be sure to stay away from them. Geoff can take you as far as the forest road, and you'll go west from there. Stick to the road and you should be okay. Now, Shaelynn?"

"Yeah?" she asked.

"I've told you about wild foods and evil beasts, right?"

"Yes, you tell me about them all the time."

"Remember what I told you. Don't trust anybody or anything, not even if they prove themselves to you. Stay away from anybody who gives you a bad feeling, no matter how nice they look. Zathos and his followers have been known to deceive even the greatest of creatures."

"I've packed you food that you can eat right away and food that you can save for a while, and Geoff will give you extra arrows. There's some flint, metal, and tinder in your pack already, Liz, and Shaelynn, I put some herbs and things in yours."

"But why are we leaving?" I asked.

"Oh, I'm sorry. I heard this morning from the trees that there's a beast Zathos has released on the land, headed straight for here. Even the spells on the grove can't hold it back well enough. I don't know what exactly it is, but I'll send word through the trees if I ever do. Just remember to listen, Liz. Now, you must be off by dawn, so hurry, hurry!"

Geoff went outside and Tayna went back to the kitchen, while I buckled the sword to my waist and Shaelynn tied her pot to her pack.

We both put our quivers on at the same time, and both of us shouldered our packs. I saw her eyeing my sword, just before she caught me looking at her pot.

"Why'd he give you that?" she asked.

"Why'd she give you that?" I asked at the same time. Shaelynn laughed.

"Go ahead," I said, gesturing at her.

"It's a spelled pot. It cleans anything that goes into it, like water or something." She tapped it, looking at my sword. "You?"

"Geoff taught me to swordfight. We just used wooden swords, but I guess this one serves me better than a wooden one." She nodded, smiling.

Tayna came in from the kitchen, a handful of food in her arms.

"Here's your breakfast," she said, handing a roll to Geoff as he came in. "You'll get the rest of yours when you return." He smiled at her, then handed us both a handful of arrows; we put them in our quivers. Once they were in, we followed Geoff out the door.

"Get on," he said when we were outside. "And hang on." We gave Tayna a quick hug and then got on Geoff's back. He took off at once at a run, Shaelynn hanging on for dear life behind me. Her grip tightened around my waist as Geoff leaped a wide creek and landed easily on the other side. I turned to look at Shaelynn; she giggled.

We ran and ran, until Geoff started to slow. The sun had come up, but there was no road in sight. I started to ask, but Geoff held up a hand for silence. He walked forward, carefully picking up and setting down each hoof.

Heads swinging side to side, we finally saw a clearing ahead of us: the road. There was nothing in sight, but still Geoff was quiet. He stopped at the edge of the trees. He listened for a moment, and we could hear a creaking sound, and voices. Then we heard hooves, and a wagon pulled by a large horse came into view down the road. They were heading west.

A man sat on top of the wagon, dressed in bright but tattered clothes. He was talking to another man and a woman who were walking next to the wagon.

"Hurry," Geoff whispered. "Run up the road a ways and make it look like they caught up to you. You're headed to Barda." We got off of him as the wagon drew nearer, and we could make out some of the words the people were saying. Geoff turned and ran back into the forest, leaving us by ourselves.

Shaelynn tugged my arm, and we both jogged up the road around a turn where they couldn't see us.

"What are we supposed to do?" she cried.

"Put your pack down and unroll one of your blankets." I said, starting to do the same.

"What?" she asked, but she bent down and started unrolling one of hers too.

"We just woke up. It's still early, right? We slept on the side of the road, and now we're getting ready to take off again." Once my blanket was unrolled, I started to roll it up again. Shaelynn had just started on hers when the wagon came around the corner again.

"Remember, we're headed to Barda, wherever that is," Shaelynn whispered.

"Oy! Who're you?" the man on the wagon had spotted us.

"Travelers!" I yelled back, starting to tie my blanket back on my pack. Shaelynn was still rolling hers.

"Where ye be going?" the man asked.

"Barda!" I said, shouldering my pack. The wagon came to a halt next to us. The man peered down at me then watched as Shaelynn shouldered her pack and walked up next to me.

"I'm Rish, and this is my cousin Tera. We're going to Barda, looking for work. And you?" I asked.

"Carthusian, merchant, heading to Barda as well. And these two traveling with me are Ternac and Vitane." I nodded to the two who peeked around the side of the wagon at their names. Shaelynn did the same.

"May we join you, then?" Shaelynn asked. "Since we are all going to the same place? That is, if it's not too much of a bother."

Carthusian thought about it for moment, and smiled. He reached down and shook her hand. "Come along, then." He flicked the reins over the horse's back and it started walking eagerly down the road. We waited until the wagon had passed us, then ran forward and fell in step next to Ternac and Vitane.

We walked for a couple more days until we reached a bustling city next to a wide river. According to the map Tayna had given us, an ocean or sea of some sort was a short way down the river. This location was obviously why Barda was so big; it must have been like a big port for ships and the goods they carried.

We crossed a bridge and entered the city after close examination from the guards at the gate. Shaelynn and I said our thank yous and goodbyes to Carthusian, Ternac, and Vitane. Once we were alone, we started off.

"What are we supposed to do, anyway?" I asked.

"Well, we don't have any money, so I guess we have to find some work. Where do you want to go?"

"I dunno. Not anywhere that we have to gut fish or something."

"No, I don't want to do that either."

We were walking through some sort of a market place, and I noticed a lot of kids running around, some of them milling innocently around some rich looking adults. Two of them talked with a man in front of us, asking him for food. He angrily swatted the kids away and they left, but his moneybag was missing. I saw the older boy toss it and catch it in front of him, then he dashed off to join his comrades.

I glanced at Shaelynn and saw that she had seen the kids too. She looked at me to see what I thought. I cocked my head.

"We could ask them where there's good work and a place to sleep for now," I suggested.

"Maybe," she replied.

When we next saw the same boy at work, this time with a few more friends, we stood to the side and watched them work until they were done. Making her mind up in an instant, Shaelynn grabbed the boy as he ran by and whirled him around. His eyes widened, then he smiled.

"Milady, would you please give us some money? My friends and I are poor and we haven't enough to buy our noonday meal." He smiled warmly. I stepped up next to Shaelynn to look at him.

I easily took a hold on the boy's sleeve as Shaelynn's hand inched away from his collar; he was watching his friends behind us. Suddenly Shaelynn reached out behind her and grabbed one of the kids' arms.

"You won't find any money on us, and don't even try to take my weapons," she said icily. I was surprised at the change in her.

"Or mine, either," I said as I felt a tiny hand pulling at my pack. I glanced at the two behind me out of the corner of my eye; they fled. Only two boys remained. The older one tried to run for it, but he didn't realize I had a hold of his sleeve. I gave a hard pull and brought him back towards me. At the same time Shaelynn's captive had tried to run, but she had him held fast by his wrist. She drug the little boy around to stand in front of her.

I let the older one go, and Shaelynn released the other. The older boy looked worried.

"Miladies, please don't hurt us; we wouldn't be able to eat otherwise."

"We're not going to hurt you, as long as you don't try to steal from us," Shaelynn said, calmer now.

"We don't have any money ourselves, and we were looking for a place to sleep for tonight," I said.

"You can sleep with us!" the little boy cried. The older one glared at him, but the younger one stood his ground.

"Everyone who ain't got their own roof sleeps where we do, down by the docks!" The older boy elbowed the younger in the ribs. "No, really," the younger cried. "They said they wasn't gonna hurt us. We'd love to have 'em. Right?"

"Well, okay." The older boy turned to us. "Me an' my gang sleep down by the docks, like he said. You can't miss us if you know where to look, but don't go down too close to the ships. Them sailors have guards on 'em, and those can be right nasty for the one that gets caught."

"Thanks," Shaelynn said. "We were also wondering if you knew where we could find work."

I dunno about that," he said, "but a few of the boys might know. You'll talk with them tonight. We might have us a small fire lit; you can look for that." A man shouted somewhere behind us.

"Gotta go," the boy said, then disappeared in an instant. Shaelynn and I did the same, just before the rich man who had been robbed earlier stomped by. Shaelynn laughed, and we headed out of town again. Once clear of the town we went straight into the forest to hunt. I came up with nothing; Shaelynn had shot what looked like a quail or something. Just before the gates closed at dusk we were back inside Barda.

We found the docks and went down by the water, steering clear of any ships. There was a small fire lit in between two unused docks, with a lot of children milled around it. We saw the boy sitting on the ground near the fire. We cautiously walked in, everyone turning to stare. I felt really uncomfortable, but Shaelynn walked on.

"Miladies, you made it!" the boy cried, standing. Everyone looked from us to him. "Everyone, this is . . . . what did you say your names were again?"

Before Shaelynn could answer I blurted out, "She's Tera, I'm Rish." I didn't want anyone to know our real names, so I stuck to the ones we had used for Carthusian. Shaelynn shot me a look, then turned back toward the boy, who was speaking again.

"Tera and Rish are friends of mine," he said. "So, everything of theirs is off limits, you hear? In return, they won't turn us in, and they have promised not to harm anyone. Right?" he turned towards us. We nodded.

"Very well then, what have we got tonight?" he asked cheerfully. All of the children milled around him and put their food at his feet, then stood back. The boy looked it over, smiling. This must have been the food they bought from the money they stole.

"Dig in!" the boy cried. He squatted down as everyone rushed in, grabbing for a piece of food. When they all had something in both hands, they backed away and sat down close to the fire. I leaned in and grabbed a half-stale roll, then sat down near the boy. Shaelynn grabbed a piece of meat and sat down by me.

I looked around at everyone. Mostly there were young boys, none of them older than the one next to me. There were some girls, but they looked as tough as any of the boys. This life must be pretty rough, I thought. I looked at Shaelynn; she was thinking along the same lines.

I was about to ask the boy something, but I realized he had never told us his name. "Hey," I said. He turned. "What's your name anyway?"

"I'm Dush!" the little boy we had seen earlier cried out.

The older one glared at him for a moment before he said, "Yeah, the pipsqueak there is Dush, he's the youngest of us. My name is Najee. I'm oldest, and I'm the leader of our little gang."

"Whatever you say, Najee. People like to listen to me too, and I still ain't no leader of anything," Dush grinned. Najee punched him in the shoulder.

"Well I'm oldest, people have to listen to me. Besides, I'm smartest, been here the longest. Without me you'd all be in prison for nicking bread off the stands, 'stead of payin for it first."

"Paid for in stolen money," Dush retorted.

"How else you gonna eat? And anyhow them rich folks is stuck up, they can afford to lose a bit of money every now and then if they're gonna be stingy with it. A regular hero, I am, for helpin' return money to the poor. And you all get to help me in my campaign, you do."

"Works for me!" Dush cried, giggling. Shaelynn and I smiled at them both.

"Say," Najee said, tapping my leg. "Didn't you tell me you were looking for work?" I nodded my head.

"Supai!" Najee called. A boy almost as old as Najee stood up and walked over and then sat down facing Najee.

"Tera and Rish were looking for work. Do you know of any place?" The boy considered us for a moment, then spoke quietly.

"Up at the stables, at the high end of town, old man Marl just released his two hands. I dunno if he found anybody yet, but you'd look there. Also, Agathla just opened a kind of jeweler's shop. She'll be looking for help."

"Thanks," Shaelynn said; Supai stood and walked back to his place and sat down, watching us. I caught Shaelynn looking at me and turned to her.

"I guess you can go to the stables and I'll work for Agathla. Mom always told me I should be a jeweler, and you're a lot better with horses than I am." I sighed.

"I don't know about the sound of 'old man Marl'."

"He's probably a little cranky, but it sounds like he's been there a while. You'll get along fine with him if you're both that horse crazy." We laughed, gaining a few people's attentions. Najee leaned over.

"When one of the sailors comes back to his ship, you'll sleep by me. You have your own blankets?" he asked.

"Yeah," Shaelynn started to say, but a small shout stopped her. Immediately a bucket of water came from out of nowhere and put out the fire, then everyone ran about for a minute and settled down for sleep. Shaelynn had grabbed my hand just in time and had somehow followed Najee. We hurriedly laid down our blankets and fell asleep. I heard footsteps a few docks over and saw a man look curiously in our general direction, shake his head, then get onto his boat.

I lay for a minute, thinking about horses and market children, then fell asleep.

Chapter 3

THE NEXT MORNING NAJEE AND Dush woke us up. We rolled our blankets up and went with Supai, who had been waiting for us. I had just finished buckling on my sword when Supai broke into a trot coming out of the docks. We entered the market place and jogged for a ways, then turned down a side street and ran up the length of another street.

We stopped by an old-looking store with newer jewelry in the small window that had a fresh sign hanging on the door. I put my hands on my knees, bent over, trying to catch my breath. I thought I was in pretty good shape from volleyball, but looking at Supai, I saw he was barely out of breath. I looked at Shaelynn, who was worse off than me. Her face was red, and she looked like she really wanted to sit down.

Leaving us a little time for rest, Supai waited a minute before he pushed open the door and walked in. He made hardly any noise, but a young woman in a maroon robe and a gold silk tie around the middle came in from the back.

"Supai," she said, "aren't you supposed to be in the marketplace?"

"Yes, milady, but I knew you were looking for work in your new shop."

"I found a young girl already; I only have room for one more," she said, looking at Shaelynn and I pointedly.

"Well, I was the one who wanted to work for you," Shaelynn put in. Agathla looked her over, pausing over her hands. She nodded, then waved Shaelynn over to her.

"What is your name?" Agathla asked.

"Tera."

"My name is Agathla. You have a room down the hall you can stay in, I'll show that to you later. You work from sunup to two hours before sundown and I'll give you money that you can spend for now. Set your things down, let me look at you."

Shaelynn gave me an excited look as Agathla waved us off with a muttered thank you to Supai. I smiled at Shaelynn, then followed Supai out of the shop. Once I was out on the street Supai took off at a jog again.

We got to the stables on the other end of town, just as an old man dressed in plain brown pants and a dark green shirt came out of a wide hallway lined with stalls. The man's hair was grey-white, with a small bald patch on top of his head. His hands were thick and rough-looking from years of hard work, holding onto a rope attached to the halter of a beautiful black horse. The horse danced eagerly next to the man, watching us as we ran into the stable yard. I saw the horse and immediately stopped in my tracks, but Supai bowled into the animal, scaring it so that it reared up on its hind legs.

The rope slipped from the man's hands, who had already pushed Supai out of the way of the horse's flailing hooves. The man stood in front of the horse, feet planted and arms low. His relaxed figure brought the horse down on four feet, where it danced in place until the man had his hand on its shoulder and his other hand on the lead rope.

The man led the horse over to Supai and I, and we helped Supai to his feet. I followed the man as he led the black horse to a kind of hitching rail and tied him there. The man abruptly turned and walked away from us, without acknowledging that we were there. We followed him into the stables, trotting to keep up with his fast pace.

"Marl! Sir!" Supai panted.

"Get outta here! I don't want no kids around here that don't know how to act around a horse."

"But sir, we didn't see you—"

"I said, get outta here! I have enough things to do as it is."

"That's why we're here, sir. Here's someone who'll work for you." The man stopped and turned with ease, which surprised me for a man his age. He looked from Supai to me, then at the black horse tied outside.

"Have you ever not scared a horse, girl?" he asked roughly. I nodded.

"I can ride too, sir, and I'm a good worker."

"Are you strong? Can you handle a horse taller than you?"

"I think so, sir."

"Call me Marl. You'll start today, but I'm taking an hour off since you're late. Don't bother me unless I need you. You work an hour before sunup and two hours after sundown. You get afternoon free time, and you can take one of the horses out if you like. Your room is upstairs, right across the hall from Shamar, my other one. For now, just brush down this black horse."

He turned to Supai. "Thank you. Now get!" Supai turned and ran, flashing a smile at me. I lifted my hand long enough for him to see it, then followed Marl to a small building to the side of the stables. He opened the door and went in; I caught the door before it hit me and followed, setting my sword, bow, and quiver next to my pack by the door.

"This'll be good enough for him," Marl said, laying a hand on a saddle. It was oddly shaped compared to the Western style I was used to. It had a rounded pommel with no saddle horn and a high cantle, with stirrups that looked like pointed cups and a string-like breast collar. There was only one girth, not a second one that I was used to.

"Here's his bridle," Marl said, lifting a thin leather headstall from a hook behind the saddle. It had no throat latch or a chain to go beneath the chin, and the reins were short. The mouth guards on either side of the bit were very large.

"The brushes here; use these ones. Here's a comb for his mane, and just get the ends of his tail. His rider is coming in an hour, and I want him warmed up as well." Marl turned and walked out of the tack room, headed for the stables again. I followed him out of the shed, then walked to the black horse, who was pulling on his lead rope.

Talking to the horse, I approached at his shoulder, a friend. He stopped dancing to look me over. I took a step closer; he lifted a hind leg, his first warning. I stepped toward his head, and his hind leg lashed out. It was only a second warning, as he did not try to reach me. I gave him a look and bared my teeth, lowering my head. He hurriedly backed away, and stood still as I approached him again.

The black let me brush him down and start to work on his mane as I quietly talked to him. When I was done with his mane I went to work on his tail. Instead of standing behind him, I pulled the end of it toward me and worked on the ends. After that was done I checked his feet; I managed not to get kicked, thank goodness.

I went back to the shed and put the brushes up, then draped his bridle over my shoulder and picked up his saddle. I shut the door behind me and walked back to him. This time he gave no warning, at least none that I could see. His head snaked down and he bit me, drawing a little blood on my arm. I dropped the saddle and looked at him angrily; he seemed to be smirking. Then I got it: he was playing with me. I was as young as him, and he wanted to play.

I cocked my head in response as his nostrils flared playfully. I grasped his nose with both hands before he could bite me, and gave it a firm squeeze: not now. Enough. His head lowered, but he still lifted a hind leg to check. I smacked his shoulder and he put it down.

The saddle was a little tough to figure out, but I got it soon enough. I put the rope halter around the black's neck and put his bridle on, or at least tried. He jerked his head up almost as soon as the bit touched his lips. I tried putting one hand on the lead rope and putting the bit in with the other, but the rope burned my hand as he jerked his head up again. I knew he wasn't playing around this time.

I patted his shoulder, then draped my right arm that held the top of the bridle over his head, behind his ears. With my left hand I put the bit in as soon as his teeth parted. My right arm kept his head from going up too far, and it worked. I placed the top of the bridle behind his ears, and he was ready to go. I looped the reins in my hand and turned him around, and saw Marl standing not too far off, watching me.

"Good!" he called. I smiled. He stepped forward, then turned and walked away. The black followed, reading the body language I couldn't understand. I followed the black, and after a moment I remembered to try to lead him instead of him leading me.

I followed Marl to a paddock in front of the stable, where he held the gate open while I led the black inside. Marl came in as well and shut the gate behind him.

"What did you say your name was?" Marl asked.

"Rish," I said.

"All right Rish, let's see how you ride. Go ahead, get on." His voice was gentler than before. It made me feel a little less nervous in front of him. I pushed it out of my mind as I patted the black, then swung up into the saddle. The black immediately took off. I stopped him and backed him up, waited a minute, then walked him around the edge of the pen. Marl had walked to the center. He had a small smile on his face, but showed no other signs of emotion.

I walked a couple of times around Marl, and then he told me to trot. I took a deep breath and clucked the black into a trot. His trot was smooth for as young a horse as he was, but it was still a little bone-jarring. I found his beat, settled into it, and started to post: every time his right foot came forward I pushed myself up a little in the saddle, and every time he put it down I let myself down.

"Good!" Marl cried. "Canter!" I clucked the black into a canter, or slow run; he leaped forward eagerly. I settled into his gait, rocking back and forth with his body, keeping my back as straight as I could with him.

We did a few more circles, did some figure eights at a trot, and then walked more circles just as a young man strode to the fence. He had dark hair and a boyish face, and was dressed a bit nicely for riding, in my opinion. He smiled at me, but only regarded Marl. I had a bad feeling about him.

"Is he ready, Marl?" the man asked. His voice was deep, but not very. Marl nodded vaguely, then motioned for me to get off. I dismounted and led the black to the gate; I almost had to drag him out of it, he didn't want to go. It was a radical change from the excited horse I'd ridden only moments ago.

"Who is this beautiful young lady?" the man asked, holding out his hand. I put mine in it, though I really didn't want to, and he bent and kissed it.

"A young lady who knows how to ride," Marl grumbled, but the man didn't take the hint. He was looking at me.

"And, she works here," Marl said pointedly. The man peeled his eyes away from me; I felt disgusted. Marl told me to give the reins to the man, named Karbab. I reluctantly handed them over.

Karbab roughly jerked the horse away, making him stutter-step. Karbab yanked hard, and the black followed far behind. When he was at the street he got on, pulling the reins too far back and landing hard in the seat. He kicked the black into a run but still held the reins tight, making the black confused, telling him to stop and run at the same time. They disappeared behind a building before I could see anything else.

I turned to Marl, angry, but he was already halfway to the stable, not turning to see if I followed or not. I ran up to him and touched his shoulder just as he walked inside.

"Why do you—" I started.

"Because," he cut me off, "I have no other choice. His father owns me and this place, so if I want to stay here with the horses I have to let him ride the black. Even if he doesn't know how to ride it. Okay?"

"Even if it makes you mad?" I asked quietly.

"Aye." He put a hand on my shoulder. "But, there is hope. I finally have a hand who can really ride." I looked up at him and smiled. He smiled back for a moment.

"Now—feeding's over, so you can check their water. Each horse has its own separate water, so if one gets sick it can't pass it on through that. You'll have to carry it one bucket at a time. Don't try two—they're heavy enough as it is. Don't worry about the horses, either. That black is the only one who'll think you're young enough to play." I smiled.

"The well is out front; you might have seen it between the corral and the stable." I nodded. He headed for a small room off to the side, calling out over his shoulder, "I'll be in here when you're done."

I walked down the wide hallway that was open at both ends, feeling the little wisps of air that floated in from outside. I started at the back, checking each stall to see if it had enough water. Whenever I found one that needed water, which was often, I made a line coming out from the stall with my toe. When I reached the front, I jogged out to the well.

There were three buckets there, all big enough to hold about five gallons each. I picked one and set it close to the edge of the well, then drew up the pail until my bucket was almost full. Picking it up, I carried it almost to the mouth of the hall until I had to stop. Picking it up again, I carried it to the last stall I had marked and let myself in.

I finished after about an hour and some, and still I had not seen Shamar, Marl's other hand. I wondered if he was off somewhere instead of here. Setting the bucket next to its friends, I turned and walked back up to the stable, turning into the side room.

Marl sat slumped over a desk, snoring. Smiling, I walked up to him and laid a hand on his shoulder. He snapped awake, eyes wild, looking around. He saw me and his eyebrows pushed together, then he recognized me.

"Sorry; must have fallen asleep," he mumbled. He stood and stretched, then walked out of the room to the first stall, checking the horse's water. He walked to one in the middle, then went to the back, picking random stalls. He walked back.

"Good." he said. "Have you seen Shamar yet, by any chance?" I shook my head; Marl looked troubled.

"Well, that's about it unless someone shows up. It's too hot to ride now; you'll exercise the horses tonight, with Shamar's help. Go and grab your things if they're still outside. I'll be here."

I turned and jogged to the shed and picked up my pack and my weapons from inside the door, putting them on as I jogged back. Marl eyed my sword and my bow, but said nothing. When I came up to him he led the way into the stables and up a narrow hall to the side that I hadn't noticed. It was in between the middle stalls, and was barely wide enough for Marl's shoulders to fit.

I followed Marl up a set of stairs, to the second story of the stables. We were standing in another hall, but this was much wider than the narrow hall downstairs. There was a door to the right and left, and two doors down the hall, also on the right and left.

Marl pushed open the one to the right, showing me a bathroom. The door to the left led to a sitting room. Down the hall, Marl skipped the door on the left—Shamar's bedroom. He opened the other on the right, revealing a room that was empty except for a small table with a washbasin and a bed. There was a window in the far wall, but no curtains.

I walked in and set my pack on the bed; a cloud of dust rose. I'd have to wash the sheets. Glancing over my shoulder, I saw Marl turn and go down the hallway. I listened to his footsteps fade as they left the narrow hallway at the bottom of the stairs. Then they disappeared altogether, and I started to unpack.

I heard the tower bell ring the noon hour and went downstairs, having just finished unpacking and examining my map. We still had a way to go before we could even think of being close to Zathos. Yet we needed money, so we had to stay here until we had enough to at least move on.

I met Marl sharing a piece of his bread with one of the older horses near his room. He looked up when he was done feeding the horse and gave me a roll and piece of meat, along with a wooden cup.

"I have a bucket of clean water right outside," he said. I followed him until he turned into his office, and I went outside. I dipped my cup in the bucket, drinking two cupfuls. Refilling it a third time, I went inside. Marl was behind his desk, leaning back in the chair. I sat in a chair too, facing him and the door.

Looking at my sword belted to my waist, he asked, "Can you use that?" I looked down at it then up at him, swallowing my mouthful of meat.

"Yes," I answered. "And I can use it very well, at that. At least my mentor told me so." He nodded, but did not ask who had taught me. He eyed my bow, then looked at me.

"It took me a while to learn, but I can use that well too. My cousin is better, though. Much better."

"Where is she?"

"She is working for Agathla at her new shop. She also started today." He nodded again then got up. As he walked out the door I heard it too: hoof beats. I hurried outside.

Karbab was trotting the black up from the road. The horse was lathered in sweat and exhausted. Karbab had the reins pulled up short again, maybe shorter than before. The black's head was up and pulled back, his ears back and the whites of his eyes showing a little.

Karbab clumsily dismounted after he had pulled the black to a halt. He tried flicking the reins over the horse's head but caught them on his ears, causing the black to jerk his head back. Karbab jerked its head down again, then brought his arm swiftly up. The black, thinking Karbab was about to strike him, reared up high.

Karbab jerked on the reins again as Marl and I ran up to the black, who started to flail his legs. A hoof nearly struck Karbab on the head, and I almost wish it had. I roughly pushed him out of the way, but he grabbed my arm on the way down. He pulled me down too, and I landed on top of him, knocking the wind out of him. I had caught myself on my elbow, and now it was hurting and bleeding, but it was just a scrape.

As he tried to catch his breath again, his arms came up and wrapped around me. I jumped up and helped Marl, who had gotten the black back down on all four feet, though he was still skittish.

"Get that saddle off," Marl said softly, keeping his eyes on the black. I hurriedly took it off, not trying to be neat. The black blew air out of his nostrils gratefully and trotted after Marl, who was leading him toward the paddock. I hitched the saddle up higher on my hip and walked toward the shed, trying to get everything on top of it so the pad could dry in the shed. Even as I carried it the blanket dripped sweat.

Coming out of the shed, I stepped down and turned to close the door. I didn't even hear Karbab behind me, but as soon as it was shut he had grabbed my arm and was pulling me behind the stables.

I kicked and pulled and tried to reach my sword, but he held the arm that could reach it and handle it better than the other. Then I resorted to talking and squealing, but he clamped a hand over my mouth and made me walk forward. When we were all the way behind the stable and out of earshot of anybody, Karbab stopped.

He took his hand off my arm, and I spun around. Before I could say anything he had roughly pushed me up against the wall and put his mouth over mine in a sloppy kiss. Screaming, I pushed him away. I started to run, but he grabbed my arm and held me fast.

Turning, I saw his face was shocked. "Why don't you want me?" he asked. Angrily I tried to jerk my arm out of his grip.

"Why don't you want me?" he asked again, pulling me toward him. "Every woman wants me. My father is rich, and I am too!" He pulled me in for another kiss, but I kicked his shin. He let go in pain and then reached for me again, but too late. My sword was drawn and pointed at his chest. He stopped short, smiling.

"Come now, I know you want me. You can't even use that, can you?" He stepped forward and reached out again. I pushed the tip of my sword to his throat, stopping it just as it touched his skin. He gulped.

"Stay away from me," I whispered. He laughed.

"And what are you going to do if I don't? Who's to say I can't tell my father? He owns Marl and every beast in here, including you."

"I swear I'll kill you, no matter what your father does. Don't touch me again." Keeping my sword drawn, I backed away from him, glancing around the corner over my shoulder. He stayed where he was, watching me. When he was out of sight I turned and ran, not sheathing my sword until I was at the shed. Marl was walking up from the paddock.

"Where's Karbab?" Marl asked. I shrugged my shoulders.

"I think he left."

"Good. That idiot doesn't know how to handle a woman, let alone a horse." I shivered at his choice of words.

"What's the matter?" Marl asked, having seen me.

"Oh, just the way he handles that horse. I'd like to treat him like that."

"I know. I would too, but we can't. Otherwise we wouldn't be here, and the horses who-knows-where." I sighed, then followed him to his office again. Glancing over my shoulder before I walked in, I saw Karbab storming out from behind the shed. He was headed for the street and into town. Trying to get him out of my head, I grabbed the rest of my bread roll and meat and sat down in my chair again.

At three Marl let me go, giving me a sweet bay gelding to ride. He was a short horse, and his gleaming red-brown coat shone in contrast to his dusty black legs and tail. Still, he was a good sound horse that would give me no trouble, Marl assured me. I quickly tacked up and was off, running for a while down the empty streets and getting to a slow trot when I neared Agathla's shop.

Tying the gelding outside, I went in. As soon as the door opened Shaelynn and another girl looked up from some shelves in the back. Shaelynn put everything she was holding down and walked over, smiling.

"Well?" She lifted an eyebrow.

"I got the job!" I said. She pulled me into a hug, squeezing tight, threatening to take my breath away. Hugging her back, I saw Agathla come out from a hallway at the back of the shop. Seeing Shaelynn and I, she smiled.

Shaelynn let go and backed up, then turned and saw Agathla behind her. She ducked her head sheepishly and headed back for her shelf, but Agathla held her arm out, stopping her.

"Are you on your break now?" Agathla asked me.

"Yes, lady," I said. "Marl lets me out at three." She nodded, then turned to Shaelynn.

"Go with your cousin, dear. You can have break with her." Shaelynn dashed down the hallway at the back of the shop; I followed her to the end of it, where I heard her moving around in a room a few doors down from me. After a moment she came into view, her quiver on her back and her bow in her hand.

"You have two hours!" Agathla called as we half-ran out of her shop. We slowed in front of the gelding and I got on, then helped Shaelynn up behind me. Pushing the bay into a trot I headed out of town, but decided against it and went back to the stable.

Marl was coming outside and looked up as we walked up the driveway. He squinted in the sun and waved at me, looking puzzled. I pulled the bay up next to him and helped Shaelynn down, then got off too.

"Back so soon, Rish?" he asked. "And with a visitor?"

"Marl, this is my cousin Tera." He held out his hand and she took it; instead of bending and kissing it, he bowed his head, and she bowed hers in response.

"Marl, Tera needs a horse. It would be too much for the bay to carry both of us. Can she use one?" Nodding, he turned and walked into the wide hall. Shaelynn followed him as I tied the gelding outside, then went in too.

Marl had stopped about halfway up the back end of the stalls and was opening one of the doors. Stepping in he called out, "A halter, please, Rish." I walked to the wall by the door and lifted a halter from a hook, then grabbed a rope from the ground. Going to the stall, I handed them to him.

He put the halter on a tall dappled grey mare with a white star on her forehead and dark grey bands on her legs. Once the halter was on he tied the rope to it and led the mare out. She danced eagerly but paid attention to Marl as he led her outside and tied her next to the bay. The mare laid her ears back against her head and the bay did the same, but that was all they did. In a moment or two they were fine.

"Rish, go ahead and grab the saddle next to the one that we used on the black this morning. Grab his bridle, too." He pulled a soft brush from a back pocket and started brushing down the grey. Shaelynn followed me to the shed.

Walking to the black's saddle, I grabbed the only one next to it and hoisted it onto my hip. Pointing to the black's bridle, I carried the saddle out of the shed. Shaelynn grabbed the bridle and followed me out.

"Were you guys busy today?" Shaelynn asked after she had closed the door.

"No, not really," I said as she fell into step next to me. "We had a guy earlier and a man and his son asking for two heavy horses for a cart, but that was all." I tried not to think about Karbab but still wondered if I should tell Shaelynn.

I set the saddle on the ground far enough away from the mare that she couldn't bother it and waited for Marl to finish brushing her down. He was done in a moment, and I quickly tacked her up. Putting her bridle on proved to be a little of a challenge, but we had it on soon enough. I was just about ready to get up on the bay when Marl stopped me.

"Get on the grey, Rish. She can be a handful sometimes. The bay will be easier for Tera." Smiling at Shaelynn, he said, "Your cousin doesn't look too experienced with horses."

"You got that right," Shaelynn said. Marl chuckled and helped her up on the bay while I got on the grey.

"What time do you have to be back at Agathla's, Tera?" Marl asked, just as we were about to leave.

"At five, she said." Marl turned to me.

"The same goes for you," he said, then turned away and headed for his office. We walked the horses out onto the street. Shaelynn kicked the bay into a trot, which surprised me but still made me smile. We trotted most of the way out of town, then went into a canter outside the gates. We ran the horses until we reached the woods, stopping at the edge of the trees to ready our bows.

Walking in, we decided to split up and meet each other in an hour at the edge of the forest, next to the road that went into Barda. There we would build a fire and eat what we caught before we had to go back into town. Shaelynn turned to the left and walked the bay on a game trail while I went straight in, climbing steadily up a hill.

The grey mare turned out to be a very good mount, especially when we started walking on rocky ground. She was sure-footed; I let her choose her own way on the rocks, but she still paid attention to my commands as we went further up the hill.

After fifteen minutes or so we had come out of the trees into a wide meadow, full of rocks and boulders strewn here and there among larger outcroppings of rock protruding from the ground. I had seen no game nor heard any sound of life at all, save for the wind in the trees and the water on the rocks. There were no birds singing now, not even a sign of a small feathered body flitting from one branch to another. It was total silence.

Dismounting from the mare, I loosened the girth to give her a rest and sat down, leaning against an outcropping of rocks and holding the end of her reins in my hand. The rock was warm from the sun, and nice and smooth. Looking at it, I noticed triangular shapes all over it from constant wind and rain streaming down its sides.

The mare stood for a moment, watching the rocks behind me, body still. After a moment she seemed to shake her head, then she went to grazing. I spread my legs out in front of me and started to lean my head back, but my bow and my quiver were in the way. Taking them off and setting them next to me, I leaned my head back and dozed.

I must not have slept for more than a few minutes when I felt the tug of the mare on the reins.

"I'm not letting you wander," I said, not opening my eyes. I started to slip back into sleep when I felt another tug, this time more persistent. Huffing out a breath, I opened my eyes.

The mare was as far away from me as she could get, and still trying to back up. Her ears were flicking back and forth, and the whites of her eyes had begun to show. I was about to get up and go to her when I felt my heart skip a beat as the rock underneath me moved.

I leaped to my feet, drawing my sword. The mare backed away as I did, straining at the reins. I glanced over my shoulder to look at her; her ears were laid back flat on her head, a rim of white was around her eyes, her body language clearly stating that she was afraid. Turning back to the rock, I had a moment's glance at a mass of green and yellow scales before I felt a blow to my head.

My sword flew from my hand, and I heard it clatter to the ground a few feet away. My other hand relaxed in my dazed state, and I heard hoof beats retreating as the mare's reins slipped out of my slackened grip. Seeing black at the edges of my vision, I looked up.

A huge beast stood before me, teeth bared, wings spread. The light on its emerald-green scales made me squint at it. It had a yellow throat and belly, dark green horns curving upward from its head, sharp black claws on all four feet, and bright yellow catlike eyes.

Smoke poured from the dragon's nostrils as it breathed out. Its attention turned from me to my sword, still on the ground. At the same instant the dragon reached for it, I had leaped.

I landed on top of it, trying to grasp the handle as the dragon roared above me. It shook me to my bones, but I had found the handle. Bringing my sword up in front of me, I stood.

The dragon was frozen, one huge talon suspended in the air above me. I was standing underneath it, my sword not a foot from its chest. I froze also, realizing the situation.

So, who will strike first? A deep voice said in my head. I looked around me, trying to see who was there; no one was around but the dragon and I. Looking up at it, I saw it watching me.

Of course! I had read quite a few books on dragons. None of them said it for sure, but most of them mentioned dragons being able to mind-speak. However, none of them had ever said anything about dragons being able to disguise themselves as rocks.

Looking at the dragon again, I saw that he was waiting on me to answer. Taking a deep breath, I hoped he understood me.

"You have the power over me, dragon. Strike me and I cannot strike back."

You speak words of truth, he said. I closed my eyes, waiting for the fatal blow.

I heard him move and shut them tighter, but no blow came. I opened my eyes just as his raised talon touched the ground and he stood before me on all four legs.

Now, we are equal. Again, who will strike first? His voice had become extremely serious. As he waited for my answer, millions of thoughts flashed through my mind, but none of them would fix on killing the dragon, or even making the first move.

"Dragon, I—I can't." I sheathed my sword, bowing my head. Watching him, I saw him pause and look me over, then he backed away a few steps—peace. I raised my head, watching him. As he shifted his weight I glanced down at his feet; he was about to put his hind leg down on my bow when I stopped him.

"Wait!" I cried, running forward. "My bow. Watch your foot or you'll crush it." He held his leg in midair as I approached his side. Putting my hand on his belly to brace myself, I leaned down to pick up my bow.

There was a flash of blinding light. My hand tried to jerk away from the dragon, but it was stuck to his hide; I couldn't move it. Then I realized that I couldn't move anything else, either. Fear surged through me, but it was quickly cut off by a voice in my head and a wave of comforting.

Be still, human. Be still, it said over and over, and I finally stopped trying to move. Voices sounded in my mind, hundreds of various names and words spoken so powerfully that it made my heart race with excitement, though I did not know why. After a minute or so the light faded and I could see the dragon. I sat stunned for a moment as the hundreds of voices echoed throughout my mind with their last unison phrase: *Ir hrathan jhere Fravid-Sorva.* Suddenly everything was still, save for my pounding heart. I pulled my hand from the dragon's side and hurriedly stood and backed away from him.

"What was that? What happened?" I asked.

Try speaking with your mind.

"What just happened?" I asked again.

Please, try to speak with your mind.

"How am I supposed to do that?" I asked angrily, but I thought I heard an echo of it in my mind. I tried again and only managed a faint whisper.

Direct your thoughts to me and speak, but not out loud.

What?—I stopped, shocked. *How did I do that? How did I do that?* I repeated.

Good, the dragon said, laughing in my head. I even felt a humorous feeling coming from him.

Wait, what just happened? How can I do this?

You and I, we are Bonded. When you touched me you were willing, as was I. We Bonded. You can hear my thoughts and feel my emotions, as I can yours.

What do you mean, I was willing?

To be my companion, and I was willing to be yours.

Your companion?

Aye. I sat myself down on the ground, thinking. So, now I was a dragon's companion. But what did that mean? What happened now? That was when I remembered that I was supposed to meet Shaelynn at the edge of the forest on the road leading to Barda. I jumped up and then paced in a circle, realizing that I'd never make it in time without the grey mare.

What is wrong? the dragon asked.

I need to get to the edge of the forest on the road leading to Barda. I was supposed to meet my cousin there. How long has it been since I came into this valley?

I'm not sure. Maybe an hour?

"Uhn," I groaned out loud. *I'm supposed to be there now. But how am I to get there? My horse ran away, and who knows where she is now? Oh, Marl is going to have my head for this if I'm late and I can't find her.*

You are forgetting something, the dragon said, maybe a little playfully.

What? I said, a little angry at his mocking tone.

We are Bonded now, and I can fly.

What? I turned around to face him, and saw that he had his wings spread, teeth bared in a grin.

Get on, he said.

I backed away, shaking my head. *No way, oh no.*

Get on, and I'll fly you to your mare.

Are you sure?

Yes, hurry! You have your cousin to meet. How else are you to get there in time? He was right. I edged toward him, looking for a place to get on. There seemed a suitable place on his shoulders, just in front of where his wings met his body. I imagined myself getting on a horse and swung one leg over.

I barely had time to position myself when he had crouched down low to the ground. He suddenly sprang up into the air, beating his wings, trying to get altitude. My scream was lost in the rush of the wind. We rose above the trees, and still higher we went.

Down far below us, I could see Barda, the sea, and the river that led to it. The road wound through the forest, coming out of it and going on to Barda. I could see a figure on the road where it came out of the forest, probably Shaelynn.

I can see your horse, the dragon said suddenly.

Where?

There. He wheeled to the right and dropped, folding his wings in. We fell diagonally, picking up speed. I couldn't help myself, and screamed yet again. Ahead I could see a white animal running on the flat area in front of the river, constantly changing direction and slowing down then speeding up; the mare was confused and scared.

The dragon landed behind a low hill and lay down where the mare couldn't see him—she was only a few hundred yards away.

I will leave you here, the dragon said quietly. He peeked up over the hill, lifting his head a little. *Your horse has stopped. Run her to the edge of the forest away from the road, then ride to the road from there. Your mare will be sweaty; think of something. Meet me at the rock valley tomorrow.*

Wait! How will I find you?

I will find you. Now, go. He watched as I walked over the hill and disappeared over the edge.

The mare jumped at the sight of me and started to run, but stopped to look at me. There was no one else around, to guide her in the correct direction so she could go home. She stood still as I approached her and let me lay a hand on her shoulder. I mounted and rode off. In the sky above me I saw the dragon flying far overhead.

I did as the dragon had said and met Shaelynn at the road, almost an hour late. We had maybe ten minutes to get back to work before it was five. I didn't tell Shaelynn anything about the dragon or where I had been; I was still unsure about it myself, half hoping it was a crazy dream.

Shaelynn had caught three birds. We had had plans of cooking them and eating them in the forest, but that was out of the question. She put them in one of the saddlebags she had on the gelding and we rode out.

Chapter 4

SHAELYNN WAS ONLY A FEW minutes late to work, but it turned out that I was over ten, since I walked the horses most of the way to give them a chance to cool off before I gave them back to Marl.

Marl was upset at the horses' conditions and at my being late, but I told him that we had lost track of time and had had to run all the way in, which was partly true. He accepted it and told me to brush them down and turn them out in the paddock, then clean up for supper before his customers started coming in.

I did as told, and we ate upstairs in the sitting room at a small table. Shamar was back; he had decided to take the day off and run around with his friends, which Marl had not approved of, he told me.

Right after we were done eating the man and his son brought back the heavy horses they had borrowed, telling Shamar that they would need them again tomorrow, early.

I went and caught the bay and the grey mare, who had been rolling in the dirt of the paddock. I quickly brushed them down again, then put them in their stalls. Marl came out to help us feed, then left Shamar and I to water them. We finished just as the sun was setting; I thought I saw a large figure wheeling in the sky, enjoying the last few moments of sunlight.

Shamar and I went up to our rooms together and got ready for bed. I was just finished getting into my night things when he knocked and came in.

"Hey," I said. He lifted his head and smiled, then sat on the floor as I sat on my bed.

"So, you're the one that started today?" Shamar asked, looking around at my few belongings. I saw his eyes linger on my weapons before I answered, taking his attention off of them.

"Yeah. I met a kid last night who said that Marl had just fired off his last two hands and hired on another. I guess that's you."

"Yeah, I used to hang out with the other two, until they started causing trouble for Marl and the horses and everyone else. I heard they got fired and I came in, and somehow got the job."

His head turned back to my weapons. "Can you really use those?" he asked, leaning back on his hands.

"Aye."

"Where'd you learn?"

"You wouldn't believe me if I told you."

"Try me."

"No. You wouldn't believe me."

"Come on. Please?"

"A centaur."

"A what?" He leaned forward, all of his attention on me.

"A centaur," I said again. "In the forest. My cousin and I were on our way here about four months ago. We met a centaur, and he and an elf taught us how to shoot a bow and arrow. He also taught me how to use a sword."

"Man, you must be an excellent fighter! I mean, learning from a centaur. They're really good at that." I laughed.

"I don't know about excellent. I'm okay."

"Yeah right!" he said. "I bet you could be the best anybody's seen." I was about to answer when a shout came up the stairs, telling us to get to bed.

"Yes, Marl!" we shouted at the same time. Shamar lifted a hand as he walked across the hall to his room, then shut his door behind him. I left mine open and blew out the light, then climbed into bed. The day's events whirled in my head until finally, I was asleep.

The next day I exercised the horses while Shamar helped Marl with anybody that came in. The bay and the grey mare had been run yesterday and we had a few more customers than yesterday, so I really didn't have that many to work out.

Karbab came in early while I was on a sorrel. Shamar brought out the black and got him ready while Karbab stared at me. I didn't even glance at him, knowing he wanted to catch my eye. When he had trotted out onto the street I looked at Shamar. He looked back, shaking his head. He frowned, then turned and left.

I had only three more horses to exercise when the lunch bell rang from the town. I'd just finished untacking a palomino, so I quickly brushed him down and put him away. Shamar was already in Marl's office room; I went in and he handed me a slice of bread, a few pieces of beef, and my cup. We walked out together to fill our cups in the well.

Marl had gone to look over the horses I had exercised. Shamar was refilling his cup for the third time when a little boy that I recognized from Najee's group came running toward us.

He skidded to a halt in front of us, out of breath.

"Sir! Milady!" he panted, "Karbab has had an accident! Some creature startled his horse. The horse ran off with him, out of the city gates, headed straight for the river!"

Shamar and I left the boy and ran into the stable. We quickly explained to Marl what the boy had told us.

"Quick," Marl said, "you two get horses. Ride bareback. I'll come with one of the heavy horses and a few ropes if we need them."

Shamar went and got two bridles while I found two horses that I had not worked today. Shamar tossed me a bridle as he went into one of the stalls, I in the other.

I was opening my door just as Shamar rode out at a run, clinging to his horse's mane. I swung up on my red roan (I'm not sure how, I've never had the strength) and started to ride out when I saw the boy still standing next to the well.

I trotted the roan over to him. "Can you ride?" I asked.

"Aye, milady." I reached down a hand and helped him up behind me, then I followed Shamar at a run. The roan was quick, and we soon caught up.

People dashed out of our way as we ran down the streets, some of them cursing at us. The guards at the city gate watched as we rode by.

"Which way?" I asked the boy. He pointed to the left; I led the way toward the river. Shamar followed behind me, looking for Karbab and the black.

We didn't see anything until we were at the bank of the river. The black had obviously tried to jump it; he was clinging to a log that was caught up on some rocks, facing upstream. Karbab was a little ways down the river, grasping the reins. The black had his neck turned around and stretched out as far as it would go, trying to make the weight of Karbab less painful.

I jumped down from the roan, leaving the boy to sit on it. Shamar did the same next to me, tossing his reins to the boy, who caught them. Shamar's brown horse danced nervously when Shamar started to climb down the bank to the very edge of the river. I followed him, holding on to his shirt in case he fell.

We reached the muddy edge, wondering what to do next. There were a few rocks between us and the black, but we would have to have had extremely good balance and some skill to get across them. Then, a thought occurred to me.

I climbed back up the bank, where the boy was still sitting on the roan. I took the brown's reins from him.

"Are there any of Najee's gang who've ever done any balancing acts before?" I asked him.

"Yeah. Dush used to perform with a traveling group. Najee did some of it too."

"Can you ride and get them for me?" I asked. "You all are small enough; the roan can carry the three of you. Put Dush in the middle, though, since he's the smallest." The boy nodded, then turned the roan and ran for the city. I slid down the bank and explained to Shamar. Then, we waited.

It was a while before anyone showed up, but they all came at around the same time. Marl arrived first on a draft horse carrying a lot of ropes and a harness, then some of the people of the town came. Shortly after the boy arrived carrying Najee behind him, Dush in the middle of the two.

Najee leaped off the roan before it was stopped, landing lightly on his feet. He bowed low, then stood straight and shook my hand. I introduced everyone quickly, then let Najee and Dush pass.

Najee took one look at the horse and Karbab, still hanging on, before he had leaped out onto the rocks. He and Dush nimbly jumped from rock to rock, until Dush stopped about halfway. Najee continued on until he had reached the horse.

Shamar went out onto a couple of rocks, and I stood on the bank. Marl got the draft horse as close to the edge of the bank as he dared and then, with the help of some of the townspeople, got ropes and a harness down to me. I passed them all except the harness on one by one to Shamar, and then from him on to Dush, and finally from Dush on to Najee.

Najee couldn't have put the harness on the black; it was too dangerous for the both of them. He had no choice but to tie the ropes around the horse's neck and onto the saddle. He couldn't get anything around the end of the horse—his body was too far out in the river.

When the ropes were secure Najee tied one around himself, tossing the end of it and the rest to Dush. Najee's rope only made it to Shamar, but the rest went far enough up to Marl that he could fasten them to the draft's harness.

Marl gave the horse a pull on his halter, and the draft leaned into the ropes. At the same time, Najee hauled on the black's reins, slowly pulling in Karbab. He grasped onto the almost unconscious man as the black made its way out of the water, too exhausted to fight.

When the black was up on the bank, Najee jumped—and plunged into the water. Shamar pulled on the rope holding Najee, but his hand started to slip. I quickly waded out into the water and grasped the rope as well. Najee surfaced from a wave that had covered him, spluttering. He was still holding Karbab.

Very slowly they came in, until Najee could stand on his feet. I went to him and took Karbab from him; Shamar jumped into the water from his rock and picked up Najee.

I half drug Karbab up the bank into the arms of the townspeople and then went back to help Shamar. He was trying to untie the knot Najee had made, but it had tightened when Shamar had pulled them in against the river's current.

A man from the village scrambled down the bank, producing a knife from his coat. He cut Najee's ropes and then carried him up the bank where he was wrapped in blankets and put in front of Marl on the draft horse. The black was standing behind the draft, covered in a heavy blanket and a few coats, legs shaking.

Marl started off at a slow walk, leading the tired black behind him. The horse's bridle was off; a rope halter had been fashioned for him. There were rub marks behind his ears where the bridle had been, where he had felt the weight of Karbab.

Dush and the boy, whose name was Tomar, rode with me on the roan. We followed the rest of the people of Barda back into the city, not speaking the whole way. Tomar showed me a lot of the side streets so we could avoid most of the crowds. I left them at a street that connected the docks to the marketplace, where Dush ran for the docks and Tomar headed into the marketplace.

I stopped by Agathla's for a few minutes to tell them what had happened and then rode the roan at a trot back to the stable. He was tired, but he didn't slow the whole way until I stopped him by the paddock, where I led him in, took the bridle off, and turned him in with Shamar's brown, who had already rolled in the dirt.

I watched the roan run his nose on the ground over the whole paddock, until he circled back to a spot on the other side of the pen. With a groan he sank to his knees and then proceeded to roll in the dirt, grunting happily. He managed to flip over once before he heaved himself to his feet, rising in a cloud of dust.

Smiling, I turned and walked into the stable. Seeing no one, I went upstairs. I found Shamar sitting on the floor by the window in the sitting room, looking outside. I was nearly standing over him before he noticed me; he started, then eased himself back against the wall again.

"You really are quiet, aren't you?" he asked. I smiled in response and sat down next to him.

"That was pretty wild today, huh?" I asked. He nodded.

"I can't believe those two boys, jumping from rock to rock like that, like a couple of deer or something!" We laughed and then were quiet. After a minute I spoke.

"Where's Marl?"

"He took care of the boy that saved Karbab, an' he left the horse here. I put a few blankets on him and gave him some feed, but I'm not sure what else." He paused. Turning to me, he said, "You wouldn't mind teaching me a little of that sword fighting, will you? I mean, in your free time, if you don't mind."

I smiled. "Yeah, I'll teach you. But first, I need to find a couple of little wooden swords. It'd be a disaster if we practiced with real ones."

"I can get some. My friend is a carpenter, learned from his father."

"Good. Not too long, though. Just simple ones, too. Nothing fancy." He nodded. "When do you want to start?"

"As soon as they're finished!" I laughed at him. A few minutes later Marl appeared on the street, and we went downstairs to help him. We put the draft horse away while he checked on the black and then we fed and watered all the horses. It was dark by the time we finished, and as I tried to get ready for bed I felt a sort of worry. I was just about to climb into bed when I heard a voice.

Human, the voice said in my head. I nearly jumped out of my clothes; I had all but forgotten about the dragon from yesterday with today's events. Sighing, I answered.

Yes, dragon?

Where were you?! He snarled in my head. *I told you to meet me in the field today, and you never came! I thought something had happened to you.*

I'm sorry. One of our customers was in the marketplace and his horse got scared by something. It took off and kept running until it tried to jump the river, and we had to rescue it.

Why didn't you tell me?

I didn't know I could. I was surprised at what he had said, but then also kind of thinking myself dumb. Of course I could talk to him from a distance. That thought made me think of something else.

Where are you, anyways? I asked.

Up on the roof, he said, a touch of humor in his voice.

What? Without waiting for him to answer I pulled on a coat over my clothes and quietly ran down the stairs. The horses were stamping their feet in their stalls, softly neighing. I went to the stall that held the bay gelding and saw that he was pacing his stall with his head high, ears back, the whites of his eyes clearly showing. He was scared.

Jogging outside, I saw a flash of green as the dragon pulled his head back from looking over the edge of the roof. I huffed out a breath of air.

What are you doing here? I asked, stepping back to see him.

I told you. I was wondering where you were, since I heard nothing of you today.

Well, you know where I was. Why are you still here, then?

I told you to meet me in the field so you could start a portion of your training. You can do that now since you didn't come today.

What training?

I have to do a part of your training to become a dragon rider. Being a dragon rider means that you watch over all peoples and fight for them, if need be.

Wait a minute, dragon. I didn't sign up for this when we 'Bonded'. I don't want to be a babysitter for anyone. I don't want to fight-

But you have to, he interrupted. *You have no choice. That is the responsibility that comes with being a rider. Now—I can do only a part of your training. After that we'll have to go to a friend of mine, who can help you complete your training.*

What part can you do?

Mostly, it is all history—of the riders.

Why do I need history?

To understand your past so that you are better prepared for your future.

Oh.

Now, the night wears on, and we need to start if I am to return you here in a few hours so you can get some sleep. With that he leaped off the top of the roof. He landed lightly and quietly next to me, then took flight again when I was on his back. I barely managed to stifle a scream, and whimpered instead. On the way to the field we talked.

So, why are you working for Marl at the stables? the dragon asked just as we had cleared the southern end of the city's wall. He flew straight for the mountains, his nearest source of cover.

How do you know of Marl? The dragon laughed in my head.

You let out a lot more than you know, at least through your thoughts. You have to remember that I can hear you. Anyway, why are you working there?

To get money, I answered. *My cousin and I are traveling to Zathos's castle, though I don't know why.*

Why would you want to go there? the dragon asked, recovering after skipping a wingbeat at my words. I tried to think of an easy way to explain it, but I found none.

It's kind of a long story, was all I managed.

Well, we can make time for that tonight. You can tell me about you, and I'll tell you about me. Go on and start. We were in the mountains now and he turned north, flying low over the trees. I told him about how my cousin and I had come to Partaenia, meeting up with Geoff and Tayna, learning to swordfight, having to leave, and coming to Barda. By the time I had finished we had been sitting in the rocky field for quite some time. The dragon lay in the grass quietly while I spoke.

After I was done he started with his own story. He had been born on an island far north up the coast. He said that it was where dragons used to live, until the island became too small for all of them and they had to move onto the mainland. His parents were there, as far as he knew, and so was his friend that would be my teacher.

I'll not tell you his name; that is his own business. The island, though, is called Amatol. He went on to say that when he had turned nine hundred years old he had been sent off to find his *Fravid-Sorva*, which was dragon talk for Dragon-Bonded. He said very few people still knew of the name, as it had been shortened to just Bonded.

He had been searching for the right companion for at least two hundred years, he said. He was there when Zathos had taken over as king and had witnessed the effects of his evil reign. He had once been to the castle, just before the heirless king had died and Zathos had crowned himself king. He remembered the rolling fields of green and the castle sitting up on a rocky hill, overlooking the land. There had been small villages everywhere, and the whole kingdom had prospered.

And now, the dragon said, *the land is dark and desolate. Evil creatures have taken over the land, and whatever buildings that were there are gone, the people killed or run off. It is our job as* Sorva di Fravid, *or Dragon and his Bonded, to restore to the land the way it once was.* (The word *Sorva* means a dragon in general, but if you are specifying a male, it is *Sorvo,* while females are still *Sorva.*)

For another hour more he talked of the first *Sorva di Fravid* and how they had defeated an evil force in the land. After this more and more dragons sought companions, until it became normal for dragons to seek their companions at nine hundred years old. They were trained under either experienced *Fravid-Sorva* or by people who knew well the ways of *Sorva di Fravid,* which the dragons called *KnukSorva,* meaning Dragon Friend.

The many *Sorva di Fravid* continued to keep peace in the land, until people thought them old and useless. They tried to tell the *Sorva di Fravid* to leave, until all of the *Sorva di Fravid* were driven out to seek faraway lands where people would want them. Peace continued without the *Sorva di Fravid*, until Zathos came and took over the land.

This was when the dragon, the one sitting next to me, decided that he would be the first, of only about thirty remaining dragons, to seek a companion to overthrow Zathos and restore the land.

The rest of the dragons either lived on the island he had come from or hid themselves away long ago and haven't been seen again. My teacher was there on the island with my dragon's parents and some of the other dragons, waiting for him to return with me so I could complete my training.

Just as he was saying this I asked, "Is my teacher a *Fravid-Sorva?*"

No, the dragon said. *He is KnukSorva, a Dragon Friend. He knew many Sorva di Fravid, and he helped to raise me under their teachings, but he is not Bonded. And please, practice mind-speech. You must get used to it.*

Aye, Sorvo, I said, grinning at my own use of words. The dragon chuckled as well.

You learn fast, Fravid-Sorvo. *I am pleased.* Warmth rushed through me at his compliment, and I smiled. As I had seen people do in a formal mood, I bowed my head to him. He bowed back, pleased.

So, what does Iri hravath jhere Fravid-Sorva *mean?* I asked, remembering the phrase from the hundreds of voices when I'd Bonded with the dragon.

It is dragon-language, a phrase almost as old as the Sorva di Fravid *themselves. After it became tradition for dragons to Bond with humans or elves, it also became a tradition that the new additions would be blessed at the time of their Bonding. Often no other* Sorva di Fravid *were present at a Bonding, and so a spell was created to recite the blessing over the dragon and Bonded, magically helping to seal the Bond as it took place. Those voices you and I heard were the voices of every* Sorva di Fravid *that has ever been, their blessings saved over time and waiting to be reactivated by a Bonding. The phrase you wonder about is what was always said at the end of each blessing to complete the spell. It literally means 'the two-legged becomes Dragon-Bonded'. However the language has changed, and* hravath *is taken to be a human whereas* elifar *means an elf; the spell has also been changed to become more personal and thus more magically significant to the new Bonded.*

Now, the dragon said, *it is late, or rather, early. I must get you back to Marl so you can sleep a little before dawn.* He slowly stood and stretched, then let me climb onto his shoulders. When I was ready he leaped into the air, gaining altitude in a few wingbeats. As it was night, we only flew about a half mile above the land. I remained silent as we came closer and closer to Barda, mulling over all I'd learned.

The dragon landed silently in the yard in front of the stables, letting me off. *Erase my claw prints before you go inside,* he said before he took off once more. I did as he asked and then quietly slipped into my room upstairs. Easing myself into my bed, I quickly fell asleep.

A few days after Karbab's accident he came up to me on my way out of the city, close to the gates. I was riding one of the horses to go and meet the dragon in the forest and was taking a shortcut past the marketplace: an alley.

I almost turned the horse to run in the other direction, but maybe he had changed after the accident. People usually did, especially after accidents as serious as his. However, I still kept a wary hand on the reins.

He slowly walked his horse to mine; it was the sweet bay that I had first taken out. Marl had told me that Karbab wasn't allowed to touch the black again if he could help it. He knew he'd lose his business over it, but a few people had rallied to him and told him that they'd take some of his horses for him. With all the people that had offered to help, all of the horses were taken care of and he had a room in one of his friend's houses. So Karbab and his father couldn't use their threats anymore.

"I heard that you saved me when the beast ran me into the river." He gave me a warm smile, though I could tell it was fake. He kicked the bay; it stepped forward, and he pulled it up sharply when he was adjacent to me. I winced when the horse grunted and stutter-stepped, pulling its head up to ease the pain in its mouth. I remembered now that the bay had a soft mouth. He was the most patient horse I had ever seen, but he wasn't used to rough handling.

Karbab spoke again, letting his hands free from the reins. As he spoke, the hand nearest me moved slowly forward.

"Well," he said softly, "Didn't you save me? I heard that you were so eager to get to me in order to come to my rescue." His hand reached my thigh, and I sidestepped my horse away from him before he could touch me.

"No, it wasn't for you." I spoke in a cold voice, trying not to let it rise into a yell. "I was worried about the black. I could have cared less about you, but common courtesy requires me to save you if you are in need."

Karbab's eyes turned hard, but the rest of his face remained pleasant. "You will want me, one of these days. And I will have you."

"Need I remind you of my promise?" I asked. I could tell that he remembered how I had told him I'd kill him if he laid a hand on me again.

"You will get over it soon, I'm sure."

"I'll never forget it."

"Need I remind you that you will soon not have a job?" he said, suddenly changing the subject. It surprised me; I had expected him to keep trying to soften me.

He went on, "Marl will not let me take the horse out, and my father is getting angry. Marl has nowhere to go unless he lets me have the beast again."

I burst out, "That 'beast' still quakes when we approach him, from what you did to him! You ruined him! You have no idea how to handle a horse as great as he. You do not deserve him."

His face turned as hard as his eyes, and his hands shook with rage. I fingered the hilt of my sword, at the same time sending a faint whisper to the dragon: *Come. I might need you.* I felt him half-respond and draw closer to me.

Karbab made a move to get his horse closer to me, but before he could hurt the bay even more I said, "No. Let's settle this on the ground. Leave our mounts out of this."

I dismounted from my gelding and let the reins fall to the ground, knowing he would stay. Karbab did the same with the bay, and the two horses stood next to each other.

For the first time I noticed a sword belted to Karbab's side. He had his hand on its hilt, and I wondered how good he was at swordplay. Slowly I drew my sword, and he did the same. Stepping away from the horses, I let him follow me farther into the alley until we were far enough away from the horses so we couldn't hurt them.

We started circling each other, until Karbab thrust his sword out at me. It wasn't very good, and I easily blocked it. I struck back at him, coming in sideways from the right. He blocked it as well, though not as easily as I could have. I thrust out at him again and he dodged it, though I still gave him a slight cut on his upper arm. He examined it for a moment while I smiled.

Then, suddenly, he thrust his sword at my own arm. I worked to block it as he came at me with a skill that I had not seen before. He was good, very good. I struggled with every blow and was only able to get in a few strikes, but they seemed feeble compared to his.

He cut me—my arm, my leg, a thin scratch on my side. The cut on my leg was deep, and it pained me. I barely blocked a blow to my head, and then Karbab quickly stepped in toward me. He brought the butt of his sword down on me, smashing it into the right side of my neck. Crying out, I fell.

I dropped my sword as I hit my knees in pain, and Karbab kicked it away as he stepped toward me again. Barely breathing hard, he knelt beside me, putting his knee into the flesh above where he cut my leg. I cringed in pain.

"You are good, for a woman," he sneered, his face close to mine. He put his sword at my throat, watching me cringe underneath it, still in pain from the blow. A sick grin escaped him, sadistically twisting his entire face. No longer was he handsome, if I would ever have believed him so.

Then he bent over me, sword still at my throat. His lips met mine, but I did not return the kiss. The sword pressed down harder on my throat and came at an angle, where it could more easily cut into me. Reluctantly, I parted my lips. His tongue had started to dart in and out of my mouth when there was a shout from the far end of the alley.

Karbab tore his lips from mine to look up at the person who had shouted. Cursing, he got up, leaning heavily on his knee that was on my leg, causing me to writhe in pain again.

Feeling the dragon's consciousness lightly touching mine, I opened my mind to him, realizing that I had blocked him from me.

I'm right above you, high up. Are you all right? I can see you on the ground.

I'm-

My thought was cut off as Karbab turned to me again. I could hear feet coming, lots of feet. He reset his grip on his sword, bracing for a thrust. Hurriedly I tried to roll out of the way, but the sword point followed me, piercing my back, going through my shoulder. I curled into a ball, screaming, as the feet came closer. I heard Karbab's footsteps, and then the clatter of hooves as he raced away.

One pair of feet ran up to me, and I felt small hands on my side and my legs. I tensed even more at the touch, but then relaxed out when I heard Najee's voice, asking if I was all right.

In a daze I rolled over to face him; I saw all the rest of the boys and the girls that he led. Behind them I heard a commotion in the marketplace as everybody wondered what had happened and why the children had all suddenly disappeared from the marketplace.

A man shouted from the street, "What's the matter?"

"Call for a healer!" I heard Dush shout. "There's been a lady hurt!"

I heard the dragon calling again, closer this time. *Are you all right? Shall I get you?*

Karbab has wounded me, but I will be okay, I think. I will be fine in the hands of the townspeople.

How bad?

His sword pierced my shoulder through my back. He cut me, but only one is deep enough to bother. He also struck me on the neck,-

All right. I can tell you are weak. Rest. I will come for you tonight.

Feeling him leave, I could tell he was still keeping himself in my head to check on me. He was right; I was weak. I could barely stand and had to be helped by two men, who had to eventually carry me. Najee, Dush and a few of the others followed me all the way to the healer's house, and Najee came in with me when I couldn't answer the healer's questions. My sight was fading, and I knew that I'd soon pass out. Najee told the healer who I was and who had been in the alley with me, along with telling him that I had kin working for Agathla. He left when the healer had to take off my shirt to tend to my shoulder, and a slight woman with dark hair came in to help him.

I heard the healer telling his assistant something about Karbab and the seriousness of my shoulder, and then I remembered nothing after that.

I woke in the night to the dragon prodding at my consciousness. No one was in the room and I felt stronger than before, so I put my shirt on over my bandages and belted on my sword. Unable to put my quiver over my head, I instead carried it out with me.

I couldn't see the dragon at first, not until he moved. In the dark he was nearly invisible, for he was crouching not ten feet away from me next to a barn.

How are you? he asked. He stood and walked to me, not having to take more than a step and a half. His immense figure towered over mine, but I went and stood closer to him.

Better, I answered.

Are you ready?

For what?

To leave. You aren't safe here any longer. We need to go to Amatol to complete your training.

And leave my cousin here? He'll kill her! I cried, thinking of Karbab's rage today.

You knew you would have to do this.

Yes, but can we take her somewhere else? Somewhere where she'll be safe?

No one can know of us. Not yet. Unless she goes of her own will, we cannot take her anywhere.

Can I have one more day, then? To warn her and let Marl know that I am leaving? He has done too much for me to leave him like this.

One more. Be ready tomorrow night. I will be here then.

All right. Thank you.

Without a word he thrust himself up into the air with a giant downbeat of his wings. I listened to his rhythmic wingbeats fade as he flew farther and farther away. Sighing, I turned and snuck back into the healer's home. In a few moments I had set everything up as it was before, and I fell asleep on the mat.

Chapter 5

T HE NEXT MORNING I WAS out of the healer's house before anyone was awake. First I had to go to Marl and get my things and my pay, and then I would go to Shaelynn.

When I was almost there I felt a slight prod at my mind.

Dragon! I called.

Yes?

What are you doing? Where are you? You sound close.

Look up. I did so, and saw a small figure high in the sky above me, small enough to be mistaken for a bird. *I will watch you for a while. Are you going to be long at Marl's?*

Most likely.

Then call me when you come back out again. I'm not letting you out of my sight while you're outside again, at least not until we are up in the air tonight.

All right, dragon. I'll call for you when I go to Agathla's.

As I turned off the road and approached the stable, I saw the figure in the sky wheel and head for the mountains. I was about half ways up to the wide hall when Shamar came out with a young woman, leading a chestnut gelding.

He started when he glanced up and saw me approaching. Hurriedly he handed the reins to the woman, wishing her a good ride. By the time she had mounted and turned her horse for the road, I was standing in front of him.

"Rish," he said, out of breath. "I heard you fought Karbab yesterday, but I thought he'd killed you."

"Obviously, he didn't kill me. He pierced my shoulder, nothing more. I can only hope it heals properly." I kept things short, not wanting to press the subject. "Where's Marl?"

"Inside, why? You're not going to try and work today, are you?"

"No. Shamar," I paused. "I have to go. I'm not safe here anymore, and I have to leave. I—I can't teach you to swordfight. I'm sorry."

"It's all right." I could tell by the way he dipped his head and slowly turned to lead me inside that everything wasn't all right. He had really wanted to learn, and I had let him down. I felt like I'd taken a kick to the gut.

Marl looked up from behind his desk when Shamar led me in. A look of surprise crossed his face, and he motioned for Shamar to leave. When Marl had shut the door behind him, he shook my good hand.

"We all thought Karbab had . . ." Marl started, but I raised a hand.

"I know. I fought him, but he was better than I had expected. A lot better," I added.

"Why did you fight?"

"He thought that we could be together." A look of confusion crossed his face, and I went on, "It started from the day we met. He dragged me behind the stable and tried to get at me, but I pulled my sword on him and vowed that if he ever touched me again, I'd kill him."

Marl frowned, shaking his head. I continued, "Yesterday in the alley he approached me again, saying how I'd saved him and him alone. When that didn't work he tried to say that I'd soon be out of a job since you aren't letting him take the black horse out. I told him I was glad and that he didn't deserve the black, and he got angry. I suggested we get off and away from the horses, and we fought. He quickly had me down. One of the street kids saw me and shouted for the rest of them, and they came to help. Karbab went to drive me through, but I rolled and he missed—and pierced my shoulder. He ran when some of the townspeople came, and I haven't seen him since.

"Marl, Barda isn't safe for me anymore. I need to leave, by tonight. I'll need my pay if I'm to get anywhere as well." My speech done, I looked at him. He sighed, and then stood.

"I knew you'd say this."

"How—?"

"It's you. You're smart, not a fool. Now me, I'd most likely stay and fight and probably be killed. I'll be losing the best hand I've ever had, though. You're good all around with horses." His compliment filled me with happiness; it was one of the best things I'd ever heard from anyone.

He went to the room in the back and came back with a chest. Opening it, he withdrew a pouch full of coins. He put a few more in, and then tied it closed. I took it and pocketed the coins, then followed him out the door.

Putting a hand on my left shoulder, he said, "You have a gift with horses, girl. You should put it to further use in the future."

As I walked up the stairs to my room I thought about Marl and Shamar and how sad I'd be to leave them. I had come to love my job here and I didn't want to leave, but I had to. I quickly packed my scattered things, for I didn't have much. Putting my pack on my good shoulder, I headed back down the stairs.

About halfway down I heard voices, ones that were angry. At the bottom of the stairs I realized that it was Marl, arguing with another man. My heart skipped a beat as I realized that the other man was Karbab.

Silently I called the dragon; I knew I'd be leaving soon anyway, whether on my own or on the run. He answered, flashing me a picture of the rocky field. He'd be here in less than three minutes.

Just as I was thinking this I felt a hand grab my pack and pull me backwards. With a grunt I was pulled into an empty stall. Whirling around, I saw Shamar crouching down, urging me to do the same.

"It's Karbab!" he whispered.

"I know," I whispered back. "I can hear him talking."

"He's here for you. Somehow he knows you're here, and he wants to find you."

"Probably to finish the job," I muttered under my breath. As I spoke the voices grew louder and angrier, especially Marl's. Then there was an audible thump, and a grunt. Feet stormed up the steps while the other person stayed. I could hear Karbab slamming doors upstairs.

Quickly unlatching the stall, I slipped out, Shamar right behind me. Marl was doubled over, moaning. Looking up, he saw Shamar and me rushing to help.

"Get out of here, girl. Quickly, before he comes downstairs."

"But you . . ."

"I'm fine, only gut-hit. Shamar, get the bridle by the door and put it on the black." When Shamar had dashed out the door, Marl turned to me.

"You've gotta get out of here, out of Barda. Karbab probably won't bother to follow you farther than a few miles, but if he does you just keep running and defend yourself if need be. You've got skills with that bow, put it to use if you have to. The black will keep you safe, but you remember to keep him out of that damned man's hands."

Footsteps sounded on the stairs, and Marl shooed me from the office. I caught a glimpse of Shamar leading the black from his stall before Karbab ran out from the narrow hallway, eyes livid. He saw me and his face curved into a nasty smile as he unsheathed his sword.

"Now I've got you, and I can finish what we started!" He seemed a mad man as he yelled, charging at me in the wide hall with stalls of anxious horses on either side. I pulled out my sword in time to block his first swing, and for a brief moment I had the upper hand on him as I delivered blow after blow, forcing him back away from me. Before the fight could turn in his favor I delievered my hardest strike yet, and on the upswing I brought my sword arm back for balance as I picked up my right foot and kicked Karbab squarely in the chest, sending him flying into the solid door of a stall.

"Liz, take the black and go!" Marl shouted, and I turned to see Shamar just behind me with the horse. Shamar tossed the reins over the black's head as I jumped on his back, and I quickly turned the horse and kicked him into a run. He was eager to leave Karbab behind, and snorted happily when we came out from the hallway and raced for the street.

As I got out onto the road I looked over my shoulder. Karbab was running for his horse, which was hastily tied to the well. By the size of the knot I knew it would take him a moment or two, but it wouldn't be long.

I kept the black at a run on the side streets. Along the way I heard a whisper in my head and briefly looked up. The dragon was there, easily gliding not too far above me. I quickly explained to him the situation, but kept the black at a run.

What are you doing? the dragon asked angrily. *Karbab is after you, and you know he's out to kill you now.*

I have to warn Shaelynn. He'll kill her too if I don't.

There's a chance he won't. But if you do not leave the city now, he'll find you.

I can't leave her for dead. I'm going to convince her to leave.

She must leave on her own, we cannot bring her with us to Amatol. The only humans allowed there are Fravid-Sorva *and* KnukSorva. *And you must not tell her about me or where we are headed.*

All right, all right. I arrived at Agathla's in a hurried trot. Quickly I tied the black on the street and ran inside. Agathla was behind her counter. She looked up, surprised, when she saw me.

"Rish, I thought you were-"

"No, but Karbab is after me. Where's Tera?"

"In the back. Why?"

"She needs to leave here before Karbab comes after her as well. Get her pay, quickly. He's not far behind me." Trotting to the back, I opened up a door and came to a hall similar to the upstairs of the stable. I called for Shaelynn and started down it.

I quickly turned when I heard a door open, and Shaelynn poked her head out of a door behind me. Running to her, I went in her room and shut the door behind me.

"Liz, what—?" she asked as I found her pack and started putting things in it. Looking around the room, I could see that she had quickly made herself at home, something I could never do in such a short amount of time.

"You have to leave. Quickly. Karbab is after me, and he'll soon be after you if you don't leave as well."

"Leave?" she cried. "Leave Barda? I can't, I'm working for Agathla, and I can't leave her. Where would I go?" She paused, then considered me again.

"Where are you going?" she asked. "Are you going to leave me?"

"It's hard to explain. I have somewhere else to go, and you can't come, I'm sorry. But please, leave Barda. Now. Karbab tried to kill me yesterday, and now he's going to try again-"

"Again? Yesterday I heard you were dead! And now you're here, telling me to move my butt out of here, but I can't go with you. Where are you going that's so special?"

"I told you, it's hard to explain. Please, you have to-"

"No, Liz, I don't. I like it here, and I'm staying."

"Shaelynn-" Even as I started to say her name she took her pack from me. Walking to her door, she opened it just wide enough for me to get through.

"Goodbye, Liz. Have fun wherever it is you're going that you can't take me." I hesitated, caught between anger and desperation. Just as my desperation kicked in she grabbed my arm and dragged me out in the hall, shutting the door in my face when I turned to talk to her again.

Trotting down the hall again, I found Agathla had come from around her counter and was standing near the door. Going to her, I started to say something, but my breath caught in my throat.

Outside, people were dashing out of the way as Karbab came flying down the street. As he roughly pulled up the bay, I said to Agathla, "Tell Shaelynn to keep the black horse, and to keep it from Karbab, no matter what he does. Watch out for her, because I can't. I must leave." Digging in my pockets for a moment, I handed my bag of coins from Marl to Agathla, wordlessly telling her that they were for Shaelynn.

Drawing my sword, I walked out the door, locking it behind me from the inside. In case Shaelynn changed her mind, I didn't want her running out to save me and get hurt, or worse.

Karbab looked surprised when he saw me approaching him, so that I got a good first hit before he could draw his sword. I came in at an angle, cutting into his left shoulder.

Enraged, his left shoulder hanging limp by his side, he came at me, one blow after another. I struggled to block every one, even though he had only one good arm, like me.

I thanked God that Geoff had taught me to fight with both hands, because my good one was unusable now. I got another hit on Karbab, on his wrist that held his sword. Though it was a weak spot for most, he kept on striking, making his blows come harder and fiercer.

Finally my hand slipped, and I was unable to block a viscous blow to my lower side. The sword pierced deep, just above my hip. It was only my lower middle, but it was a bad injury all the same.

As I fell I heard Karbab laugh. He took a step toward me, sword raised. Then people started to scream and back away. Looking up, Karbab did the same, disappearing behind one of the buildings. I turned my head, but all I could see was Shaelynn standing in the window of Agathla's shop, looking shocked and hurt. Then I heard the whoosh of leathery wings, and I was enveloped by the dragon's claws.

In an instant I was lifted from the ground and flying fast from the city, headed for the ocean.

I regained consciousness when the dragon landed, and then I wished that I hadn't. The pain from my wound mounted suddenly, pushing down on my brain, almost enough to make me pass out again. Looking down at my hand, I saw that I still had my sword clenched in it. The dragon slowly let me down, gently sliding his razor-sharp claws out from under my body.

Delicately lifting my shirt to examine the wound, the dragon said, *I have to heal this. If we leave it you will bleed to death.*

All right, heal it then.

I have to use my flame. It will burn and leave a scar.

Just do it. A scar will be better than dying.

The dragon put the flat of one claw on my leg, the other on top of my shoulder, making sure I wouldn't move under him. Taking a deep breath, he made a hole between his scaly lips. As he let the air out an orange-blue flame came with it, scalding my skin. I twisted under the dragon's grip, but I couldn't move very much at all. In a moment he stopped the flame and released me. I writhed on the ground while he tried to examine his work.

It is healed. It will give you no more trouble.

What did you do?! That hurt more than I thought it would.

I breathed my flame on it. It has healing properties when it is hot. When it is white-hot, it can heal almost anything, even injuries implied by magic. Now—you were almost killed, and you were lucky I was there. And to what? I never saw your cousin leave, and I can tell from your feelings that she didn't have plans to.

No, I couldn't talk her into leaving. When I said I had to go somewhere she couldn't, it offended her. We're close, and we've always done everything together. It hurt her to know that I wanted us to be apart.

I see. His voice was sad as he regarded me. I was still recounting the events of the past half hour.

Before I met Karbab in front of the store I told Agathla to watch her for me and to keep and guard the black horse.

Aye. That was wise. But meeting him wasn't so much.

Yes, it was. There's no other way out of that shop than the front door. If he'd come in, he would have easily cornered me. I thought it was better to fight where you could help, and you did.

But I only did when you were in mortal danger. We were seen, and now word will spread to the sorcerer king that we are here. You are lucky that your place of training is protected, on an island far out in the ocean.

Are we near it? I pulled my map from my pack, examining it for any islands in the sea that took up the entire left side of the map. The only islands I saw were a small cluster of them to the south.

You won't find it on there, the dragon laughed. *It is in the northern waters, hidden from passing trade ships by enchantments. It will take us more than a few days to get there. We will travel up the coast to a certain place, then fly out over the ocean until we reach the island—Amatol. Your teacher is there, waiting.*

What is his name?

You know that I will not tell it to you. As for me, I feel the time is right. Now listen human, to every word I say: Dragons never give their names to anyone unless they form such an intimate relationship, like when we bond or mate. KnukSorva that have helped raise us since hatchlings may also know our names, but few dragons have been raised by humans along with their dragon parents, as I was.

He paused to collect his thoughts and went on, *A dragon's name is his soul, more than just an identifying name. Knowing a dragon's name gives you complete control over the dragon, if you wish to. By giving it to you I also take our bonding a step further: I will feel all of your pain now, and you will feel mine. This is why we never give our names away as easily as humans do. My name, then, is Honoras. Use it to call me if you are in real need of me. It is stronger than just trying mind-speech, and I can respond from a much greater distance. By knowing my name, you can also borrow strength from me when you need it, and I from you. Now—what is your true name?*

My name is Elizabeth; most people call me Liz. We humans do not have to conceal our names for so much reason as dragons do, but it's also dangerous to give our real names to the wrong person. That's why you knew me as Rish. My cousin and I took on fake names when we entered Barda.

That is wise Elizabeth. I am very glad to know your name, it is quite beautiful. Now—we have far to go, and you need to recover. Rest now and we will continue tomorrow.

But where? I can't sleep on the beach.

Come here. Lying down far enough away that the tide would not bother us, Honoras hooked a claw on the strap on my pack and dragged it over as I limped to him. Unsure, I dropped to my knees by his chest.

No. Lay down by my belly. My flame will keep you warm. Slowly standing up again, I shuffled around his forelegs and lay down next to his belly.

Put your head on my elbow . . . . There. Now stretch your body out, yes. He chuckled as I struggled to do as he asked, then finally got into the right position, which turned out to be extremely comfortable. As soon as I was still for a moment he lay his head down on the sand, pillowing it with a scaly foreleg. When his head was in place he stretched his wing out over me, enveloping me in a tent of warmth.

Closing my eyes, I could see Shaelynn standing in the window of Agathla's shop. I saw her face, a mixture of anger, surprise, and guilt. I wondered what she thought of Honoras, if maybe she thought that the dragon had killed me, or if she had figured it out. I also wondered if she was all right. Thinking back, I saw that it was dumb to fight Karbab in front of Agathla's shop, where he could easily figure that it was important to me, and he would know from people around Barda that I had family working there.

Rest, said a voice in my head.

I'm worrying about my cousin, if she's all right.

I know. I have been listening to you. One thing about humans is that they let their thoughts wander too freely. They never keep them to themselves.

Will I learn to control them? Sighing exasperatedly, Honoras lifted his wing up enough to peek at me.

Yes, you will learn. Now, rest. There will be time for questions later, my human. Sleep. I smiled at him as he lowered his wing again. Trying to focus on sleep, I closed my eyes, but I still saw Shaelynn there in the window. Again I heard her voice, refusing to leave. I saw Agathla standing by her window, looking up the street as Karbab approached. I remembered what I had told her, and how I had locked the door behind me as I went out to meet him.

I relived the fight, sinking into a fitful sleep. My slight victory, then again having to go up against his unbelievable skill. His sword slashing through my side-

I woke with a jerk, breathing hard, my body covered in sweat. Afraid to close my eyes again, I sat up in my warm shelter, trying to erase the memories fresh in my mind. I heard Honoras stir, and then wake when he realized that I was not asleep.

You did not sleep very long, Elizabeth.

Call me Liz, I grumbled. Honoras chuckled softly.

I shall call you by your true name whilst I am speaking directly to you.

But only my parents call me Elizabeth . . . and old people.

Are you implying that I am old? he grinned a toothy grin at me.

Of course you are, I grinned back. Sighing, I looked out across the ocean at the restless black waters and the white-crested waves that crashed onto the shore, a constant roar of rushing water and foam.

You are tired, Honoras remarked. *Why can't you sleep?*

The events of today came back at me too vividly.

Do you want me to help, my gliad?

What's a gliad?

It is a word we dragons use for someone young and green but dear, like a hatchling or fledgling.

Hmm. So, how can you help me sleep?

I know a few dragon lullabies. I promise you will sleep peacefully.

I'd be glad if you did. Thank you, Honoras. He started to hum deep in his throat, slightly vibrating my tent. The pitches of the song rose and fell, easily flowing together. Instantly I felt my eyes droop sleepily, and I lay down again by his belly, resting my head on his elbow and stretching my body out along the ground close to his body.

As I was almost asleep I asked, *Honoras?*

Yes?

What's the dragon word for someone I would look up to like a parent?

Wyrla. Why?

I am your gliad. You are my wyrla. Honoras chuckled, then continued his lullaby. It wasn't long before I drifted off into sleep.

The next morning I woke to find Honoras watching me. He had folded his wing and had drawn his legs up close to him, but the rest of his body was as it was when I had fallen asleep.

I sat up, feeling a slight pain in my side that quickly mounted, but subsided after a minute or two. Seeing me up, Honoras gathered his legs under him and stood, shaking his body like a dog to get the sand out of his scales.

When I struggled to stand Honoras offered me his head; I grabbed onto the base of his curved horns with my good arm and held on as he lifted me. *How are you feeling, Elizabeth?* Honoras asked, turning his gaze to the flat ocean horizon.

Call me Liz, I asked. *I'm feeling better than I expected I would, actually. But still not as good as I could be.*

That is understandable, he said, still watching the horizon. After a moment more he looked at me and then examined the land around us; I did the same to see what he was looking for.

As if reading my thoughts Honoras said, *I have been watching the horizons since dawn, which was several hours ago.*

Several hours? I slept that long?

Yes, my gliad. You were more exhausted than you thought you were.

Why are you watching the horizons?

To see if anyone approached in search of us. Are you ready?

What, to go? Already?

Aye. I am hungry, and I know you are too. We will fly up the coast; there is a forest not too far away from here.

As I struggled up onto his back Honoras picked up my pack, hooking his claws through both straps. Leaping into the air, he beat his wings vigorously to gain enough altitude to fly fast over the ground, not even a hundred feet below.

We flew faster than I thought we could, and soon I could see a forest whose trees marched right down to the water itself. As I looked at it I saw large birds flying above it while the smaller ones flitted from treetop to treetop to get out of sight of the birds of prey that circled above.

Honoras found a suitable clearing and landed, leaving my pack on the ground. Tossing my sword on top of it, I lifted my bow over my head, also pulling out an arrow and nocking it. Agreeing to keep our contact with each other open at all times, I set out into the forest while Honoras took flight and headed in the opposite direction.

I caught a few choice birds and headed for the clearing again to meet Honoras, who had already caught a couple of deer. As I walked out of the trees I saw him swallow a leg whole and then lick his claws, having eaten the last of the deer. Smiling, I approached him and sat down with a grunt on the ground.

Honoras watched as I plucked the birds, continually commenting on how dragons ate birds raw, feathers and all. He also suggested once that I try it and save some time, but I continued on until I had all four birds plucked. After this I cut off all the meat I could get from them, tossing the remains to Honoras, who quickly ate them up even after eating two deer.

Instead of trying to build a fire and roast the birds I set them on the ground and stood back as Honoras roasted them for me. In under a minute they were all well done. Being hungrier than I thought I was, I easily ate all the meat.

When I was nearly finished Honoras took flight for a moment, letting only his head clear the canopy of the trees. As the force of the wind from his wings beat down on me, I could feel him tense in my mind. Quickly he descended again, landing neatly next to me.

There are creatures in the sky, flying in this direction. Most likely they are Zathos's slaves, searching for us. He sounded extremely worried. He went on, *I hadn't planned on him sending out spies this early. That means that he found out quicker than I expected, and that can only be a spy, someone placed in the village that saw us. I had planned on staying in a rocky part of the shore until they came, where I could easily disguise myself.*

Now, Elizabeth, I must go. I will not fly, but I must find a rockier place in the forest to hide. You will find a dense thicket less than a quarter of a mile from here, heading that way. With a curved claw he pointed in the direction of the ocean. *Hide there, and go, quickly!*

He gave me my pack and my weapons, then gave me a nudge in the right direction. As soon as I had taken a few steps I felt the earth tremble as he trotted off in the opposite direction. I grumbled at his calling me Elizabeth again, but did as he told me to and I soon came to a thicket that was denser than I had pictured. There was a game trail that went through it, but it had been made by deer. I had to carry my pack in front of me and half-run doubled over, feeling twigs snagging at my clothes from all sides.

Inside the thicket it opened up a little, and I stopped there, gratefully setting my pack down. It was thick enough for what Honoras had wanted; I was unable to see the sky, save for a few slivers in between some of the branches above. The thicket was dark due to the lack of sunlight, darker than the cloudiest day. I could almost have believed it was night.

Sitting down, I waited for a sign—of the spies, from Honoras, or any sign of danger. In about five minutes I heard squawks above as birds flitted and flew to their nests, getting out of sight from the approachers. Even through the branches I could hear wing beats. They were powerful, but never as powerful as any dragon's. Through the spaces in the branches I could see the slivers of sky blocked out by feathers. As the creature moved I could see that the feathers glistened black in the sun like a raven's.

The creature stopped and hovered in the air above me. Catching my breath, I saw a head adorned with slim feathers that curved off its head, sitting atop a neck much like a swan's. Its long beak was as black as its feathers, with an eagle's curved end, coming to a wickedly sharp point.

Another bird joined the first, but I could only see that its legs were like that of a heron's. This bird was also black, like the first. They both hovered for a moment, the first moving its head in all directions. There was an evil cry from far away, then another, and another. The two birds above me voiced a raspy sound, like a command. Then the two flew down the coast where Honoras and I had come from, and the evil cries subsided.

All right, said Honoras in my head after a long moment. *It is safe, my gliad. Come out; I am close.* With a grunt both in my head for Honoras and one out loud, I stood and put my pack back on my front and hobbled out of the thicket. About halfway through the tunnel I felt the ground shake underneath me as Honoras landed in the trees ahead. It startled me and I lifted my head, getting my hair and my bow caught in the branches.

Sighing with frustration, I stumbled out of the tunnel, letting the branches take my hair out of the leather cord. My quiver stayed on my back, though I later had to clean a mess of broken branches out of it.

Honoras was waiting directly in front of the tunnel entrance. He took my pack when I held it out to him and waited patiently as I tried to get my hair to cooperate enough to tie back into a ponytail.

What were those bird things? I asked as I raked my fingers through my hair.

A race of phoenix that Zathos has enslaved. They once lived with the red and brown phoenixes, but years ago they separated from the rest. Zathos took that opportunity and welcomed them to him, and he has used them as spies of the air since. The black phoenixes were once very noble creatures, but Zathos has corrupted them.

That's a sad story.

I know, my gliad. I know. Now—they are far down the coast now, and we must fly hard and fast to Amatol. He looked through the tress, north towards the ocean.

How far is it? To Amatol, I mean.

A week's leisurely flight, four days for us who are in a hurry. In three days time we'll reach the northernmost point of the mainland that we will go. After that it's nearly a whole day's flight over the ocean.

But, he said, *that is enough questions for now. We must be on our way. Are you ready?*

I suppose so. Letting him take hold of my pack, I clambered up onto his back again. When I was in place he walked back to the clearing, where we immediately took off. Honoras flew low to the ground to gain speed, beating his wings faster and faster until they settled into an easy beat.

By nightfall we had traveled many miles, but Honoras said we had far to go still. He went hunting for both of us, bringing back the choice cuts from an elk. He dried them for me when I had eaten my fill, and once they had cooled I put them into my pack for later.

I fell asleep next to Honoras's belly again, enclosed in the tent made by his wing. We continued on like this for two more days, always watching for more of Zathos's spies. There were no more of them after the black phoenixes, and one day Honoras told me that we had reached the spot where we would rest before we flew to Amatol.

We will rest for the night and then head out before dawn, he said as we made camp at sunset. He hummed another lullaby for me as I fell asleep next to him under the shelter of his wing, but I knew that he'd be staying awake for most of the night to keep watch.

Zathos will have his spies here for us, Honoras had said before we'd landed. *He knows we must come to this spot before we fly for Amatol. Sleep lightly tonight my gliad. He might come for us then.*

I was nearly asleep when I recalled him saying that, and I immediately snapped out of sleepiness, startling Honoras.

What is it, gliad?

If Zathos or his spies come for us in the night, what will you do?

I will wake you and we will fly for Amatol. The spies will be left behind or outdistanced and will perish over the ocean.

Will you be strong enough to make it all the way under chase?

I will if I must. His words comforted me, and I let myself fall asleep as Honoras picked up his humming where he had left off.

Honoras told me later that I had been asleep for only an hour when they came. He had not seen them until it was too late, and he said that their numbers were too large for anyone to have held them off, or even to have out-flown them.

The latharks attacked just after Honoras had woken me, before I had time even to shoulder my pack. Latharks look like extremely bony horses with wings, but have sleek bat-like bodies with no hair. Their wings are clawed at the top and the ends of each "finger", and their bodies are brown, black, or stone-grey. They have a doglike snout with long sharp canines, the rest of their teeth being pointed and serrated, and they have no hair on their ropy tails. As for where they came from, it is said that Zathos rallied them to his side from a distant land.

They had begun to swarm around us when Honoras lifted me in his claws leaving everything but ourselves, taking to the air, flying over the ocean fast and hard, but the latharks kept up with his fiery pace. When they had surrounded us again some of them began to swoop in, trying to get at me, until Honoras caught one in his teeth. The lathark roared in anger before it was flung aside; it fell into the ocean and sank beneath the waves.

After this the latharks tried to weary Honoras, coming in at all angles and in large numbers at a time. The rest of the flying latharks picked up the pace, leaving enough room for Honoras in the front and driving him faster from behind.

Honoras was soon tired; after an hour of hard flying he was skipping wing beats and huffing for breath. His grip on me became weaker, but he never let it slip. The latharks came closer and closer to him, until they were free to attack as they wished. They bit him—on his shoulders where his wings met his body, on his neck, on his legs, and on his sides.

They couldn't get to me; it seemed the only thing Honoras was able to do but fly: to protect me still.

Then Honoras turned inland and back toward our camp, seeming to find his second wind. His wings beat faster and faster and he flew lower and lower above the water. He spread his body out horizontally, streamlining it. We flew faster than I had ever thought possible, faster than any jet. Were it not for Honoras holding me and his body partly sheltering me, I would have been ripped away by the force of the wind he created.

We passed our camp, and he turned back down the coast the way we had come. Then we passed our camp from two nights ago, then the forest we had hidden in. We sped like a bullet, until Honoras started to slow at a town I recognized that was a days' flight from Barda. High above the town he slowed and wheeled to face the latharks, who were but a few hundred or so feet behind us, even at the speed we had been going.

As they approached Honoras said, *No matter what happens, do not give anything up.*

What are you talking about?

I am weak, weaker than I ever thought possible, he said, just as a lathark hit him head-on. He grunted from the effort of recovering enough to stay in the sky. *They might capture you, but not if I can help it. All the same we cannot ignore the obvious. They are stronger than we, and there are more of them than I can handle.* Another lathark battered him from the side. They were all here now, and they came in all at once from all directions.

Trying to shake them off, Honoras suddenly took off to the side. It worked for a moment until the latharks recovered. They left Honoras's belly clear and attacked his top, all except for one jet-black lathark. It skirted around the rest and came up from underneath us as the rest of them held Honoras's attention. I cried out to Honoras as I saw its glassy black eyes blinking at me, its sinewy muscles rippling under its thin, tightly stretched skin.

Honoras's head dived down from the swarm of latharks, his open mouth reaching for the black one's body. It moved easily out of the way, seeming to bare its teeth in a grin. Honoras was suddenly pushed from above, knocking him off balance. I heard a ripping sound from above and felt Honoras's pain as the latharks bit into and tore the thin membranes of his wings. Unable to fly, we plummeted toward the earth at a frightening rate.

At the last moment Honoras turned in the air, putting me above him so he wouldn't flatten me underneath him. We hit earth, hard. I heard a few bones snap and break as Honoras landed on his back. We bounced and hit again from the force of the impact, skidding across the ground to a halt.

Honoras! I cried. There was no answer from the lifeless dragon under me. I tried getting out from his claws, but they were clamped shut. *Honoras, answer me! Please, no-*

My thought was cut off as a lathark pried open Honoras's claws. Backing up against the wall of Honoras's talon, I saw the lathark stretching its twisted head toward me. In a final attempt to wake Honoras, I delved into his mind, letting my mind become his. There was a spark of life and a feeling of anger and desperation and fear, and then there was black.

Chapter 6

SHAELYNN LAY IN HER BED for the second day in a row, thinking about nothing, really. She knew Agathla wanted her in the shop, helping, but she couldn't bring herself to do anything. Agathla had saved the black horse Liz had ridden on and that Liz had said it was hers, but she couldn't get herself to get up and care for it, even though her heart soared at owning such an animal as him. Agathla had told her that Liz had given her her pay from Marl, but Shaelynn had not accepted the small pouch of coins.

It had been three days since Liz had died. Shaelynn remembered it vividly: Karbab had fatally wounded her in the street, and then the dragon had come and taken her, probably to finish the job. Her bones were probably picked clean by now, bleaching in the sun.

Tears welled in Shaelynn's eyes as they did every time she thought of her lost cousin. She angrily wiped them away; she did not deserve the right to feel sad for Liz. The last thing she had probably remembered was that her cousin had deserted her. The last sight she probably saw was her standing in the window of Agathla's shop. Shaelynn had never told her sorry; she had just stared and done nothing as Karbab fought and defeated her and when the dragon had come for her.

Frustrated with herself, she got up and paced the room, another thing she had done for the past two days. There was a soft knock at the door, which she had locked. Shaelynn stopped as Agathla's voice came through it.

"Tera, dear, do you feel like coming out yet? I have a meal here for you."

"No."

"Tera, you need to eat. I know you're hurting, but starving yourself won't make the pain better."

"Maybe I can join my cousin."

"No, Tera. Don't think like that, not ever. Let me in."

"No. You'll drag me out of here."

"I won't. Make you eat, I will, but you can stay in your room if you like. Let me in. We need to talk." Sighing, Shaelynn dragged herself to the door and undid the latch. Opening it, she saw Agathla standing in the doorway, holding a plate of food.

Wordlessly Agathla handed her the plate. Shaelynn took it as Agathla closed the door behind her and went to sit on the edge of the bed.

"You know Rish wanted you to leave. To get away from Karbab, where you would be safe."

"She wanted me to leave alone while she went somewhere else. Somewhere that she couldn't take even me, her cousin."

"But she wanted you safe. It would have done her a world of good if you had told her yes, even if you had stayed. She could have run." Her words split Shaelynn wide open as she realized what she had done, and her tears streamed down her face, unchecked. "She was desperate, Shaelynn. As desperate as you are now, probably even more. She wanted to know that you would be safe from him."

"Well, she knew you'd keep me safe from him, even if he caught her. Why did she fight him instead of running when I told her no in the first place?"

"Tera!" Agathla scolded. "How can you say that? She had fought him before, so it's not like she stumbled into it blindly. She knew he would defeat her. She wanted to take his attention off of you to save you." Shaelynn was about to say something, but then stopped. Taking a deep breath, Agathla continued.

"She loved you enough to do that. Many people, even me, would never be able to do that for anyone. How can you honor her when you are starving yourself, locked up in your room?

"You can have today to think and mourn. Tomorrow I expect you back to work, or I will personally escort you out of the city to carry out Rish's last wish." Getting up, Agathla crossed the room and shut the door behind her, leaving Shaelynn with her plate of food. Shaelynn stood for a moment and then took a bite of bread, sitting on the floor.

When she was done she cried for a good while until she had no more tears to cry.

The next morning she reluctantly woke and got ready, just as she would have any morning before Liz was killed. She cried twice in the process, but managed to eat breakfast with Agathla and Leona, the other girl who helped in the store. They watched Shaelynn to see what she would do, but she appeared as normal as was expected for her present state.

Shaelynn worked quietly the whole day, until she got her afternoon break. She got the black horse ready in Agathla's neighbor's barn, which was close to the shop. When he was saddled as best as she could get him, she swung up in the saddle and rode the fidgety horse to the marketplace in search of Najee and Dush.

She found them stealing money from rich people as usual. Najee was talking to an extremely fat man, and Dush was walking away from a snobby-looking woman, tossing her coin purse in the air and catching it before he pocketed it. A moment later he had disappeared with the rest of the people there and the woman had discovered her loss. There was a squeal of rage from the woman, and a few of the usual merchants hid their grins.

"Hey, Tera." The voice came from her left side, surprising her. Looking down, she saw Supai standing next to the black with a steady hand on its shoulder. The black had turned his head to examine the young boy without her noticing; it turned its head to face forward, where she saw Dush standing with a wide grin on his face.

"Hey, guys," she said, glancing up to see Najee walking away from them as the fat man behind him reached for a coin purse that wasn't there. Najee quickly turned and dodged into a merchant's stall as the fat man came trotting his way. Laughing, Shaelynn turned back to Supai and Dush, who were also grinning.

Suddenly the black threw up his head and pulled his ears back, looking behind him. Shaelynn and the two boys turned to look; Najee was standing behind the black, playfully pulling his tail. The black warningly cocked a hind leg, and Najee bared his teeth, making horse ears out of his cupped hands. In an instant he had turned them backward, still baring his teeth. The black read his message and put his leg down, dipping his head shamefully to the ground.

Najee came forward, putting his horse ears forward again in a friendly way. The black lifted his head again as Najee took light, dancing steps toward the black. Playfully the black snaked his head out and nipped Najee's hair, being careful not to pull it.

Shaelynn watched the two communicate, mesmerized first by Najee's sudden appearance and then by the way he talked and played with the black. In response to the black Najee reached out and tugged a lock of the black's hair. The horse danced underneath Shaelynn, unsettling her. Cautiously she grabbed the black's mane.

Najee quickly stepped back from the black and bared his teeth again. The horse became still, and Shaelynn relaxed again. "Thanks, Najee."

"No problem. How are you? After Rish, I mean," he said softly, indicating with his tone that he didn't mean to set her off.

"I wasn't looking good until Agathla came in and talked to me yesterday, but I am better now. I'm still sad, but not so much now that it overpowers me."

"Good. I'm glad you're recovering. All of us, my gang, I mean, we're sorry. We liked Rish a lot. It's a pity she had to go like that."

"She was protecting me. She knew he'd defeat her, Agathla said. But she wanted me to be okay."

"And you will be. We are watching you as closely as Agathla, even if you don't realize it." It was Supai that said this, and he stepped closer to Najee, putting a hand on his shoulder.

"Yeah," said Dush, moving around the black to stand in front of them. "I been watching the shop 'till you came out yesterday, even spoke to Agathla."

"And I been following you since you left the shop," Supai put in.

"Thanks guys, but I really . . . I don't need-" Najee held up a hand, cutting her off.

"I told them to watch you for good reason. Agathla was right. Rish knew what she was getting into. She knows how to fight. I mean, she really knows. And Karbab still did that to her. I watched them fight in the alley, before I realized that it was them. He had her down in under half a minute. You wouldn't stand a chance. He's way too skilled."

Shaelynn stopped, considering what Najee had said. He was right—Liz had told her that Geoff himself had taught her to fight, and Karbab was still the better by a long shot. She had watched the fight in the street, before Liz had been wounded. Liz had been good, but Karbab was better.

"Thank you," Shaelynn finally, said, bowing her head to the three of them. "I greatly appreciate your concern and would be grateful if you could keep watching me when Agathla is not there." Just as she finished speaking there was a yell from behind her. It sounded female, and it was angry. With quick bows to Shaelynn and a few grins, they dashed away and easily disappeared. As Shaelynn got her horse out of the way of the snobby woman Dush had robbed earlier, Shaelynn saw Najee reappear a few stalls ahead of her with Supai. They talked with an elderly man, who gave them a few coins from his purse. They smiled gratefully, bowing to the man. They left his coin purse alone.

Laughing, Shaelynn rode the black out of the marketplace, seeing for the first time Supai darting in and out of her vision from the corners of her eyes. She rode to the stable that Liz had worked at, where she saw Supai disappear to wait behind one of the buildings.

"I won't be long, Supai," she called over her shoulder. As Shaelynn approached the stable Marl walked out from the wide hall, smiling. It was a grim smile, but a smile all the same, and it was good to see it coming from Marl. Dismounting, she returned his embrace. Marl led the black in for her as she walked next to him. Wordlessly she helped to take off the saddle and quickly brush him down.

Then Marl led her to his office, shutting the door behind them. He crossed the room to sit behind his desk while she took a seat in front of it.

"So," Marl started, clasping his hands together, "Rish gave you the black?"

"Yes, she told Agathla he was mine before she met Karbab."

"Why did she go to see you? She knew Karbab was after her."

"She did?"

"Aye, he chased her from here. She came early, just after we opened. She came in telling me she'd leave, then asked for her wages. She went upstairs to get her things, and Karbab showed up. She and Shamar ran downstairs and hid in a stall. Karbab struck me and went upstairs to look for her, then I got her up on the black. She was almost out when Karbab saw her coming down the stairs, and she took off with him right after her."

"I didn't know that. She came to talk to me to tell me to leave. I couldn't go with her, she said. I had to leave and go on my own."

"Really?"

"Yes. She said it was hard to explain, and I couldn't go with her."

"She wanted you to leave so you'd be safe from Karbab?"

"Yes. But I stalled her because we argued, and she couldn't run."

"No, Tera. Don't blame yourself for it. It was her fate, and nothing could control that."

"I know; it's just hard to understand it."

"Aye. Things will heal in time, though, as long as you don't let it linger over you." Without saying anything else besides a "take care of yourself," and, "you're welcome here anytime," Marl helped Shaelynn saddle the black up again.

"Take care of this horse, now," Marl said after she had mounted. He patted it on the shoulder and said, "He's a good horse, only gets a little scared sometimes, just like everyone else. If you ask right, he'll do anything for you. If you need any help with him, come see me."

Shaelynn went onto the street at a trot, slowing down when she remembered that Supai had been waiting on her. She saw him out the corner of her eye not ten feet behind her and relaxed in the saddle, somehow reassured that he was there to watch her.

She went straight to the barn that housed the black, as she was a few minutes past her break time. She slid the saddle off his back and put it back in the corner where she had found it and brushed him down with a handful of hay as she had seen Marl do. Hurriedly she trotted up the street and entered Agathla's shop, seeing Supai dart away after she shut the door behind her.

"You're late," Agathla said from behind the counter. Shaelynn was about to call over her shoulder on her way to her room when she saw that she had a customer who was looking at a necklace. Shaelynn knew that Agathla wouldn't want to listen until the customer had left, so she went to her room and changed out of her breeches and back into her maroon robe.

She liked this robe; for one, it was comfortable, and another, she liked the way it looked. It had sleeves that went halfway down her arms, a squared collar that went down a ways but not too far down, and it had a golden sash that went good with a necklace she had bought from Agathla with her wages.

Half-trotting down the hall, she stopped at the end of it and closed the door to the hall behind her. Shaelynn heard someone clear their throat expectantly, and she turned. The person at the counter was still there, except she was now wearing the necklace she had been looking at.

"Why were you late, Tera?" Agathla asked.

"I went to Marl's stable to talk with him, and it took longer than I expected."

"Ah. I have heard tell that you were in the marketplace as well." Shaelynn looked at the woman, seeing her for the first time. She was the snobby woman that Dush had robbed.

Agathla went on, "Ms. Vaught says that she saw you sitting your horse, talking with the boy who robbed her." Shaelynn's breath caught in her throat as she realized what they were getting at, but she held her tongue.

"Yes, he was asking me for money as well," she said, amazed at her ability to come up with such things so fast. "He and the other two. You saw them as well, didn't you, Ms. Vaught?" Shaelynn grinned inwardly at her achievement of turning the conversation on her so smoothly.

"Why, yes, I did see the other two. Did they rob you as they did me? You seemed to be laughing with them at some joke right before you left with them."

"I was laughing at them, Ms. Vaught. I saw the boy rob you, yes, and I was laughing at them when you discovered your loss and started chasing them." Again she smiled inside. She had just easily thought up another lie that fit perfectly. The woman stood there gaping for a moment, unable to think of anything to say. Then she snapped her mouth shut and tramped out of the store, mumbling a thank you to Agathla before she shut the door behind her.

Shaelynn let her smiles escape her in a wide grin, until she saw Agathla looking at her accusingly. The smile vanished.

"Tera, what were you doing in the marketplace? That's the one place you're bound to find Karbab."

"I had to see Najee. Dush was there too; he was the one who robbed Ms. Vaught. I saw Supai there as well. It turns out that Dush has been watching me here since Liz's death, and Supai followed me today. Najee said he'll have somebody watching me when you're not here."

Smiling with approval, Agathla said, "Aye, Najee has always been loyal to any close friends he makes. You are lucky to have him and his comrades watching you. With as many connections as they have, you will be safe anywhere.

"Tomorrow, however," she said sternly, "I expect you to be riding in on your horse with fifteen minutes to spare, that way you have time to unsaddle him and change your clothes before you report back to work." She walked around from behind the counter, taking Shaelynn by the elbow and leading her to a shelf on the far wall.

"Now," Agathla said, "I don't know what to put on this shelf now that the necklace is gone. Can you help me pick one out? And I don't like these earrings here . . ."

===

I woke in a dark, damp place, feeling very cold and hungry. As I moved to stand I heard a laugh coming from somewhere, but the close walls around me made it echo, seeming to come from everywhere at once. Startled, I scuffled backwards until I hit a wall; I didn't have to go very far. Reaching out with my left hand, I groped for another wall.

A rough hand grabbed my arm, letting it go as I jerked it back and scooted back in the opposite direction, finding a corner. The person laughed again, a wicked, cold laugh.

"Are you scared of me, *Fravid-Sorva*?" I recognized the name from what Honoras had told me. As I remained silent the man laughed again, for now that he spoke I realized that he was a man.

"Who are you?" I croaked, astonished at my voice that was usually strong.

Laughing again, the man replied, "The man you will wish you had never met. I am Avernus, Zathos's personal servant. You are here, in his dungeon, deep underground, where your dragon can never get to you." With a wicked laugh I saw light flood the room as Avernus opened a door and left. Before he shut the door he turned to once more look at me. He wore a blood red robe and had white eyes and jet-black hair. Then he turned away and with a thud the door shut, enveloping me in darkness.

===

Honoras's senses told him that he was in trouble even before he realized he was awake. He could feel walls all around him and shackles on his talons. He could feel the presence of many other minds around him. Smelling, he realized they were humans, and they were close, but not too close for him to identify any one person.

As he stirred he could hear the chink of chains on stone. Feeling past his scales, he realized that he was lying on a stone-filled floor. He heard people audibly gasp and the shuffle of their feet as they backed away even further. Opening his eyes, he could see high walls all around him. The thick chains that held him to the wall were bolted in place. Several chains spread out from each talon, and they even had shackles put at the bases of his wings and one around his neck.

Looking above and around him, he saw an open roof crowded with people and windows around him that people had gaped through, at least until he had moved and they had backed away. Seeing the wide doors in front of him and the daylight past the windows, he realized that he was in their public prison. That meant that these walls were at least a few feet thick and strongly made. Getting out would be rough.

He heard the whispers of people around and above him, but he did not bother to make out their language. Instead he tried repositioning his body into a more comfortable position. He got half ways comfortable at least, so he laid his head on his talons and stared at the wall in front of him, thinking.

Maybe, if he didn't do anything stupid, the people of this town would become comfortable enough around him that they would either let him go or he could be free enough to get away. He could try communicating with one of them through mind-speech, but it would be difficult. One thing he was sure of, at least: he had to get out quickly to find Elizabeth before she was hurt or killed.

He knew that the latharks would have taken her to Zathos, but from there he wasn't sure. He knew she'd be close to the king, maybe in his dungeons. He was sure she'd be tortured; he knew that she wouldn't give anything up and for that Zathos would surely inflict pain. Honoras only wished he could get there before Zathos or one of his servants started, for he like he had told Elizabeth, once Bonded by will and by name, dragon and human felt each other's pain to the fullest extent.

Just then, a voice called from above Honoras: "Dragon! I know you can understand me, for I know of your kind. Can you make the human-talk?" Honoras thought for a moment, deciding whether or not he should answer. He shook his head.

He sensed the man's disappointment as he thought that all hope of communicating with the dragon was gone. Honoras thought for a good moment, going back and forth in his mind. Finally, he decided to do it.

Delving into the man's open thoughts, he said, *I can't make the man-talk, but I can mind-speak.* He saw the man whirl in place, looking to see who had spoken to him. His eyes finally settled on Honoras, who was looking intently up at him.

"Did you just speak to me? In my head?" The man was astonished; he had never heard of dragons communicating through mind-speech before. He watched, amazed, as Honoras dipped his head in a slow nod.

You can as well, if you wish. But if you are more comfortable speaking aloud, that is fine with me. I only wish that we speak in private, Dragon-Knower. The man's face slacked as he tried to concentrate on the dragon's words, which were barely more than a whisper in his mind. His face became troubled as he slowly interpreted Honoras's message.

Turning to an old man next to him, he said to him, "The dragon wants to speak to me, in private." The old man nodded, gesturing for the prison's guards to run everybody off. The man walked downstairs with everybody else, pausing at the wide doors to the cell until everybody had left. When he was sure that even the guards had gone, he cracked one of the heavy doors open enough for him to slip through. Legs and hands shaking, he turned his back on the waiting dragon to push the door shut, hoping that what he had learned was true and the dragon wouldn't strike him while his back was turned.

Honoras did not move from his position as he watched the man shake, feeling his fear reverberate from him like waves of thunder in a cloud. The man turned around again to find that the dragon had not moved. Heaving a sigh of relief, he sunk down to the ground, leaning his back against the door.

"So, dragon. Why are you here?"

I would rather not give you all the details, but I and my Bonded were attacked in the sky, by a swarm of latharks.

"Latharks?" the man interrupted. "They have not been seen since the old days."

Aye, I lived through those days. They were sent by Zathos.

"That is hardly surprising. If you are Bonded, then it is no wonder Zathos is after you. A dragon and his *Fravid-Sorvo* would be dangerous to his rule."

I see you are familiar with the old name as well as the dragon language, Honoras said with satisfaction in his voice, noticing how he specified that Elizabeth was Bonded to him, a male dragon.

"Yes. I have tried to learn everything about dragons, but I see I have not." Honoras made a frightening sound deep in his chest. It startled the man, until he realized that the dragon was laughing.

Countless humans have tried, but none have ever succeeded. It is an impossible task. However, we are straying from our subject. The latharks overpowered my Bonded and me while we flew over the ocean, but I found a new strength and headed back for civilization, looking for help. Once I found this town, I was surprised that I was still able to stay in the sky.

The latharks attacked again, most of them from the top, while another circled under me to try and get my Bonded from me. I brought my head underneath me to defend my Bonded, which was exactly what they wanted. They knocked me off balance and ripped my wings so that I was unable to fly. I put myself underneath my Bonded to help break the fall, and that is the last I remembered.

"That is quite a story. Are you all right?"

I know that I have broken a few bones in my back from the fall, but they will heal on their own with a little of my own help. I am most worried about my wings, for if they do not heal correctly they will be of little use.

Honoras raised his wings with some difficulty to show the man his tattered membranes. The man gaped at Honoras's wing span and then got to his feet. "May I?" he asked, gesturing at Honoras's wings. Honoras nodded, and the man stepped forward.

As he wordlessly examined his wings Honoras asked him, *If I may ask, can you give me a name I can call you by? It doesn't have to be your real name if you wish.*

"I am Riman. And you, what may I call you, if I dare ask?"

You know that I cannot grant you my true name, but you can call me whatever name you wish, if you can think of one. Honoras jerked his wing inward as Riman touched the edge of a tear.

"Sorry about that," Riman said quietly.

It is all right; it is only still tender. Have you thought of anything?

"Mmmm, I will call you . . . well, I guess I could just call you Sorvo. That's your word for dragon, isn't it?"

It will do, if that is all you can possibly think of.

The man laughed out loud and said, "Sorvo, you are too much. I had expected a dragon your size to be more serious."

Am I supposed to be? Riman laughed again, shaking his head.

"You only surprised me. I didn't think dragons had a sense of humor."

Why not? We are as complex as any human, capable of any emotion and personality you are. Another thing you fail to realize is that we are just as intelligent as you are. But do not worry; as you said, you have much to learn. You and every other human.

"Where are the other dragons? You can't be the only one."

Most of us fled north or south, away from certain destruction by Zathos and abandonment by the people. But a few of us remain on an island, though I will not say where.

"Is this the island you and your Bonded were going to?"

Aye.

"For what reason?"

To complete her training.

"Training? What, is she not yet trained? How old is she? Who is she? And where is she?"

You humans and your questions. My companion has even more than you. No, she is not yet trained. She has only begun. She is young by even your standards, but I will not say who she is. I shall not give that away. But I can tell you that she was taken to Zathos by the latharks when we were attacked, probably after I fell. As for exactly where, I do not know.

"She is in the hands of Zathos? You need to get to her, quickly." Turning to leave, Riman said, "I will see what I can arrange. Hopefully you will be out of here by tomorrow. I must go; I will send a healer to tend to your wings."

Tell the healer that I swear on my being that I will not harm them.

Riman paused at the door. "I'm not so sure that will work. We may have to dart you, just to make the people comfortable. Please do not be angry."

It is all right; I understand. Do what you must to heal them, though. Leave, quickly, and try to convince your people. With a firm nod Riman opened the door and left, pulling it shut behind him, leaving Honoras alone in his small cell.

About an hour later there was a commotion outside the wide doors. Honoras sensed many people, all of them nervous. The door cracked open, and with a whoosh a small dart, half the size of an arrow, came flying in. As it clacked off Honoras's hard scales he saw that the tip had been dipped in a bluish fluid. Sniffing it, he realized that it was made from a plant he knew had enough strength to knock him out if it hit him right.

Going against his better judgment, Honoras roared loudly and stood on his hind legs, exposing his chest and flanks, the only place he was not shielded by harder scales. Another dart came flying in, going faster than the first. As he had intended, the human had put more force behind the dart due to his roar.

The dart sunk into the flesh of his right flank. Honoras roared again as he felt the full force of the herbs quickly take effect. In less than a minute he had toppled to the ground, unconscious.

The man who had shot the darts peeked in through the crack in the wide doors. The dragon had fallen forward on its stomach, straining at the chains around its neck and the bases of its wings. Its forelegs had been pulled under itself by the shackles attached to the walls. He waited for a moment to see if the dragon would move again, quickly stepping in and nudging it with his foot. Nothing happened.

"He's out, but I can't tell for how long. We put enough in there to kill a whale." After he had said this the healer cautiously stepped in, a small, slight woman no more than twenty years old. She looked at the dragon lying on the ground before her, awed at his size and at his very existence.

Feeling the stares of the armed men behind her and the dart man standing in front of her, she looked away from the dragon. "Go, all of you. I will be fine." Bowing, unconvinced, the dart man stepped out of the room and pulled the door shut behind him. She waited until she heard no noises from outside, and then knelt beside the dragon.

Just to be sure, she expanded her mind just far enough to check if anyone was close enough to see or hear anything. She felt no other presences around her but the dragon. Satisfied, she opened her pack. Taking out her smelling salts, she set them next to her, along with a healing salve a real healer had given her once. Standing, she went to the dragon's side where the dart protruded from his flank.

Closing her eyes and focusing on the dragon, she felt the knockout herbs' power all over his body. Concentrating, she drew every trace of it she could find in him to the point of the dart inside his flank. Willing it to remain clustered on the point, she pulled the roughly made thing out of his side. For a moment she could see what she had gathered, then it fell and scattered on the ground.

Walking back to the dragon's head, she opened the top to the jar of smelling salts and placed it under the dragon's nose, far enough away that they wouldn't affect him too badly. The dragon took two slow breaths before he sucked in an enormous amount of air and spat it back out, opening his eyes and lifting his head, shaking it wildly.

He continued on for a moment, batting at his muzzle with his talons, before he calmed and his eyes settled on the healer. *Why am I? How did you—*

Hush, Sorvo, she said, raising a hand. Honoras considered her again, realizing that she had used mind-speech. What surprised him was that her voice was clear in his head, not just a mumble that he usually got when other humans besides Elizabeth spoke to him through mind-speech.

The woman went on, *I removed the herbs' power from you and pulled it out along with the dart. See for yourself.* Honoras shifted enough to see his flank and the dart lying on the ground next to it.

Dipping his head low, Honoras said, *I thank you. But I must ask: how can anyone but a magic-user draw that out of my body?*

I can perform a few healing tasks, but I am no healer, the woman said, smiling. *I was trained in the use of magic, though I am no great sorceress. I merely do things that are just above what normal humans can accomplish.*

Still, it is better than most can say. If I may ask, who taught you?

His schooling was excellent, before he turned for the worse. The woman scowled, not looking at Honoras. *His name was Markus, but we now know him as Zathos.* Honoras quickly stood and backed away from the woman, as far away as the chains would let him go. He growled viciously at the woman.

Go, now, one who learned from my enemy.

Should you judge me by who I learned from? He was not your enemy at that time, merely a man learned in the arcane arts.

You still were with him, no matter who he was then. He may have influenced you, and I'll have no part of you.

How shall you make me leave, Sorvo? You cannot leave this place, the townspeople here have made sure of that. Even you with your strength cannot break those chains. Nor are you able to fly, for that matter. You need me.

With a shudder of acceptance Honoras realized that she was right. He needed her to heal him if he had any chance of quickly reaching Elizabeth, whether or not the townspeople released him. If his wings did not heal properly, he would have troubles flying the rest of his life.

His own magic allowed him to heal a few things, and he would use that to heal his back, which ached him from as much as he had moved today, though it was little. Yet he could not use it to heal both; he did not have enough. Whether he liked it or not, he needed her help.

Relaxing his position to a more comfortable spot lying on his side, he allowed her to approach him. He spread a wing out for her as best as he could.

I will use both magic and herbs to heal these tears, the woman told him.

If it will not interrupt your work, may I work on my own back with my own magic?

I did not know that dragons could use magic.

We have very little, but it is enough to help.

Aye, you may. With that they both set to work. The woman carefully put on the herb cream, trying not to cause the dragon pain and interrupt his work. Honoras had difficulty drawing on his magic, but once he found it and directed it to the bones in his back it wasn't as hard as he had expected. Just as the other dragons had taught him, he willed the magic to do what he wanted, whispering a few dragon words in his head to help it along.

After the woman had put the salve on every tear she could find, she herself submerged her mind in her magic, directing it to the edges of the tears, willing the salve to work faster than normal. A few smaller tears healed completely, and the bigger ones were reduced to a much smaller size. In a few minutes every tear but two larger ones had totally healed.

Sitting to rest and to wait for the dragon to finish his work, she examined the chains bolted into the wall. They were strong, but she could snap them with her magic if she needed to. Deciding that that would drain too much of her strength from her, she looked at the shackles fastened to the dragon. She could cut them with magic, but not all at once. She could weaken them, however. Maybe once the dragon was healed and his strength had returned he could break them once she had weakened them.

She knew the dragon had to get to his Bonded one, for Riman had told her what he and the dragon had discussed. She also knew that Zathos was impatient and if the dragon's Bonded did not give him the answers he wanted, the dragon would soon be going through almost the same thing as his Bonded was, far away. Like Riman, she wanted the dragon to be set free as soon as possible.

She was startled out of her thoughts as the dragon nudged her with the flat of a claw. *I am finished, and my bones are healed.*

Shall I start on the other wing?

Aye, if you have the strength for it.

I do. Sorvo?

Yes?

I was thinking: If I weakened your shackles, would you be able to break them once your strength has returned? I mean, if the townspeople will not release you soon.

Why are you concerned about me?

I know what you and Riman talked about. He told me.

Ah. I see. Yes, I would be able to. You are right; I would like to be out of here soon.

Have you ever felt it? The pain of your Bonded?

A little in the past few days with her, but not enough to really bother. She was wounded, you see, in Barda, and I healed her before we exchanged our real names, creating that bond.

In Barda, did you say?

Aye.

I was there when a young lady came in to the healer there. She had been pierced through the shoulder with sword. The young boy who came in with her said that she'd been in a swordfight with some man.

What was his name? Was it Karbab?

Aye, that is what the boy said. She had fought Karbab and he had overpowered her. How did you know?

Honoras hesitated, and then decided to tell her the truth. After all, she had already healed one of his wings. He answered, *She is my Bonded, the girl who came to you and the healer. The boy I do not know of; he might have been one of the younglings from the marketplace that she spoke of.*

Aye. The boy was Najee, the leader or the marketplace children. They beg money from the rich people there and rob them when they don't give it to them. The merchants there enjoy it somewhat; everybody thinks that people that arrogant deserve to lose however little of their money.

She continued, *I had wondered what had happened to her. One night we left her in the main room on a bed, and the next morning she had disappeared. Right after that I left for here. What happened to her?*

The man Karbab chased her from the stables, where she had been working. She went to her cousin at another store to beg her to leave Karbab's wrath, but her cousin refused. Not wanting to be cornered in the store by Karbab, my Bonded faced him in the street. She was badly wounded, but I rescued her and we fled for an island of safety I know of. Zathos's spies found us and chased us from about four day's flight from here. We were surrounded and attacked and she was taken from me. And of course, Riman has told you the rest.

Yes, he has. I think I will start on your other wing now.

Please do so. He repositioned himself to make his wing more available to her and fell silent as she began her work. She quickly finished and within a half-hour they had exchanged a few more words and she left.

Chapter 7

I WAS LEFT IN THE CELL for a few more hours before Avernus came for me again. I had been thinking about the bracelet, which I somehow still had on. I remembered how I had liked it when I found it at the mall, and how reading the tag that was now in my pack had brought Shaelynn and me here. I remembered our first night here in Partaenia, the griffin and Geoff the following morning, and Tayna. I remembered their hospitality and what they had taught us.

The light from the open door nearly blinded me from hours in the dark. Feeling my heart jump in my chest, I tried to back even further into my corner, wishing I could melt into the stone walls around me. My heart leaped further up into my throat when I saw the burly man that accompanied Avernus.

Avernus laughed, saying, "Are you ready to feel the power of Zathos, *Fravid-Sorva?*" I let a quiet whimper escape me as Avernus flicked a finger over the lock of my cell; it clicked open without him touching it, and the burly man stepped into the cell.

The man roughly grasped my elbow and dragged me out of the cell to Avernus. He laughed as I squirmed in the man's grasp, trying to break free, though I knew that I never could break from the man's grasp.

Avernus waved his hand in a strange way; I felt a strong force, stronger than any man, lift me from the ground by my head. My face became just lower than Avernus' before he clenched it into a fist, and I was held in place. Keeping his left hand clenched, he brought his right hand up to my face. He held out a claw-like fingernail and then quickly raked it across my left cheek, leaving a deep scratch. As I gasped and squirmed in the hold of his magic, I felt blood start to run down my neck.

A grin playing on his lips, Avernus gestured to the man and released his magic's grip on me. I dropped to the ground and the burly man dragged me out the door and up a flight of stairs. I fought endlessly all the way up, squinting in the torchlight. We stopped at the top of the stairs before a heavy, soundproof oak door.

The door opened seemingly of its own accord, and the man dragged me inside the room. At the opposite end was a similar oak door; sitting in a chair in the center of the room was a man dressed in black. He sat in the chair as if it were a throne; a feeling of evil seemed to vibrate from the man himself.

The man holding me let me go and left the room at the evil man's gesture. Avernus bowed low, almost brushing his nose to the floor.

"My king, Zathos," he murmured. I felt my heart skip a beat as I realized who the black-clothed man was. Avernus closed the oak door with a flick of his wrist and backed into a corner, keeping his eyes on Zathos as he held his head down.

Zathos turned his attention to me, saying, "So, *Fravid-Sorva*, we meet at last. I have heard about you, however little it may be. I wonder where your dragon is. Are you willing to tell me?" I clamped my mouth shut even though every fiber of my being told me to tell him so he wouldn't hurt me, but my love of Honoras kept it closed.

"Is there anything at all, girl?" Zathos's voice had raised a little, giving away his emotions. I thought desperately of Honoras, lying motionless in the dirt as latharks surrounded us. Defiantly I shook my head once.

With an angry yell Zathos's hand flashed up and contorted in an odd way. In the same instant I toppled to the ground in pain, squirming and writhing on the floor as the feeling of millions of tiny daggers pierced my body in every place imaginable. The daggers pierced deeper with every second, seeming to cut through my very soul. Then the pain was released as Zathos lowered his hand, an amused look on his face. I continued to twist on the ground as some of the excruciating pain lingered.

"Have you remembered anything yet, weak human?" As I continued to twist on the ground I looked at Avernus in the corner, who had raised his head to watch. With a feeling of grim satisfaction I shook my head again; Avernus' eyes flashed with an obvious glee. Turning to look at Zathos, I saw him stand and approach me.

He held out his hand low and slowly raised it. His magic drew me up until my feet were hanging a foot over the ground. With a smile his other hand jabbed at my stomach. My muscles locked themselves up as electricity surged through my body, collecting in my middle. My throat refused to let me scream as I held my breath, at the same time trying to let it burst from my body as I felt the full force of Zathos's power.

===

Honoras was lying quietly, examining the woman's work on his wings when it happened. He felt his heart jump and a strong feeling of dread, then a sting on his face like a whiplash. He roared from the unexpected pain and felt more men approach from the outside.

Riman and the woman had appeared in the barred windows next to him, their faces worried. He was about to speak to the woman when an excruciating pain seized his entire body. His heart nearly stopped as he felt hundreds of millions of spears pierce him all the way through, far enough to touch his very heart, it seemed.

He roared at the top of his lungs with the pain as it mounted every second, growing more and more powerful. He spread his wings out and dug his claws into the earth, his tail lashing back and forth through the air. Then it stopped, though much of the pain lingered. He tried to relax and found himself shaking from his spikes to the tip of his tail. Looking down, he saw his talons had been buried in the patches of gouged earth he had created.

It has started, he groaned to both Riman and the woman. *Yet these are no torture devices; this is the work of a*—He sucked in a breath as his body raised itself a few feet off the ground of its own accord. In an instant an electrical current raced through his body, starting, ending, and collecting in his abdomen. His muscles bunched up and locked in place, refusing to let him roar or even breathe. The breath he had sucked in beat against the walls of his lungs, refusing to be held in.

As his body was raised even higher the force of the electricity increased. His shackles strained at his body, tearing into the bases of his wings and cutting the circulation off in all of his talons, starting to suffocate him, even though the magic was already doing that.

When he knew he could hold his breath no longer the magic was released and he fell to the ground with a thud. The direction of his fall had taken him far sideways, and he realized with a jolt that the shackles around his neck were suffocating him. He strained to get his body backwards so he could breathe, but he had no strength left in him.

He felt a magic in the room, a strong one. As his vision clouded the shackle itself snapped, setting his neck free. Without moving he sucked in huge breaths, grateful for whoever it was that had broken the shackle.

There were yells, and a woman.

"He would have died!" It was the sorceress, and she was defending herself. Lifting his head enough to see, he saw that some armed men had grabbed her at the elbows and were dragging her away.

No! Let her stay. Let her explain to you—Honoras started to say to the men, who stopped at the sound of his voice in their heads. The woman had begun to smile at him, but another wave of pain swept over him, the same feeling of hundreds of millions of spears piercing him everywhere. He moaned and twisted on the ground, straining at his remaining chains. He rolled on the ground as the pain grew more and more, faster and more powerful than the first time.

The magic continued its grip on him longer than any of the other two; he knew it would stop any second as Elizabeth died from its force, for no human could withstand this and live. It continued for a moment more, then slowly ebbed away. He felt a pang in his shoulder; Elizabeth must have fallen to the ground, unconscious. His hocks burned and ached along with his lower leg muscles; Elizabeth was being dragged away.

He felt an ache in his heart for her, more than pity or sorrow. More than likely his companion was close to death, far away in the hands of Zathos. Still out of breath, he wearily tried to stand and move closer to Riman and the woman, whom the armed men had let stay. He had barely gotten all of his weight on all four legs when they buckled, and he went down. Lifting a talon, he saw his whole leg was shaking violently. He opened his mind to his entire body, and saw that his very insides were trembling. His whole being had been shaken.

Are you all right? asked a tentative voice in his mind.

Give me time, he responded. *It is for my Bonded that I worry. The pain just ebbed away and I felt her collapse and be dragged away, but I do not know if she will still be of the living.*

I am sure she will live. From what I saw of her in Barda, she is strong.

Aye, but only when her fear has run out. She was still very afraid. I felt her heart jump many times in fear of the people around her, whoever they may be. She didn't respond, but instead relayed their words to Riman and the other men there.

Then Honoras heard the words, "Was that magic you used when the dragon was suffocating?"

There was a pause from the woman, and then she said, "Aye, it was. I had to break the chains on his neck before he was killed."

And I thank you for it, Honoras said quietly. *How can I repay you? I owe you my life.*

Just do one thing for me.

Anything. I am in your debt.

Get her out of there as soon as I can convince them to let you go. No girl that young deserves to go through that. And make sure whoever was responsible is killed.

I will see it done, Honoras said, inclining his head to her, completing the vow. He half-listened to their conversation as the men asked Riman and the woman questions about him and they answered, conveying most of his story to them. With worried faces some of the men left, on their way to tell their leader about the dragon.

Riman, the woman, and the remaining men stayed with Honoras, making sure that he was all right. After water and leftover meat from the butcher was brought to him, his shaking subsided to a small tremble. His breath became less ragged, and he held his head a little higher than he had before.

Several times Honoras tried reaching Elizabeth through her mind, but the combination of distance and unconsciousness refused to let him feel even the slightest hint of her. He had lost count of the times he had tried when he gave up, exhausted. Only Riman and the woman remained; the armed men had left.

"I'm sure your Bonded will live, if you get to her in time," Riman said after his wings had drooped for about the eleventh time. The dragon wearily looked up at them, standing half-asleep in front of the barred windows.

Thank you, both of you, for your kindness and support for me. Not very many humans would do that.

"Not many humans would desert you after seeing what you went through," the woman said, "knowing that your Bonded received the worst of it."

Go, both of you, Honoras said. *You are tired, and there is nothing more you can do. I will probably be awake by the time you come tomorrow, don't worry.*

Reluctantly they both left after more of his urging, and he lay awake for most of the night, thinking about his Bonded. A few more times he tried to seek out Elizabeth, but there was still no sign of life from her, at least none that he could detect. Troubled, he fell into a light sleep.

===

Shaelynn was running. She had the black going as fast as he could through the city. Najee and Supai ran beside her on foot, Supai slightly ahead, leading the way. All she had with her was some spare money, her bow and quiver of arrows, and a cloak.

Karbab had stormed through Agathla's shop, looking for her, but one of the marketplace children had seen him coming and reported it to Agathla, who had immediately sent word through Supai what he was doing. Shaelynn had been talking with Najee in the marketplace when Supai came flying toward them.

Shaelynn had had to fight to keep the black from taking her with him at a run, but Supai had grasped his reins and had yanked him around. Giving Najee a look, they'd run with her since, taking her out of the city on the fastest route possible.

They were nearly at the city gates when Karbab's bay stepped out in front of them from a side alley Najee had not considered. He had his sword drawn and was making the bay step out into the street. As they neared him he raised his arm and put the bay in position, ready to strike Shaelynn out of the saddle when she was in the right spot.

At the last possible moment Najee yelled, "I got him!" and picked up his pace, turning quickly away from Shaelynn. He rammed himself into both the horse and the man, knocking them both off balance. Just as Shaelynn and Supai flew by the bay crashed to the ground and Najee dashed down the side street Karbab had used.

As Shaelynn and Supai approached the gates, Supai suddenly skipped a step and planted his feet together, leaping up. He landed halfway up on the black; Shaelynn helped him up as the black started to show signs of bucking.

Quickly Supai uttered a low nicker, and the black balked, receiving his message. He ran on out of the gate, flying past the guards. They yelled at the two, but Shaelynn kept the black going at full speed.

They had come out of the north gate, opposite the direction she and Liz had first come to Barda. The road curved up to the base of a low hill and disappeared around the side of the hill, where it reentered the forest. Shaelynn kept the black going until they were far into the woods, letting the black's hoof prints mingle with the many others that were present from the travelers that came back and forth from Barda. About a half-mile in Shaelynn stopped the black and backed him up for a few feet. After this she turned him into the woods, quickly dismounting and erasing the tracks.

"Walk him on until you can't see me," Shaelynn said to Supai. He did as she said without asking any questions. She stayed where she was just off the road until she heard the black stop, and then went after them on foot, quickly erasing more of the black's prints for a while. She leaped from rock to rock as often as she could; in other places she picked her way along, stepping in clumps of grass and small bushes.

When she was standing in front of Supai and the black she looked behind her; there were no visible tracks she could see, only the black's small prints. Satisfied, she and Supai quietly walked farther in the forest, at least until they could hear approaching hooves.

Supai heard them first; he held up a hand and stopped the black, dismounting. He made an odd gesture to the black, and he fell completely still, not shifting his feet or champing his teeth for once. Supai and Shaelynn squatted behind a couple of trees, both straining their ears to listen.

The pounding hooves slowed and stopped. For a long moment Shaelynn expected to hear the hoof beats start up again and head in their direction. Then she heard the hoof beats start again, and her heart leaped to her throat, but they continued on north and faded away.

Breathing a sigh of relief, she relaxed her knees and sat down in between the tree's roots, leaning on its trunk. Supai held his position, watching her. The black strained at the reins in his hand, trying to get to good grass, but Supai held him firmly in place. When his piercing stare finally started to bother her, she turned to him.

"What are you staring at me for?"

"Why didn't you leave when Rish told you to?" he countered. "She knew this would happen."

"Just leave me alone," she grumbled, closing her eyes.

"I need to know," Supai said, not letting the subject drop. "Why didn't you do as Rish asked? She's dead because of you. You held her up when she could have—"

"She could have run, I know!" she finished, sitting up, eyes flashing. "I was hurt by what she said, okay? She told me I couldn't go with her, and I just blocked her out after that."

"You were hurt?" he asked, unbelieving. "She was killed because she *hurt* you? All Rish wanted was for you to be safe!"

"Stop calling her that!"

"Stop calling her what?" His tone had softened slightly.

"Her name isn't Rish. It's—never mind. You don't care."

"Don't tell me I didn't care about her." Supai's voice had turned cold and hard. "She meant as much to me as she did to you. She meant a lot to all of us—Najee, Dush, everybody. She meant a lot to Marl. Do you know what he told her before Karbab discovered her there the day she was killed? Marl told her she was damn good with horses, and he'd be losing the best hand he'd ever had."

This shocked Shaelynn. She didn't know anyone but herself had been close to Liz. Supai continued in the same icy tone, "She was supposed to teach Shamar to sword fight, before she fought Karbab. She was the one who helped save the black's life. Don't tell me I don't care and that no one else but you cared. But tell me: what was her real name, if it wasn't Rish? What other secrets do you have?"

Hesitating, Shaelynn replied, "Her name was Elizabeth, or just Liz. My name is Shaelynn. We came to Barda looking for money so we could travel toward Zathos and face him head-on." Supai's expression changed to a look of total shock. Shaelynn went on to tell him everything, all the way from Liz buying the bracelet to when they had met.

It was almost dark when she finished. Supai had a few questions before they came to their senses and decided to get firewood to start a fire. Shaelynn set off hunting, and she came back with a couple of small birds. It was late when they finally tied the black to a tree not far off and lay down on Shaelynn's cloak.

Supai watched Shaelynn from the corner of his eyes as she fell into a fitful sleep. She had woken twice, breathing hard, when he himself finally fell asleep, keeping an ear and an eye open.

==

Honoras saw Elizabeth, crumpled in a corner in a dark room. A door opened, filling the small room with a blinding light. The room, he saw, was a cell, a human cage. Elizabeth did not stir as a tall man wearing a red and black robe entered the room. His black fingernails had been sharpened to claws; for the first time he noticed a deep scratch on Elizabeth's left cheek.

The man flicked a finger at the lock on the cell door; it clanked open, and Honoras realized with rage that the man was a sorcerer. But he could tell it wasn't Zathos. The man raised his arm, and Elizabeth was lifted from the ground to hover a few feet over the stone floor.

She made no move of her own until she twitched and shook violently as pain wracked her body. Her eyes flew open and her mouth opened in a scream; the man's face formed a wicked grin.

Honoras's own eyes opened as the same pain wracked his body. It seized his brain and froze his body after a moment, but he was still able to open his mouth and bellow at the top of his lungs. His vision soon clouded; all he could see was black. His muscles started to cramp from being locked in the same position.

He had started to hear commotions outside when he listened past his own roar. He stopped for breath and had just sucked in another amount of air when his strength failed him. Blind, he hung limp in the magic's hold as the pain continued on but his mind shut down almost completely. His unconscious mind briefly registered something he wouldn't remember when he woke: he could feel Elizabeth's presence in his mind.

==

My eyes snapped open as the horrible pain returned. My limbs shook of their own accord and nothing registered in my mind except Avernus before me, causing me pain, his hand outstretched. The other thing was the faint flicker of Honoras in my mind. Half-conscious, I reached out to him.

I felt his presence all around my mind, but there was no response from him. Suddenly a new wave of pain swept over me, bringing me back to my own self. My lungs filled with air of their own accord, and my throat opened itself. A piercing scream erupted from my body; I felt the sound waves reverberate around the room from its force. I saw Avernus' grin spread wider as his forehead wrinkled with concentration.

You cannot escape, said his evil voice in my head. The pain mounted, and then stopped. Gasping for breath, I looked back down at Avernus. His concentration had ceased, and he was watching me. Gleefully his arm shot down, pummeling me into the stone floor, knocking the wind out of me.

Avernus stepped forward until he was standing right over me. His hand came forward, stopping directly above my chest. He stopped to watch me try to sit up, but no grin crossed his face now. Anger flooded him, and his hand shot out, his fingers tightening into a half-fist.

My throat tightened in the grip of Avernus' magic, cutting off my air. My fear kicked in and I scrabbled on the ground, clutching at my throat, no matter how much my body ached from trying to recover at the same time. After a moment my vision blacked, and then my body stilled. Unconscious yet again, I fell to the floor.

Lazily, Avernus leaned against the filthy bars, half-concentrating on his magic as he watched her body start to twitch as pain gripped her again.

==

The woman cautiously approached Sorvo, fearful the magic might stop and he'd fall on top of her. She touched a finger to the tip of his wing, the closest thing to her. She jerked it back as millions of knife-points started to pierce her as well. Taking a deep breath, she let her magic lightly touch his mind.

She recoiled from the sudden pain, then pushed deeper into his mind as the knives drove deeper into her being. And then suddenly, she felt briefly, another presence. Before she could grasp at who it was, it quickly disappeared.

Overwhelmed by the pain she received from being in the Sorvo's mind, she collected her magic back up inside herself. With a shudder she felt the last of the pain ebb away. Suddenly hands grabbed her from behind and dragged her back. A split second later, Sorvo dropped heavily to the ground. Thankfully, he landed on his side, where none of his limbs could be broken underneath him and he was able to fall safely on his wing without shattering it as well.

Turning to see who had grabbed her, she saw Riman behind her, trying to hide a nervous grin. Releasing the breath she had held, she gave him a shaky smile as well.

"The girl was there, in his mind," she told him as she walked over to the dragon before her. Cautiously, she reached out a hand to him, but the pain had stopped ravaging his body. She put a hand over his racing heart. It seemed to be starting to slow down, but then he was gasping for breath all over again.

The woman turned to look at Riman. Behind her, she heard the dragon move. Turning back, she saw his throat pinched in one spot, strangling him. The dragon squirmed and thrashed on the ground. His air finally ran out, and he lay still on the floor once more. As Riman and the woman watched, his tail, his foot, a forearm twitched a little more violently than expected.

The woman approached the beast and lightly touched the tip of a claw on a talon that had just twitched. Surprised, she again jerked back from the sudden impulse of pain, though it was light. Angry, she stomped back to Riman and sat by him, leaning her back against the far wall.

"What is it?" Riman quietly asked. She quickly explained what had occurred, ending with a huffy remark.

"Even when they escape to their own minds," she said, "he still causes them pain."

"Is there anything you can do?" Riman asked.

"I could wake him, but—" she hesitated, and then went on, "For a moment I entered his mind, to see what was the matter, and I felt another presence, most likely the girl."

"Yes, you told me."

"Well, if I could help Sorvo find that connection, he or I could speak with her and find out the information we need. It would be dangerous, though."

"How?"

"I could have the wrong mind, for one. Or, Sorvo or I could delve too deeply into her mind and we'd be vulnerable to anything—her pain, her state of consciousness, even the penetration of another evil mind. We'd be as much of a prisoner as she is."

"No. I say, no, no, no. Definitely not. We can't afford to lose either one of you, not right now."

"But Riman, it's the only way I know of to get her whereabouts at least, so he could find her."

"Wake Sorvo, then, and ask him. But I say no." Sighing, she got up as he stayed by the wall, watching her. Who was she anyway? He'd only known her for a few days, but she had appeared as an innocent healer that had come up from Barda. Then suddenly she knew magic and could talk to the dragon.

Uneasily, she approached the shaking dragon. Lightly she brushed his mind—only the slight pain and an unconscious mind. Carefully, she drew her magic from herself and gave some of it to Sorvo, willing him to wake.

Sorvo's eyes flew open, and he immediately sucked in a breath and bellowed. Still bellowing, he tried to get up, in vain. His shaking limbs would not hold him up long enough to get his full weight on them, and he sank back to the ground, breathing hard. He jerked at the woman's touch, but relaxed when he realized it was her.

I am sorry. What we've gone through, it just-

I understand. Riman and I are here, we have been here since you were, ah, woken last. You nearly crushed me when you fell.

Again, my apologies.

It is all right. I felt your pain as well. I touched you several times, and the magic or something caused me to feel it.

I have a feeling that there is more than that to tell.

Yes—I touched your mind at first, and delved into it; my apologies. I found someone there with you, but they left before I could know who it was.

And you have come up with a plan. You will help me find the connection to speak with my Bonded.

How did you know?

You humans let your thoughts wander too freely. He chuckled ever so softly as she sheepishly grinned.

Do you know the risks? he asked, carefully lifting his head to look at her better.

I know some. I could become bound with her mind or I could have the wrong mind, and if I did I could be mentally captured or worse.

Correct. But if we tried to do so and she is killed in the same instant, we would most likely be killed also. Or if we are in her mind and she is knocked unconscious, we would be unconscious, trapped in her mind until she wakes. Are you sure you want to try this? I have been trying on my own in vain.

But if we combined our two strengths, we could do it. You said dragons do not have very much of their own magic. I have more; we could make contact if we tried.

It is a worthy debate; I am still not sure.

About what? You could find out where she is and immediately go to her.

I am not sure about you. You once trained under Zathos; he knows you and could easily influence you, or even break into and control your mind.

No, never. I would kill myself before I let him do that. I would never let him take me over, never.

If you are determined, then I will try with you. You are right; it is better than me trying to find out on my own. But not now; I have not the strength. Give me a few hours, if nothing more happens.

Very well, Sorvo. At dusk, as it is midday now. She relayed their conversation to Riman, and they left for lunch. Some meat and some water were brought to the dragon, and he ate a little. Dusk came.

The woman entered the stone room with a sly half-smile on her face. Honoras chuckled slightly at her expression, and then asked, *What has made you so happy? Even I cannot tell.*

The town leader has granted me permission to take off your shackles; I told him of the situation whenever the magic controls you through your Bonded. Without another word she held out her arms, clasping her hands together. Concentrating, she flung them apart, and all of his shackles were cracked open. With some of the woman's help, they bent them enough so they could fall with a clatter to the ground.

Honoras happily tossed them against the wall that they were attached to, letting out a satisfied grunt. As he lay still for a moment every once in a while the woman noticed that his muscles twitched or his face grimaced.

"Is the pain still bothering you?" she asked out loud.

Aye, but I prefer however much of it compared to what I experienced a while ago. And, at least my Bonded is unconscious, so she feels it, but not as badly as if she were awake. I can still feel it though, since I am awake.

"Will you be able to concentrate? Maybe we should do this tomorrow."

No. I do not have that much time. I am ready now, and if we wait I may not be as ready then. We must try now.

"Very well. Now, gather your magic, centering it in your mind. I will bind mine with yours, so do not be startled when you feel it." They both concentrated, and after a short moment Honoras felt her magic touching his own within his mind. Half-startled, he held his concentration as she wove their magic together as if it were a rope, making them both stronger together.

Speaking with her mind now, she said, *Search for her. I will help you by letting your mind travel farther.* Honoras did as she said, flinging out his presence to any sign of Elizabeth. At first, there was nothing, and then he touched on something familiar. He battered Elizabeth's mental defenses she had instinctively set up until he found a weak spot and dashed through.

All he met was her unconscious mind, but he still found something there. As he tried to reach it he felt his concentration slip, but the woman caught his magic and held it in place. Knowing that he risked falling into Elizabeth's unconsciousness, he reached for the little bit of life in her mind.

It responded to him immediately, though it could not speak directly with him. It flashed him a picture of Zathos in a room with a thick rug and a throne-like chair, standing over her along with another man in dark red and black robes. Another picture: A castle up on a rocky hill in the middle of a dark land that he knew had once been filled with rolling fields of green. A narrow trail filled with switchbacks led to thc castle, and a similar one led around the very front of the castle, following the bases of the stone walls.

And then another: There was a tower in the center of the castle, with a wide platform that was open to the skies. He flew down a flight of stairs that led from the top of the platform to a spiral staircase. He went straight down three more flights, until the only light was torchlight. There was a hall with an open room at one end and another flight of spiraling stairs to his left; next to the stairs was a small set of steps that led to a tightly shut door. Honoras knew that beyond the door was the cell that Elizabeth was being held in.

Suddenly, Elizabeth's unconscious mind sped away, and a cold voice spoke. *Ah, dragon. At last you seek your Bonded. I knew you would come.* Hurriedly Honoras scrambled out of Elizabeth's mind and back into his own, blocking his mind from anyone until he felt the evil mind retreat, having failed at finding anything out.

Honoras felt a blow to the side of his neck, just above his left shoulder blade. He roared, tearing his and the woman's magic apart. She stumbled backwards, afraid he might be lifted by magic and fall on her. Only after the pain had subsided did he tell the woman everything he had found out.

She was shocked to find that another mind had spoken to Honoras. "He must have been keeping watch over your Bonded, or he wouldn't have known you were there. She was unconscious still, you say?"

Yes. All I met was the unconscious part of her mind. It could not speak to me, as I said, but it sent me pictures. I know where to find her.

"So? Where do you think she is? You never told me that much."

She is being held in the lowest chamber in the dungeons, in Zathos's castle. The woman gasped, clapping a hand to her mouth and shaking her head violently.

"No," she breathed. "It cannot be. Are you sure?"

It is what her mind showed me. I have been to the castle, and I remember it well. I am sure she is there, though I wish she wasn't. It will be trouble enough just getting there. After that I will have to get her out safely.

"It won't be just you." She looked down, glancing up at his curious eyes. He looked at her as if she was a little girl and he was her parent, knowing she planned on doing something dangerous. She continued, "Riman and I have decided that we will accompany you. He's a good fighter, and I am skilled in magic, and we can help you retrieve your Bonded."

Where is Riman now? Honoras only now realized that the man was gone.

"He is getting ready. We haven't really cleared it with the town yet, so, he's settling that." At the stern look Honoras gave her she quickly said, "They decided to let you go, you know. You can leave tomorrow, if you wish. He is only there now to see if we can leave with you also."

I see. Thank you for your efforts, but I really don't-

"This isn't your decision, Sorvo," she said. "We are going with you to help the girl, and even you cannot stop us from pursuing her with you. We made this decision for ourselves."

Honoras chuckled, and said, *You two are determined, aren't you? Very well; you can accompany me. I can use your help, brave ones.* He bowed his head to her, and she inclined hers in return. She left at his bidding to go and help Riman, leaving Honoras alone.

He decided that if he were to leave tomorrow, he'd need to be strong enough. He only hoped that the sorcerer that held Elizabeth, whoever he was, wouldn't do anything to her while he was on his way to her. It could slow them a lot if he wasn't able to fly.

He had once been taught to draw strength from other things, even living ones. He preferred things like rocks and water; if he drew too much strength from things like trees or animals or even humans he'd kill them immediately. To see if he remembered his lessons, he focused on the stones around him, trying to find the heart of their strength.

Once he found it he drew it to him, feeling their strength helping his own. When he had drawn enough but not too much to crumble the walls around him, he released the rest of their strength back to them. He almost heard them sigh with relief; he knew they wanted to keep holding the stone wall together and keep it strong.

If he had another attack of pain from the sorcerer he could quickly draw strength from the things around him. There was sure to be something around, even if it was the ground.

Satisfied with himself, he let himself fall completely asleep, grateful for whatever rest he could get.

Chapter 8

SUPAI WOKE BEFORE DAWN; HE got up and stretched, careful not to disturb the sleeping girl next to him. As he remembered her tale she had told him last night, he still couldn't really believe it. According to her, she and Liz were from another world entirely different from his.

He watched her start to moan and roll over on the cloak, dragging it up around her legs, tangling herself in it. He knew she was having a bad dream, but about what he could only guess. She was probably reliving the day of her cousin's death.

She woke suddenly, her eyes snapping open as she sat up on the ground, breathing hard. Her face was red and flushed, and she was covered in sweat. Thinking she'd need to be left alone for a moment, he let her briefly see him as he pretended to be just waking up and walking off.

A moment later he came back from a stream, having just splashed his face. His hair was dripping wet and by the color difference on his shirt Shaelynn could tell that he had used it to dry his face.

He looked through the black's small saddlebags to see if there was anything useful in them, but he came up with next to nothing, save for a water skin. He went and filled it at the stream; Shaelynn silently followed and splashed her face as well, getting a drink.

She came back to their small camp a few minutes after he had to find that he'd already started to light a small fire. He was striking two different rocks together, bending over and blowing on the small sparks, trying to get them to light.

He succeeded after a few tries, and the fire easily caught on the small branches. It slowly grew until Supai thought it was big enough for larger branches. Shaelynn stared into the fire for a few minutes, unblinking. She watched the flames be created and travel up, disappearing into a thin trail of smoke. She watched the sparks that flew from the top of the fire; they drifted lazily on the air until they put themselves out, and she could see them no more.

Supai watched her for a moment as she stared blankly into the flames. After a while she noticed him watching her. "What?" she asked irritably.

"What's the matter?" Supai asked, but then immediately regretted it.

"What's the matter? Everything! My cousin just died, I was chased from the city by the man who killed her, I lost my job and a few good friends, and you ask what's wrong?" Tears streamed down her face, and she quickly walked to the black. He danced, nervous from her tone of voice but quieted and stood still when she buried her face in his shoulder, trying to hide her tears.

Sighing at last, Shaelynn picked up her bow and quiver of arrows from next to the cloak on the ground. Giving Supai a quick look of explanation, she quietly stalked into the forest around them, nocking an arrow.

As soon as she was away from Supai and the black and the camp and everything else, Shaelynn immediately felt better. She loved hunting, and she loved walking through the woods, alone. Quietly walking forward, she savored the moment when she was standing right behind a quail, just before it noticed her at last and took flight. Her arrow followed it and released itself almost of its own accord, and the bird went down in a flurry of feathers.

She went to it, picking it up and examining it. It was large for a quail, but that was to be expected with the abundance of the forest it lived in. She lashed it to a loop on her waist with a leather thong and went on.

Again she was amazed at her own ability: she was standing not three feet away from a rabbit, and it was facing her, quietly grazing. Then it looked up and quickly dashed away, running in a zigzag pattern, trying to throw her off. It had not gone another yard before her arrow hit home and the rabbit fell, kicking out a hind leg. She picked it up and lashed it and the quail together, careful of its dripping blood.

She caught another rabbit, a small thing. Satisfied, she silently went back to camp, surprising Supai by her sudden appearance. She tossed the two rabbits at the ground next to him as she sat against a tree and started to pluck the feathers from her quail. When it was ready to cook she put it on a spit and held it over the fire, turning it around on the two forked branches that held it up.

Supai ate one rabbit and most of another, and Shaelynn shared a little of her quail with him. She finished the rest of the last rabbit, and they got ready to go.

"Where do you think we should go?" Shaelynn asked Supai as he put out the fire and she saddled the black. "I don't know the land; I'm not from here."

"I don't know much of it either, mostly places to the south and east of here; that's where I'm from. I know there's a city a day or two away from here if you go north, and we could get supplies there with the money you have if we need to."

"We could use some blankets, I think. The black can carry us both, and I don't have enough money to buy another horse anyway. We can find our own food and water. We need a map too, I suppose, if we can find one."

"Those can be hard to come by," Supai said suddenly. "Especially with the evil king—I won't say his name. People are afraid to make maps of the country anymore in case it gets in the wrong hands. They say that the king can track people by seeing them on a map, even if it's just paper and ink." Shaelynn thought about this as they traveled on through the woods, keeping the road just in sight.

Anytime anyone came down the road, they stopped and hid, silently waiting for them to pass. On one unlucky occasion they were stopped half a day and all night because a merchant decided to stop early for the day and rest.

Eventually they reached a town much smaller than Barda, called Mechem. It seemed to be a tense town, and Shaelynn and Supai decided not to get involved in it. Local men guarded the city gates, and everyone kept their faces hidden. There was a large jail off to one side of the city, where a lot of people were congregated.

As they approached it on their way to the small marketplace, everyone suddenly left, climbing down from the roof and flooding through the doors, while armed men entered it.

"I wonder what's going on?" Supai asked. He noticed the wide double doors that must lead to a large room. It was probably made of thick stone walls, from what he could see. He wondered what was in there. After a brief moment the guards and another man came out of the prison. The guards left for the center of the town, while the man cracked open a wide door and entered the room alone.

Seeing nothing else happen, Shaelynn gave Supai a few coins, telling him to get them a room at the cheapest hotel he could find, but not one so bad it was disgusting. She left to barter at the marketplace, something Supai would have rather done, but he did not object. He liked the opportunity to go back and check out the prison.

He left and got them a suitable room at an inn and then quickly left for the prison at a jog. He stopped behind a building that was closest to the jail, watching the door. In a few minutes the same man came out, looking more relaxed than he had before. Supai had noticed his hands violently shaking when he had first gone in.

The man walked back into the city; Supai did not want to follow him or ask questions to raise any suspicion. He and Shaelynn needed to stay low for as long a time as they could. Instead he leaned against the wall of the building and half-dozed.

At about an hour later the man, a small woman he recognized as the healer's assistant from Barda, and some armed men approached the prison. They cracked open the great doors, and one man leaned over in front of the opening, using something like an odd crossbow to shoot a dart in at whatever was in there. There was a brief moment of silence, and then a roar that shook Supai to his very bones, even from where he was.

The man shot another dart in, drawing the crossbow farther back to hit harder. There was a loud thud, and then the man went in. He quickly returned and said something to the rest of them, who opened the door wider for them to get through, though Supai still could not see what was in there. In a moment all but the woman he recognized came back out. The armed men left, and the man stayed. He seemed calm enough, but he still looked a little worried.

When more time had passed and nothing happened, Supai went back to the city gate he and Shaelynn had come through. She was waiting for him there, and he told her what room he had gotten. She left for the inn as he left for the forest around the city to retrieve the black and everything else they had with them.

He returned a few minutes before the gates shut at dusk, and he led the black up the city streets, untacking him at the stable attached to the inn. He watched as the horse thankfully sank to its knees and lay there, grateful for a stall once more.

Supai went to their room, where Shaelynn was already in the one bed. Smiling to himself, Supai grabbed her cloak and spread it out on the floor, wrapping it around himself when he'd laid down.

The next morning Supai said nothing of what he'd heard and seen the previous day. He decided not to tell Shaelynn until they were far from the city; he had an idea of what was in the prison and did not want her to overreact and cause trouble. Instead he went and did more bartering while she got everything ready, hoping she wouldn't pass by the prison while whatever was in there was making noise.

He used two more of her coins to buy a bunch of dried meat from the local butcher. Shaelynn said she'd not found a map, and he had had no luck so far. A few hours after sunrise he gave up on it and went to meet her at the inn, where she was supposed to be. The owner said she'd left a while ago when he asked him.

Supai dashed away to the marketplace, thinking she'd have thought to meet him there. None of the merchants had seen her there, and neither had the guards at one of the city gates. They ran him off, telling him to look for his girlfriend elsewhere.

Supai ran all out for the prison, where he saw her standing with the black behind the same building he had been sitting by yesterday. She started when she saw him suddenly standing next to her, jerking on the black's reins. His head went up, and his forelegs became light on the ground, daring to rise onto his hind legs. Supai and Shaelynn backed away from him as he reared up, rising to his full height.

His forelegs kicked out and he held his head high and back, so that he threatened to fall over backwards. The reins had flown from Shaelynn's hands as the horse had risen; Supai dashed under his flailing hooves and grabbed them, sharply pulling down. The black's head came down from the force, and the rest of his body followed. His hooves touched for an instant before they came back up again, but Supai held the reins, showing his teeth and angry eyes. The black touched down again and stayed down, but he still danced nervously in Supai's grip.

Soft applause came from behind them, and Supai and Shaelynn turned. The healer's assistant, the slight woman Supai had seen, was standing behind them.

"That was an amazing display of horsemanship," she said approvingly. Supai blushed and handed the reins to Shaelynn.

"It was nothing," he said.

"No, really. You understood that horse and made him understand you. How do you know what to say to him?"

"All of my friends know how to deal with animals." Her gaze strayed to Shaelynn, and he quickly said, "Some of my other friends that I used to know. It's a long story."

"Ah. I see. Well, I have other business to attend to. I shall see you around, perhaps." As she started to walk away Shaelynn started to say something, but Supai clamped a hand over her mouth. The woman looked at him quizzically.

"We are traveling," he said quickly.

"Have a safe journey, then," she said, inclining her head. Shaelynn did the same once Supai had taken his hand off her mouth, while he dipped into a graceful bow, coming back up with a flourish, making her smile. She turned and walked back into the city.

Shaelynn whirled on Supai, saying, "I was going to ask her what was in there! I heard it as I walked by on my way to meet you."

"I know, and I think it best not to meddle now, not until we are far away. I don't want anyone to know we are here. She may have recognized me—she was the healer's assistant when Liz was injured. I saw her there, and she saw me, I think."

He continued, "Besides, you may not want to know what is in there. I don't want you to do anything stupid and attract attention." She scowled and started to say something in retaliation, but he raised a hand, cutting her off. Wordlessly he turned with the black and led him away, leaving her to follow. They exited the city gates without much commotion and continued in the forest, following the road from a distance. At dusk they stopped and made camp.

They were getting ready to cook dinner when a roar of some beast rang through the air. It was far away, but the pain in it was evident. The black jerked and pulled on his reins, which were tied to a tree. His eyes rolled in his head, showing the whites; his limbs shook and he had his ears back. Shaelynn could easily tell he was very scared.

Supai went to him and quieted him with low nickers, much like a mother would quiet her baby. The roars continued on for a brief moment, and then they stopped. In a few minutes they picked up again, the pain even more evident. It sent chills down Shaelynn's spine, and Supai had to quiet the black again. After a long minute or so they stopped, and they didn't hear them for the rest of the evening.

Both Shaelynn and Supai had trouble going to sleep, and they both knew it, even though they didn't tell each other. About halfway through the night they sat up from their blankets at the same time. They looked at each other, unsure about what had woken them.

It was silent all around them, and then, far away again, the roar. It rose to a bellow in excruciating pain, filling them both with despair. Shaelynn covered her ears; the night made it seem as if the beast were only a mile away. It ended abruptly, but Shaelynn held her position in her blankets: she was curled into a ball with her arms wrapped around her head.

The black stamped nervously, but Supai left him be as he rolled over, turning his back to where the sound had come from, trying to sleep. They both fell into a light, worried rest, waking frequently until dawn.

There were no more of the pained roars when they got ready to leave, and Shaelynn and Supai mounted the black together, leaving at a brisk trot. Neither wanted to speak of the sounds of the previous night, and not even Shaelynn wanted to ask Supai if he knew what the beast in the prison was.

They traveled on until lunch, when Shaelynn managed to shoot two rabbits mounted on top of the black as they bounded away from them. They quickly skinned and roasted them, eating the meat along with some bread Shaelynn had gotten.

It was well after dark when Supai decided that they stop; they had met travelers at around dusk just as they had been setting up their camp. Supai wanted to be as far away from their camp as possible.

"Do you want to hunt now? I can go without food until morning if you don't want to," Supai said to Shaelynn once they had tied the black up and had gotten their blankets on the ground.

"I can hunt just as well in the dark as I can in the day," she answered. "I can see almost just as well."

"All right, but don't go far. You may be able to see, but that will not keep you from getting lost."

"Of course." She shouldered her quiver and picked up her bow, thinking of when Tayna and Geoff had given them to her. Liz had received her own as well, along with a sword from Geoff. She had asked around Barda if anyone had seen or picked up Liz's weapons after her death, but everyone had told her that she had had her pack and her bow and quiver when the dragon had taken her. They had also told her that she'd had her sword clenched in her hand when she had been picked up.

Shaelynn had not noticed these things herself. She had only seen Liz's face, looking desperately at her own. Then the dragon had turned toward the sea, and its green bulk had hidden her cousin from her sight.

Without realizing it, she had stopped in midstride at the edge of camp. Supai looked at her quizzically; she had been staring at him the whole time. Shaking her head, she watched the ground in front of her as she walked away from the firelight.

The moon lit her path as bright as the sun would on a cloudy day. Shaelynn heard the forest alive around her. An owl screeched, another answered; she heard grasses rustle near her as small animals hid from her as she approached. She heard a few sets of hooves far to her right, where a herd of deer had noticed her presence and had bounded away. She heard a final, irritated snort from a buck, and then the hoof beats were gone.

Focusing on her task, she nocked an arrow on her bowstring and drew it back, watching for any small game. There weren't many birds out now, except for the hunters that lived only in the night. The rabbits had been out since dusk, and now they should be going back to their burrows.

She caught no rabbits, but had luck with a large quail that was returning to its nest. Holding it in her hand, she turned back the way she had come. After walking a few yards, she could see the light from the campfire Supai had started; she was astonished and scared that the fire was so far to her left. If she had done that and Supai had not had a fire going, she would have been lost, like he'd said.

Not telling him of her short experience, she plucked the fat bird and gave it to Supai who cut off its head, lower legs, and wings. He put it on a spit and roasted it over the fire. Once Shaelynn saw him lick his lips in anticipation; it brought a small smile to her lips.

They quietly ate the rich meat, licking their fingers when they had finished. They got water from their skins, and fell asleep in their blankets after that. Shaelynn tried not to think of the pained bellows from the previous night, but lying in her blankets with nothing else to think of, she couldn't help it.

She felt sorry for whatever animal it was, and she knew it was the beast they had heard in the prison. Shaelynn searched her mind for what it could be, but she kept coming up with the same answer. No other animal but a dragon could make a roar like that and have it carry over miles of land through a forest.

Numbly she thought of the dragon that had taken her cousin from her, wondering if it was the same one that was in the prison. She hoped that they weren't torturing it there; it had finished off her cousin, she was sure, but it could not help it. It was only an animal, after all, and it had acted on instinct, even if it was a bit bold for an animal like it. Most predatory animals, as far as she knew, preferred to hunt in quieter areas. As far as she knew, it would have rather not have swooped down in the middle of a crowded street just to get one meal.

Thinking about it brought tears to her eyes. Normally she would have angrily wiped them away, but she knew now that the best way was to let them come. And she did, quietly sobbing with Supai next to her in his blankets. Supai said nothing but pretended to be asleep.

Shaelynn and Supai continued on for a couple more weeks, heading north up the coast. It was the only way they knew of to get north, but they asked no one how to get to Zathos's castle. At every town they stopped at, though, they asked if there was another farther north, so that they didn't go too far north and run into a barren or foreign land.

They stopped in the towns only to hear of talk; they had little money left, so they didn't want to waste it on rooms at inns. After their first stop where they had purchased blankets and other things, they needed nothing else. Shaelynn hunted food, and they both cooked it. They met a stream or creek wherever they went, so they had plenty of water. They made good time while riding on the black, if they weren't held up somewhere.

At one town they stopped at, after two weeks and a few days of riding from Barda, they heard some interesting information. People said that they had found a pack full of different things, among them dried meat that had been cooked by a fire. This was nearly impossible to do unless the fire was very hot, and no campfire could be that hot.

They had also found numerous gouges in the earth that they claimed to be the claw marks of some large beast. There were marks of where it had laid down, and right next to them were marks of a human lying down as well. There were plenty of footprints, one set, with large feet, but not large enough for a man.

Near a town off to the south they had found similar marks when they were informed of the mysterious findings. At the southern town there had been blood and tracks of elk, but they led nowhere, as if the animals had been lifted out of the sky.

Supai wanted to leave the town immediately, but Shaelynn refused to go. "Those prints were made by a girl who was alive and comfortable with a dragon. I'm going to ask what they found in the pack." She stormed away from him, half-dragging the black behind her. She kept up the pace around the corner of a building they had hidden behind. The black tugged sharply on the reins; she slowed her fast walk.

Shaelynn tied the black outside of a tavern, where Supai had first heard the men talking. Pushing open the door and quietly going inside, she sat at a table near the men.

". . . . an' there was a bow with a quiver o' arrows next to the pack, made by hands I've never seen. The feathers on the arrows are black-brown, and the bow itself is a longbow, hard to pull. Some o' our men could barely handle the thing. Whoever that girl was, she was strong." Shaelynn's breath caught in her throat, catching their attention. Pretending to double over and cough, she let them continue talking.

"Anyway," one man with a scraggly brown beard said, "that girl had been lying down right up close to that creature. An' do you know what I think it is?" The men in front of him leaned forward in anticipation.

"A dragon." One man cursed, another's jaw dropped, and another shook his head, closing his eyes and leaning back in his chair.

"How do you figure that?" said the man who had leaned back. His eyes darted warily around the room as he leaned back on the table, resting on his elbows. He quickly shook his long black hair out of his face and said, "The *Sorva di Fravid* haven't been seen in over half a century." At the men's confused looks, he explained.

"My granddad told me once that his great granddad's four times great granddad had trained under a man when he was a boy. This man's father had been one of the ones to run off the last *Sorva di Fravid*. The Bonded's name was Anna; she had tried to stay and make the people understand that they had needed the *Sorva di Fravid*." The men's looks were even more confused.

"Don't you know the old stories?" the man half-yelled, exasperated. The men around him shook their heads. Sighing, the man went on in a softer tone, "The words *Sorva di Fravid* mean Dragon and its Bonded. It was also the name of the whole group of them, who rose up against an evil force in the land long, long ago and defeated it. They vowed to protect the land and its people from any harm. After a while, peace reigned in the land with or without the *Sorva di Fravid*'s help. The people tried telling the *Sorva di Fravid* to leave, that they didn't need them anymore.

"The *Sorva di Fravid* refused to leave, insisting that someday they would be needed. Zathos had somewhat risen to power by then, and he led the people in a revolt against the *Sorva di Fravid*. They fled, going to far, far away lands where the people there would accept them, if there were any.

"After this the former king died. Zathos crowned himself king and slowly spread his evil throughout the land. The woman Anna stayed behind, trying to convince the people that they needed her and the other Dragon-Bonded. But they were blind to Zathos's evil, and nearly killed her before she fled to some distant island. She was the last *Sorva di Fravid* to be seen since then, and was never seen again.

"I think that the markings you people found were that of a dragon and its Bonded." With his last statement, the man leaned back, watching the men around him and around the room to see what they would do. By this time the whole room had become extremely quiet, listening to the man's story. Slowly people turned back to their friends, and the usual buzz of conversation picked up.

"But what does it mean?" asked one man quietly. Shaelynn leaned closer to the table to hear the man's whispered answer.

"They will rid us of Zathos and destroy the evil he has created. The land will be restored, and a new, right king will be placed on the throne, though I don't know who it will be." Shaelynn quickly turned her back to the men as they leaned away from the speaker and looked around the room for anyone listening.

With a shiver she remembered a line from the spell that was on the tag of the bracelet Liz had bought: "Restore a lost land to return home . . ." That meant that, if the girl and the dragon succeeded, she could go home. Her heart soared at the thought.

But then, she realized, she would have to face her own world without Liz, and no one would ever believe what had happened to her. She'd have to keep everything a secret unless she wanted to be locked up in a mental hospital. And then they'd still look for Liz, and they'd go after Shaelynn first. What would she say to their questions? It might be better to just stay here.

All of a sudden she didn't want the girl and her dragon to succeed. If they did, she'd be in a world of trouble at home. She liked it here, and she could get used to it, if they weren't on their way to find Zathos and at the same time being on the run from Karbab.

Then she countered herself: If Zathos were gone, these people would finally be able to live in peace. She didn't want to get in the way of that. It was their only hope.

Deciding to leave things be, she decided to also find out more about this girl and her dragon. Maybe they could lead her to Zathos. As she was thinking this, all of the men left but the one who had been talking. He again flipped his black hair out of his face and let his eyes wander around the room warily. His eyes caught Shaelynn's and they held their gazes for a moment, until the man looked away at someone behind her who had come in the door.

Shaelynn glanced behind her only to see some burly man walk in and sit at another table. Getting up, she walked over and sat down in front of the man's table.

"What else do you know of the-" she hesitated, trying to remember the words. "*Sorva di Fravid?*" she guessed. A small smirk appeared on the man's face.

Leaning forward once more, he said in a low voice, "Aye, they were called the *Sorva di Fravid.* It is dragon-speak, and it means Dragon and its Bonded. The person Bonded to the dragon is called *Fravid-Sorva,* or

Dragon-Bonded. *Sorva* in itself means a dragon in general or a female dragon; males are called *Sorvo*. They formed thousands of thousands of years ago when an evil force had its hold on the land. The dragons had just found the ability to bond with humans, elves, sorcerers, or even dwarfs, though that was rare. Three *Sorva di Fravid* were created, and they defeated the evil force, though no one knows what it was or how they did it.

"After this many dragons bound themselves to other beings, and they kept peace in the land. As I said before, when Zathos had started his rise to power the people had begun to believe that peace could be kept in the land without them. Zathos helped them run off the *Sorva di Fravid,* and crowned himself king. After this the people realized their mistake, but it was only after they had nearly killed Anna, the last Bonded. They wished for the *Sorva di Fravid* to return, but in vain.

"Some say that a few dragons remained, but there had to be no more than fifty of them. Most of them hid themselves away, but a few remained on an island heard only of in rumors—Amatol. No one even knows where it is, if it really exists."

"But how could fifty dragons stay hidden for so long?" Shaelynn asked the man.

"Dragons are like elves—they take forever to age and can live for thousands of years, if not forever. No one really knows, as they never had the chance to find out. Dragons can also disguise themselves very well—rocks, hills, deadfall—they could be anywhere. As for being on the island, maybe a dragon has finally found its Bonded and he or she has at last completed their training. It can take years for a dragon to find the right companion, even longer for their Bonded to complete their training."

"How do you know all this?" Shaelynn asked. The man's eyes hardened, and his eyes darted around the room once more.

"I have seen some things and known a few people. And you? Why are you so interested?" In return Shaelynn's entire face turned hard as stone.

Looking away, she said quietly, "My cousin was taken by a dragon some weeks ago. She's dead now."

"How do you know she is?" the man asked, not unkindly. This thought had occurred to Shaelynn many times.

"She was fatally wounded in a swordfight, just before the dragon took her. I watched the fight, and I watched as the dragon lifted her in its claws. I saw her face seeing mine; it was one of the last things she probably saw." For a moment tears threatened to come, but she held them down. The man did not reply; he only sat back in his chair, rubbing his clean-shaven face, as if there had once been a beard there.

The man was quiet for a few minutes until he finally asked, "Where did it take place?"

"On a city street—I'll not say which city."

"No need. I've heard some rumors. That is unusual for dragons. Was the street crowded?"

"Yes."

"Hmmmm. That is very strange. Dragons do not normally risk being seen, and they'd rather avoid humanity, unless they are seeking a companion, but even then they meet the human alone."

"Again I have to ask—how do you know all of this? You seem to know everything about dragons and the *Sorva di Fravid*." The man laughed, catching the attention of some of the people in the room. He let their eyes turn back to other things before he continued.

"It would be impossible for even a dragon to know everything about itself," he said. "There are so many things about them that they have no idea about. Most of the time they discover new abilities by complete accident. The *Sorva di Fravid* I do know a little about, but not as much as I would like to."

"Do you know anything about the pack that they found?"

"Just what they've told me. I'm not from here, just traveling around wherever I can. It was somewhere next to the ocean on a rockier part of the coast where a few of the men here go to fish."

"Did you find out if there was a bracelet in it?"

"No, why?"

"The bow and quiver of arrows the man said they had found next to the pack? They sound like they were my cousin's. We received them from a friend, far from here. I have one also—look." She turned and lifted her bow over her head, laying it on the table. The man picked it up eagerly and examined every inch of it, turning it over and over. When he tried the string, Shaelynn found that he had a little trouble pulling it far enough back. He gave it back to her, and she lifted it over her head, pulling on the string over her chest to get the bow settled into place on her back.

"Aye, that looks like the one they found—they let me see it to see if I could identify its make, but I couldn't. Where did you say you got it?"

"I told you—a friend, far from here. I won't say who."

"My apologies. And the arrows that were found, what do you think they were made of?"

"Made from turkey feathers, if I'm not mistaken. Mine are pheasant, I think."

"Aye, they were turkey. Come; I will show them to you." He stood and walked from the room. Shaelynn followed, blushing at the looks some of the people in the tavern gave her.

She followed the man to a large building in the center of the city, probably where the town leader lived. At the third set of doors they came to there were armed men guarding it. The man made Shaelynn stay back while he gave a quiet explanation for the guards. Shaelynn didn't hear what they said, but they let them in.

Inside was a large room full of odds and ends, and right in front of them, in the center of the room, were about seven or eight men clustered around a table on which something lay. They looked up when the heavy cedar doors shut behind them.

"Jacey, who is this?" asked one tall man. The rest of them moved around to stand in front of the table, blocking any view of whatever was on it. Shaelynn stepped out from behind Jacey.

"I am Tera," she said.

"She may have known the owner of the pack found on the beach. She identified the feathers on the arrows, and she hasn't seen them yet." Looks of surprise crossed the men's faces.

"What are they, then? And who made them?" asked the tall man.

"They're turkey. We got them from a friend, but like I said to Jacey, I won't say who. I have a bow as well." Lifting it over her head once more, she tossed it to the man, who caught it and examined it carefully. "Is it similar?" she asked.

"Yes, very similar," said the man after a little while. The rest of the men crowded around him, revealing Liz's bow, her quiver, and the rest of the pack. Laid on top of the quiver was the map Tayna and Geoff had given them.

"Hey, that's our map," Shaelynn said, stepping forward. One of the men snatched it up and stuffed it in the pack, trying to hide it from her sight. Shaelynn was already there. Fighting off the man, she pulled the map out and examined it.

The tall man made to grab it from her, but Jacey's hand on his arm stopped him. The man looked furious. "Oh, come on, Sert'da. She knew the owner of the pack, can't you see?"

"Well, whose is it, then?" Sert'da asked Shaelynn.

"It was my cousin's."

"Was?"

"For all I know, she's dead. But that seems impossible now, though she'd have to be. She was fatally wounded in a swordfight. There's no way she could have survived it."

"Where, in Barda? We heard tell of that. She fought Karbab, didn't she?"

"How do you know of Karbab?" Shaelynn asked, stepping away from him, eyes cold.

"Peace, I mean you no harm. He is the son of a wealthy ruler, who was once ruler of half the land. We heard of it through the merchants; he is nowhere near here, not that I would know of."

"Yes, she fought him. The fight you heard of was the second. The first was in an alley, and the marketplace children saved her. She was sent to the healer, and she was gone the next day. She had gone to her workplace to request her wages and get her pack, the one you have here. She went to me to convince me to leave, and we argued. I-" she stopped and took a breath before going on, "I held her too long. Karbab had come after her again, and she met him in the street. They fought, and he ran her through in the middle, off to one side. Then a dragon carried her off, and I thought she was dead.

"But," she said, turning to the pack on the table, "I'd have no idea of how it got so far up the coast unless she was alive. And her tracks were there, weren't they?" The men nodded. "A dead girl doesn't leave tracks, I suppose. It's too confusing."

Shaking her head, she sat down on the floor before she fell. She was dizzy; she felt disoriented, struck dumb by the obvious fact that her cousin was alive. It couldn't be, yet here it was. Who else would have had her pack, used her bow, and left those tracks? And what of her lying right next to a dragon? What did that mean? Was Liz *Sorva di Fravid*? No. It wasn't possible.

Another wave of dizziness came over her. This couldn't be real. Her cousin had died almost two weeks ago. There was no way she could be alive now. Shaelynn had just gotten done mourning her loss. This couldn't be happening.

Looking up, she saw Jacey was kneeling next to her and the men were gathered around her. Shaking her head to try to get some of the dizziness out of it, she tried to stand, but had to be helped up by Jacey.

"Are you all right?" asked Sert'da. Slowly, Shaelynn shook her head no.

"Not for a while. I'd accepted her death, after a week; the first few days I nearly killed myself from isolation. I've just finished grieving. It's just so hard to accept."

"I see," said Sert'da.

"So, does this mean that my cousin could be Bonded to a dragon?" Her question rang in the silence, hanging in the tension of the air.

"How do you know of the *Sorva di Fravid*?" A man standing behind Sert'da whispered. Shaelynn's eyes flicked to Jacey next to her, and then back to the man who had spoken.

"I've heard some stories here and there, but I wasn't sure if they were true, until now."

"What do you know of them?" Shaelynn tried not to glance at Jacey for support when she answered.

"Well, they disappeared a long time ago. When they were first created, they defeated an evil force in the land. Peace was kept with or without them, so the people told them to leave. There was a bit of a fight, and the *Sorva di Fravid* left. They haven't been seen since."

"At least, no idea of them existing again has come to anyone's thoughts until now with this discovery," said Sert'da. The men behind him nodded and turned back toward the pack and its contents lying on the table, blocking her view from it once more.

"When we are through examining them and have an answer to this, you may have your cousin's possessions back," Sert'da said before turning his back on them to join the men clustered around the table once more. It was his way of dismissing them.

Silently Jacey helped Shaelynn out of the room and back out into the city. He took her back to the tavern, but they didn't go inside. Supai was sitting underneath the black, having been waiting on them to show. When he saw them he touched the black's belly before crawling out from under him.

"Where've you been? I waited for an hour an' a half, then went in. Some big man told me you'd been in there and then left with some man. I've been waiting here for at least another hour."

"Sorry," Shaelynn said. "They found Br— . . . my cousin's pack. I had to go and identify it. But I can't tell you now, it'll have to wait." She stepped out from underneath Jacey to stand by the black while she untied him.

"Thanks, Jacey," Shaelynn said over her shoulder when she was almost finished. Slipping the reins from the rail, she turned back toward him, but he was gone. Astonished, she turned toward Supai, who had moved to the opposite side of the black.

"Where'd he go?" she asked him. He shrugged his shoulders.

"I dunno. I been standing here, I didn't see anyone."

"Well, let's go. It's almost dark." They left the city just as the gates were closing. They kept on riding the black until the city was a faint dot through the trees below them. There they camped; Shaelynn shot a grouse, which was enough for both of them for the night. While they ate she explained everything to Supai.

"So, we're going to have to wait until they're finished with Liz's things until we can leave?" Supai asked, licking the juices from his fingers.

"Yes. We need that map, and I want Liz's pack with me instead of with those people."

"Can't you get them from them sooner?"

"No, they're as confused as I am. I guess they think Liz's things can point something out."

"Wow. I never imagined this, not ever. I thought she was dead, and here she is leaving tracks next to those of a dragon's. Maybe the days of the *Sorva di Fravid* have finally returned."

"Maybe," Shaelynn said. "I'm tired. Goodnight, Supai."

"G'night, Shaelynn," Supai said just before stifling a yawn. They both went to their blankets and almost instantly fell asleep.

Chapter 9

I SAW SHAELYNN, SITTING ON THE ground, looking dazed. She had a hand up to her forehead, as if she wasn't feeling well. There were men around her, one of them in his twenties. He had black hair that he constantly flipped out of his face and eyes that saw everything. He knelt beside Shaelynn; she looked up as if realizing for the first time that he was there.

He helped her up, and she hobbled to a table, losing her balance frequently. She had to be supported by the twenty-year-old man. She fingered something on the table, but she was in my way and I couldn't see. Then she stepped back, and I saw my pack on the table, with its contents lying near it.

My bow and quiver of arrows were on the table as well, and my map was lying on my quiver. She examined it for a moment, then the men clustered around the table once more. A tall man stood in front of them and spoke to Shaelynn and the twenty-year-old man; they left when the tall man turned his back on them.

The man helped Shaelynn through a town until they reached a tavern, where I could see the black horse tied to a post, Supai sitting underneath his belly in the shade. Supai got out carefully from underneath the black, trying not to startle him. Supai looked worried; he spoke fervently to Shaelynn before the man left.

I followed the man, seeing Shaelynn and Supai heading out of the city behind me. The man looked warily around him, and then ducked between two buildings, running down the narrow space until he came out the other end. Still following, I saw him running out of a gate in the city's wall, heading for the coast—one that I recognized.

It was the beach that Honoras and I had stopped at before we would have gone on to Amatol, where the latharks had attacked us. The man easily ran and jumped from rock to rock, passing the place where Honoras and I had slept with hardly a glance.

He continued on up the coast, leaping from rock to rock as they got more and more lumpy and ragged-edged. Suddenly he stopped before one of them and, looking around him once more, bowed deeply to the rock.

The rock moved, changing shape and color. What was once a dull tan rock turned to a brilliant blue-green shimmering mass of scales. A massive dragon, two times bigger than Honoras, rose from the ground and stood before the man. Slowly it returned the bow with a solemn dip of its head.

Briefly I wondered if the man was a *Fravid-Sorva*, but any evidence was almost immediately erased. While Honoras and I communicated through mind-speech, this man spoke to the dragon out loud. He also didn't act as if the dragon was the closest thing to a magician able to read your every thought, Bonded to one another, like Honoras and I.

As the man talked with the dragon, keeping his eyes low, he pointed down the coast in the direction of the place where Honoras and I had stopped and slept. The dragon looked toward it, and then its head turned to the man's right, where I was. The dragon met my eyes and stared into them, as if searching my soul.

Its eyes narrowed in anger and suspicion. An instant later they widened in shock, and recognition flowed through me. In a moment I was gone, back in my own mind in the dungeon of Zathos's castle.

With a jolt I sat up, knocking my head in the corner of the cell. Moaning softly, I felt a throbbing pain, realizing that I had been feeling it for quite some time. Soreness racked my body; my muscles shrieked in pain as I tried to sit up against the wall.

A soft laugh echoed in the room, making my heart jump in fear. As I tried to scramble back even farther into my corner I heard Avernus say, "It is about time you woke. It has been over two weeks since I had my last fun." Suddenly electricity surged through my body.

I squirmed and thrashed on the ground and heard Avernus laugh ever so softly. The electricity ebbed away as a picture flashed in my mind, along with a feeling of desperation and fear. It was of Honoras in the sky, trying to land as the electricity seized hold of his body, too.

With a pang I remembered what he had told me when we had revealed our names to each other. Now that we were Bonded by both soul and name, we could feel each other's pain, he said, to the fullest extent. Whatever I went through, he went through as well.

Praying for Honoras's safety, I watched as Avernus waved a hand over the lock, opening it with his magic. He pushed the door open, letting the burly man in with him, whom I had not seen lurking in the shadows.

My heart jumped to my throat as the man came toward me, roughly jerking me to the door of the cell. I screamed and lunged and tugged, trying to get away from him, but his grip was like iron. Avernus met me in the door while the man held me before him, keeping me immovable by twisting my arms behind my back.

Avernus held out a finger, touching it to my forehead. It stuck to it as if it were glued there, and he smiled. With a sharp thrust upward my head was thrown up and my mind into blackness.

I woke in another dark room, but it was not nearly as dark as the former cell. It was darker, so dark I could see nothing. The floor was stone as well, but I could tell that the walls were not all stone. I could also tell that there were people in the room with me.

My first instinct was to crawl backwards until I found a wall, but I didn't know how big the room was or where the people were at. I could run into Zathos himself. Instead I kept still, hoping to feign unconsciousness for as long as I could.

"Now. She is awake," said a cold voice to my left. Whirling to face it, I felt something collide with my face, catching my jaw and throwing me to one side. I shrieked and impulsively backed away, instinct taking over logic. Another fist hit me full in the side, cutting upwards, toward my ribs. I looked wildly around, but could see nothing. Everything was black; I couldn't have seen my hand if it was in front of my face.

I heard voices laughing, those of men. Footsteps approached me, and I tried to back away from them. There were footsteps behind me, and hands grabbed me from behind, wrenching my hands behind my back.

Somebody slapped my face, and I sagged in the man's grip. A foot connected with my leg, and then another with my side, both at almost the same instant. There were at least three men in the room with me.

Two more feet kicked me, again in my side and another on my arm, near my elbow. I heard a rib crack from the force of the kick. I screamed, which made it hurt worse. It was hard for me to breathe; every shuddering breath I sucked in seemed like a knife slicing through my side. The man behind me let my arms go, and the footsteps retreated as I writhed on the ground in pain, even though moving the slightest bit hurt me.

They let me lay there for a few minutes, and then another fist smashed into my face, throwing me on my stomach. A second later, two fists pounded into my back, one after the other. I was flipped over, and then received a few more punches. I was kicked again, and then was lifted up by the collar of my shirt, just enough that my upper body was off the ground.

Honoras! I cried out as a final blow was inflicted to the side of my face, leaving me immovable with pain and shock. The footsteps left and a door was opened, but I saw no light enter from the door, no light blinding me with its brightness as usual. I looked straight toward the sounds, hoping to see at least some filtered light coming down from above, but there was no flicker of light anywhere. I could see no more things in the room than I did before.

My heart skipped a beat as two answers floated to the surface: one, I was so far underground that even when a door was opened no light came in from a tunnel or other doorway, or two, I had been blinded somehow. I realized numbly that it had to be the latter; how else could the men have seen me or the door in the room?

Slowly I shut my eyes and focused on the blackness there, and then I opened them, but there was no change in the amount of light. I ran a hand in front of my face. Nothing. My instinct taking over again, I crawled backward, ignoring the searing pain in my side as I moved and breathed, until I reached a wall. After this I moved away from the direction where the sounds of the door had come from until I hit another wall. As I had in my cell, I tried to back into the corner as far as I could, wishing I could melt into it.

Eventually my adrenaline and numbness wore off, and the pain from my broken rib came back all at once. It was like I was being run through with Karbab's sword all over again. Every breath I took brought the sharp pang, and my breathing became shallower and shallower as I tried to ease the pain. Every small movement I made brought a stab of discomfort, to say the least.

Sucking in a breath as I lifted my shirt, I felt a swollen lump on my side. Touching it even a little hurt. Easing my shirt down again I leaned back in the corner, letting my shoulders rest on the two walls.

They came again a little while later, maybe after an hour or so. I heard the door open, and again there was no flicker of light anywhere around me; I was still blind. The door shut, and it was quiet for a moment. Then there were hurried footsteps to my right and left. Before I could do anything two people had grasped my arms at the shoulders and had drug me toward the center of the room.

I tried to fight, but my broken rib prevented me from doing much. I jerked hard to the left, trying to wrench myself free of their grasp. My side seared with pain as if I had been touched by a white-hot rod. I sagged in the two people's grip, gasping for breath.

"I see my men have done well on you, *Fravid-Sorva*." My breath caught in my throat as I realized who the speaker was. "Are you ready now to give anything up?" asked Zathos.

I said nothing. In a moment I felt fire; it was soft at first, and I felt it in my foot. And then it grew, suddenly racing up my veins and all through my body. It was burning me from the inside out. It burned hotter and hotter as if it had set my blood on fire. I squirmed in the men's grip, feeling the sudden lashes of pain from my broken rib. My throat finally opened for me to breathe; I screamed and screamed, trying to release the burning energy within me.

When it felt like my skin was on fire it stopped, leaving me weak and gasping for air. I sucked in every breath and held it as the pain in my side returned, trying to slowly let it out before I was forced to suck another one in.

"Anything come to mind yet?" Zathos asked, his voice cold and hard. My logical self, the part of me that I normally listened to, screamed at me to tell him everything so he would stop hurting me. But the stubborn part of me that I had inherited from my parents held, keeping my mouth clamped shut. I loved Honoras more than any friend I had known, and I wasn't about to get both of us and the rest of the dragons killed because of me. That was what Zathos had in mind:

if he could find out where the dragons were and how to get there, he would either call them to his side or, if they refused, kill them.

I felt the tension from the men around me grow as I remained silent and the minutes lengthened. My body screamed at me to tell him something, but I held my tongue for Honoras's sake. I wasn't about to hand him over to this man. I felt sweat drip from the tip of my nose onto the ground as I kept my head down. Finally I heard a muffled roar of rage. I felt a blow to my face, and then I heard Zathos turn and then take a few steps. They turned back toward me and stopped just in front of me.

"You will be sorry, *Fravid-Sorva*. I will find out where your dragon is, and I will find where the other dragons are. I will drive the sword through your heart that will kill you and your dragon, and I will make sure that your spirits stay trapped here forever." The footsteps whirled and quickly walked away from me, but the men holding me did not let go. I heard the door open across the room. "Do what you want with her, but make sure she lives," said Zathos as the door shut behind him.

Desperately I flung out my mind, searching for Honoras, crying out, *Help me! Honoras, please,* over and over. I felt the men's grip tighten on my arms as I was drug even further forward, probably more toward the center of the room. Low, evil laughs sounded around me as the first punch was inflicted on my face.

==

Honoras felt the surge of electricity just as he had started to think of Elizabeth once more. It seized his body, freezing his muscles at first so that he had the two humans with him dropped a few hundred feet in the air. As he regained control of himself he flapped hard, trying to get low enough to land before something else much worse happened.

The surge of electricity ended after a short moment, and he was able to land before he felt magic pressing at his forehead. His head was snapped backward, and all he could see was blackness. He blinked over and over, but all he could see was the total darkness. He turned his eyes to where the sun should have been, but there was nothing.

Roaring with rage, he tramped around, blundering into rocks and trees, paying no heed to the frightened humans, who had both managed to jump off of him immediately after he'd landed.

Riman was pulled out of the way by the woman behind him; Sorvo ran by at nearly a full run, barreling into a rock face. He froze, out of breath and energy. He sank to his belly, lowering his head between his talons.

Cautiously the woman and Riman approached him, trying to see if he'd get up and charge them again. He remained motionless except for his heaving sides, sensing them slowly coming forward.

The woman stopped next to his shoulder, reaching out a hand to him. He flinched at her touch, but relaxed. "What is it?" she quietly asked.

The sorcerer has blinded my Bonded. I can see nothing, and neither can she, whatever they are doing to her. His words troubled her, and she relayed them to Riman. He put a hand on the dragon's shoulder as well, feeling him jerk at his touch as he had with the woman.

"What are you going to do?" Riman asked. Honoras told the woman, who told Riman.

"He says that we could wait, but he does not know how long they'll be blinded. It could be until she is dead or it may be just so she can't briefly see something. If it keeps on, we'll have to lead him on, going on foot."

"But either way we lose time, and she could be killed by then. Is there a way he can get around the blindness?" He waited a moment for Sorvo's answer.

"No, there is no way he can think of. Once a dragon and companion are Bonded by soul and name, they share each other's pain and experiences to the fullest extent, as if they were one. If she is blind, he is blind. If pain is inflicted, he feels it as well. But, he says, while she may faint or break bones from experiences, he might not because he is stronger than she."

"Well, are there no other ways we can travel? It will take us too long to get there on foot. She'd be killed by the time we got there."

"There is slim chance of her being killed, he says. Zathos wants her alive so she can tell them where he is as well as where the other dragons are. She is the only source he has of discovering their location. Once he finds them he'll command them to fight for him, and he'll kill any that don't agree, which will be most of the dragons, if not all of them. None of them will willingly serve him. It would be the end of their race. As long as the girl doesn't give it up, he will keep her alive, because if she is killed then Sorvo will die also, erasing any chance of him finding out the information he wants.

"As for traveling, he says, he can think of no other way unless he gets his sight back. There's no way he can fly now even if we are his-" she stopped, holding a finger up in the air. An idea had just struck her. She was about to tell Riman that there was no way they could be Sorvo's eyes and allow him to fly, but there was a way. She turned toward the dragon again, leaving Riman in the silence she had created.

Sorvo, maybe I can be your eyes. There is a spell—

Yes, I know. But it would be difficult for me, let alone for you. Do you even know it?

Yes, but I've never tried it. If it will work, though, you could still fly.

Try it now. I don't want a disaster in the air.

Very well.

Focusing on her store of magic, she muttered the words. Opening her eyes, she saw that her vision had enhanced greatly. Looking to the sun, she could see the ball of fire in the sky, all the time looking at it without blinking. Looking around the clearing, she could see the individual blades of grass move as a mouse, which she could clearly see from a hundred feet away, stirred in the grass and darted into its hole.

Turning back to Riman, she saw a small bug, smaller than anything she could have normally seen, crawling up his shirt. Looking closer, she saw others in his hair and the woven fibers of his pants. Examining a blade of grass, she saw the little aphids moving underneath it.

Sorvo, can you see this? she asked, gazing with awe at the new things she could see that she had never noticed before.

My own eyes cannot see it, but through your mind I can see what you do. Experimentally she waved a hand in front of his staring eyes; he did not stir, only laughed at her intentions.

It is odd, seeing myself like that. It is like I have traveled outside of my body.

Can you fly like this?

Can you keep up the spell?

Aye, for a while.

When you feel your magic start to fail, tell me. I will land until you can get your strength back.

As you wish. Turning back to Riman, she was surprised again to see how many things on him stood out that she had never noticed before. "Come, we have found a way." She turned to get back up on the dragon's back, but he stopped her.

You must ride below me in my claws. I cannot see well enough to fly when you are behind my head. But do not worry; you will be safe.

Uneasily, she watched as Riman clambered up and looked at her expectantly. She explained to him what was going on while the dragon shakily stood on all four legs. The dragon nodded, and she stepped toward his claws. He sat back on his hind legs, bringing his forelegs out. He put his claws together to form a kind of net for her.

Look down at my claws so I can see what I am doing, Honoras said. The woman did as he asked, climbing backwards into his talons. Putting her hand on a claw while she pushed herself inside the net, she found that it was razor sharp.

Are you sure your claws won't slice me to pieces? she asked, unsure.

Hush. My Bonded has ridden in my claws before, and nothing happened to her. Now, look to the skies. He leapt into the air, unfurling his great wings. The sun hit them, and they sparkled emerald green from its light. The dragon pumped his wings, gaining altitude with every beat. When they were a few hundred feet above the ground he started to level out, rising higher all the while.

Look around so I can see the skies better. The woman turned her head from side to side. Far off in the distance was a rainstorm, heading their way. By looking at the thunderheads she could see them moving and building, shifting with the wind. Sorvo told her that it would reach them by late tonight. His wings rose and fell with an easy beat, pushing them on and on.

After a half hour of flying the dragon's head was pushed sideways with such energy that he was knocked off course, leaving the wind to throw them as it willed. His wings were battered from it, and they sank quickly toward the ground. He roared in pain again, stopping his wingbeats just long enough for them to fall again. He regained control, trying to fly in the right direction while the woman's sight in his mind whirled this way and that, trying to find their attackers.

Look straight ahead. It is from my Bonded; she is being beaten. He roared again as another blast of pain came from his jaw. *No one is attacking us; look ahead! I need to see where I am.* Pain exploded from his ribs, such a pain that he knew Elizabeth's rib had been broken. The pain speared him again and again as she moved, and then it quieted a little, only hurting periodically as she breathed. There were a few more stabs of pain as she moved even more, but there were no more inflicted blows made upon her.

It is stopped, he told the woman. *For now at least, I will keep flying.* They flew fast, but they had only put about thirty miles behind them when it started to get dark and the woman could feel her magic starting to fade.

How long can you hold it? Honoras asked.

Maybe another few minutes. We must land quickly.

Very well. Look to the ground ahead of us. No, farther ahead than that. I must find a clearing. There; about a mile ahead. It will do. The dragon folded his wings in a little, pointing his body downward as he dived down, down, closer and closer to the tops of the trees. When they were just above them he leveled out, keeping his momentum from his dive. Just as the rock wall on the far end of the clearing came into view Honoras froze, feeling pain lash in his side. It ached more, and more, and then there was the worst pain, like being scalded with a line of fire.

He folded his wings into a dive, knowing what was coming. He plunged into the trees far before the edge of the clearing, striking their trunks once—twice—a third time knocking him off course. He fell to his side on the ground at the same time that the feeling of fire ignited within his body, growing in an instant.

The flame inside him spread throughout his body, racing through his veins. Vaguely he felt Riman leap off and run to his talons, which he had clenched with the pain. The woman was still inside, barely able to move.

Fighting against his body, he released his savage grip just long enough for the woman to scramble out before they closed completely. The fire seared white-hot, and he thought his blood would start to boil and his scales would melt off him.

The fire ended, giving him a chance to catch his breath and roll over to his belly. A minute went by, and then two, as Honoras waited expectantly for more sorcery to inflict more pain. After almost five minutes he heard Elizabeth.

Help me! Honoras, please, help, her voice said desperately. He felt a blow to his face, and others, beating his shoulders and sides, kicks to his legs, and he heard Elizabeth's voice in his head all the while, calling him to come and help her. He lay on the ground the whole while, feeling her pain. It did not hurt him as much as it probably hurt her, save for the pain of her broken rib as she moved and as it was struck.

The beating continued for nearly ten minutes, until he felt nothing more from Elizabeth. There was only the throbbing pain left to remind him that they were both alive. He slowly relaxed his tense body; extending his hind legs out, he found that he had been close to hitting a very large tree.

"Sorvo? Are you all right?" asked a timid voice. It was the woman, and she sounded shaken. Honoras nodded his head carefully before letting it rest on his forelegs. He felt the vibrations in the earth as she approached, something he had only vaguely noticed before.

I will be fine, he answered, *but I worry about my companion. She was beaten badly.* The woman relayed the information to Riman. Thunder rumbled in the distance, reminding Honoras of the approaching storm he and the woman had seen from the sky. Lifting a wing, he told them, *Come, I will give you some shelter.* They cautiously approached, until the thunder clapped close to them. They hurried under his wing and sat down next to his warm belly as he lowered his wing over them, encasing them in warmth.

Honoras tucked his head under his wing as well, adding to their warmth with his smoky breath. He drew his legs and tail up around the two humans, creating a protective wall around them. Riman almost immediately fell asleep, leaning his back against one of the dragon's massive hind legs.

The woman flashed Sorvo a picture of Riman asleep through her mind. The dragon softly chuckled. *Tell me, woman,* he said, *what is your name?*

I haven't told you? It is Dasriel.

It is a beautiful name.

Thank you. My mother named me after a sorceress of long ago.

Yes, I have heard of her. She fought in the battle that helped the first few Sorva di Fravid *defeat the evil that was in the land.*

Sorvo? Something just occurred to me.

What is it?

Do you think that history is repeating itself? Are you and your Bonded destined to be the ones to defeat Zathos? To be the first Sorva di Fravid *in over a century?*

I do not know. I will be happy just to rescue her from him, but it is our duty to take care of Partaenia. If we must, we will. However, my Bonded is still untrained. That in itself will take a year at the very least. To himself he thought, she is in no condition to fight. She does not yet know what she can do.

But yes, he said, *we are indeed the first* Sorva di Fravid *in many centuries. That much we have accomplished, however little it may be.*

It is much, Dasriel said. *Once people learn of you, their hearts will be filled with hope, even more so when you defeat Zathos.*

That much is yet to be proven. For now, I still have my doubts. The people did not accept us before. They ran us off, he said, his voice suddenly full of anger. He stopped himself before he went on, afraid he wouldn't be able to stop his rant.

He felt a drop of water on his back and jumped severely, awakening Riman for a moment. Dasriel quieted him as more and more drops fell, and he fell asleep again just before the clouds above them opened wide. It was a downpour; the rain thundered on Honoras's wings, and he was glad he had thought to hide his head under them. Drowsily he felt Dasriel lean back, resting on his shoulder, close to his head. After a few minutes he lightly touched her mind. She was asleep; he withdrew quietly, not wanting to disturb her. After a few more minutes the rain let up a little, and he was able to sleep at last.

==

I woke, terribly hungry, cold, and thirsty. I had gone who knows how many days without either food or water, and I knew I was dehydrated. If I didn't get at least some water in a day, maybe two, I'd die. I already felt sick to my stomach, as if I would throw up, but I had nothing in my stomach to bring up.

"Water," I croaked, hoping someone would hear me. For the first time I felt another presence in the room. It stirred, and then the door opened and closed again; someone had gone out. Feeling around with my mind since I still could not see, I found no one else in the room.

My mind searched my body, and I realized that I was lying on my back, probably somewhere in the middle of the room. I was bruised, I could tell. My whole body ached, and my side still stung when I breathed. I had received a bad beating and I wasn't ready for another, but I did not retreat to a corner. I was too weak to do so anyway. So I lay where I was in the open until I heard the door open again.

There were two or three sets of footsteps; I had trouble discerning the shuffling feet from one or another. They came close. I stirred a little, trying to get my sore body to move, but it refused my commands. They chuckled; they were men, I could tell. I felt the splash of water on my face, and I eagerly opened my lips, but I only received a small mouthful. Yet it helped. I kept my mouth open, ready for the next splash.

"She don't need more'n that," said a gruff voice.

"The King said to keep her alive. Give it to her."

"No. She don't need more'n that," the first man repeated. His footsteps retreated a little, but there was a small struggle as the other man tried to stop him. There were grunts as I heard their feet shuffle around, and then there was a final grunt. I heard water slosh slightly and something heavy fall to the ground. Wondering who had won, I waited in anticipation.

Feet approached at my head, and I heard the second voice say, "Open your mouth, girl." I opened my mouth as far as it would go, and water was carefully poured into it. I heard the other man get up and walk for the door as another mouthful of water was poured in.

"Thank you," I said, my voice sounding better, but still no more than a croak. There was no answer, only the kinder man's footsteps going to the door and disappearing behind it. Before he left, something whooshed through the air and landed not too far away. Crawling to it, I felt a piece of rough bread lying on the floor. Though it was stale, I eagerly bit into it.

===

Honoras's side flared with pain during the night, and he tried not to wake the humans still leaning against his body, sleeping. Carefully he cast out for Elizabeth's mind. The connection was so faint, but he could tell she was awake. Feeling his slight presence there, she lashed out at first, screaming at him, *Get away, sorcerer! Leave me be!*

Elizabeth, he said, loudly so she might hear him. Even her shouts of fear and anger were mere whispers, but Honoras was excited by the strength of the connection all the same. It was stronger than when he was in the prison, by however little. It encouraged him.

Honoras! Where are you? Stay away from here. Zathos wants you. I'm in his dungeons.

I know. And do not tell me what to do. I am coming for you, no matter what happens. I have two humans with me as well; they will help. I am close to you, but still a few days away. How are you faring?

You know of the torture. I would have died of lack of food and water, but I was taken care of today, a little at least. One of—men here is good.—rib is—and I—blind,——know of—.

Yes, he said, his heart full of longing and sadness. *I must go; it is hard to keep the connection for long. Please, though, warn me if they come again. I have found a way to fly, and I don't want to be caught in the air again.*

Yes,——.—bye, Honoras.

Goodbye. Reluctantly he broke the weak connection and settled back into sleep. Before long it was dawn.

===

I was still eating the stale bread when I felt someone else's consciousness lightly touching mine, prodding at it, sort of. I lashed out at it, knowing it was Avernus. *Get away, sorcerer! Leave me be!* I was surprised at my own bravery, or foolishness.

Elizabeth, a voice faintly whispered. It was Honoras! I spoke with him, though I could barely hear anything he said. I had to shout to him to make him hear me, and I was only able to catch the most important points of his sentences. He was on his way to rescue me, and he said he had someone with him that would help. I told him to stay away, but he refused. He told me to warn him when something was about to happen. I wasn't sure if I could, but I told him I would. He was having trouble keeping the connection, so we said goodnight. As soon as I felt his presence fade, I remembered the odd dream I had had with the man and the dragon by the ocean.

Frantically I reached out for him, but I could not send out my mind far enough; I still wasn't strong. I panicked for a moment, dropping the bread and letting my breathing become heavy, even though it hurt my side terribly. What if I couldn't reach him again when the torture started once more? What if he was flying, and he crashed because of me? What if he died? What would happen to me? Would I die as well?

Stop it, I told myself, trying to keep the flood of What ifs from taking control again. If you panic, you'll die, I told myself. And you might kill Honoras in the process. Another question fought its way to the surface of my mind, and I squashed it down again, telling myself over and over again, Don't panic, don't panic. Honoras is coming.

Chapter 10

SHAELYNN WOKE TO THE SUN already in the sky, peeking through the trees and bathing her in warmth. She sat up, looking around. Supai was sitting by a fire, trying to dry his pants. Shaelynn sheepishly looked away, and realized that she was damp as well. It must have rained a little during the night. She put a hand on her blankets; the tops were almost soaked. They were lucky the blankets were thick, otherwise they would be worse off than just being damp.

Stealing a look over her shoulder, she saw that Supai had seen her and was hurriedly putting his pants on. Pretending to be just looking around, she waited until he had them all the way on until she turned toward him.

"Morning," she said, making her voice sound surprised, as if she had just noticed him. He replied with a sheepish nod, his face red. She got up and folded her blankets, carrying them to where the black was. Supai's blankets were already there, far enough away from the horse that he couldn't bother them.

She found her bow and started to set off, but Supai called her name. Carefully, she turned back toward him.

"I went and got breakfast already. I used your bow, if you don't mind," he said. Reaching on the ground close to the fire, he picked up the choice cuts from a rabbit that was lying on a rock. She took it; the meat was already cooked for her, and it was still warm. Supai sat down close to the fire.

Shaelynn sat down as well, on the other side of the fire from Supai. She wanted to watch him. He had never hunted before. He had cooked it most of the time, yes, but Shaelynn had always done the hunting. She didn't even know he knew how to use a bow and arrow. She watched him closely, but his face remained impassive as he warmed himself.

Finally she asked him, "I didn't know you knew how to shoot a bow."

"Well, yeah," he said a bit defensively. "I had to eat on the way from my birth town to Barda somehow, didn't I? Besides, you'd be hard pressed to find someone who don't know how to use one."

"I just haven't ever seen you with one, so I didn't know if you knew how."

"Well, now you know. Anyway, my old bow broke—it was a gift from a friend. He helped me get out of that place and on my way somewhere else. I haven't seen him since." They remained quiet; Supai scolded himself for giving too much away. I barely even now her, he told himself. I'm just helping her get to Zathos, even though I know I'm crazy for it.

Yet he knew what he said to himself was a lie. He did know her. She had told him her whole story, and he had known a lot about her from his first look at her; it was one of his gifts, reading people.

They sat in silence, Shaelynn eating the meat and Supai occasionally changing positions to warm himself better, though he was warm enough already. He just didn't want to move away from Shaelynn and offend her. There was a scuffle behind them, startling them both into looking up at the branches of a tree.

A squirrel, bright red in color, swiftly backed up out of a knot in the tree, squeaking indignantly. Shaelynn could almost imagine what it must have been saying. A dark brown squirrel came out after the red one, barking in anger. The red one went down on all fours, pointing its ears aggressively forward and puffing its tail up. The dark brown squirrel puffed up as well, causing the fur on his back to rise also. It barked once, twice, advancing on the red squirrel with each bark. The red one gave up and jumped down to a close but lower branch, running for the trunk of the tree. The dark brown one followed from above, making sure the red one didn't try to get in again.

The red squirrel, seeing the darker one above, thought better of the situation and ran down the tree headfirst. The dark brown one leaped onto the trunk and raced after him to be sure he would stay away. When the squirrel hit the bottom of the tree, he raced along the ground, heading straight for Shaelynn and Supai. When it saw them, it stopped and whirled away back toward the tree, but then it saw the brown squirrel waiting for him. The red squirrel froze in fear, barely breathing.

The dark brown squirrel turned and raced up the tree, disappearing back into its hole. The red squirrel stayed, still frozen in place. Shaelynn watched it from the corner of her eye, not wanting to scare it away too soon. And then, the squirrel's small shoulders sagged as if in relief. It turned toward Shaelynn and Supai.

Shaelynn jumped severely when it said, "Good gods. I been tryin' to get outta there for months. Hated that guy, I did. Always took more nuts than he needed to." Supai and Shaelynn stared at the squirrel, not believing their own ears. The squirrel walked toward the fire, stopping in between the two of them. He went on, "I hooked up with him a year ago, ya know. I didn't know how to find a good hole, nice and high up, so he let me bunk with 'im. It was nice of him, up 'till I didn't like 'im anymore. Been trying to get him to run me out for months."

Shaelynn watched the squirrel, dumbfounded. It sat down close but not too close to the fire, pulling his tail up around him, softly running his paws over it. It looked at Supai, and then at Shaelynn.

"What, you've never met a talking squirrel?" it asked. "Sorry if I missed introductions. I am Avinret, red squirrel of the Great Forest in the North." He bowed as gracefully as a squirrel could to both Supai and Shaelynn. "And, you are? . . . ," he asked politely.

"Um, Shaelynn," she answered. Looking to Supai, she told him, "We're not still asleep, are we?" Supai shook his head slowly as the squirrel turned to him.

"I—I'm Supai," he said shakily. "And since when do squirrels talk?"

"Why, since this bloody place was here," Avinret said, sounding a little annoyed. For the first time Shaelynn realized that somehow Avinret had a strong British accent. Avinret stomped a foot forcefully at Supai, saying, "Consider yourself lucky, boy, to be speaking with a squirrel such as me. We're hard to come by, you know. There aren't as many of us as there used to be, though I wish there was. It might make this world come to some sense." He muttered on as Supai and Shaelynn exchanged looks.

Suddenly the two of them burst out laughing, though neither knew why. A smile spread across Avinret's face, at least from what

Shaelynn could tell. "It's about time I made you two laugh. I've given who knows how many punch lines already. I forgot how slow humans were." Shaelynn and Supai laughed even harder, tears at the corners of their eyes. Shaelynn sucked in a breath, feeling a little dizzy.

Eagerly Avinret scampered to Shaelynn, swiftly climbing up her shirt. He was sitting on her shoulder before she realized he was there. "So, where might you be headed this late in summer?" he asked.

She hesitated, but Supai put in, "It's a bit of a touchy matter, if you know what we mean. It's far north, so much as you know."

"What would you want to do way up there? There's no trees or even any grass for hundreds of miles up there, and then you run into that bloody castle on the mountain where that idiot of a king lives." He hesitated, looking between the two of them suspiciously. "Say, what would you want to do up there? Nothin' good ever comes outta that place, or wants to go in."

"You've been there before? You know of it?" Shaelynn asked, realizing for the first time that he had given them a detailed and knowing description, for a squirrel.

"Well, yeah, that's where I was born, before them bloody monsters and those stupid spells tore up the place. I used to know how to get around by heart, 'fore me mum ran me outta there."

"Wait. You said you were *born* there, before Zathos took over?"

"That's what 'is name is! Been tryin' to figure it out for years, now."

"No, you just said you were born there. And you knew it by heart."

"Yeah, that's what I said. Didn't you hear me?" Shaelynn sighed exasperatedly. Supai turned to the squirrel.

"What she means is, can you get back up there if you wanted to? We don't know how."

"Well, yeah, I could, but why in the bloody 'ell would I want to? You humans must be harder of hearing than I thought. I said—"

"I know what you said. Can you take us up there or not?"

"I could, yeah, but I told ya, there's no *trees* for hundreds of miles! What am I supposed to do? Walk and sleep on the ground?" Supai looked uncomfortable, unable to answer. Shaelynn thought of something.

"If you lead us up there, you can ride on the horse, if he lets you. You can even sleep up on him where you have a good view, and you're off the ground." Avinret was about to make another loud protest, but stopped with a paw frozen in the air. Slowly he lowered it and shut his open mouth. He crossed his arms in a very humanlike way.

"I might be able to," he said slowly.

"And, all the way until we get there," Supai added, "you can do everything with us, okay, friend?"

"You mean, I can help you find a good place to sleep and set up camp, and everything like that? As if I were one of you?"

"Yes." Avinret jumped into the air, punching it with his fist. "I've always wanted to be like a human, since I'm different and all," he said a little more quietly. "Not many animals can talk, and most of them that can aren't very nice, but some humans are. I've hated being different, but now it's paid off!"

Supai gave me a quick look that was smug, as if he'd known that that was how the squirrel felt and he had said that on purpose in order to get him to cooperate. He probably had known which things to say to the squirrel after he first started to talk. She wished she could learn to interpret people like that.

"What're you two lookin' at each other like that for?" Avinret asked suspiciously. Then a wide smile broke out on his face, and he said happily, "Oh, you two *fancy* each other! I get it now!" Both Supai and Shaelynn looked away and blushed horribly, their cheeks hot. Avinret curled into a ball, rolling over and laughing. His laughter carried on into most of the night, picking up again whenever he saw the two humans trying to look at one another. It bugged Shaelynn, really. After they had retrieved Liz's pack from the town, they went on their way north as they followed the map, still intact.

They made good time with Avinret's help, better than they would have expected. There were places in the forest where Avinret led them to some of the most treacherous-looking paths Shaelynn had seen, but with his guidance they got through them faster than they would have if they'd gone around.

Soon they had gone through the last town they would meet in the north, and they stocked up well on preservable food, using the last of Shaelynn's coins. And, even sooner, it seemed, they reached the edge of the trees.

==

Honoras balked at what he saw through Dasriel's eyes. He skipped a wingbeat, dropping them about seventy-five feet in the air. Dasriel shut her eyes, cutting off his view of anything. Riman yelped.

Open your eyes so I can see, he told Dasriel irritably. He picked up his pace again, turning in slow circles to make sure if what he saw was true.

Just below him the line of trees stopped. The line formed a great arc, and no trees grew anywhere past it, not even from where he could see a couple of miles up. There were simply no trees for hundreds of miles.

And the colors were odd too. He was sure it wasn't Dasriel's vision. The ground was tinted gray, and the sky seemed the same as well. The blanket of clouds over him did not help either. Brittle grass covered the ground where he remembered softly rolling hills in between forest land. There were no roads anywhere, no footprints in the ground, no signs of life at all.

Yet, he realized, his memory had not failed him. If he found the road, he could head northeast from it. And, he saw the road was to his left, just in front of the horizon. He banked to the right, and then picked up his steady pace to something a little faster. They were almost there.

==

After a day riding in the open, both humans as well as the squirrel longed for trees. The wind blew around them relentlessly, and there was nothing to stop it. Day and night they felt exposed from lack of cover.

The next morning, they were reluctant to travel any farther, but they packed up camp nonetheless and headed out. Avinret was asleep and snoring, curled up on the black's muscled rump. Supai held the reins, and Shaelynn sat behind him. Her arms were wrapped loosely around his waist, and she had laid her head on Supai's back, just under his shoulder to keep the wind out of her face. She stared blankly at the slowly passing ground.

Supai kept the black going at a steady walk. He must have been tired, for he had been carrying them both for almost a month now.

Supai decided that anything more than a brisk walk would tire him out too much.

At what Supai guessed was midday they stopped for a while to let the black eat whatever grass there was, and for them to get something to eat as well. They had been saving the bought food for this open area, where they knew they could find nothing else to eat. They had just not expected it to be so desolate.

Supai and Shaelynn ate bread and the one chunk of cheese. They had to eat this first, otherwise it would spoil later on. Avinret sat on Shaelynn's shoulder, eating a small piece of bread. They drank only as much water as they needed, and then went on again. Nobody spoke for quite a while.

Suddenly, Avinret sat up attentively. He cocked his head to the side, trying to listen past the wind. No one had noticed him yet, so he scampered up Shaelynn's back to sit on her shoulder.

"Do we know of any large birds around here?" he asked.

"No, I don't think so," Shaelynn answered. She tapped Supai's shoulder, and he turned to face her. "Do you think there would be any large birds around here?"

"Prob'ly not. Ask Avinret."

"He's the one that wants to know."

"Why?" Wordlessly Shaelynn put Avinret on Supai's shoulder.

"Oh, I just thought I heard something like wingbeats, that's all. Really big wings, at that," the squirrel said.

"You're hearing things," Supai said. "That's what happens when-" He stopped in midsentence and cocked his head. Shaelynn heard it too, just as Avinret looked up. Supai and Shaelynn followed suit.

"I told you I heard something," Avinret said smugly. Something huge was just above them, pumping its bat-like wings. Its regal head surveyed them from about three hundred feet in the air. Its long tail was held lazily out behind it, and it seemed to be carrying something in its front claws. Shaelynn looked closer. It was a woman.

Immediately Supai dug his heels into the black. He leaped forward into a frightened gallop, his tiredness vanishing as he realized the danger above him. Supai went with his motion, but Shaelynn was jerked backward and Avinret flew from Supai's shoulder and caught on to Shaelynn by his claws. Shaelynn screamed half in terror and half in pain as the squirrel's claws bit into her skin. She reached up and grabbed him, holding him to her chest.

The black stumbled, and they went down. Supai managed to leap off before his leg was smashed under the horse's weight, and Shaelynn and Avinret were thrown ten and some feet. The black screamed; it was a high pitched, anguish-filled scream that chilled Shaelynn's blood.

Shaelynn landed on her back, and she felt her breath whoosh out of her chest. She rolled over once more from the momentum, while trying to get her breath back again. Supai was doing the same, rubbing his shoulder. Avinret was picking himself up. The black was lying on his side, breathing hard and moaning softly. Shaelynn crawled on hands and knees over to him and Supai by his side.

White bone protruded slightly from just under the knee on one of the black's legs. It was bleeding a lot, and the black wasn't trying to move it. It was broken, probably shattered. "Aw, no," Supai groaned. He threw his head back, and he saw the dragon again. Shaelynn and Avinret remembered it at almost the same time as Supai; Avinret dived between Shaelynn and Supai, and the two humans clutched the trembling horse tighter. As they watched, the dragon landed on its back legs to keep from smashing the woman in its claws.

Gingerly it set her down, and she walked over to them while the dragon settled itself. There was another man atop the dragon who was getting down. The dragon kept its head low but cocked, listening. It was a glittering grass-green color, with a yellow underside. Yellowish scales mixed somewhat with the green. It was almost big as a house.

The woman approached them cautiously, her hands out in a sign of peace. She saw the black's shattered leg and hurried forward. Supai somehow jumped over the black's neck from a squatted position, a snarl on his face.

"Get any closer woman, and I'll kill you. Take your dragon and leave. You've caused enough harm to us and our horse."

"I doubt you could keep that promise, boy. Besides, I mean you no harm."

"Look what you've caused!" he yelled, pointing to the leg.

"What if she said she could heal it?" a new voice said. It was the man; he had walked around the front of the dragon and had seen the black's leg. Supai stopped, shocked.

"That can't be true," he murmured. He turned to the woman and asked, "Is it? Can you really heal him?"

"Yes. I am a sorceress." Supai nearly fell backward.

What she says is true, a deep voice said in Shaelynn's head. It was faint; she wasn't sure if she had heard it. *She healed my tattered wings after I was attacked.* Supai whirled, looking for the voice. It had said 'my' wings. That could only mean-

"Is the dragon speaking to you?" the woman asked. Shaelynn nodded, but Supai only stared blankly at the beast.

"You can speak?" he asked the dragon. It did not look at him, but nodded its head.

I can speak nearly every language, but the human language I must speak with my mind. Again it did not look at him, but stared ahead.

"Well, dragon, can you face me when you speak? I do not enjoy looking at the side of your head." As soon as Supai had said it, he regretted it instantly. The dragon roared unexpectedly and whirled around, snarling. Past his fear, he saw that even now the dragon's eyes were blank and did not focus on him.

That, human, is because I am blind. I must use that woman there to see. Without her, I would still be stuck in the forest miles away. You do not understand. Most humans don't. The massive dragon settled down once more, but still faced Supai. The woman turned toward Shaelynn and the dragon said, *I know you, girl. You are the cousin of my Bonded. Perhaps you remember me.*

Shaelynn looked around anxiously at being singled out. It seemed as if she were the only one that heard the dragon now. She thought for a moment before she finally realized what the dragon was talking about.

Anger rose to the brimming point, and she stood up and walked around the black. Briefly she looked at the woman, who was taking the opportunity to examine the black's leg. She seemed to stop herself, and then she walked with Shaelynn toward the dragon and stood by his head, facing her. Shaelynn did not get as close.

Shaelynn opened her mouth to speak; she had imagined more of a yell, actually. But the dragon lifted a single claw, stopping her. *I can hear your thoughts already, but they are jumbled and confused. Organize them first, and then try to yell with your mind rather than with your mouth. It will make the conversation private, so focus on me when you do.*

Stunned, she just stood there stupidly. But, she thought, what the heck? She tried it, and it actually worked. *You're the one that killed my cousin! I saw you pick her up in the street, and then you carried her off and ate her!*

Not true, the dragon said calmly. *She is alive now. Anyway, I hate the taste of human. Your race is too . . . . well, shall we say, dirty, to eat.*

You're lying! I know she's dead, and I know you killed her!

Not true, the dragon repeated.

Where is she, then?

It is a bit of a long story. But I can tell you, she is alive. In fact, she is the reason for my blindness, though it was not her fault. Shaelynn heard a hint of sadness in the dragon's voice for the first time. She held back the stream of angry thoughts in her head. Then she thought of something else.

If it is a long story, I can make time. I need to know.

Very well. I will tell you, but I must hurry to help her. We are only two days' flight from her, and that will be enough time. Ride with me, and I will tell you our story.

What about Supai, and the black? And Avinret?

They can continue on foot. But, did you say Avinret? The squirrel that speaks?

Yes, why?

I know him. Dasriel turned to the squirrel, still hiding by the black. *It has been a long time, my old friend.*

Avinret poked his head up from behind one of the black's hind legs. "Green Dragon, is that you?" The dragon bared his teeth in a smile.

Aye.

"Where have you been? It has been long!" Their conversation continued on, and Shaelynn blocked it out to go and see Supai.

"Well, what do you make of all this?" she asked him. He seemed to have been glaring at the woman, who had sat down in the arch of the black's neck. His head was behind her, his injured leg before her, where she could easily work. Both hers and the black's eyes were closed, hers in concentration. A faint glow issued from her steady hands, held just over his injured leg.

"I can't believe it. A sorceress, and a dragon. Working together. The *Sorva di Fravid* have returned at last."

"Those two?" she asked, gesturing at the sorceress and the dragon. He nodded. "They aren't together, umm, Bonded. That's the word, right?" Supai nodded, confused. Shaelynn went on, "They're traveling together, looking for Liz. That's what the dragon said. He said she was the one Bonded to him."

"What? This is Liz's dragon? Where is she?"

"The dragon hasn't said anything to clear it up, but he said he'd explain it to me on the way. He's trying to reach Liz as fast as possible. I guess she's in trouble."

"What, are we traveling with him now?" Supai sounded irritated.

Shaelynn hesitated. "He said I could go with him while he told me what happened to Liz. He said you and Avinret could catch up on foot." She flinched at the reaction she knew would come. Supai blew up.

"On foot? What are we, the packhorses? The little ones that can't go with the big guys? He can carry all of us, I know he can!" He flung his hands up in the air and proceeded to stomp around in circles, muttering to himself and cursing under his breath.

By now, he had caught the dragon's attention. He sat in place to their side, not moving. But they could still hear him. *Calm yourself, young one. It will be more dangerous than you think. You see, my Bonded is being held by Zathos in his dungeon. I cannot risk you and Elizabeth's cousin going in with me to be killed. That is why you will be on foot. With the help of the sorceress, your horse will be faster, almost as fast as me. When I drop Elizabeth's cousin off, you will be but a day behind.*

I and the sorceress will go in after my Bonded, with the man to help us. Elizabeth's cousin will wait for you with the remainder of my burdens, and you will wait with her until we arrive again. If we do not return within three days' time, you will turn south and go back to Barda. Do you understand me?

Supai held his tongue for a moment to let his first wave of anger subside. He did understand. He and Shaelynn would be useless in the attack, and they would definitely be outmatched by the evil king. There was nothing they could possibly do to help. He hung his head. "Aye, dragon. I understand you. We will not interfere."

Thank you, young one. I know how hard that is for you. Supai realized that the remark had been aimed at him only. Satisfaction invaded his tired body. He smiled at the dragon, even though he knew he couldn't see it.

The man, who had been standing next to the sorceress, moved toward the dragon and the two teenagers. "Would you like something to eat? We have some supplies to share. I think Dasriel's almost done with your horse."

"Yes. We have some supplies of our own, but we can return the favor later on," Shaelynn said. Supai nodded his agreement. The man nodded, and walked to the packs strapped to the dragon.

The dragon cocked his head to the side, as if he were confused. *I'm sorry, did I miss introductions? What a fool of me. The sorceress is Dasriel, and the man is Riman. I will not share my name, but the humans call me Sorvo.*

Sorvo, my name is Shaelynn. The boy is Supai. He is from the town where Liz and I were staying before she was—injured, I guess.

Correct, Sorvo said with a nod of approval. *She was wounded by the man Karbab, and I rescued her and healed her. But that will be left until tomorrow. Now, eat.* Riman had returned with bread, a skin of water, and some preserved meat, probably pork, by the way it tasted. Riman said that they had had cheese at the beginning of their journey, but it was gone now.

Dasriel had finished with the black, and she was now famished. Before she ate, though, she stood by Sorvo, her hand on his cheek. She stood there for a minute before returning to the humans.

"What did you do?" Shaelynn asked her.

"I removed the spell that allows him to see through me. I am still getting used to it. If I can make magical contact with his mind, it allows me to be his eyes, literally," she explained. "I can see with his normal vision, which is much better than mine. That is what I am still getting used to. But if I didn't see with his vision, it would have been much harder for us to navigate, and we wouldn't have met you. Lucky we did, eh?"

Supai turned his gaze over to the black's sleeping form, making sure that Dasriel saw him. "Oh, yes. Well, that couldn't be helped. But I promise you, he will be well enough tomorrow, even to run. Which he will do, with my help. Did Sorvo tell you of our plan?"

"Aye, he told me," Supai said, still unhappy about it. Dasriel leaned forward and put a hand on his shoulder.

"It's for your own good," she told him with a smile. "Your day will come, though hopefully not anytime soon."

"But how will I know when it will come?" he asked anxiously.

"You will know. Trust me." With that she settled to concentrating on her food. Supai moodily did the same.

Meanwhile, Shaelynn had been watching Sorvo and Avinret swapping stories, though most of them made no sense at all to her. When they were done laughing at something she hadn't found funny, she spoke.

"So, how do you guys know each other?" Avinret turned to her, still smiling. Sorvo dipped his head to hide his own grin.

I visited the castle once, before Zathos became king. On my way up I was alone, and I got a little lost. Avinret found me. We've been friends since, though we lost touch quite a while ago.

"Yeah, suddenly this bloke just disappeared. That's when my problems started, see," Avinret put in. "But now, he turns back up! And I got by best bud back. Ain't it great?" Shaelynn laughed, seeing Sorvo shaking his head. Avinret turned to him and patted him on his forearm, where he was resting. Sorvo bared his teeth playfully.

They sat for a few minutes in silence, each one thinking about something or other. Thoughtfully, Sorvo lifted a talon, gesturing at Shaelynn and Supai. *Tell me, younglings, what brings you this far north?*

Shaelynn balked inwardly at the question. She wasn't so sure herself. She looked around; everyone but the dragon was watching her. Taking a deep, steadying breath, she said, "When Liz and I were in our own time, we went shopping once. Liz bought-"

An enchanted bracelet, Sorvo finished. *And by reading the spell on a full moon, you and Elizabeth were brought here. Aye; Elizabeth told me of it when we shared our stories.*

"Yeah. That's right. It brought us here. Somehow Liz managed to keep it, and we found out from some friends of ours that it was created and sent to her by Zathos. I wanted to know why, so I decided to leave for his castle. It was stupid, I know."

"Well, you hadn't really decided yet," Supai said. At the inquisitive looks he received, he went on, "I was a street kid in Barda. Me and the rest of the boys were set to watching Shaelynn after Liz's . . . . fight. One day some of the other boys seen Karbab coming after her. Me and another boy helped her out of Barda, and I came with her. We lost Karbab outside of Barda."

"That's an interesting story," Dasriel said. Suddenly she smiled, as if realizing something. "Now I know where I've seen you two before! You were outside the prison where Sorvo was, in Mechem. You were having trouble with your horse."

"You were in there, Sorvo?" Shaelynn asked, astounded. "We passed right by you?" The dragon nodded.

"I knew he was in there," Supai said quietly. He stared at the ground as all eyes turned on him.

"How did you know?" Dasriel asked.

"And why didn't you tell me?" Shaelynn asked, her short temper rising.

"I heard Sorvo in the prison. When he roared; Shaelynn was at the inn we were staying at. The next morning we were going to leave, but Shaelynn went over to the prison. That was when you found us there, Dasriel. Shaelynn wanted to find out what was in there, but I said to leave it until later. We heard Sorvo's roars again that night, but Shaelynn thought it was some other animal, and I let it go at that." He turned to Shaelynn uncomfortably.

"I didn't tell you he was in there because I knew you were still upset about what you thought was Liz's death. I know you get mad really easy, and I didn't want you to do anything stupid. I didn't know it was Sorvo, but I knew it was a dragon."

But how did you know I was one of my kind? Sorvo asked, curious. *We haven't been seen by humans for centuries. That is, except for me.*

Supai shrugged. "I knew it wasn't any other normal kind of animal. And no magical creatures that I know of can make that kind of sound, except for dragons." And besides, he thought to himself, he had seen another dragon besides Sorvo. There was a sleeping one by his birth town. It lived in a cave, and Supai and some of his friends had stumbled upon it in the mountains close to the town. But it looked nothing like Sorvo. It was a golden brown color, like a really rich cedar wood. Its head was more blunted than Sorvo's; it didn't taper to a beak like his but curved to a snout like an alligator's. And it was bigger, much bigger.

The conversation continued after he had fallen silent, but Sorvo wasn't paying attention, as if he were distracted. Supai guarded his thoughts carefully, to let nothing out that the dragon could hear. Still, the dragon seemed distracted, and even troubled, now, it seemed.

As Supai watched, the dragon's eyes widened and muscles tensed in horror. Much quicker than Supai would ever have imagined, the dragon got to his feet and scrambled backward, almost tripping over himself. Dasriel and Riman leapt to their feet, Shaelynn and Supai not far behind them.

It is Elizabeth! he cried desperately, still scooting backward, farther away from them. *It's about to happen again*—He cut himself off with a roar, from deep within himself. A roar of pain, the same as the ones Shaelynn and Supai heard in the forest after they had gone through Mechem.

Sorvo's muscles bunched up with the intense pain, which was setting every one of his nerves on fire, it seemed. Soon his muscles started to twitch from being constrained like that for so long, and he jerked uncontrollably on the ground. The wave passed after almost a minute, and Sorvo was able to sit up and breathe.

Dasriel and Riman finally rushed forward to examine him, but Shaelynn and Supai simply stood there, shocked. "What just happened?" Supai asked faintly. Shaelynn hadn't found her voice yet.

Elizabeth is being imprisoned by Zathos. It was worse at first, but it is less often now. He paused to take a few deep breaths, and then he went on, *We are more closely Bonded than you think. Our minds are Bonded, yes, but it is much deeper than that. Our own beings have almost been fused together. We can feel each other's pain, we go through everything that the other does. To put it shortly, when she is tortured, I feel it as extensively as she does. That is why I am blind; Zathos blinded her almost a week ago, probably through magic. I do not think it is permanent. I hope it is not.*

He stopped then, and crossed his forelegs together in front of him, much like a dog. He laid his head upon them and rested. Dasriel and Riman ushered the children away from the dragon and closer to the small fire.

"I'm sorry," Dasriel started.

"We're sorry," Riman corrected her. "We should have told you earlier. It happens every so often, every time Zathos feels like trying to get something out of Liz, most likely. That was the roars you heard the night after you visited Mechem. That was probably the worst one; there were two different types of torture."

Both Shaelynn's and Supai's eyes widened at this thought. Supai shook his head and muttered something, then got up and went to take the saddle off the black. Dasriel had to magically lift the black for him so he could get it off without trying to wrestle with the black's weight. He was a light horse, but he still weighed several hundred pounds.

Once the saddle was off, Supai brought it closer to the fire. He went through the saddlebags a little bit before he found the cloak. He untied the blankets from the back of the saddle, took one, and curled up a little ways from the fire where he could be closer to the black.

Shaelynn stayed with Dasriel and Riman; they asked about the journey up here, and she relayed it to them as best as she could. When she was finished she was barely keeping herself awake, and Dasriel and Riman didn't seem much better off. Shaelynn announced she was going to sleep too, and the two adults instantly agreed. The small fire was doused with dirt, and soon everyone was asleep.

The next morning, Sorvo, Dasriel, and Riman were the first up. Their activity roused Supai and the black, who shied at the dragon so badly that Supai had to restrain him while Sorvo spoke to him and assured him no harm. Finally, after a few minutes of this, the black was more relaxed around the massive dragon.

Thirty minutes after the sun had come up, Dasriel had put a fast-traveling spell on the black, and had put the seeing spell on herself that worked between her and Sorvo. Supai had had trouble restraining the black after the spell had been put on him, so he left a few minutes before the rest of them. Supai and Avinret were nearly thrown backwards off the black as he took off. Even at a slow run he was moving three times faster than he did at an all-out gallop. Shaelynn marveled at it from atop Sorvo's back, just before they took off.

Once they were in the air, Shaelynn's heart settled from what it was when the dragon had first leapt into the air. He had simply crouched low and then sprang upward, and already they had been nearly sixty feet in the air. One beat of his great wings, and they had been a hundred feet up.

When they had risen to over a mile up Sorvo had leveled out and was flying forward fast. The ground whizzed past beneath her, and she could see Supai and Avinret on the black, still a little ways ahead of them. But soon they had passed over them, and they started to fade in the distance.

Elizabeth met me one day when you and her went out hunting in the forest outside of Barda, Sorvo said privately sometime after they had flown over the black and his riders. *She said the two of you had split up; you went across the bottom of the hill while she went up it. She rode her horse up to where I was, in a rocky field. I had disguised myself as one of the rocks; it is one of our many talents.*

Anyway, she sat down to rest and let her horse graze. She must have dozed; when I revealed myself, she didn't stir until her horse was at the point of running away. She woke up and let the horse go, and then pulled out her sword; her bow and arrows were underneath me.

From some odd events, we came to a standpoint. If I tried to kill her, she could take me with her, and I likewise. I asked her who would strike first, and she found that she didn't have the heart to. When she touched me while leaning down to pick up her bow and arrows, we Bonded, though not fully.

Wait, Shaelynn interrupted. She noticed Riman jump next to her and look around.

Focus on me when you speak, Sorvo said gently. *Don't worry; Elizabeth was a little worse than you. It will take some getting used to. Go on.*

Sorry, she said, embarrassed. *But anyway, she touched you, and then you two just Bonded? Just like that?*

It takes willingness for a companionship from both sides. But this is dragon history. Let us move on. As I was saying, we Bonded. I met her on the roof of the stable the next night. She hadn't come to me during her break; Karbab had been ridden into the river by that black horse behind us.

I remember that, Shaelynn said reflectively. *Gosh, it seems ages ago. Sorry. Go on.*

Yes, it does, Sorvo agreed. *After that, she and Karbab fought in an alley where they had happened to meet. She was wounded, and when she was well enough we talked. I knew we had to leave for her sake, but she wanted to delay another day to say goodbye, to you and to Marl and Shamar.*

That was when we had our fight, Shaelynn said softly. *She said she was going away, and I couldn't go. Where were you going? And what happened that Zathos has her?*

I'm getting to that, don't worry. I was in the sky the whole time. I saw her go into the shop, and I saw Karbab approaching. When Karbab wounded her, I had no choice but to rescue her and get us as far away from there as possible. We were headed to a place where she could train to be Sorva di Fravid. *That is why you couldn't come.*

Oh, Shaelynn said. Her heart felt as if it had dropped in her chest. She had caused Liz to be wounded because she had been selfish.

You were not being selfish, Sorvo said. *Yes, I heard your thoughts. But her injury was not your fault. You didn't know. I told her not to tell even you. I knew you would be angry with her for not telling you everything. I am sorry. But I could not risk it; even if you let it out accidentally that we, I, existed, we would have been hunted down like dogs. Do you know why there are no dragons in the land, besides me and a few hidden others?*

Yes. I heard from a man in one of the towns south from here. He said that the people ran the dragons off and Zathos crowned himself king. I understand why you didn't want Liz to tell me. I'm sorry.

No. What is done is past. We cannot change it, no matter how we wish it. But even after all that, we can still manage to get Elizabeth back. And after time, the remaining Sorva di Fravid *may come back to Partaenia as well.*

Will you get rid of Zathos?

I am not sure of that. If we must try, Elizabeth and I will have to do it ourselves, because the other Sorva di Fravid *will not come back until he is gone and they are sure they will not be driven out again. I do not want to think of what will happen when we try, though. That will come later. Now, I will go back to our story.*

Once I had rescued Elizabeth, I flew her to the shore and healed her—my fire has healing powers, if used right. Anyhow, we decided to go through with our plan and go to her place of training. We were close to being there, under a day's flight away. We were attacked by Zathos's latharks—large bat-like carnivore horses with fangs. To try and get away from them, I flew back the way we had come, using a special dragon method; we covered four days' worth of flying in under an hour. But still the latharks caught us, and they attacked me from all over. They shredded the membrane in my wings, sending us to the earth from over a mile up.

To protect Elizabeth, I turned my back to the ground and put her above me. When we landed, I broke several bones in my back and was knocked unconscious for nearly a day. In that time the latharks took Elizabeth and flew her to Zathos's castle. I received help from Riman, and then from the sorceress Dasriel. Some time after you and Supai came through the town, we left to get Elizabeth back. She was blinded by Zathos, affecting me about halfway through our journey. Dasriel found a way for me to still fly, and we came to meet you.

That is quite a story, Shaelynn said, not wanting to believe it but knowing it was true. *And to think, five months ago I was in my own home, in a different place than this. And now look how far Liz and I have come.*

I only wish her situation was different, Sorvo said before falling silent for a long while. Shaelynn did the same, using the time to think about what she had learned.

==

I sat in the corner of the room, slowly chewing the worst piece of bread they had given me so far. There were two other men in the room with me, but they hadn't touched me yet. They were there to watch me.

I'd heard whispers from one of them that Zathos and Avernus thought they could get Honoras's location from me right away, and in the process of torture they forgot to give me any food or water. I had gone two weeks without them. I had nearly died. But being unconscious for most of it had saved me. So, now they were watching me to make sure I ate the food and drank the water so I wouldn't keel over dead on them.

I saw something the last time Avernus tortured me with a spell. Avernus had just taken the pain spell off when I collapsed to the ground, and blacked out briefly, maybe for a second. But in that second, I saw Honoras with Shaelynn, Supai, and two other adults. And I knew they were on their way to get me, to finally rescue me from this place.

==

Najee was marching, with about five thousand other people, headed to Zathos's castle in the north. They were getting closer to the edge of the trees and to their destination. He had rallied these people mostly by himself, and there were more to come.

He had heard the news from an elf and the centaur she was traveling with: Rish and Tera had been sent here by Zathos for some unknown reason, and they had gone through Barda on their way to go to his castle. The elf said that Rish and Tera, whose names were really Liz and Shaelynn, had stayed them for a few months while they were new to the land. She had told them they would find reason for their coming on the way, and they had.

The elf said the trees could tell her any news from any distance away. And these trees had told her that Liz had met a dragon. Liz had Bonded with the dragon, and it was this dragon that had saved her after she was wounded by Karbab; the dragon had not killed her as everyone suspected. They also said that both Liz and her dragon had been attacked by Zathos's latharks, and Liz had been taken to his castle. So Liz's dragon was on his way after her, and Shaelynn was going in the same direction, for other reasons.

The elf and the centaur had been gathering people to help with the fight to come, and now Najee was as well, after he had learned all this. If he could briefly explain it to the people, and tell it the right way, they would be jumping to help him. And he had about five thousand people with him now, and they were to meet with the elf, Tayna, and the centaur, Geoff, with the rest of the people they had convinced to come. And then they would all go to the castle to fight in the battle. Tayna said that it was sure to happen anytime soon.

Chapter 11

HONORAS LANDED AS SOON AS he caught a glimpse of the castle. Shaelynn saw it too before he landed, somehow dropping over a mile straight down and landing lightly. The castle was set in the side of a mountain, high up on its hill. A winding road led up to it, and long-abandoned fields were to its left. The castle itself was huge, four stories tall and at most three stories below ground, Sorvo said. It sat just in front of a rock face, and Sorvo said another escape route was probably blasted through it and came out somewhere else.

Honoras crouched silently for the humans to get off, after he had let Dasriel out of his claws. He had been inside the castle before; the hallways were large enough for him to walk comfortably with room on either side of him for a human to walk. He had grown since then, but he was sure he could still fit with his wings tightly folded, even if his sides brushed the walls. And he could probably carry a few people on his back without their heads touching the ceiling.

If he remembered right, he'd entered through the front of the castle, and there had been an inner courtyard inside. Two staircases branched off from the courtyard and led to the hallways that could take you either downstairs or upstairs to different rooms. And inside the courtyard were rooms on two sides, a stable on another, and workers' rooms next to them. The towers and defense wall were accessible from staircases just inside the castle entrance, though he never did fit in those. They were too narrow.

There was also a tower on the castle's right front corner, with a wide platform and an open top, with no walls on the edges. It was made as a place for dragons to land. A ramp led from this platform to the courtyard for leisurely visits, before Zathos had become king.

Another platform was on top of the castle's keep as well. There was another staircase that led from the platform to an inner hall where the king's hall, the infirmary, and the dungeons were immediately accessible, whatever the case of the visit may be.

Honoras came back to the present, realizing that the humans had been conversing with each other and had now fallen silent to let him speak. He shook his head to rid himself of other thoughts.

We will all camp here for the evening. Supai and Avinret will be here in an hour or so on the black. Dasriel, Riman, and I have made the plans already, and we cannot risk waiting. We will head out tonight. If we have not returned by noon the day after tomorrow, leave for the south, with haste. Zathos will have been awakened and he might set out on the rest of the land if we fail. But we'll leave that until tonight. For now, we wait for Supai.

Then Honoras turned to Shaelynn. *You must remember not to try and follow us, no matter what might cross your mind. You are young, and it will be no place for you. You and Supai will stay here with Avinret and our belongings. Am I understood?*

Yes, Shaelynn grudgingly said. If it was no place for her, why was Liz there, then? she was thinking, but she tried hard not to let it escape her thoughts for Sorvo to hear. If he did hear it, he gave no outward signs. After she had answered him, he stood quietly while Dasriel and Riman took their gear off him. Shaelynn helped to unload them too, after a moment. They did not have much, mostly the same kinds of things she and Supai had.

After everything was unloaded off Sorvo and onto the ground, everyone settled down to wait. Dasriel and Sorvo sat by themselves quietly, and Riman and Shaelynn talked with each other and puzzled about magic and all its quirks.

Honoras sat away from the humans, even from Dasriel. He badly wanted to speak to Elizabeth. He knew he could, but he didn't want to risk it. If the sorcerer was there, he could easily hear her thoughts if he wanted to. Or, if he let her know he was close, she might attract attention to herself in some way. Then Zathos would know he was near. They needed the advantage of surprise just now.

Honoras's prediction turned out to be true: in little over an hour Supai and Avinret arrived on the black, who was lathered in sweat but still favored remarkably well considering how fast he had traveled.

The sun was starting to sink in the sky, and they ate a hurried dinner. Honoras went without food; he couldn't eat Avinret or the black, and there was nothing else. Maybe he could find something in the castle.

He tried to swallow the fear that rose within his chest, but it rose again and again, every time he tried not to think about what might happen tonight. If he tried to distract himself, it would well up stronger than the last time. Honoras knew that fear was good; it made you cautious. But it did not help him now.

Finally his attention could be completely focused on the humans. They had finished eating, and Dasriel had said that the castle was probably quiet. "If there are any guards," she said, "they probably won't be expecting us. It'll be just the same as another night, to them." Honoras nodded thoughtfully, knowing that now was their best chance.

He told the two younglings again to stay put and leave if they didn't return. This thought sent a spike of fear through his middle, but he didn't let the humans see it. He was leading this mission; he needed to be strong for them. The two nodded reluctant agreement, but understood the situation.

Dasriel got on Honoras's back at his request. *Once it starts, there will be no chance to stay in my claws, and there will be no time to switch positions. Just lean over my shoulder as much as you can, and I will keep my head low for you to look over top. Whatever you do, do not fall. If you fall, we all do.*

All right, Dasriel responded mechanically. She shook her head to try and clear it of the thoughts racing through her brain. Once Sorvo had taken flight, though, she found her mind strangely clear and calm.

Shaelynn watched Sorvo leap into the air and soar silently away, carrying Dasriel on his back rather than in his claws. She supposed it must be better for her to ride there than in his claws, where she would be less vulnerable.

Thinking of what they were about to do sent a flood of anger through her once more. She should be with them, going to rescue her cousin. But she had to stay here. Yet she would be no use to them: she'd probably freak out. The thought made her angrier.

She whirled to see Supai sitting on the ground, staring at nothing. Avinret was on his shoulder, watching the skies. "I'm going for a walk," she said abruptly and started off.

"Don't go far. There's no fire to mark our spot, and the moon isn't out yet. You'll get lost easy, especially when everything's flat." Supai still sat on the ground, but he was looking at her with concern. Avinret was nodding agreement, half-focused on the subject.

Supai's kind tone softened Shaelynn's mood a little. "I'll be careful," she promised. Supai nodded and then turned around to stare at the ground again. Shaelynn walked quickly, letting the motion melt the anger away. Soon her mind was calm again. She stopped and looked around. Supai was just in sight behind her.

Untying her scarf, she drove the corner of it into the ground with the point of her knife, draping it over the top of the handle to make it more visible. Then she set off in the same direction she had been going.

She stared at the dry, cracked ground as she walked, occasionally checking to make sure she could still see her scarf behind her. When it was just in sight as well, she lay down on the ground and looked up at the stars, watching them turn across the sky. After a while she sat up again and focused on the place where the sky met the ground, some miles away ahead of her.

She didn't know how long she had been staring at the horizon, but presently she noticed a white shape just starting to come over the top. It was probably the moon, finally rising.

Yet as she watched, the white shape became tall and thin, and it was moving toward her. It glowed silver white, and there was a small point of light seeming to float above it. She watched it, mystified. Soon it started to resemble some sort of animal, with long legs that carried it quickly toward her.

Just then, when it was not more than a half-mile from her, Shaelynn realized what it was: a unicorn, galloping straight toward her. The point of light floating above it was the tip of its horn, nearly two and a half feet long. Its coat was of the purest white, with no spots or flaws whatsoever.

When it was thirty feet from her, it slowed to a graceful trot, its muscled body seemingly floating on air. It stopped directly in front of her and regarded her with a piercing gaze. Shaelynn felt dirty and impure being close to it.

"Do you know what I am, human?" it asked in a deep male voice. His voice lingered in the air, as if the air itself wanted to absorb the musical sound.

"Yes," Shaelynn answered, still entranced. "You're a unicorn."

"Correct, and the most sought-after magical species in all time. I have been watching the events of the past few thousand years, human, and I see what my world is coming to. There will be a great and terrible battle soon, in the very place you and I are standing. I will fight in it, for my land and for my kind. I need a Guide, and I have chosen you, Shaelynn, cousin of Elizabeth, companion of the green dragon you call Sorvo."

Shaelynn staggered backward, shocked at his knowledge of who she was, and what he had told her. "Wh—what?" she stammered. "A battle? Me, a Guide? You?" The spell the unicorn had first cast on her had now faded. All that was left was disbelief.

"You've got the wrong girl, unicorn. I can't be your Guide. I can't fight, in a—a battle!" The unicorn closed his eyes and tucked his head in close to his chest as if stung. Without realizing it, Shaelynn realized that his horn was very close to her forehead. He suddenly took a step forward, and its tip pushed against her skin. The point of light grew in an instant to a blinding flash, and in her mind's eye she saw vividly herself upon the unicorn, fighting in a battle against other terrible beasts. But alongside her was Tayna and Geoff, both brandishing swords alongside her bow and arrows. Above her was Liz aboard Sorvo, who was breathing fire upon the enemy. And behind her were ordinary townspeople, led by Najee. The rest of his boys were there, and so was Agathla, Marl, and Shamar, the other stable hand.

The blinding light faded as the unicorn stepped away, withdrawing the contact between her and his horn. "Sit down, quickly," he said calmly. Shaelynn did so, not knowing why she obeyed him, but she was about halfway down to the ground when she collapsed the rest of the way. She felt suddenly drained and out of breath. The unicorn seemed the same way, but he remained standing.

"My horn's contact with humans can have that affect," he explained. "I am used to it, and someday you will be too, perhaps." This statement brought her back to reality and she remembered what he had told her.

"That can't be true," she whispered.

"But it will be so, and soon. I need to know now: are you with me or not? Will you be my Guide?" She was about to protest again, but his stern look stopped her. "You can't evade the inevitable, Shaelynn. You will be in that battle, whether I am with you or not. I have been watching you closely, girl, even at the moment you came to Partaenia. You have what it takes."

She remained silent, her mind whirling. Millions of thoughts raced by and by, though she tried to get them all in order. "I suppose being with you will be better than trying to fight by myself," she said, after giving up trying to settle her mind. The unicorn seemed to smile.

"Good. We will meet again, and soon, Shaelynn. I will see you then." He turned to leave, again giving the impression of floating on the air.

"Wait," Shaelynn called after he had taken only a few steps. The unicorn turned around once more. "What's your name, since you already know mine?"

"Ilian." Once he had said this, he turned and left, gliding over the ground, until he disappeared once more looking like a faint ray of moonlight. After he had disappeared over the horizon far away, the moon finally rose.

===

Honoras flew on silent wings, hardly moving the rest of his tense body. The moon had finally risen to the east, and he could see the castle below him more clearly. Indeed, no guards were to be seen on the top of the defenders' wall. Dasriel had been right.

He went over his mental map of the interior of the castle, once more checking for anything he might have left out. Dasriel and Riman gazed at the castle, whispering quietly to each other about what might be inside.

I will land in the courtyard as quietly as I can, he said to Dasriel, who told Riman. *There will be a staircase leading up that will take us to a hall. I should just fit, but keep your heads low. There will be another staircase leading down at the end of this hallway, and that will lead us to the dungeons. I will mentally search for Elizabeth. Once we have found her, we must go back up the way we came. They will have noticed us by then, and the hallway will be blocked. I'll get rid of them as best I can, and from there you must help as well. I will get to the courtyard, and hopefully we will be able to take flight.*

Remember that Elizabeth will be weak, so you must not let her fall or be taken. Zathos himself or another sorcerer might come to fight against us as well, so be ready for that, he warned. A moment later he stooped into a dive, and the courtyard came into view. He silently opened his wings; air rushed into them and slowed them instantly. They were in the courtyard.

Without a word Honoras trotted to the staircase, just where he had remembered it to be. He listened intently, but no shouts came up until he had just gotten into the hallway. Hurriedly he trotted down the long hallway as best he could. Dasriel had hunched down to avoid the ceiling, but she still enabled him to see. He quickly made his way to the end of the hall, going at just under a trot.

There was the staircase at the end, the only one leading down. The steepness of the stairs and the width of the steps only enabled him to scrabble down as best he could. Still, he made it to the bottom with no troubles.

Elizabeth! he called, sending the sound only to her. He could feel her, close.

Honoras! I don't know where I'm at, I can't see, I said.

Neither can I, he responded. *Just feel for me. Search for me.*

Okay, I said, trying to let no outward expression show as I searched for Honoras the way I had searched for him many times. The men were still in the room with me, at least two of them. I relayed this to Honoras.

A moment later, Honoras told me to brace myself. I balled up in my corner as there was an explosion; Honoras must have knocked the door off its hinges. I heard it clatter against the wall not far from me at the same time I heard shouts from the men. There were two, as I thought.

I heard surprised gasps, from the men. Then it was quiet, save for a commotion outside. The two guards had been killed. I felt, rather than heard, Honoras come forward and nuzzle me. Instantly, my vision returned, as did his. The light from torches somewhere above was almost blinding, yet it must have been a low light, being underground. I covered my head with my hands as Honoras lifted me to his back with a talon. The feeling of his claws around me again was wonderful. Being upon his back once more was even better.

Elizabeth, there are two humans aboard with you as well. If there is any trouble, we will take care of it. Focus only on staying on. We must go up a flight of stairs, into a hallway, and into a courtyard. From there we should be okay.

All right, I said, trusting myself to peek open an eye for a moment to look around. Honoras was already up the stairs and in the hallway he had explained. Waiting for us was Avernus and Zathos's soldiers. As Avernus stepped forward, my heart nearly stopped in my chest. *Honoras, this is the sorcerer that blinded me,* I told him. *Be careful; he is powerful.*

Don't worry, he said, though he sounded uncertain. I had opened my eyes fully by now, and the woman next to me had just begun to stir. I was in between her and another man, who was behind me.

"Dragon, it was good of you to come," Avernus said, giving him a smile that wasn't warm. The sight of him sent chills of fear down my spine. I tried not to show it. Avernus went on, "When your Bonded wouldn't tell us where you and the other dragons were, we decided to keep her and lure you here. It worked nicely." I felt a wave of pride from Honoras, but at the sorcerer's last words it stopped. Honoras shifted his feet, and Avernus' grin turned wicked. He lifted a hand.

The archers behind him lifted their bows and found their targets. Honoras did not move, and neither did the woman or the man. Avernus lowered his hand forcefully, and the arrows shot forward. At the same moment, Honoras reared, ducking his head forward because of the ceiling. With the breath he had sucked in, it poured out as a greenish-yellow fire that burned the arrows to crisps and hit most of the soldiers behind the sorcerer. While the soldiers were either dead or rolling on the ground in pain, Avernus was still standing, because he had shielded himself with his magic.

"Well done." Avernus stepped forward from the corpses immediately behind him. Some of the other soldiers were recovering and were starting to nock their bows once more. "It is interesting, though, that you carry one of the King's students upon your back." I looked around me in shock, but no one said anything.

"He trained me well through the person he once was. I want nothing to do with who he is now," the woman in front of me said loudly. He trained her? I thought. But he was a sorcerer, and that meant—"Our being able to perform magic connects us in no way," the woman finished. I was stunned. Honoras had found a sorceress to fight alongside him.

"He will be upset to hear this," Avernus said. Then suddenly, his hand flicked forward and then up. An incredible pain seized my brain and seemed to choke it, as if Avernus had somehow reached his hand inside my head and had clenched it around my brain. Honoras felt it too, and nearly collapsed. And then, after only a moment, it stopped. My head cleared slowly, and when it did I realized that the sorceress in front of me was sitting very tense. She had her hands outstretched in front of her, her fists clenched, trying to hold Avernus' magic back.

Honoras recovered relatively quickly, and charged forward, sending before him another blast of green fire. Avernus disappeared just before the fire was to strike him, releasing the sorceress from her counter spell. She sagged forward on Honoras's shoulders, and I caught her before she could fall too far. I held her close to me as Honoras bowled past the two or three remaining soldiers, of which there had been nearly thirty. He scrabbled down the staircase into the moonlit courtyard, where archers awaited us.

He took flight instantly, beating his wings hard to get as much altitude as fast as he could. Still, there was a volley of arrows that were sent out while we were still in range. I feared we would be hit; the sorceress suddenly sat up and flung her arms out. The arrows changed direction instantly, hurtling down faster and faster to those people who had shot them. Cries of pain echoed up to us from two hundred feet below. The sorceress, her job done, slumped back against me again. I wrapped one arm around her middle and put the other hand comfortably on Honoras's scaly withers, where it belonged.

We landed about a half-hour later on the treeless plain around us. I had looked at it in despair, knowing that Zathos had done this to the land. Honoras landed near a horse and two young adults, but before I could make them out he had landed with his wings up just so I couldn't see them.

The man, who told me his name was Riman, hurriedly got off first to lift the woman down, whose name I found out was Dasriel. She was still unconscious from the effort of holding Avernus' magic back. I felt much the same way from simply trying to stay on Honoras's back.

Honoras helped me down, holding me carefully in his talon. Once he set me down, I could see who had set up camp here. It was Shaelynn and Supai, come all the way up from Barda. That seemed ages ago.

Shaelynn and I faced each other, looking the other up and down. Everyone hesitated, waiting to see our reactions. But a moment later, we rushed into each other's arms, tears on our faces.

"I thought you were dead," Shaelynn wept into my shoulder.

"I thought I was too," I cried back.

"No more secrets, okay?" she suggested after we had recovered and stepped back from each other.

"Okay," I nodded, wiping tears off my face.

"Sorvo already told me everything, about what happened in Barda up 'till now," she said.

"You need to tell me why you're here, then," I told her in return.

I think that can wait until later, Honoras said. I noticed that Shaelynn, Supai, and Riman turned to him at the same time I did. They must have been able to hear him, too. *Dasriel was weakened by fending off another sorcerer's magic,* he told Supai. *He tried to hold us up by using another form of torture on Elizabeth, but Dasriel held it off. She also repelled the arrows that the archers shot at us while we were in the air and still in range. Riman, set up her blankets for her. Supai and Shaelynn, help him get her into them. She will be fine with some rest.*

You need rest as well, Honoras told me after everyone else had nodded acknowledgement and went to help Dasriel get comfortable.

I know, I said, feeling my exhaustion once more. He shifted around to lie on his side and lifted a wing welcomingly. Grateful, I started toward it. I stopped for a moment to say, "Shaelynn, I'm going to rest, okay?" She looked up from Dasriel and nodded with a smile, seeing where I was going to sleep. Supai and Riman smiled as well, seeing things going smoothly between us.

I lay down next to him, as he lowered his wing over me. He tucked his head inside his tent, grinning at me. *It is good to do this again, my gliad.*

Aye, Wyrla. Thank you. Very soon after this I fell asleep.

Shaelynn watched Sorvo lift is wing up for Liz as she climbed over his foreleg to lay down by his side. She caught one last glimpse of her face and again saw the thin line of a scar running down her left cheek.

==

The centaur and the elf were leading the ten thousand people across the empty plain, another obvious sign of Zathos's too-long rule. It was night and the moon had not yet risen; still they marched on, and nobody minded in the least. They had a mission.

Just as a thin sliver of moonlight started to peek over the horizon, Tayna and Geoff called a halt to the march for the night. The people behind them set up tents and blankets and then built small fires here and there. Everyone crowding around the fires to cook their food made them undetectable.

They were too busy to notice the thin sliver of moonlight coming towards them instead of rising like the moon was supposed to. Tayna and Geoff watched the people behind them to make sure they still did not notice it, and no one did. They were too busy. Tayna and Geoff walked out onto the plain together while it stayed that way.

Najee noticed them, though, and silently crept away from his friends around their fire. No one noticed him. He walked silently behind the elf and the centaur as they met the unicorn far from the people. The real moon had just started to rise.

"Tayna, Geoff," the unicorn said, nodding his head to them in turn. They nodded their welcome as well. "How have things gone so far? How many of the people are here now?"

"Over ten thousand, Ilian," Tayna responded. The unicorn's eyes widened in amazement.

"Goodness, how did you get so many to come?"

"We went first to Barda, the closest town to us. That was where Liz and Shaelynn were staying, and they had made friends among the street children. Their leader Najee was eager to help, and so we assigned him to gather people on his way north while we went southward. We met at the edge of the trees, and have gone on from there together."

"I suppose that is Najee just behind you there?" Ilian asked. Tayna and Geoff turned to see Najee there, watching in awe. Tayna nodded to Ilian that it was him and stepped back as the unicorn moved toward the boy.

"Najee of Barda, leader of the many street children, I give my thanks to you for helping Tayna and Geoff collect so many of the people to fight in the coming battle. I am in your debt." After he had said this Ilian bowed to him by lowering himself to one knee.

Najee was simply shocked, but managed a small, "You're welcome." Ilian raised himself from his bow and gestured Najee forward to talk with him and Tayna and Geoff. Before anything could be said Najee asked tentatively, "If it doesn't bother you, sir, could I ask how Liz and Shaelynn are faring?"

"Yes, how are they?" Geoff asked, and Tayna nodded in agreement. Ilian thought for a moment, lifting his head to the sky a little.

"Liz is okay, considering her position. Her dragon and two humans, one of them a sorceress, have just rescued her. Supai is with Shaelynn, and they have stayed behind during the rescue. They are now waiting for the dragon and the humans to return with Liz; they are on their way now." Ilian turned toward them once more. "I met Shaelynn just a little while ago. I explained most of the situation to her, and she has agreed to be my Guide."

Tayna and Geoff grinned with joy, looking to each other, to Ilian, and then to Najee, who looked extremely confused. Ilian looked to Tayna and Geoff and asked them, "What, you have not explained everything to him?"

"Most of it," Tayna said.

"We told him while we were in Barda, and there wasn't time to tell him everything," Geoff put in. He turned toward Najee. "We met Ilian before Liz and Shaelynn ever came. He told us that they would come from another time, and that they would be the ones to play the biggest role in saving the land. He told us to take them in and teach them how to survive in this time, but not to reveal anything to them. He told us to send them on their way to Zathos's castle after a time, telling them that they would probably find reason for their coming here along the way."

"And they did," Ilian said. "I followed them all the way, sending messages to Tayna and Geoff through the trees. Though when they split, I had to follow Shaelynn. She and Supai went on northward after they parted from you. Once they almost met Liz's dragon, but Supai knew her temper would keep the better of the situation from happening and kept her away. They met a talking squirrel who led them across this plain. They met with Liz's dragon and the two other humans. And tonight they stayed behind during the rescue."

"Which reminds me," Ilian said, turning toward Tayna and Geoff. He hesitated for a moment, and then said, "Well, I suppose you can know now too, Najee." He nodded to the boy and then went on, "There is another dragon headed this way from Amatol. I believe it is Liz's dragon's mother. She is traveling with a human inhabitant of their island, and they are on their way to meet her son before the battle starts. They will pass overhead tonight in the early hours; make sure no one sees them."

Tayna, Geoff, and Najee nodded, and the unicorn turned and ran into the rising moon to mask himself. By the time its lower edge had risen from the horizon, he had disappeared. Najee walked with the elf and the centaur back to the people, who had not noticed their disappearance. The three split up to make their rounds and make sure everyone was all right.

Chapter 12

WHEN ELIZABETH WAS ASLEEP HONORAS took his head out from under his wing to watch the humans finish getting Dasriel comfortable in her blankets. When they were done Riman went to lay out his own blankets; he was soon asleep, lying close to Dasriel. Supai laid out his blankets out as well, close to the black, who had lain down with the boy.

Shaelynn went to Honoras, who was watching the black and Supai settle down close to each other. *That boy knows very much of animals,* Honoras told Shaelynn. She looked to the two as well.

Yes. He and the black have always understood each other. Once, in a town, I came back from another place to find him lying down in the shade, underneath the black's belly. Liz told me once that it takes a lot of trust from a horse to let you do that.

She is correct, he said, turning to look at her. *What did you want to speak to me about?*

When you and Dasriel and Riman left to rescue Liz, I had some mixed emotions about not being able to help. I got angry at myself, and I walked eastward, I supposed, far enough away that I had to put a marker in the ground so I wouldn't get lost.

That was not very smart, Honoras said. To Shaelynn, he sounded like her mother. But then he said, *And I suppose you're going to argue about your point, am I right?*

She laughed softly with him and said, *Yes. Anyway, I met someone out there. He said there was to be a battle soon, and everyone is going to fight in it, even some of our friends from Barda. I saw it.*

The only 'someone' that would enable you to see a coming battle would be a unicorn. How did you come to meet him?

He came to me, she said, sitting down so she wouldn't have to stand while she told her story. *I was out there trying to cool down, and I thought I saw the moon coming up over the horizon. After a while, I realized it wasn't the moon, and the shape became a unicorn. He knew who I was, and who you and Liz were. He asked if I would be his Guide.*

And what did you say?

I wasn't sure. I was shocked, and I told him he had the wrong person. He said I was to lead him in battle, and still I told him no. Then he touched his horn to my head, and I saw the battle. It was on the plain, close to the castle. I was on him, and there were a lot of people fighting against these horrible beasts. Najee and the rest of the street kids were there fighting too, and Tayna, and Geoff. You and Liz were in the air over the battle, and you were breathing fire on the enemy.

Is that all you saw?

Yes. It was only a glimpse he gave me. It left me tired, and him too.

Aye, that can happen, I've heard. Unicorns can see the certain future, you know. They can see anything, really. They always know what is happening because they can see everything at once, I think. My mother told me of them.

So they know everything that is going to happen?

Not everything. I said they could see the certain future: things that will happen that cannot be changed. Beyond that, I am not sure. Did he say when the battle was?

He only said it was soon, and he would see me again, sooner than that.

Well, what did you say to being his Guide?

I still wasn't sure, even after seeing the vision. He told me that I would be in the battle, with him or not. I supposed I would rather fight with him than alone, and I said yes. Then he left.

You are lucky, you know that?

Why so, other than being a unicorn's Guide?

A bond with a unicorn is just as strong as a Bond between a dragon and rider. But they are different. A dragon and rider are simply close companions who know each other completely. But a unicorn and Guide form a more intimate relationship, more like lovers than anything else. The relationship lasts forever, beyond death. Being a Guide also means that you will help guide him through his life; without you he would wander aimlessly, as he did before he met you.

Wow, was all she could manage. She got up to head for her blankets as well.

What was his name? Honoras asked before she could leave.

Ilian, he said. Honoras nodded for her to go, thinking about the name. Shaelynn laid out her blankets between him, Riman and Dasriel, and Supai and the black, in the center of their camp. She fell asleep almost as fast as Elizabeth had. Honoras stayed awake a little while longer, watching the skies, before he too fell asleep.

===

Najee watched the huge dragon fly on silent wings far overhead, knowing that Tayna and Geoff watched as well. No one else but they were awake. The dragon was enormous, larger even the dragon that had taken—or no, rescued—Liz. This dragon must have been twice as big. It was hard to tell in the dark, but from the remaining light of the moon it looked to be a blue-green color. Its wings were white, as was its belly and neck scales. It could have easily blended in with the ocean water itself.

===

Honoras woke me in my sleep, urgently nudging me, barely at the point of gentleness. Reminded for a second of Avernus and still being held in the dungeons, I nearly fell over myself getting to a corner, causing my ribs to shriek in pain. Honoras steadied me, already standing up, his wings spread. The soft leathery fringe on his neck was extended.

I looked to Dasriel; she was still fast asleep, but Riman was getting up at Supai shaking him. When he was sure Riman was awake, Supai turned to look south. I turned as well to see what he and Honoras were looking at.

Shaelynn was standing about fifty feet off from camp, face-to-face with a pure-white horse that had a gleaming silvery-golden horn protruding from its forehead. The unicorn had noticed the rest of us moving around, and was staring directly at me. He spoke to Shaelynn it seemed; she nodded, and she followed behind him as he walked to me. At the same time I noticed Honoras stepping forward to stand directly behind me.

"Elizabeth and Sorvo, most recent *Sorva di Fravid,* I greet you. I am Shaelynn's Follower, Ilian. Sorvo, you have heard of me."

I have heard your name before, yes, Honoras replied in an even tone.

"And Shaelynn has already told you that she has agreed to be my Guide. Liz, you have not heard. You were asleep at the time, I think." I turned to Honoras.

What does he mean? I asked him privately.

After you had fallen asleep Shaelynn told me that she was his Guide.

Oh. I suppose you'll tell me more about it later?

Aye.

Ilian had watched them converse silently, already knowing what they spoke of. When the two turned toward him again, he said, "Sorvo, Shaelynn also told you that I told her there was to be a battle that would take place soon. No doubt she told you what I let her see." Honoras dipped his head in a nod.

Again, I'll tell you later, he said. I sighed mentally at not knowing what was going on. He chuckled a little.

"There is something, though, that she did not know of and you don't know," Ilian continued. "I have seen another dragon, headed this way. A man rides her, though he is not her Bonded. She is a dragon you know, Sorvo. She has swirls of blue, green, and white on her hide, and the membranes of her wings are white as well as her belly and neck." Honoras froze.

My mother? he asked. Ilian nodded in a very humanlike way.

"Wait," I said. "I know that dragon. I was hallucinating, or dreaming, or whatever, when Zathos had me in the dungeon. I saw Shaelynn talking to some man in a town, and then she left with Supai. I followed the man, who went to the beach. He passed the last spot H— . . er, Sorvo and I slept at before we were attacked, but he kept going, at least a half-mile up the coast. Then he bowed to a rock, and the rock turned into a dragon just like what you said. The man and the dragon talked, and he pointed down the coast to our sleeping spot. And then the dragon looked right at me, as if she could see me. Then the dream ended."

"When did you see this?" Ilian asked. Shaelynn looked curious as well. I looked to Honoras; he did too. I shrugged my shoulders.

"I don't know. It was before I talked to Sorvo, when Avernus was torturing me. Sorvo felt it too, and it caught him while he was flying. I don't think I'd been blinded yet."

Ilian looked to Honoras. "It must have been at least a half a month ago. That was when I recognized that happening."

"A half a month?" I asked, astonished. "How long was I there?"

"Over one month," Ilian said quietly. "You nearly died of dehydration; you did not eat or drink for three weeks, which is longer than any human I've known to do. I think it was while you were unconscious for two weeks that your body shut down and didn't need anything." With a shiver I remembered Avernus telling me: "It is about time you woke. It has been over two weeks since I had my last fun." It was then that he had sent the electricity surging through my body, and Honoras had been caught in the sky when it happened. My heart raced and my breathing quickened at the memory.

You can tell me in private, Ilian, Honoras said. *Elizabeth is starting to recollect on past experiences.*

"I can help her then." He turned toward me. I trembled with the memories that had come flooding back, and now I had just started to shake violently. "Shaelynn," Ilian said, gesturing to me. She rushed forward, holding me tight, hiding the unicorn from my vision. I felt a small tip touch the back of my head, and then I remembered nothing.

Ilian touched the tip of his horn to the back of Elizabeth's head, pouring all of his will for her to sleep peacefully into it. As soon as it touched her, she fell limp in her cousin's arms. She stopped shaking and adopted the peaceful look of sleep on her face. Honoras laid down where he was and laid her down next to him where she was more comfortable.

Ilian nodded to Shaelynn and she went to Riman and Supai, who watched nearly the whole thing. She knew what to do without any question; she just knew what Ilian wanted of her. She explained what was going on to the other two while Ilian and Honoras talked privately with each other.

"Sorvo" Ilian said, "there are two sorcerers in that castle: Zathos, and the one that you escaped from yesterday. His name is Avernus, and he is almost as powerful as Zathos, if not as powerful, I do not know. And Dasriel trained under Zathos. You must watch her carefully. She had close ties with Markus, the old Zathos, but they are ties all the same. Do you know what happens when a sorcerer takes on a novice?"

Honoras shook his head. Ilian went on, "They become his apprentice, and he immediately sets to knowing everything about them, for training purposes. In turn the apprentice forms a close bond with the mentor. Zathos knows everything about her; he knows how she acts, how she thinks things out, how she reacts to certain things. It is something he was not likely to forget. He can use any of these things to take advantage over her at any time. Just be careful.

"Your mother is coming soon; she will be here within the hour. She recognized Liz when she was dreaming, and she will want to help to briefly train her for the coming battle, and she will help to fight. The man that is riding her is Jacey."

The shipwrecked boy? Honoras asked. Ilian nodded.

"It seems he has some sort of talent, and no one else was available to come and train Liz," he said. "While we are on the subject, I must take Shaelynn and do the same. May I?" he asked, seeing that she was done explaining to the other two.

Yes. But send word, at least, of how soon the battle will be.

"I still am not sure, but it will be within the week. Zathos is preparing for it now, but even he is not sure when to attack. He does not know of the army coming this way. The elf and centaur that helped Liz and Shaelynn have gathered ten thousand common folk willing enough to fight Zathos."

Shaelynn said she had seen them in the vision you revealed to her. Very well. You need not return until you two are ready, just don't be too late.

"Have no worries on you, friend," Ilian said. He looked to Shaelynn; she turned to him in an instant and came to his side. "Are you ready?" he asked her. She nodded and climbed on his back a little unsteadily.

"Liz will wake a few minutes before your mother's arrival," Ilian said. Shaelynn gasped.

"Wait!" she cried, leaping off Ilian. She rushed to her own pack and picked up another one. Honoras recognized it as Elizabeth's. She handed it to Honoras, who took it in a talon. Shaelynn got back on Ilian. "Her map, and her bow and arrows are there, along with everything else. I don't know where her sword is."

Honoras nodded. *It was lost when we fled the latharks,* he explained. She nodded, and then Ilian turned west and raced off. Honoras soon lost sight of him. He turned to the two humans, who were seeing to Dasriel.

Riman, Supai, he called, being louder than usual so they could hear him. They looked up at him and quickly came over. *There will be another dragon come to see us in under an hour. She is my mother, and the ones who accompanies her is a friend.* They nodded.

"When will Liz wake?" Supai asked.

Just before my mother comes.

"All right," Riman said. "How do you think Dasriel is faring?"

The sorcerer that she held off was much more powerful than I thought, almost as powerful as Zathos. She will most likely be asleep for the rest of the night and most of tomorrow. For now, see if she will take any water. She is only extremely exhausted, I think. Riman nodded and left to see to her. Supai stayed.

"What else will happen when your mom comes?" he asked. "It can't be a friendly family visit." Honoras chuckled.

You are sharp and full of knowledge for a youngling. My mother and my friend have come to help train Elizabeth a little before the battle that is coming. There is something else too. Najee, I think his name is, is coming with the rest of your friends to help. As I understand it, he helped to collect over five thousand people to fight.

"Really?" Honoras nodded. He was about to say something else, but then he stopped himself. He thought for a moment before he spoke.

Supai, do you think you and Riman could join them? Dasriel would be better off with them, and you and Riman wouldn't be alone anymore. And, Elizabeth and I could have space far enough from the castle to train.

"Aye. I think that would be okay," he said.

Very well. When my mother arrives, I will explain the situation to her. She can help move you three and everything else to the camp. Our things will be better off there as well.

Supai nodded and went to tell Riman. He looked up to Honoras and nodded agreement too. They stood up from Dasriel's bedside together to get everything packed.

I woke of my own accord, surrounded by green. I looked around, forgetting for a moment where I was. I realized that I was under Honoras's wing. The fingers on it were a dark, dark green, while the membrane in between was illuminated a silvery green by the light of the moon outside. I felt Honoras stir next to me. He lifted his wing to look at me. I could feel his happiness reverberating through my mind.

It is good to have you sleep by me again, he said. I nodded, smiling. He moved his foreleg from around me to let me out while he turned his head to look behind him. He must have said something to Riman and Supai, for I heard quick responses and movement. I stepped out from under Honoras's wing and walked around in front of him.

The other two had everything all packed up and ready to go, though I wasn't sure to where. Dasriel was on a stretcher that could be carried in Honoras's claws, and a cloth sling had been made for the black. Everything else was piled up together.

My mother is coming, as you heard, before Ilian put you to sleep.

Aye. But why is she coming? What is going on?

She is coming to train you, a little at least, before the battle. I and the two humans decided that it would be better for all if they joined the fighting force Tayna and Geoff gathered. They are camped little under half a day's flight south of us.

This left me even more confused, and he could tell. *That's right,* he said. *I said I would tell you. Yesterday while you were asleep, Shaelynn told me how she met Ilian after we'd left to rescue you. He asked her to be his Guide, and she accepted. A Guide is much like how a rider is to a horse. Without a Guide, Ilian would be wandering aimlessly through his life. He needs Shaelynn to direct him down the right path.*

Ilian also let her see a small vision of the future to help her with her decision. She saw a battle on this plain, just in front of the castle. She said she saw ordinary people fighting against Zathos's army of beasts. Najee was there with the rest of his gang, and also Tayna, Geoff, Agathla, Marl, and Shamar. She saw you on me; we were in the sky, and she also saw herself fighting upon Ilian. The battle is supposed to take place within the week.

But how does he know that? How could she have seen that?

Unicorns are gifted with being able to see everything in the present time at once, and also being able to see the certain future: the things that are sure to happen, the events that cannot be changed.

That's how he knew what happened to me, even though he'd never met me before?

Aye. He picked up something from the ground near him and handed it to me; it was my pack. Shaelynn must have found it somehow. *Your cousin left you this. She said your bow and arrows are in it, and your map, and whatever else was in there.* I took it and put it on my shoulders, grimacing at the twinge in my ribs caused by the movement.

There was a faint beating rhythm from the south; I was not able to hear it, but was somehow able to through Honoras. He lifted his head high to hear better. The beating grew louder, and I recognized it as wingbeats.

Chapter 13

MY MOTHER COMES, HONORAS SAID. I knew I wasn't the only one to hear the rhythm of heavy wingbeats; Riman and Supai came to stand by us, looking to the starry sky above. The wingbeats grew louder and louder, until at last a massive dragon appeared seemingly out of nowhere. She was twice as large as Honoras, and a different color than he, just as I had remembered. The man I had seen in the dream was on her back.

She landed heavily, making the ground tremble underneath them. She laid down flat on her stomach to let the man get off, still having to help him down with a talon. Once he was off and headed toward us, she did the same.

When she landed, she had had to land at least a hundred feet away because of her size. But now that her wings were neatly folded at her sides, she could stand right next to us. With a careful eye she looked Honoras over. They held a private discussion, I could tell; they kept cocking their heads this way and that and gesturing with their claws. Finally, after a few minutes, Honoras gestured to me. Politely he stepped back so his mother could see me better.

Come closer Liz, she told me. Her voice was deep, but not so much that it seemed manly. There was a firm gentleness in it, and also a kindness. I did as she told me; she lifted my chin a little with a claw twice the size of any of Honoras's. I didn't flinch in the least. She grinned a dragon grin, flashing her teeth for a moment.

Good spirit, though a little too determined, enough to be stubborn, she remarked to Honoras, letting me hear as well. He chuckled, nodding. I smiled. *Now, turn round, slowly. Let me see you, girl.* Again, I did as asked. She made small chirping sounds as she looked me up and down.

She is a good companion, she announced for everyone to hear. Honoras let out a little roar, and the man that rode Honoras's mother jumped up, punching a fist in the air. Riman and Supai smiled, as did the dragon before me.

It is the tradition of Sorva di Fravid *that the dragon's parent announces their approval of a new companion,* Honoras explained to me.

Honoras stepped closer to his mother, and they talked privately for another few minutes. He must have been explaining our plans. I saw her nod her approval enthusiastically. The man that was with her joined them after this; I saw him agreeing as well. They came back to the rest of us. I saw Honoras's mother look over at Dasriel for the first time. No emotion showed on her face.

So, I guess we are transporting everyone and everything but Liz to the human camp to the south? she asked. We all nodded. *Load us up, then,* she said. Riman, Supai, and the man hurried to do it. Soon everything was packed on top of Honoras's mother, while everyone rode on Honoras. He had to stand on his hind legs to take off because of Dasriel in the stretcher grasped in his claws. His mother held the ends of the black's sling in her claws. The black had been put to sleep by some herbs Supai had found and identified in Dasirel's pack.

They took flight, the female dragon going first. *We did not want them to know, but we will reveal ourselves to the humans. We will land at the edge of the camp, where the leaders should be. It will be a mess, but the leaders should be calm and will help,* Honoras said just when we had caught sight of the camp. The two flew on and landed as quietly as they could, though they still woke everyone up on that side of the camp. Word of their arrival spread quickly, and soon the whole camp was awake.

By this time, Tayna, Geoff, and Najee had come out from the mess of confused people. Supai, Riman, and the man had gotten everything unloaded off Honoras's mother and had out everything close to the blankets and few tents scattered over the ground. Dasriel had been taken out of the sling and carried to a nearby tent, whose owner was willing enough to give it up. Tayna followed Dasriel inside while the tent's owner went to go and sleep under her blankets. The black had been laid down and was still sleeping in the sling.

"Liz!" I heard Geoff say as I got off Honoras. I turned to look at him.

"Geoff?" I asked.

"You've aged years since I last saw you," he joked. He held a hand out, and I shook it. He held me at arm's length, looking me over in wonder. He looked up at Honoras, who was standing close behind me. "That's a nice dragon you've got there," he said.

May I request a nickname of you, dragon? Geoff asked Honoras.

The other humans call me Sorvo, he said.

Sorvo, I honor you for taking Liz to be your companion and Bonded. And I thank you for saving her from Zathos. I am sure you two will make an excellent addition of the Sorva di Fravid.

Your praise is taken well, and thank you for your approval. I also hope we will be able to help the Sorva di Fravid.

Once their formal greetings were made, I was sure they would talk of something I would find no interest in. I left them to say hello to Najee, who was already looking my way; Supai had brought his attention to me. We smiled at each other, but then gave up formalities and rushed into each other's arms. Najee fake-choked as I gave him a bear hug.

"It's so good to see you again," he said. "I thought you were dead."

"I came pretty close." We let go of each other.

"And I thought your name was Rish," he laughed. "Oh well; you had good reason."

I looked around at the camp. Everyone was out of their tents, gawking at Honoras. "How many people are here?" I asked.

"Ten thousand, at least," Najee said. "And I gathered a good half of them. The elf and the centaur came to Barda, looking for people that wanted to fight. I heard about it of course, and went to talk with them. They said that two young women had come through, and one of them had found a dragon: you, Liz. They said that you were now being held in his dungeon, waiting for your dragon to come. They said there'd be a battle, and if enough people fought, we'd be able to defeat Zathos's reign. I was interested, and asked who the girls were. They wouldn't give it up at first, but eventually they did.

"So, I was all ears, you know. I wanted to help as much as I could. I told Agathla and Marl, who wanted to help too. Shamar heard of it, and he wanted in, too. So, we talked with Tayna and Geoff. They said they'd go south to look for people, and we could hit all the northern towns, and we'd meet on the road at the very edge of the trees. So, we did. And here we are now."

"Who else is here that I know?"

"Well, all my gang are here—they were really worked up when Tayna and Geoff tried to tell them they were too young, until one of them tried to take on Geoff. Guess who it was."

"It wasn't Dush, was it?"

"Yup. 'Bout had him at first, but Geoff has two extra limbs to his advantage. He said to be really careful, but we were okay. I guess we'll be toward the back, where we're safer, but at least we'll be fighting." I was looking around at everyone again, seeing Dush and some of the others by a ragged tent made out of everyone's blankets, it seemed. They grinned and waved, and I waved back.

There was movement in the tent Dasriel had been taken to, and I watched as Tayna climbed out with another person, probably another healer. She said goodbye to him and came to me.

"Liz, who is the sorcerer that attacked Dasriel?" I knew she was glad to see me, even though she didn't sound it; she was busy now.

"He told me his name was Avernus." I was surprised that the mention of his name didn't bring back another flood of memories, only the one of when he gave me the scar on my cheek. I could see her staring at it.

"Did he give you that?" she asked. I nodded. She touched it softly at first, and then ran her finger down it. It felt odd.

"There," she said, satisfied. "It had a small spell on it, but it is gone now. It should give you no problems, other than being a scar."

"Thank you."

"You're a brave girl, you know that?" she said, putting an arm around my shoulder. "I'm proud of you." She smiled at me warmly, creating another feeling of warmth and peace in me, just as I had experienced the first time I had met her.

Tayna walked to the two dragons, who were listening to Geoff, eager to hear what was going on. The man who rode Honoras's mother was there as well. When Tayna got their attention and told them of Dasriel's condition, the man came over to me.

"You're the one who saw us in your dream, aren't you?" he asked. I nodded and held out my hand.

"My name is Liz. And yours?"

"Jacey, and your dragon's mother you can call Wraetha."

"Jacey, good to meet you." We shook hands. "You can call my dragon Sorvo—it is the only thing the man traveling with us could come up with when looking for another name for him." We both laughed. Honoras and Wraetha looked over, curious, but we only waved them off.

"So, where is your cousin that I met along her way north? She spoke of you and identified your pack, but she said you were dead."

"She thought Sorvo killed me when really he was rescuing me. Yesterday she met a unicorn by the name of Ilian. She agreed to be his Guide, and she's with him now."

Did you say Ilian? Wraetha asked. I nodded. *The unicorn? Your cousin is his Guide?* Again, I nodded. *Interesting,* she remarked to herself, though she let us hear. She turned back to her previous conversation.

"Anyway, when did she meet Ilian?"

"Early last night, I guess. While Sorvo was rescuing me." He nodded, and we both looked to the two dragons talking with Tayna and Geoff. They finished their conversation, saying a few last words to one another. There were nods, and then the dragons turned to us.

Are you ready, gliad? Honoras asked. Wraetha must have heard him; happiness radiated through my mind. Jacey smiled as he got on her back. Honoras got down low so I could get on as well. With final goodbyes, we took flight and headed north once more.

Since we didn't have a camp anymore, and we didn't want to be so close to the castle, we headed east, opposite the direction Shaelynn and Ilian had gone to train. The dragons flew on for half a day; the sun rose while we were in the air, the first sunrise I had seen in a month. It was beautiful, the sky various colors of coral and rosy pinks, oranges, and reds. It would have been better, in my opinion, with a few mountain silhouettes.

When we stopped we unloaded everything from the dragons, which wasn't much. I had my pack, and Jacey had packed only what was necessary for himself. We shared his food while the dragons discussed what would be covered in only a few days.

Tayna and Geoff had provided some strong leather while we were at the camp. Wraetha directed Jacey and I on how to make a harness for Honoras, just something to strap me on to with enough strength to keep me on while Honoras executed certain maneuvers.

There was one strap that acted like a girth; it went around Honoras's middle and let the other straps attach to it. Two more straps went from the saddle down both sides of Honoras's neck over his shoulders and met with each other to connect to the girth, much like the breast collar on a horse's saddle. From the leather seat, small buckles could be tightened around my legs to hold them in place. There were also stirrups put on for my feet to go in when I didn't need the leg buckles.

When we were done, we put it on Honoras. It looked good, I thought. Wraetha looked it over, occasionally tugging on it here or there to see if it would hold. *It will do,* she said finally. *Liz, go ahead and get on.* I did as asked, and Jacey helped me to get the straps tight enough.

Good, now go and try it out. Do a few turns, and a flip or two.

"What?" I said out loud. "A flip or two? What if I fall?"

Nonsense, dear, and speak with your mind. That should come naturally. And don't worry; you aren't likely to fall, and if you do, you do trust my son enough that he will catch you?

Aye.

Very well then, go on. As soon as she had given the word, Honoras leapt into the air and took about three wingbeats to get enough altitude to be safe. He flew forward as fast as he could and then suddenly banked sharply to the right; I was jerked sideways, but remained in place. He did the same, banking to the left this time, with the same results.

After he had done this, he flew forward again. I thought that he would do more banking, but suddenly he gained speed, flew straight up, and then glided backward in a complete circle, putting me upside down for a second—I screamed.

He came out of the flip at a faster speed than I would have expected, and then he went and did it again. This time I was expecting it, and I didn't scream. I actually liked it. It was a thrill.

Honoras laughed in my mind. *I see you enjoyed it that time. Shall we do it once more?*

Yes! He pumped his wings hard to gain speed, angled his wings upward, and then spread them out as he glided backwards, swooping down and righting himself again. He continued the glide back down to his mother, and landed lightly on the ground, back-winging to get himself straight.

Very well done, Wraetha said. *Now—Sorvo and I have agreed that we are hungry, and we cannot be expected to fight after over a week of fasting, and you two need to work on some long-distance flying and flying tactics. We will fly to another part of the forest to the east where we may hunt. There is also an old village there, I don't know if it still stands. But it was once a village that helped the* Sorva di Fravid. *They made armor.*

All right, I said.

I agree as well, Jacey said, surprising me by mind-speaking. I stayed on Honoras while Jacey got on Wraetha. I noticed that she didn't have a harness for him to ride on. I asked him why when we took flight.

I have no need of it: I've been around dragons most of my life. I was found shipwrecked on the coast of Amatol; Wraetha and her companion found me. They said I was only four or five years old. I don't remember it at all. Since I knew about the dragons I couldn't go back to the mainland, but I grew used to it quickly. Wraetha schooled me, as did the other dragons. I grew up on their backs. I have no need of a saddle.

Where is her companion now? Shouldn't he be with her?

Right now he's teaching one of our very young dragons, and couldn't be spared for the task. He asked me to go with Wraetha, and I agreed.

Another thing, how can you mind-speak so clearly? You aren't Fravid-Sorva, *are you?*

No. None of the dragons on Amatol have chosen me for their Bonded. Most dragons will rarely choose anyone so close to them anyway. They prefer to find someone on the mainland who is suitable enough. They like to teach their companions, and what good will I do for them?

True enough, though I'm sorry to hear it. It'd be neat if you were Bonded. Then, maybe we could go flying together. After all this is over, maybe.

Aye. After all this is over, perhaps the other dragons that were run off will return. Then, maybe, one of them will choose me. It's a possibility.

I hope it'll happen to you.

I do, too. I'd like that. We talked of other things along the journey, which was long. Wraetha had Honoras and I do various things, from flying spirals in the air and diving and then pulling up again. In between exercises, Honoras simply glided, trying to save his energy, using a wingbeat here and there to give him a push.

When we finally stopped for the two dragons to hunt, Jacey helped me down; I was still exhausted and had fallen asleep along the way. He had had to wake me up when we landed. Honoras said he'd wear the harness while he hunted, so Jacey and I simply lay against a tree while they went off in separate directions. They were quick about it; in under half an hour they returned, licking their chops happily.

We are off the plain, but we still have far to go, Wraetha said.

How far? I asked.

We have gone about forty miles, and we have almost another thirty to go.

Nearly seventy miles? I asked in disbelief.

Aye. And we must be back at your campsite for your training by tomorrow afternoon.

Do not worry, gliad, I can handle it, Honoras said playfully. Jacey smiled; Honoras had not made his remark private. I scowled at him and he laughed, a deep rumbling sound.

I got back on Honoras and did the buckles around my legs without Jacey's help. He stood next to me to see if I had fastened them right, and then quickly got on Wraetha. Honoras was already in the air; he hovered for a moment while his mother got airborne. When she was close, he beat his wings to get more altitude and speed.

The time passed a little more quickly, now that there was some diversity in the landscape below us. It was uninhabited as far as I could tell, but it had once held many people. Many large clearings were checkered among the trees, remains of crop fields long forgotten. Lakes passed beneath us, and Honoras and Wraetha dipped low over the water, dragging their claws over its surface. Honoras would occasionally flick water up at me or toward his mother. The last time he did she quickly dipped her head down, getting a mouthful of water, and squirted it in his face.

When the sun had started to set I could see a large tower in the distance, still some miles away. We quickly reached it, and just on its other side were the ruins of a once-great city. There were many streets and two—or three-story buildings that led up to a four-story temple-like building.

This is Zaniel, the elves' capital city, or it was, Honoras told me.

I thought you said this was a small village.

Well, most of elves had fled when I last came here. There were only a hundred or so of them.

Can we still find some here?

Perhaps, but there can't be more than three or four. This place is regularly visited by Zathos's creatures on their way in and out of his castle. But don't worry; they aren't likely to come now. Zathos has been expecting this battle, and he'd have already called them to him.

He knew the battle was going to happen?

Oh, yes. He can't have not known. By kidnapping you, he was luring me to him in order to rescue you. If he had succeeded, he would have held us under threat of our life to get the rest of the dragons to come out of hiding. To keep that kind of force from knocking down his walls, he would have needed his creatures to fight for him. He knew there would be some kind of fight, though I don't think he expected this.

That makes sense, though. I wouldn't have thought that out like that.

You are still young; that is why you need training. In time it will come.

We found a clearing by the city big enough for both dragons to land, though they were a little uncomfortable. Once they had folded their wings up close to their bodies, they were fine.

The clearing was meant for dragons to land in, Wraetha told us. It was close to the city, and a wide path through the houses led to the four-story temple. She said the city was built for dragons of all ages and sizes. Even her large bulk fit nicely in the path. Honoras followed her to the temple.

When we reached the temple, there was a large platform on the north side where both dragons could stand. There was a wide hallway that went all the way through the base of the temple, which was actually a smithery where the armor was made. The platform was where the dragons could stand while the elves got their measurements and could make armor to their size. Wraetha could not fit in the hallway, though, and neither could Honoras; he was just big enough to not fit. Instead, Jacey and I went in, keeping an open connection with both dragons.

Time seemed frozen here, as if the ruins were holding their breath, waiting for something to happen. Tools still laid on low brick walls surrounding a place for a fire, the bellows still intact. Scraps of metal were piled on the floor, and some pieces of armor, probably for humans, were still lying on some of the anvils. There was a door off to the side of one of the rooms, the only one out of all the stalls. Jacey and I went to it; the door was cracked open a little.

I stood just behind Jacey as he opened the door; it opened easier than either he or I thought it would, with not a creak in the hinges at all. Inside was a long storage room. There were abstract piles of formed metal everywhere, propped up against the walls and stacked chest-high on the floor. But now that I looked closer, I saw that the piles of formed metal were piles of armor, of every size and make.

Just in front of me, Jacey moved into the room slowly, looking at all the armor. "Everything in this room must be hundreds of years old, if not thousands, some of it." I moved into the room as well. On the floor in front of me, propped up against a stack of armor, was a faceplate for a dragon, I think. It certainly was the right size for Honoras. I picked it up to look at it.

Jacey stopped trying to move around one of the piles and froze. I looked up at him; a thin metal spear was pointed at him, hovering over his chest. I moved backward the tiniest bit and felt a sharp point aimed at the base of my neck. I could feel another at my back. I watched Jacey to see what he would do, and saw one of the spears pointed at his head drop as the elf holding it stepped forward to speak.

"You were right, human, this armor is old. And we are older. You have no right to be here, in this place. Why have you come?" His voice had an evilly calm tone, until the question came: then his tone was angry and he almost spat the words out.

"We need armor for our dragons and weapons for ourselves. There is a battle coming within the week, and we are fighting to defeat Zathos and his followers," Jacey said quietly, just enough for everyone to hear.

"Your dragons?" The elf inquired. "Where are they? And who are you?"

"They are outside on the large platform, waiting for us. I am Jacey, a shipwrecked boy rescued by Wraetha, as I call her, of Amatol Island. I am not her Bonded, simply a close friend."

"And who are you, youngling?" The elf asked, turning to me.

I answered quickly, trying to think of what to say about myself at the same time. "I am Liz, sent here from another time by Zathos. I am Bonded to Sorvo, as I call my dragon. He is also of Amatol but left there recently to seek a companion."

"Brought here from another time, eh? And by Zathos? Now what reasons would he have for that?"

"He must have known that Sorvo would Bond with me, and sent me here to do that. He captured me and kept me within his castle for over a month to lure my dragon into coming and getting the whereabouts of the other dragons. He wanted the dragons to serve him."

"I see. May we see these dragons of yours?"

"What does it matter to you?" Jacey asked. The elf whirled on him, his spear resting on Jacey's collarbone. The tip was pointed at his throat. Another elf stepped out of the darkness to reveal himself. Jacey's eyes were going back and forth from right to left on either side of me. There must have been more elves behind me that had revealed themselves.

"It matters," a female voice said behind me, "in the way that if there truly are two dragons outside and the girl is indeed *Fravid-Sorva,* then our years of waiting in exile are over. It means that the dragons have finally returned."

"Oh. Well, not all of the dragons have returned—not any of the *Sorva di Fravid* from long ago that you speak of. If Zathos is defeated, then yes, perhaps they will return. We are only trying to make that happen."

"Then, let us see your dragons. If they are indeed real, we will help you in as many ways as we can."

"All right," Jacey said, and the two elves backed off enough to give him room to move around. I felt the spears move away from me and turned around to see three more elves, two of them female. They turned and walked out the door, and I did the same. Behind me, I heard Jacey's shuffling feet making soft sounds as he tried to maneuver around the piles of armor; I heard nothing from the elves with him.

The elves silently gestured for Jacey and I to walk out first. We did, and Wraetha and Honoras turned to us, having been looking out over the forest from the edge of the platform.

Did you find anything? Honoras asked both of us. I nodded; Jacey pointed behind us, and the elves stepped out into the remaining sunlight. For the first time I noticed what they were wearing: simple leather strips that covered only enough to make them modest. The women wore their hair long, but it was tied with leather cords just like the ones Tayna had given Shaelynn and I. Absentmindedly my hand strayed to my ponytail, and I found that it still held my hair up.

Honoras and Wraetha gave their full attention to the elves, and both dragons picked out one to talk to. At the same time the female elf who had spoken behind me came towards me, staring at my wrist. She must have seen the bracelet when I reached for the leather strip that held up my hair. I was shocked that it was still there at all, with all I'd been through.

"Where did you get that bracelet, exactly?" she asked me, grabbing my wrist a little roughly to examine it.

"I found it a long time ago; it had to be almost half a year. It was what brought my cousin and I here."

"Who sent it to you?" she asked.

"What?"

"It has been sent through time, and I want to know who sent it and why they wanted you and your cousin here. This bracelet was meant to be activated through a simple spell, and I want to know that as well."

"How do you know that?"

"Tell me what I want to know and I'll tell you about this bracelet." It agitated me, but I admired her negotiating terms. I wouldn't get what I wanted until she did, and that put her in control.

"Zathos sent it to my time. I was at a store, and I saw on the counter, and paid for it along with everything else I had. The spell was written on paper that I thought was the tag. It said-"

"Wait. Take the bracelet off and put it on the ground before you do. It could still be activated by it." I did as she said, and thought for a moment about the words.

"On the full moon shining, dreams shall take flight. Back to a place of old, wonders shall be seen. Recover the rightful one to the throne; restore a lost land to return home. One may be lost, many will fall; Hardships will come, friendships tried. Defeat the evil one, to close the gap, and a lost land will be restored anew."

"Let me guess: you happened to read it aloud on a full moon."

"Yes. It took us here, and we met a centaur, Geoff, who saved us from a griffin. After that he took us to his grove where we met Tayna, another elf. She and Geoff took us in when we first came here. They kept us in their house for a few months and taught us what we needed to know. When she heard from the trees that something was coming for us, she sent us on our way to Zathos's castle, although that something never came. Anyway, she said we'd find reason for coming here along the way. And we did. I'm Bonded to Sorvo, and Shaelynn is now a unicorn's Guide."

"What, you are *Sorva di Fravid,* and now a new Guide? Something must surely be happening in the world out there."

"Hush, you fool," said another. "Think for a moment about why we don't know what's going on."

"All of you, hush," the female on the ground said quietly, and they obeyed. She looked at me once more. "The third thing I asked you about—why Zathos wants you here. Tell me that." She seemed to have forgotten that I'd already told them that. I was about to tell her again, but Honoras answered the question before I could speak.

He knew Elizabeth would Bond with me, and he wanted her in his hands to lure me to him. One way or the other, he thought that he could get the information about where the other dragons are. He would command them to his side; if they refused, he would most likely kill them. But he never got the information. I and two other humans helped Elizabeth to escape. Honoras had come over with the rest of the elves; Wraetha was trying to see into the smithery.

Well, can you help us or not? she asked abruptly. *We need to get moving. Liz has to fit most of several years' training into less than a week. We need armor for the battle, and a few more weapons as well.*

"Our people were exiled from this place by Zathos, but we stayed, hoping the *Sorva di Fravid* would come once again. Now this day is here. We will not refuse service to you." The female stood up, without help from anyone, and walked to the smithery alone, leaving everyone else to follow. "Trius, look for any acceptable pieces in the storage. See what you can find that will fit these two, and find some upper body plates for the humans."

The elf that had spoken to Jacey in the room looked the four of us over in turn, and then quickly rushed to the room with another elf. The female elf looked over the two remaining elves. "Jiade, you and Koina work on a faceplate for Wraetha; Jacey, you will join them. Liz, come help me make one for Sorvo." The two elves nodded, beckoning Wraetha to bring her head further into the smithery. The female elf grabbed a sheet of metal and a hammer and quickly dashed outside with Honoras before Wraetha's head blocked her way.

"Bring your head down, dragon. Let me get the right fit for you." Honoras did as she asked, and she had me hold the sheet just in front of his head while she walked from one side to the other, comparing the sheet to the shape of Honoras's head. Just when my arms started to tire, she easily took the sheet from me and laid it on the ground a little ways away from both dragons to give her room to work.

She took out the hammer and beat out a square at the corner of the sheet, and then made other marks that started to resemble Honoras's head, or at least the front of it. I looked from the sheet to Honoras, and back again.

"Isn't that too big?" I asked.

"No. With the curves of his face, if I make it the right size now that it's flat it will be too small. I oversize it now so that when it is shaped, it will fit perfectly." When she was finished she took up the sheet again into the smithery and started a fire, heating it with the bellows. Just as she had started to work them Trius and the other elf came out loaded down with armor. Trius squeezed past Wraetha's head while the other one stopped in front of her to unload the armor he held. Wraetha shifted her head again, and I couldn't see anything inside past her.

Trius stopped just in front of Honoras and carefully set the armor down. He looked over Honoras once more.

"I see you have a saddle for yourself, though it could be better," he remarked. Jacey glared at him.

"We made it using all we had available. And it will hold Liz."

"It does its job well then, doesn't it?" Trius smiled a little and picked up the topmost piece. He took it to Honoras's side and held it up for a moment, then quickly set it down and went to the pile again, rummaging through it until he found a piece similar to the first. This one had leather straps on it. I looked at the other piece, which had buckles.

"I think I know where that goes, and how it goes on," I said.

"Good. Get up on your dragon and help me then." I did as he said. "Now, move to his back, but watch out for the spines."

"I know," I said irritably. I did as told as Trius came to Honoras's left side, where he held up the piece with the leather straps. I took hold of them and held it up where he had had it, with some difficulty. Truis picked up the other piece and walked to the near side.

"Help her hold it up, boy, don't stand there," Truis barked. Jacey jumped forward and held the piece in place for me. Trius lifted the other for me, and I put the straps through the buckles, connecting the pieces.

"How far up should they be?" I asked Trius.

"Just where the tops are near his spines but won't be in danger of bothering them." I tightened them as he wanted, and did up the buckles. Trius had Honoras bend from side to side. The armor didn't bother his movement at all. When Trius had checked it three times, he tightened the buckles that went around Honoras's middle to secure the armor from the bottom. Next, Trius picked out two more identical pieces. These he carried to Honoras's back legs, where they went over top of his hips and connected the same way as the side pieces. I found that there were two buckles on the upper parts of the side pieces. The straps on the hip pieces fit them perfectly, and kept them from sliding around as Honoras moved. Trius had Honoras test them again, and all was well.

The last piece was a breast plate, with shoulder pieces attached so that they were flexible as well. A beautiful green gem sat in the center of the golden-embroidered chest plate. Trius had me sit in the saddle to attach this piece because it joined to the saddle, and I needed to be comfortable enough as well. There were no buckles or straps on the saddle, so I had to tie secure double-knots to attach the breast plate to it. Honoras tested it once more, and found it to be a perfect fit.

I quite like it, he said cheerfully to me when Trius turned to leave.

"Go and try it out then, but quickly. Your faceplate should be nearly done," Trius told him before going back inside. I smiled, and climbed up in the saddle. Honoras took off from the platform without a word, but I could tell by his movements that he was excited to try it out as well.

The armor was designed to give him full movement, and it moved easily with him as he executed every maneuver he could think of, after I had buckled the leg straps, or some of them. He said it was light enough for him to wear all the time, but he said it would protect him in battle as well as any other kind of armor.

So, Honoras said, *for those reasons, and because of the hassle of trying to put it all on, I think my mother and I will wear them until the battle, whenever it is. It will not bother us in the least.*

We landed again on the platform, and Trius came out to meet us. Wraetha had all her armor on, and she took off before we landed to try it out as well. Jacey was on her, smiling and waving at me. I waved back as they whipped by.

"Come, Sorvo, Desarti has your faceplate ready," Truis said. I realized belatedly that that was the female elf's name. I unfastened the leg buckles and got off Honoras, pushing past his head a little to get in the smithery. Desarti made a few last bangs on a shaped piece of metal, and picked it up to carry it to Honoras.

"Well, here you go. I hope you like it; I made it in record time." Desarti held it up so that Honoras and I could see it. It was shaped well; the forehead was raised above the cheek plate, and the top of it curved to fit around the bases of Honoras's horns. The bottom came to a tip that would rest just in between Honoras's nostrils. It was bordered by medium-sized gold lines, with an intricate pattern of thin gold lines over the forehead and down the nose.

"It's beautiful," I said.

Indeed. I like it. Thank you, Desarti.

"You're welcome." She handed the faceplate to me, and I saw more straps and buckles hanging off it. "You can do the honors, Liz. Riders usually do anyway."

"Really?"

"Aye. It's tradition."

And a dragon's faceplate is his own, because it is made especially for him. No other dragon can wear another's faceplate.

"What he says is true," Desarti said. "Now, see if you can figure it out." I smiled and put the faceplate up to Honoras's head, fumbling with the straps and buckles until I could see where they went. It fit kind of like a horse's halter, really. There was a long strap that went behind Honoras's horns and fit just right between two spikes, and it buckled on the side of his face. There were two more straps, one that went under his throat and another smaller one that went under his jaw, farther down and just in front of his chin. I stepped back and smiled.

It fits you, somehow.

Well, it is the size of my face.

No! Silly. I meant it somehow shows some of you.

I know. I was teasing. Do you really think so?

Aye. It was meant for you.

Good. I suppose she did a good job, then.

Behind us, Wraetha landed with Jacey. Her armor was a copper-ish bronze color, rather than the silver of Honoras's armor. It too, had some pretty designs on it. Jacey got off her and came over to us. Both of them examined Honoras's armor, and both approved of it.

"The faceplate is perfect," Jacey said. He turned to Desarti. "How long did it take you?"

"Nearly an hour. I'm sorry; we have no jewels I could have put into it."

"Jewels?" I asked.

"Most faceplates will have a jewel in the forehead that matches the jewel on the breastplate. This one is emerald, which is hard to come by anyway." Desarti pointed to the green gem in Honoras's breastplate.

That will be fine, don't worry, Honoras said. *There is no time for luxuries now.*

"Yes. It doesn't matter to me," I agreed. Desarti nodded.

"Very well. I guess it'll work, then." She smiled and walked away to help the other elves finish with Wraetha's faceplate. "It's almost done, Wraetha," she called over her shoulder.

Trius came over at this time, with the other elf. Both were carrying another armful of armor. Trius went to Jacey, while the other went to me. He set down his armful, which was smaller than the one Truis had. He picked up two pieces, the largest ones.

"Turn 'round," he told me, "and we'll see if this will fit you." I did as asked, and felt him holding one of the pieces up to my back after a moment. He held it there, then set it down. He turned me around again and held up another plate, this one shaped for a woman. I took it and held it up against myself.

"It looks all right, I suppose. It'll hold up in battle, anyway. Now, hold that and turn around again." He attached the two pieces together somehow; I couldn't see. It felt a little tight, but I could move around all right. The armor was lighter than I had expected. I mentioned this to the elf.

"Well, it's made for our maidens, and they need to be able to fight, right? They're trained to be flexible, and heavy armor can't let them do that. Hence, the lightness, and the flexibility. Twist around a bit. There you go. See? You can move just as well with it as you can without it." He picked up another piece, examined it for a moment, then went to my right side.

"Hold your arm out. There you go. Now—these pieces just snap around your arm, see? Just like that. You'll need your man there to help you get these on before the fight, and you'll have to help him with his. They're impossible to get on yourself, but when you fight you won't know they're there."

"Neat. Thank you." He took the arm plates off, and then had me take off the chest and back plates to see if I could do it, which I did. He nodded happily, and then went off to help finish Wraetha's faceplate. I could see Desarti working the bellows inside.

I turned to Jacey, who had just taken off his armor. The elf that was helping him had just left to follow Trius into the smithery. He looked at me and grinned. "Does your armor fit all right?" he asked.

"Yeah. And yours?"

"It fit okay. It's a little loose, but it'll do."

I turned to Wraetha, who was trying to peek into the smithery without bothering us. *What will we do after this?*

We will fly back out onto the edge of the plain tomorrow, and we will begin your training. We will work on yours and Sorvo's abilities, some that you do not know of. It will be these that we will focus on the most. I think your fighting skills will need to be practiced a little, but Sorvo has told me that you are quite good already.

But I lost to Karbab twice. She shook her head in a funny way.

Your new abilities should be able to help you there. We will see.

What new abilities?

You will see, she repeated. I sighed, knowing that she would not tell me.

The elves came out, and the two called Jiade and Koina were behind the rest of them, carrying a huge copper piece of metal: Wraetha's faceplate. The other elves stepped away from Jiade and Koina, and the two held it out. Happiness reverberated from Wraetha.

The faceplate was the same copper-ish bronze as her armor, and it had silver designs swirling around it that were similar to the style on her armor and mimicked the swirls of white on her scales, both at once. Jacey smiled and took it. Honoras had to help him hold it up.

"Wraetha, I am not your Bonded, but you have known me since I was small and have helped me grow. Since your Bonded is not here, I will do this for him, and partly for myself." Honoras held it up to her face while he did the buckles. It was perfect.

Now, Honoras said, *I think that Elizabeth and Jacey will need some weapons.* He nodded to me and said quietly, *Tell them what you need.*

I turned to Desarti and the others and said, "I use a sword and a bow and arrow, but all I need are some more arrows for that. My sword was lost in a flight far to the south, and so I need a new one."

"That is all I use as well," Jacey said, "besides my fists. They are in good shape." The dragons and I laughed, and the elves smiled. Desarti looked me over for a moment.

"What size sword did you use?" she asked. I described it to her and showed her how long it was, hilt and all. She nodded and followed the others, who disappeared through another door somewhere to the right.

We waited for a little while before they came back up, two of them carrying nearly an armful of arrows. Desarti had two swords in her hand, and two others had a handful of various bows for Jacey. Desarti handed him the longer sword. He tried it out, fighting the air. I was surprised at his skill. He smiled and thanked her for it. The other two elves brought forward their bows for him to try.

Desarti and the elves with the arrows came to me. "What feathers did your arrows have on them?" Koina asked.

"Turkey, I think," I told them, pulling out one of my remaining arrows. She looked at it for a moment, and then they both starting rummaging through their armfuls for the right ones. They handed me a good bunch of them, more than I'd ever had at once. I put them in my quiver, which I found to be at the bottom of my pack. Now that I looked through it properly, I saw that everything had been stuffed inside. All my old arrows were loose with everything else. I put them in my quiver as well and put it on my back with my bow.

"Will this work for you?" Desarti asked, handing me the remaining sword. I tried it out just as Jacey had, and found it perfect. Desarti watched me handle the sword.

"That is a different style than we elves use, though some of it is familiar. I could tell from the arrows and the make of the bow that Tayna made them for you, but who taught you to swordfight?"

"A centaur named Geoff. He lives with her."

"That's right; you said something of him. Interesting. I was surprised at how well you handled it. The sword is worthy of you, then." She smiled as I put it at my waist, in the sheath that was also somehow still there. She saw my bracelet once more and said, "Would you like for me to tell you what that bracelet can do?"

"Yes, please."

"It has magical properties, you know, but more than you think."

"How can you tell?"

"Come now, I am an elf, am I not?"

"Yes. Sorry; please go on."

"As I said, it has more magical uses than just to transport you through time by using a spell. If you will it to, you can make it do nearly everything. It can heal, give you some few abilities, and maybe even let you change shapes briefly."

"Like what abilities?" I asked.

"You could probably turn transparent, or fly, if you wanted to."

"Neat. How can I make it do that?"

"You cannot make that bracelet do anything. You must ask it, and it must agree."

"How, though?"

She took it carefully and said, "Like this." She closed her eyes, her brow furrowed; she was concentrating hard. Then her face relaxed, and in an instant she faded out of sight. My eyes widened and I could hear her laughing. I felt something touch my shoulder and jumped back. I saw a faint outline moving and realized that it was her.

"Are you still, like, there?" I asked, reaching out. She laughed and the outline moved again. A hand grabbed my own. I groped up her shoulder and I could feel her, I only couldn't see her. It was really weird.

Desarti came back into focus and handed me the bracelet. "Now you try. Close your eyes, and talk to the bracelet like you do Sorvo. Tell it, 'I wish to turn transparent.' It will reply by letting you do it or not." I held it in my hand and closed my eyes, reaching out for something within it.

"Do not search for a mind but something that is different than beads and string," Desarti offered. I did as told, and found something entirely different than anything I'd ever felt. It seemed intelligent, but was not human and did not really think at all. That was why I couldn't find it at first.

I wish to turn transparent, I told the bracelet. I felt a wave of icy coldness run down my spine and opened my eyes. Everything was in shades of black and white and mixed blues, but I could tell everything apart from something else, just as I could normally.

"Put your hand in front of your face," Desarti said. I couldn't see it at all, only that same faint outline. This time, though, it glowed a light purple. I looked down at the rest of my body. The same outline of purple was there. Everything else was not.

As I looked all over my transparent body, feeling myself to make sure I was still there, I saw the outline disappear and the rest of my body reappear. I looked up at Desarti and saw that everyone else was watching me.

"What happened?" I asked. "I didn't want to be visible yet."

"You broke your concentration," Desarti said. "To keep it up, you must keep your concentration up as well. If you practice this every night and try to do something else as well, you will learn to be able to direct some of your concentration elsewhere and still be able to hold enough of your attention on being transparent."

Elizabeth, do you feel any weaker than you did before, by chance? Honoras asked, coming over. He gestured, and I took the bracelet off for him to hold. I focused on myself: I was a bit more tired, but then again it was getting dark and close to bedtime.

"Yeah, a little bit, I guess," I said.

"That will be something else that is sure to happen," Jiade put in. "Any use of magic seeps energy from you. Different spells have different amounts of energy needed, and it will take that energy from you. If it uses all your energy, it'll kill you. You must be careful."

"He's right," Desarti said. "You must learn the spells well and learn your limits as well."

You will be learning your limits soon enough, Wraetha told me. I turned to Desarti.

"What spells take the most energy?" I asked.

"Moving something twice your size or larger, changing into something entirely different from your human form, and taking a life."

"Killing someone?" I asked.

"Aye. That is the hardest thing to do, emotionally and physically. It takes a toll on your entire body, your mind most of all. Killing a person through magic has killed the magic user before. The ones that live usually lose their minds. You must learn to be strong enough if you are to defeat Zathos. He will be the hardest on you to kill." I swallowed in fear. If I killed Zathos through magic, I'd either die or go crazy. And there's probably no other way to kill him; he's too powerful.

I will be there to help you, Honoras said.

"That's right. If Sorvo helps you, both of you will be strong enough to defeat him. Remember that." I looked up at Honoras after Desarti's words and smiled. I sent a wave of gratefulness through to him.

He blinked in surprise. *You are learning fast, my gliad. Most Fravid-Sorva cannot purposely send emotions until a few years of training and experience.*

But I've sent fear through to you before.

Fear is easiest to send. Every time you were scared before we were Bonded, you flung out your fear to anyone near. You just didn't know it. People do it all the time.

It just takes a dragon to notice?

He chuckled. *Aye.*

We looked to Wraetha and Jacey, who were talking to the elves. "We must get going," Jacey was saying. "Liz needs training, all she can get."

"Very well. Perhaps, then, we will see each other on the battlefield?" Desarti asked. Jacey smiled and shook her hand.

"Yes, perhaps," he said enthusiastically. He shook the rest of the elves' hands, and I did the same. Honoras and Wraetha bowed their heads to each of them in turn.

Thank you for your help, KnukSorva. You will be remembered among us.

Yes, Honoras put in after his mother had spoken. *We hope that your people will be able to recover from their banishment and this capital will soon be as it once was.*

"That is all we can hope for," Desarti answered.

"Aye, and that the *Sorva di Fravid* will soon return to Partaenia," said Koina. The others nodded.

"Good luck, Liz," Jiade said.

"Yes, the best of luck to all of you," the rest of them said in unison. The dragons held our armor for us; we got on, and took off from the platform. When I turned back to look at the ruins, the elves were gone. No firelight flickered from inside the smithery. Just as it had before, it showed no signs of life. But I knew they were there.

Chapter 14

SHAELYNN LOWERED HER ARMS WEARILY, and the rock before her ceased its color-changing. She had finished her last lesson for the second day, and she was more tired than she could have ever believed. But she was proud of herself as well. She had finally done it.

For the past two days she had been practicing using magic on a large stone. Today she had finally achieved what Ilian had wanted: to change the stone's natural color to a color as blue as the sky.

"Good, very good indeed," Ilian said, obvious pride and praise in his voice. It made the effort worth it to Shaelynn. She smiled.

"Okay, now I've colored the rock like you told me to," she said, sitting down on the ground. "What will we do tomorrow?"

"We will work with the stone again." Shaelynn sighed. She was extremely tired of the rock. "Do not worry; you will not spend the whole day changing its color again," Ilian said, lying down next to her. "You've shown me that you are able to direct your magic to a specific task and hold your concentration for long amounts of time. And so tomorrow, you'll spend the whole day doing something else." She groaned and leaned back on his stomach while he laughed.

"This will pay off in the coming battle; I promise you." Shaelynn leaned forward and turned around to look at him.

"Have you seen it?" she asked. "Will I fight well?"

"That is something I cannot tell you. Some parts of the future aren't meant to be revealed. Besides, it's jumbled. Anything can change the outcome." Shaelynn sighed and leaned back against Ilian, looking at a single star that had managed to come out before the sun had set. The moon was out as well; it was a perfect crescent moon with an edge that curved nearly all the way around. The star was directly to the left of it.

"Ilian, what is that star?" she asked the unicorn.

"It tells the time of year. When you came here, you first saw that same moon, but the star was to its right, am I correct?"

"Yes."

"Now it is to the left of it, and the season is moving into autumn."

"How does it work?"

"As the moon circles the land, it takes a different path throughout the year. As it moves around the sky, the star seems to move in circles around the moon. At the top, it is winter. It moves to the right; it is spring. At the bottom is summer, and to the left is autumn. In the far north and south, I have heard that the star hides behind the moon in winter but will remain visible most of the day in the summer. It is peculiar."

"That's neat."

"Yes, it is. Now, get some rest. You have much more to do tomorrow." With a groan she settled herself and both were soon asleep.

The next morning, Shaelynn was nudged awake by Ilian's velvety muzzle. Grudgingly she blinked her eyes open to the sun, just risen. She slowly stretched and got to her feet, leaning on Ilian until she was awake enough to regain her balance.

"Today, you'll be working with the stone again, as I said before, but you won't be coloring it," Ilian started, kicking the stone towards her. Shaelynn rubbed the sleep out of her eyes, barely paying attention. She blinked her eyes rapidly to try and get them to stay open.

"You'll be becoming the stone today, Shaelynn."

Belatedly, she started. "What?"

"You will be becoming the stone. Your mind will enter it, you will explore its depths, and if it were a person or creature, you will learn how to search its being and be able to know its every move."

"But it's a rock, Ilian. I already know what it's going to do: it'll sit there unless *I* move it."

"True. But everything has life, even the stone. You will search for it. Now—sit down, right next to the stone. There. Close your eyes-"

"Ilian?" Shaelynn interrupted.

"Yes?"

"Why can't I do this on you?"

Ilian hesitated. He said slowly, "My mind is too . . . . complex, I guess you could say. Since I can see and do so much, it would be too much for your own mind. It would overwhelm you, and I am not sure what will happen to you, but it cannot be good." He stopped, trying to think of something to compare it to that she could understand.

"Shaelynn, did Sorvo ever tell you about when he and Dasriel tried to put their minds together in order to reach Liz's mental connection?"

"Um, I think so."

"Well, they did it. With their two minds combined, they had enough strength to stretch a connection over hundreds of miles."

"So? What about it?"

"When they reached Liz's mind, Avernus, Zathos's servant sorcerer, was waiting for them. He was in Liz's mind as well. He spoke to them, but they broke the connection quickly enough for Avernus to fail."

"Fail at what?"

"Capturing them. Through Liz's mind, he could have captured their minds. They would be mentally connected to Liz as long as he held them there. Their bodies would have been trapped in the cell Sorvo was being held in, and their minds would have been enslaved by Avernus."

"Can he really do that?"

"Oh, yes. If he had trapped them there in Liz's mind, anything he did to her they would have suffered also. If they had been captured, Avernus could have killed your cousin and killed the other two at the same time. Such is the power of mind and magic, it is not something easily trifled with."

Shaelynn remained silent, thinking. After a moment she said, "I think I understand what you said about your mind now. I'll work with the rock as best I can." Ilian nodded and helped her through the first part of the lesson.

"Now, concentrate, and focus on the rock. Let your hands feel it for now. It will help. Allow your mind to travel down your body, down one of your arms, into your fingertips, and into the rock. Slowly, at first. When you have done it, let your mind open up to the rock, and search for anything interesting you can tell me about."

He stood silently for a good half hour, letting her work in peace. Finally, she spoke. Her eyes flew open and she said, "Ilian, I did it!

When my mind reached the rock, it was like running into a brick wall, but I got around it, sort of. Then it was just, like, empty, but it was still there, in a way. There was something that felt different than the rest, I don't know how, but I could tell it was different. It was hard to get to it, but it was like the rock had a mind."

Ilian nodded appraisingly. "Very good. That was something like the stone's spirit that you ran into. As I told you, everything has a spirit, even the ground you sit on. Search for it."

Shaelynn did as told, letting her mind travel down her left arm and into her palm, which she held to the ground. She let her mind enter a small portion of the ground, and it spread all through it. There—that same feeling as she had felt with the rock. Something knowing, something alive. It was everywhere. She pulled her mind back to herself and opened her eyes again.

"You were right. Even the ground does," she told him.

"Yes. Everything has a spirit of its own, and so you can search anything you wish to, as long as it isn't something like me that could ruin you. Through this searching, you can enter the object's spirit, as you did with the stone, and know its thoughts, how it acts, how it reacts. Try the sand now, not just the ground in general. When you come back to yourself, make sure that you know what it will do in case of a heavy rain, or what it used to do."

Shaelynn nodded and closed her eyes. She let her mind travel into the ground, but she kept it to the surface. Letting her mind do what she wanted it to in this way was easier now. It traveled to the ground faster and searched the sand faster. She wondered how good at this she could eventually get.

She found the sand's spirit. It was easy enough to find, but it felt extremely stubborn to her. She had to almost beat her way in, if that made sense. A flood of—thoughts, she supposed—came at her. She filtered through them a little slowly, trying to find the one Ilian had told her. Then she found it.

It seemed to be yelling, in a quiet kind of way. Still, it was strong in her mind. *The rains have not come! Time has passed, long time. Rains not come! Wait for rain, lot of rain. Spread out in water, soak up, let grass grow again!* It seemed to be louder, but the thought was only repeating itself, so Shaelynn went back to herself.

"It wants the rains to come. It said it had been a long time, and the rains had not come. It waits for it. It said it would spread out and soak it up, and it wanted that to happen so the grass could grow back." She opened her eyes after saying this, and saw Ilian's muzzle to the ground. She was about to say something about him ignoring her, until she noticed the ground he was inspecting—it was glowing, a faint yellow-white. It disappeared after a moment, and Ilian seemed to snap out of his reverie. He looked at her, his eyes wide.

"What happened?" Shaelynn asked nervously at the look he was giving her. "Why was the ground glowing like that?" Wordlessly Ilian walked to her and gently pressed his horn to her forehead. The same blinding light filled her eyes as it had before the first time he had done this to her, and she closed them to shut it out.

Words filled her mind, spoken by a woman: "For as she trains for the battle, she will become stronger, more powerful than any we have known. Spirits will alight at the touch of her mind, and nearly anything will do her bidding. She is destined to save Partaenia from corruption, from the evil that has taken over. Watch over her, Ilian, Unicorn of the Far West, In the Lands Unknown, for her life depends on you."

The words stopped, and the light faded. Shaelynn's head spun, and Ilian almost fell to the ground in exhaustion, barely able to get his legs folded underneath him in time. It scared Shaelynn.

"Are you all right, Ilian?" she asked.

"Yes. That took more out of me than I expected it would, that is all."

"Ilian, was that about me? What that woman said?"

"I did not think that it was, but now I see that it is. The girl she spoke of is you." Silently Shaelynn reflected on the words in disbelief. That was her? More powerful than anyone ever known? There had to be a mistake, but Ilian had said that it was her, and why would he say that to her if it wasn't real?

"So—the ground glowing—that was the sand's spirit?"

"The part of it that you touched, yes. If you had spread your mind out even farther, more of it would have glowed."

"Who was that woman? When did she tell you that?"

"She is a fortuneteller, of sorts. She told me that years ago."

"How could she know I would come? I haven't been here a year, even."

"She is the one that all unicorns go to, to learn about themselves. It is then that a unicorn learns about finding a Guide and being a Follower. He learns where he came from, and he learns who he is to be."

"What is her name? This woman?"

"You will meet her someday. You will learn then."

"All right. So—this thing she said about me—what does it mean? Why did she say it?"

"You are the one that will destroy Zathos, and in the process, rid the entire land of everything he has touched. Everything will be returned to the way it was before. She told me that in hopes that I would someday find you. You are the only one that can do it."

"If she told you about me, why didn't you know it was me first off?"

"She said I had to find the person; I thought it was Elizabeth. The shaman didn't tell me that this person would be my Guide. I thought that my Guide would lead me to her. And you did, in a way."

"So, my cousin isn't going to be the one to fight Zathos like she thought?"

"Correct. You will fight him. How it turns out, I do not know."

"But the woman said I was the one that would defeat him."

"You will most likely defeat him, yes, but he might take you down with him."

"Can't you see it?"

"No. There are too many factors. It is not even a jumble in my mind, like some other things can be. This one does not even take a form yet. It is impossible to tell."

"Ilian?"

"Yes?" he asked, hearing the worry in her voice.

"What will happen to you if I die?"

He didn't say anything for a while, he only stared into her eyes unblinking for a long time. Finally he seemed to wake up. "Without you, I will die as well. When you die, I will follow soon after. A unicorn can rarely live out the rest of his life without his Guide. We seek Guides to find purpose in our lives. Without them, we are lost. Once we have them, our lives finally make sense. When we lose what we have once had, our life is meaningless, worse than before. There is no point in it, and we wither away."

"What about dragons and their Bonded? What happens when one dies?"

"If either dies, the other dies at that same instant. It does not matter if it is the rider or the dragon. Both die at the exact moment the other does. It is their one weakness."

"That's why Zathos didn't kill Liz? He needed her alive if he wanted Sorvo alive? So he could find out where the dragons are hidden, right?"

"Yes. If he had killed Liz, Sorvo would have died, and he would have had to wait until another dragon revealed itself, if it ever did. The problem, though, was that he almost did kill her. He expected Sorvo to come running to save her, but he didn't expect Sorvo to be captured. In his haste, he forgot to keep Liz alive if he needed her to be. He tortured her endlessly, and didn't give her any food or water. If Avernus hadn't knocked her out for over two weeks, and her body hadn't shut itself down, she would have died of starvation, dehydration, or both."

He stopped and climbed to his feet wearily, a little out of breath when he was on all four feet. "Now—since I know who you are, I can finally train you the right way. I have helped you some, but we must continue. Come now, stand up."

Shaelynn stood, still in shock, but was able to register the rock lying at her feet. "What you did with the sand," Ilian told her, "do with the stone. I want to see that whole thing glowing, okay?"

"Sure." She knelt down and placed her hands on the rock. Her mind traveled down both arms this time, flowing out of her palms and into the rock. She kept her eyes open, and her concentration was just as good as with her eyes closed. Her mind found the rock's spirit and butted through its brick wall. As she watched, the rock took on a faint shimmer that grew to a brilliant glow as her mind spread through the whole rock. She felt like she knew the rock better than herself. For an instant, she felt she was the rock. In that instant, the rock's glow grew to a blinding light, a pure, white light, different from the yellowish glow.

The rock exploded in her hands, but its pieces somehow missed her and Ilian. Shaelynn looked down at her hands. Only dust remained. She looked around her, and all she could see was a lot of dust blowing away in the wind. It cleared, and Ilian was standing in front of her. He had backed away a little.

"That was much more than I could have expected on the third day of training," he said. "Did you feel as if you were the stone for a moment?"

"Yes."

"That is what I thought. When you take on the mind of an object in the way that you did, it exists no more. You have taken it on. In the future you may find yourself a bit more like a rock—solid, stubborn, determined."

"Can I use that to defeat Zathos?"

"It would not be safe. Like I said, when you do that, you have taken it on mentally. He could find a way to eventually take you over."

"What can I do, then?"

"I teach you how to use your abilities and your strengths. You figure it out from there."

"How did I get these abilities, anyway? And why can't you tell me what I'm supposed to do?"

"You decided to take this on, and you found those abilities inside yourself. When I told you to change the color of the stone on the first day, you simply had to think of changing brown to blue. You called your own magic to the surface, and you knew how to use it. I only needed to help it along. And I can't tell you what you're supposed to do because I don't know. I can't see that. You need to figure it out for yourself."

"I had the magic inside me?" Shaelynn asked, Ilian's answer to her second question forgotten.

"Everyone and everything does. They just have to find it—and learn how to use it."

Chapter 15

WE FLEW FOR HOURS, HEADING in a general southern direction. Honoras said the change of plans was for more things for me to work with. When the time for the battle came, we would fly over the army Tayna and Geoff had gathered.

So when we finally stopped in the forest just at the edge of the plain, Honoras said we were directly south of the camp, and only thirty or so miles away. We would be able to reach it in under an hour if need be.

We have five days at the most, Wraetha said when we had landed and gotten everything unloaded. *We will work assuming we have three days. Liz, you go and find a good branch full of green leaves, say from an aspen. And Jacey, find a couple of fighting staves as well. Liz, if you've found a branch and he isn't done, just come back. Sorvo and I will teach you today.*

All right. I walked with Jacey into the woods. All the branches on the aspens had a few leaves, but Jacey said they were too small for what Wraetha wanted.

"What am I supposed to do with it, anyway?" I asked.

"They're going to have you change it," he said simply.

"Change it?" I asked.

Without speaking he plucked a leaf from a branch close to his head, holding it out in his palm. He stared at it for a moment, then I began to see spots of brown appear on the leaves, following the pattern of its veins.

"I direct my magic to the cells of the leaf, and take away the green from inside. They'll ask you to do this, and other things."

"What other kinds of things have you learned?" I asked, curious.

"Watch." Jacey picked up one of the fist-sized rocks and handed it to me, and then backed up a few steps. When he was about ten feet away he said, "Throw it at me." I tossed the rock at him. He caught it and threw it back hard so that I had to scramble to get out of its way.

"Get another one and *throw* it," he said. I picked up another rock at my foot and hurled it straight at him. I watched it to make sure I didn't hit him and couldn't believe what I saw.

The rock stopped in midair, of its own accord. Jacey stared at me as it turned circles around his head. Then it came to me and did the same thing. After a few circles it dropped to the ground.

"You'll learn more in time." He reached to a branch at about hip-level, a small aspen branch full of leaves. "This'll do. Take it to them." Still wondering at Jacey's performance, I walked back to the dragons in the clearing they had picked.

I suppose he had to show off for you? Wraetha asked as soon as I walked into sight.

Yes. Was that magic he used? I bent down and put the rock on the ground between us.

Aye, Honoras said. *And you will be using it as well. Jacey has ruined the lesson a little bit, but it will be all right. Now—I want you to take a leaf in your hand, and for a moment just explore it with your mind. Focus on it, put your mind over it, in it, throughout it. I want you to learn to direct your mind to the leaf. This will direct your magic there as well.*

Like you told me to when I learned to mind-speak?

Aye. Concentrate like that. Focus on letting your mind ecplore the leaf.

Okay, I said uncertainly. I stared at the leaf and willed my mind to enter it. Nothing happened.

Don't just will it, make it. Closing your hand lightly over the leaf will help direct the magic to it. I did so, and felt something like a stream of energy collecting in the center of my palm. Again I stared at the leaf, and let my mind wander into it. I entered a center vein of the leaf, following it all the way to its outer edge. The veins fed the cells around them, and the cells channeled their own products into the veins. Going backwards from a cell to the stem of the leaf, I found different types of veins within the leaf, each designed to carry something different than the others. When I was done I looked up at Honoras, smiling excitedly.

Good, now I want you to find the source of the green within the cells of the leaf. Pick a cell, enter it, and remove its green, redirecting it backwards through the veins until it comes out the stem and onto your hand. Then do it again, until a whole section of the leaf has turned brown and you have a visible green substance in your hand.

I let my mind enter the leaf again, exploring the closest cell until I found small chambers of green where energy was converted inside the cell. I felt a weight pulling at my arm and at my mind, but the color left the cell and began to travel down to the stem. In a few minutes I had a visible section of the leaf turned brown and a growing mass of fine green substance at the stem's end, though not onto my palm yet. Shortly after this my concentration broke, and the section of leaf regained its color.

That's all right, Wraetha said encouragingly.

Just like with the bracelet, Liz, don't let your concentration slip. Keep it up, and it will get better. I tried three times before I could get the green to stay outside of the leaf, and finally moved it out onto my palm: a tiny amount of fine green substance. Beads of sweat had formed on my brow when Honoras told me I could drop the leaf onto the forest floor. Exhausted, I sank onto a rock and let go of the leaf, most of it a light brown color now.

All right, Wraetha said. *We are here to find your strengths, and enhance them. Something you don't realize is that you now have more abilities than you know, more than magic and more than that bracelet.*

What are they, then? Where did I get them?

First, we need to find out what they are. They could be anything. But where you got them from, is my son. Dragons give their Bonded two abilities, or Gifts, and only two. They could be anything—shape shifting, flying, invisibility, mastery of the elements, communication, locating, healing, anything. We hope to help you learn how to use these Gifts so you can use them effectively in battle.

This portion of training can take years at best. Trainers will take their time with the trainees, having them do simple tasks in different ways to see if anything unusual appears.

But, they can also look to the dragons that gave them the Gifts. Whatever the dragon favors, it is likely that the rider's Gifts will match that. So, we will look to the both of you.

After she had said this Jacey appeared, as if right on cue. They started questioning us both, and at the same time, having us do something else. Jacey had me practice sword fighting with him, and Wraetha took Honoras into the sky, but I could hear them a little and knew that she was interrogating him just as Jacey was interrogating me.

He thrust his stave at me for the fifteenth time and asked another question: "When Zathos had you, did you experience any weird feelings?"

I blocked his blow and thrust my own stave at him and answered, "Right now, all I can remember was when I was knocked out and somehow I saw you and Wraetha, and she somehow saw me."

"Yeah, that was pretty weird. We might look into that. Anything else that comes to mind?"

"No, not really, unless trying to melt into a wall is unusual, especially if an evil sorcerer is trying to kill you, or so you think."

"True enough. How about in Barda?"

"Um, I'm not sure. Let me think." We fought each other for a few more minutes. "All I can really think of in Barda," I said, after a while, "is my two fights with Karbab. He beat me both times, and both times he was set on killing me. Uh . . . I felt close to the horses at the stable, but I always feel like that around horses."

"You always feel like how?" he asked, blocking another one of my blows. He spun around and tried to take me by surprise with a strike from the left hand. I blocked it a little uneasily. He was getting better.

"I feel like I know them, like I'm one of them. But I'm supposed to think like a horse if I'm going to ride it, right? And I need to understand them too. So that explains that."

"Perhaps. Sometimes a rider's Gifts can reflect the rider's interests. Anything else come to mind? How about at different places of the town? Anything weird there?"

"Um, no, I don't think so. Not that I remember right now." Jacey rapped my arm with his stave. Instead of flinching, I spun to get away from it and rapped him back. Jacey smiled.

"Retaliation is good," he remarked. He spun in another circle, feinted a left-handed strike, and knocked my shoulder with his right hand while I was trying to block the feint. He went for my middle, I blocked it. He went for my shoulder again; I spun this time, with my foot out. It connected with his chest, knocking him to the ground, winded. I leapt on top of him and held my stave at his chest.

"As I thought," he smiled. "Just like a horse." He got to his feet with my help, and then we both looked to the skies. Wraetha and Honoras were wrestling with each other in the sky. Honoras was doing well, given that his mother was twice his size. It made him faster, at least.

"Can you hear what they're saying?" Jacey asked me.

I listened for a moment and said, "Yeah. She's asking him most of the same questions you were asking me, how he felt about being in the prison and stuff like that. Can't you hear them? They're loud enough."

"No. I can't." I turned to him, shocked.

"You must be able to. I heard them earlier, too, before we started fighting."

"No. Only you can. I can't," he repeated. "That's your Gift. You can hear animals. Dragons for now, but you can hear all of them if you wanted to. Try it. Listen for—a bird, or something. I bet you can understand them if you try."

I let my mind wander around the forest around me, looking for an animal that hadn't been scared off by us. I found one—a bird, small. Maybe a finch or something, loudly chirping. It was young, just out of the nest. It was scared, because it knew to be scared of humans. But it had never seen anything like the big ones, and his mother hadn't told him of them either. They terrified him.

'It's all right,' I told him. 'They're dragons, but they won't hurt you. And neither will we.' The finch flew off, to a safer place where humans didn't talk to him. I frowned and looked at Jacey. He was smiling.

"What?" I asked, irritated at his look.

"Do you know what you just did?"

"I listened to the bird."

"And you talked to him. You tweeted just like a bird, it was so weird. So, what did he say? And what'd you tell him?"

"He was scared of us, and he'd never seen a dragon. I told him we were all right, and he flew off where 'humans didn't talk to him,' as he put it. That's all."

"Can you do that again? But talk to those two up there? Tell them we've found out one of your Gifts." I nodded, and tried to focus on them again. As before, I could hear them talking. They were arguing about something he'd done at the town he'd been held at.

'Wraetha, Sorvo, I've found one of my Gifts,' I told them loudly, so they could hear. I looked to Jacey for approval. He had his hands over his ears.

"Don't ever shout in dragon," he told me. "You're a lot louder than you think."

The two dragons in the sky stopped in midair, sinking about a hundred feet before they caught themselves. *I'll say you've found it,* Honoras said, laughing. I smiled as he landed next to me. He folded his wings in tight while his mother landed too.

How did you find it? Wraetha asked Jacey while Honoras had me do a demonstration of a dragon call for new hatchlings. Jacey didn't want to shout I suppose, so while he used mind-speech I listened intently over the sound of my own noise when he answered.

We were fighting, and I was asking her a lot of questions, just like you were asking Sorvo. I rapped her arm, and she rapped it back—retaliation. Stubbornness. I spun and whapped her shoulder. She spun around and kicked me, throwing me back on the ground and winding me—just like a horse. She'd told me earlier that she felt closer to horses than really anything, and sometimes she felt like one of them. That was what tipped me off. Then she said that she could hear you two clearly, even though you were keeping your conversation to yourself.

Very good, Jacey. Now, we have one more thing to work with. That reminds me: how are her skills?

"They are excellent," he said aloud now that I was quiet, "but they need to be kept in shape and improved a little. Mostly it is in her mind. She got nervous when I gave more of myself to the fight."

That can only be expected, Honoras said protectively. *She was nearly killed twice by the same man. Both times he overpowered her with his skill. What else can she do?*

I could get over it, I said. Everyone's eyes were on me, and I tried to ignore them. *I could learn to just ignore it and keep fighting. Can't my abilities and the magic, and the bracelet help me anyway?*

True enough. But like Jacey said, it is all mostly in your mind. You need to learn to control that emotion. Nothing whatsoever should be bothering you while you are in combat.

All right. Before I practice with the bracelet at night, Jacey and I can practice, and he can get better than me. I'll improve with him, hopefully, and I'll be good to go.

If you think that will work, then we will do it. Wraetha nodded with me at Honoras's words, as did Jacey. Wraetha then turned to me.

Your communicating skills we can work on later as well. For now, I need both of you—no, all of you,—in the air so we can find out your second Gift. Liz, don't fasten the leg buckles. Most of the time fear and anger can help these kind of discoveries along. I gulped and nodded, and then got on Honoras. I felt vulnerable without the buckles.

Do you really think I would let you fall? he asked me privately. *Don't worry; trust me, and all will go well.*

Through his words I could hear Wraetha talking to Jacey while they took off. She was telling him that while she was questioning him, he kept coming back to someone that would enjoy flying with him.

When he was a fledgling, she said, *he loved flying. But he was the only young dragon there. I asked him what he wished for most in a companion, and he said someone who enjoys the same kinds of things that he does. Maybe her Gift is flying.*

I tuned them out, overjoyed at this possibility. What if I really could go flying with Honoras like he wanted to? I was about to tell him what I had learned, but Wraetha came close to talk to us.

We will go high, maybe five and a half miles up. There are some maneuvers that require some room to do them.

Are you ready, Elizabeth? Honoras asked.

I told you to call me Liz, I grumbled in response, making him laugh. His mother let him rise first; he turned almost vertical to the ground, beating his wings hard. We flew high, and the oxygen became thin.

Watch the air, Honoras said. *At the land's high altitude plus our height, there is less air, and it can affect you.*

Finally he leveled out and flew in slow circles. Wraetha came up a minute later, speeding past us, still going up. Sharply she turned and leveled out, but from a hundred yards straight above us, I saw Jacey slip and fall.

He plummeted toward us; Honoras moved to catch him, but missed. I reached out at the same time, and he reached out to me. We locked wrists, but I couldn't hold myself on to Honoras. I was jerked off his back, and fell with Jacey.

Honoras roared and was about to dive for us, but his mother stopped and hovered next to him, and he stopped too, reluctantly.

I was still holding on to Jacey and we were still falling. Seeing Honoras stopping himself from rescuing me tore my heart apart and nearly stopped it. The wind from our fall flipped us over and I could see the ground rushing up to meet me. Any other thoughts flew from my mind; the only ones that remained were those of dying and of Honoras stopping himself. I panicked, shut my eyes, and held on tighter to Jacey for some support.

Just as I expected my body to smash into the ground at a hundred miles an hour, I felt a change in my body. It was like a tickling sensation in my shoulders. I felt my body stop in the air and a burning near my shoulder blades as whatever was there caught my body. I felt myself moving forward, instead of down. My eyes flew open to find myself just above the treetops.

One particular tree stood about seven feet above the rest, and I was headed straight for it. Without pause, I shifted my shoulders and my body sideways. I veered to the right and missed the tree.

Wondering how I did that, I turned to look at what had saved me. I saw a flash of feathers and then I was falling again; I shut my eyes and Jacey yelled in surprise. Somehow I shifted my body without thinking and righted myself, but when I opened my eyes I saw I was beginning to sink lower and lower.

Carefully I took a quick glance at my back again. Ash-grey wings had sprouted from my back, both of them six feet in length. Again I realized I was losing altitude.

"Liz, flap them!" Jacey yelled at me. Somehow we were still holding on to each other. Oddly enough, he felt light.

I snapped back to reality after my foot grazed a treetop. The second I thought of flapping my wings, they obeyed. Shocked, the thought flew from my mind and they stopped flapping. Desperately I thought hard of flapping them. They immediately obeyed once again. Just to see if it would work, I thought about flying back up to Honoras and Wraetha. My body pointed itself upward, and my wings flapped harder, quickly carrying me up to them.

Elizabeth, they're wonderful! Honoras yelled gleefully in my mind. *You look beautiful with them.*

Yeah, but never do that again, I snapped irritably. I looked at Wraetha, who was staring at them. *Catch,* I yelled at her, and flung Jacey high above her head. He arced in the air and fell downward once again. He pointed himself at her tail, and grabbed on to it. She bent it downward with his momentum and slowed him, and then she whipped it back up. Jacey sailed over her back, just above her wings. He did a showy flip in the air and landed on her back.

He smiled smugly at me, wiping away any satisfaction I had gotten from flinging him through the air. *Nice try*, he said.

It's getting dark, Wraetha said. *Land in the clearing.* She glided down. Just for kicks, Jacey stood up and waved at me as she did so.

I was about to follow them when Honoras stopped me. *Elizabeth, stay up here. Let's see how your new wings are.* I knew he meant to be serious, but the joy in his voice was evident. It was enough to help me agree and fly over the trees.

Not too long, Honoras, Wraetha said. I knew she kept it private; Jacey's thoughts gave nothing away that he had heard Honoras's real name. I let Honoras lead the way in various maneuvers, most of which I could do. It was odd; I simply thought of wanting to do something like he did, and I did it. The split second that I thought of doing something, my wings obeyed. I told Honoras of this.

You are lucky. Dragons can use sheer instincts to save themselves if they must, but we must move our wings the same way we do everything else. It is much like how you humans learn to walk. It is difficult, but it gets so easy that we do not think of it. I think it might get that way for you, eventually. I think your wings move automatically for now because they had to in order to catch you when you were falling.

You didn't know they were going to do that, did you? I asked him. He knew immediately that I was talking about him not catching me.

No. But you heard them talking, didn't you? Your elation was evident before Jacey dropped.

Yes. She said when she was talking with you, you kept coming back to flying. And you said you wanted a companion that would enjoy the same things you did.

True. And I am happy that you can now fly with me. But it broke my heart when my mother ordered me to stop and not rescue you. Even as he spoke I could feel his grief.

What did she tell you? I asked him, looking him straight in the eye. *Because my heart nearly stopped. And what you did tore it wide open. I thought I would die, and you would let me.*

She said to wait. To see what you would do. When you got where you did when your wings sprouted, she had just told me that I could go for the both of you. I would never willingly let you die. Did I tell you what happens when one of a Bonded dies?

No.

When one dies, it does not matter which, the other dies in the same instant. That is how I knew you were alive when you were in Zathos's hands—I was not dead as well. And that is why the bond is close; if one dies, so does the other. We must keep each other alive. It is also our weakness. Even an evil dragon will not trade off its rider's life, nor vice versa.

He turned in a tight circle and waited for me to follow. I did so easily. *Honoras?*

Yes?

Did you choose this Gift for me, and did I choose the other?

No. These Gifts have been evident ever since the first Sorva di Fravid *Bonded to one another. We aren't sure what creates the Gifts, but we know that one cannot command them to appear. Many dragons say that the Gifts reveal themselves according to what will best serve the two in the future, and so they say that they are Gifts from unicorns. On the other hand, other dragons argue that whatever is wished for most in the two companions' lives is given. But the thought must be purely subconscious. They say that the powers of the mind enable them to appear. If we try to make it happen with our normal thoughts, it will not happen. These thoughts are the ones that can create evil, and so it penetrates that power and that Gift cannot be bestowed.*

So your wants were totally subconscious? If you said them to Wraetha, how did it happen?

Your Gifts had already started to appear. And I was only stating the emotions I had been feeling since I was a fledgling. I had no affect on them.

Honoras, Wraetha's voice floated up from below us. *She needs to practice. It is getting darker and soon they won't be able to see to swordfight.*

Yes, mother. Hey, Elizabeth, he said, turning to me excitedly. *Try this before we land.* He pumped his wings in a way I recognized, gained speed, and then spread his wings as they carried him in a loop through the air. As he came out of it he beat his wings again and sped forward. He pulled himself up and nodded for me to go.

I thought of flying forward, fast. In a millisecond my wings had started pumping. I thought of doing a loop. They fanned out, and carried me upside down. Just as Honoras had, I pumped my wings again as I came out of the curve, but then I kept their fast rhythm going and did it again.

Honoras laughed out loud, a kind of barking sound. *That is one of the reasons I chose you,* he said, gliding down in a spiral. *You can be spontaneous sometimes.*

What's another reason? I asked, interested. He chuckled in my mind when he answered.

You've got spunk. He laughed again and landed. I grinned and followed suit. When I started to fold my wings, Wraetha stopped me.

Keep them open, and hover above the ground. I want to see how they move. She came close to me, as did Jacey. While Jacey walked circles around me to see how the rest of my body moved with them, Wraetha could simply move her head around either side of me.

They're extremely flexible, and will obey you at the slightest thought, am I right? Wraetha asked. I nodded.

"Think fast!" Jacey yelled, throwing a punch at my face. Without thinking I blocked it and kicked him in return. I sent him flying fifteen feet back. I was sitting on top of him in the next instant. My mind had never registered any thought at all. I had just done it.

"Oh, man. You got a lot stronger than I thought you did," he said, wheezing. He sat up, wincing and holding his side. "I don't think you broke anything, but they're bruised all the same."

"I got stronger?" I asked him, still trying to remember when I had thought of kicking him.

"Aye." I helped him to his feet. "When we were falling, you had a death grip on me. As soon as your wings appeared, your grip slackened but you were still holding on to me. And when you threw me in the air, even I couldn't have thrown you the way you threw me."

Your thinking has become faster as well, Honoras observed.

"That will help in battle," Jacey said. "I'll bet in one night you can improve by a landslide."

Aye, you need to practice. First do it on your feet, and then in the air. You need to get your coordination down. I nodded at Honoras. Jacey led the way across our clearing, away from the dragons and the fire they had started to make. At the edge of the trees we found a couple of wooden staves. I folded my wings tightly and told them to stay there.

Jacey threw the first blow. I parried without thinking, already watching him to calculate his next move. I struck back in the fashion that he had. He parried as well, then spun a circle, feinted a left, and struck at my right side. Again I parried with hardly any thought, and repeated his move, but instead of feinting like he had, I struck at his left for real, which was not what he was expecting, I could tell. My stave whapped his side.

"Very good!" he panted. "One more time on the ground, and then you can use your wings." While he was finishing his sentence, he tried to take me by surprise. It almost worked, but I struck back at the same instant I had blocked it. We held each other off for a minute or two, and then his skill improved by a mile. I could still tell, though, that it was not his best.

It was more of a challenge now, but my new thinking allowed me to learn fast. I had beaten him again in another minute. He stood with his hands on his knees, catching his breath. He looked up at me and held the base of his neck, where I had hit him a little too hard. I could see a red mark.

"I wouldn't want to fight you with real swords," he said quietly. "That would have easily taken someone's head clean off." I was taken aback. He was scared of me now? "You can use your wings now," he was saying, "but in a few minutes. Let me catch my breath." He walked to the fire, and I followed. Jacey sat down, holding his side and his breath while he did it. I knew what he felt.

"Perhaps I can heal that, before the battle," I offered. "If I can figure out the bracelet."

"That would be good," he said.

Just be careful with it. Practice many times before you try to heal someone else. Many things can go wrong, Wraetha said.

Practice now, while you are waiting on him, Honoras said. *Come here. I'll make a shallow cut. That way if it doesn't work, it won't bother you.* I went to him and held out my arm. He took it and carefully made a small cut on it with one of his claws. It was enough to draw a little blood.

Remember what Desarti told you. Concentrate. I sat down by him and took the bracelet in my hand. I want the wound healed, I told it.

The beads glowed, and the cut was shortened a little, but most of it was still there. *Try putting it on the wound,* Honoras suggested. I did so and asked the bracelet again. The carvings glowed, and the cut closed itself. I rubbed the skin. It was flawless.

Try it again, Honoras said. *Careful, I'll make it deeper and longer. Give me the other arm.* I held it out, without question. If Honoras recommended it, I'd do it. Quickly he slashed my arm. I flinched, but it was not too bad.

I placed the bracelet over most of the cut, and asked it to heal the wound. Again the beads glowed, and again the wound quickly healed. No marks were present, except for the blood that had run on my arm a little. I wiped it off and showed everyone.

"I'd still like you to practice a little," Jacey said, though he was impressed. "Those are surface wounds. Bruised ribs are underneath the skin."

He's right, Honoras said. *Those kinds of wounds are hardest, because you cannot see them. You must tell the bracelet exactly what you want it to do.*

"Are you ready?" Jacey asked. In answer I opened my wings and picked myself up off the ground with them. He smiled, shaking his head. "Let's go at it, then." He leaped for his stave and brandished it at me. We fought for a while, and he pulled out all the stops. Finally, after both of us were tiring, he managed to jab my lower side.

"You almost had me, but not quite," he said gleefully. "You're improving by the second, though. You're three times better than you were when you fought Karbab. If he could see you now, he'd make a run for it, I'm sure." We laughed. I knew he meant well, but the memories weren't pleasant. Still, I kept my thoughts to myself and did not tell him. Exhausted, we sat down by the fire. I had just closed my wings and was about to sit down as well when Wraetha spoke.

Wait, you said you would practice with the bracelet, she reminded me. *You told me that after you practiced with Jacey, you would practice with the bracelet.*

But I already did.

That was to see if it would let you heal. Desarti said to try and concentrate on other things and keep your original task going. It is something all of us think you need to master. The other two nodded when she said this. I sighed, and then opened my wings once again, taking flight.

I'll find another clearing nearby, I told them. Honoras nodded at me, and then turned back to his mother, who had started a conversation with them. She was saying something about what Zathos would most likely do for the battle, what creatures would be present, how he would set up his troops, and things like that. It didn't interest me at the moment, though it should have, so I tuned them out.

I flew high at first, the waning moon creating a crescent shape just like the one that Shaelynn and I had seen on our first night in Partaenia. The star that had been to the right of the moon was now directly to the left of it. I stared at it for a while, bewildered. In three days it waned from a full moon to a crescent, and now I saw that the star moved around it. Shaking my head to clear my mind, I focused it on the bracelet. I wish to turn transparent, I told it. In a moment the colors of the land had changed, and the same faint purple glow I had seen the first time outlined my body. I took a quick glance at my wings. They had turned transparent as well.

From this high, I could see small campfires on the horizon, to the north. It was the camp we had left Dasriel at. As I thought of this, my transparency flickered. I held on to it, and gave most of my attention to keeping it going, the other small part focused on keeping my wings beating. After a few minutes of this, I flew in circles and kept up the transparency.

When I had gotten to flying flips and sharp turns in the air, I was confident that I could keep it up and check on everyone I knew at the camp. What would it hurt? I mean, they couldn't see me, and I'd stay up high enough. Deciding that it was all right, and it would be good practice for my concentration and my wings, I headed for the small campfires in the distance.

Chapter 16

THE SMALL POINTS OF LIGHT from the campfires quickly got closer, and I could see the vast number of people Tayna, Geoff, and Najee had gathered. Tents were everywhere. Some weren't tents but cloaks held up on branches. And still some had no tents and slept in the open.

There weren't very many children to be seen, so it was easy enough for me to spot Najee and his gang. They had gathered wooden staves and were practicing just as Jacey and I had. They were very good. Three or four of them would stand in the center, and the rest would form a circle around them. Four were in the center now: Dush, another boy, and two girls. They faced outward, each of them taking on three or four of their own. If one went down, the one who had beaten him would take the other's place and the other would switch with his defeater. Dush was up against Supai and two girls. He focused on Supai, but one of the girls took the advantage over him. He smiled and laughed with them as he went to the outside and the girl went to the center. Without missing a beat, the fight would be picked up again.

I watched them, still keeping the transparency up. I really didn't need to; no one was looking up. They were either asleep or occupied. I just wanted to be able to concentrate on multiple things at once like Desarti had told me.

For an instant I thought of going and visiting Dasriel or Tayna and Geoff, or maybe even Marl and Shamar, but the thought of showing them my wings on the battlefield erased any temptations of showing them now. It would be a surprise.

I watched the camp for a little while more. The children's tents were in the center of the camp. Marl, Shamar, Agathla, and others I recognized from Barda were near the children and watching them as well. Tayna, Geoff, and Dasriel had their tents together at the far north end of the camp.

After about a half hour, I flew back toward the forest to find a clearing close to the one Honoras and Wraetha had picked, like I told them I would. I found a reasonably close enough one that was small and quiet, and a stream ran on the east end of it. It provided just enough noise to make it comfortable.

I sat cross-legged, still holding my transparency. I thought of other things Desarti had said the bracelet might let me do. The first thing I thought of was shape shifting, but that was a little too difficult for now. There was no point in getting it to make me fly, or in understanding animals. Then I thought of night vision, like an owl's.

Let me be able to see clearly in the dark, I told the bracelet, still keeping a little strand of thought on being transparent. I opened my eyes (I had shut them in case it worked too quickly) and saw everything around me as though it were daylight. I looked down at my faint purple outline. It was clearer than I had ever seen it, though it still seemed faint compared to everything else around me.

I looked around the forest, seeing animals that I had never seen before due to the fact that they were nocturnal. I saw a tiny squirrel, just out of its home and just getting used to the world. An owl flew by and picked it up. It wings were so silent that I had expected to hear it as its wings fluttered down to the squirrel and then took off again, but no sound was made. I almost didn't register that it had been there, save for the fact that I had seen it.

Far off in the trees, where it was thick enough that I could barely tell they were there, a small herd of deer picked their way through the trees, probably headed for the stream. They stopped and looked in my direction. I heard thoughts run through every one of their minds; they could smell me, but they didn't know what I was or where I was. They took a quick sip from the stream and hurriedly left. The young buck that was with them stood and looked in my direction for a long while, and then left after his does.

Just to see what would happen, I made a rabbit's distress call after I knew the owl was done with the squirrel he had caught. In a moment he flew into the clearing, his wings as silent as ever. My elation wiped out my transparency, and I materialized before him. In a heartbeat he had changed direction and was flapping hard for the trees once more, screeching loudly. I could tell that I had scared him badly.

'I meant you no harm,' I told him. He felt better, but still made his way to his nest. Deciding that I had had enough practice and that I had done well, I got up and flew for our clearing again. I listened to their thoughts as I approached. They had been talking of the way Zathos had handled me when I was his captive, but then Honoras heard me coming. He picked up on another subject, thinking I had not heard them. I pretended not to notice as I landed in front of them.

Before they could say anything, I turned transparent in front of them. I acquired my night vision, and silently walked up behind Jacey, who was staring at the spot where I had been. I tickled the back of his neck, took flight when he whipped around, and flew up to brush my feet on the tops of Honoras's wings. He quickly turned in my direction, and I giggled. I turned visible again and landed in front of them again.

Very well done, Honoras said. *What else have you figured out?*

Well, watch this. I turned to where the does had been in the last clearing, knowing they were headed this way. I saw them stopped fifty feet from the edge of our camp. Listening to the buck's thoughts, I knew he was proud of his does and would fight for them. Turning to everyone else, I motioned for them to be quiet.

I let them watch me walk halfway to the other end of the clearing, so they could see my general direction. After this I turned transparent again. When I was in the trees again, I called to the buck.

'Will you fight for your does, young one?' I asked him in my best adult deer voice. I pawed the ground as he came closer.

'It is not season yet, old one,' the buck returned. 'Why do you wish for them now?' I listened to his thoughts to see what answer he expected that would get him going.

'When the season comes,' I told him, 'it is good to have some for myself.' I could hear his bewilderment as he looked for me but could not see me. Still, he was getting worked up.

'How brave are you, young one?' I asked. 'Let me see. Show yourself to the monsters. If you can do that, I will leave you be.'

I knew he did not want to fight, but he wanted to get rid of me. This was another way out of it. I heard him think it over, and then he told his does to stay put. He would come around the other side and call them from there.

I tiptoed to the edge of the trees just as the buck bounded out of the trees and skittered across the clearing. Near the middle, he stopped and looked straight at the other three, and then he barreled off into the trees once more.

'Very well, brave one,' I said. He called his does over, and they left. I walked, still transparent, to the fire and materialized again, smiling. Jacey burst out laughing, and the other two laughed as well.

That was quite a show. What did you tell him to get him to do that? Honoras asked.

I laughed thinking of it, and then told them of my conversation with the deer.

I see you have learned much, Wraetha said. *But tomorrow, I challenge you to learn twice as much.*

Very well. We laughed some more, and then went to bed. It was late; Honoras told me it was already almost the peak of the night. Jacey curled up next to Wraetha in much the same way I did, but with Honoras and I it was different. We were closer than he was to Wraetha. Just before her wing lowered over him, he smiled at me, silently laughing. Wraetha shook her head and tapped the back of his head with the flat of her claw, playfully scolding him. I saw him turn and give her the stink-eye just before she tucked her head under her wing as well.

They're not Bonded, but they're still close, I told Honoras. He nodded and lowered his wing over us too. He tucked his head underneath it and shifted himself a little to get comfortable, and then he relaxed.

Aye. He is KnukSorva, *but still more than that. It is strange to say. I suppose you could say they are almost related. And very close friends at the same time. On a close level to us, they are* wyrla *and* gliad. *Just like you and I.*

Yes, my wyrla. I am glad to have you.

As am I, my gliad.

It is good to call each other that again. It has been long since we have.

Aye, it has. I think I can now call you gliad-Orthis. You are accomplished, but still learning. And you are still dear to me.

Whatever works for you. I yawned. *Can I call you anything else than* wyrla?

No.

Are there no other words?

No, I just like wyrla. Now go to sleep. You can ask more of your endless questions tomorrow. He chuckled at the look I indignantly gave him.

Honoras?

Yes?

Can you sing another dragon lullaby? I've missed them.

Sure. Will you go to sleep, and finally be quiet?

I will. He nudged me gently, and started humming deep in his throat, so that it vibrated his stomach and me as well. In a few minutes I was asleep. Before I nodded off, though, I registered the fact that the lullaby had put Wraetha and Jacey to sleep, too.

The next morning, Wraetha had me up before the sun. I could tell Honoras had been asleep, too. His thoughts murmured in my mind before he could clear them up.

'Uhnnn,' he moaned in his mind. 'Quit nudging me already.' But out loud, he said to his mother, *What's wrong?*

Wake her; it's time to start for the day. I was already awake, and I heard his grumbling before he lifted his wing and gently butted me with his nose, blowing his smoky breath on me.

Time to get up, gliad. It is time to start the day.

Why so early? I asked, sitting up. I yawned.

There is a lot of work to do. Now, up. He lifted a talon and pushed me to my feet. I staggered and gave him a look. He smiled, playfully showing his teeth.

In the air, everyone, Wraetha said. *Liz, go ahead and get on Honoras. No need for the buckles anymore. If you fall, catch yourself and get back on. I want you to be able to ride like Jacey here soon.*

All right, let's do it then. I got on as asked, and we took off. Wraetha worked us hard, even herself. We stayed in the air for hours, doing different maneuvers. There was one that we practiced over the plain, where there was less of a chance of danger. We flew together, side by side, and the two dragons breathed fire upon the ground below, each taking turns to make a continuous line.

Looking behind us, I saw that the fire caught on the grass, but there wasn't enough of it to sustain a flame. It burned for a moment, and then smoldered out, leaving a thin line of smoke rising from the ground. The next time I looked, I realized the different colors of fire that came from the two dragons: green from Honoras, and blue from Wraetha.

Jacey noticed me looking and said, *You should see some of our celebrations we have above the island sometimes. There are dragons of different colors, and so they usually put on a show using their different colors of fire.*

Focus, you two, Wraetha said, signaling to Honoras. At the same time, both of them pulled up sharply. Jacey managed to stop with them, but I kept going. I had to snap my wings open to catch myself and get back on. I sighed to myself; that was the third time I had done that.

Just pay attention, Honoras said.

I'm trying, I said exasperatedly. I could hear him thinking for a moment of what to say. I couldn't get anything out of it until he said it directly to me.

When you ride horses, you must be able to interpret their movements, so you can keep your balance and stay on. Right?

Sure.

If one blows up on you, you must move with it to stay on. You must move with it. Do that now. Pretend I am a horse, if you must. Read my thoughts. Know my movements. Move with me.

Thanks. Things went better from there. I did as Honoras said and pictured him as a horse and used my legs and my head to feel for his movements so I could interpret them and stay with him on everything he did. I fell once; we were flying upside down, and my legs were tired from gripping.

Give them a rest and work your wings, Honoras suggested. *Practice flying with us. When your legs aren't so tired, you can get back on.*

Why do you think of everything?

Because I'm nearly a thousand years older than you, that's why. He grinned again, and we went on flying. Wraetha let us stop for a quick snack for lunch. Jacey caught two rabbits, and Wraetha cooked them. He and I shared them while she and Honoras went hunting. All of us finished around the same time, and we were in the air again.

I managed to stay on Honoras when I was supposed to, but the last part of the day was spent building my endurance. I had to carry Jacey in my arms while maneuvering around Honoras and Wraetha for nearly an hour straight. With my new strength, it was no problem at first, but after forty-five minutes my arms and my wings were aching, and my thoughts were getting fuzzy. I found it hard to concentrate on my pattern. Finally, after ten minutes of this, Wraetha let me land in the clearing once more.

Jacey had to hunt our meal again, and it was again two rabbits. "I wish I had your night vision," he grumbled when he came back carrying them. "I heard loads of things around me, but these two were the only things I could see good enough to shoot." I smiled, and he handed them to Honoras, who cooked them this time. My fingers wouldn't cooperate with me; Jacey had to take it apart and hand me the pieces I could tear apart and eat.

"Looks like you'll be on foot when we practice tonight," he said a little gleefully.

"Shut up. I had you working hard last night before you would let me use them."

"True. But it still wasn't my best."

I think she only has enough energy tonight for working with the bracelet, Honoras said.

"But she needs the practice."

If she had you at nearly your best on the first night, I think she can afford one night's rest from sword fighting. Besides; she'll be in the air most of the time. She'll need her magic, her abilities, and her bow and arrows.

Except when I go up against Zathos, I told him privately. *I'll need everything then.*

Aye. But Jacey is one of the best we've ever seen, even against the centaurs and a few others. If you can be as good as him by the end of tomorrow that is the best we can do. It might make it a fair enough fight then. Besides, you won't be alone. I'll be there helping.

Thank you. He nodded in acknowledgement. Wraetha was talking to Jacey privately, but it was over similar things Honoras and I had just talked of. I tuned them out and listened to the forest around me for a moment.

Voices were everywhere, but nowhere close to here. The closest ones—squirrels, of course—were quiet and cautious. They were fifty yards off in a tree, trying to find a way to get to another one where they were sure there was food. And then, they fought about whether or not there was food there at all. Laughing silently, I listened to other animals.

A herd of cow elk were following the stream a good way off. They could see the flicker of our fire and knew to stay away from it. Leaving the stream, they headed in another direction. The owl I had seen last night was flying behind me; I heard his thoughts snap to attention as he spotted some rodent on the ground. Quickly and efficiently he calculated the right way to get it. In a moment I could hear the satisfaction in his mind after he had caught it.

"Liz?" Jacey asked, bringing me to attention. "You all right?"

"Yeah," I mumbled. "Just listening. It's loud out there, for a forest. Nothing much going on, though."

"Good. Wraetha said to go to your same little clearing."

And remember my challenge, she reminded me. *Learn twice as much as you did last night.*

"All right." Wearily I opened my wings and flew to the treetops, staying just above them as I searched for my clearing. I found it, and glided down in slow circles. I barely caught myself on landing and sat down again. What else would the bracelet let me do?

The first thing that came to mind was energy. For the heck of it, I put it on my wrist. Give me energy to focus on what I'm doing, I told it. A funny feeling ran up my arm and spread throughout my body. It was odd; I knew I was tired and I knew I was sore, but I didn't feel it. It was as if I had just woken up after a good night of sleep.

Keeping up the energy, I let it help me think of other things it would let me do. In a short time I was satisfied with myself and flew back to camp. I could tell that they could immediately see a difference in me: I actually flapped coming down, and my movements weren't as sluggish as they had been before.

You've found energy in it; good, Honoras remarked. I nodded, smiling.

"Honoras, would you like to know what Najee and his gang are doing right now?" I asked. He nodded, smiling in the way he does. I walked to him and placed my hand on his shoulder.

"Close your eyes," I said. He did so, and I called up a vision of the boys and the few girls. They were practicing as they had been when I had seen them. This time all the girls were in the middle. At almost the same instant, all of them beat their opponents and some of the boys had to grudgingly switch with them.

How about Dasriel and Riman? he asked me when the image faded. I called up a vision of them. They were in a tent with Tayna and Geoff, and were heatedly talking about something. Tayna had a map laid out on the ground, and they were all squatted next to it; Geoff was standing and using his hooves to point out something to them.

I'll have to assume that was real, he said, *but I know it is.*

Liz, could you show me someone? Well, both Jacey and I? Wraetha asked.

Yes, who?

Come here. I went to her and placed my hands on both of them. An image of a man appeared in my mind. *He is my Bonded,* she said. I focused hard. It was difficult to find someone I didn't know, but I figured it out all the same. The image that appeared was blurred at first, but it became clear in an instant.

A man dressed in dark robes appeared, sitting on a bed in a small house. He had his head in his hands, but he was staring at a candle in the corner opposite him. The flame flickered, but did not go out. For a minute we watched him staring into it, lost in thought. Wraetha's thoughts were jumbled, but she was telling someone something. The man looked up, straight at where we were seeing him from. He squinted, and then recognition was showing in his weathered face.

So you are the one Honoras chose, he said to me. I searched Wraetha's and Jacey's thoughts, but they said nothing that indicated that they had heard him.

Do not worry, I am making this private. I will not give his name away, not even to Jacey. You have no fear.

Thank you. Who are you?

Wraetha, as you call her, has said so already. I am her Bonded. My name is Yuriel. In case you were wondering, I approve of Honoras's choice. You will do this world good, and you will make us here at Amatol proud. I am sure of that. But you are running out of energy for this. We will see each other soon, Liz. He turned his back and waved his hand, and the image disappeared. I opened my eyes again, and everyone was staring at me.

"He spoke with me," I said softly.

In your mind, Elizabeth. It makes it easier. Honoras called me to him, and I sat down by his side.

Wraetha said something to someone, and he looked straight at me, and he spoke to me.

242

I told him to look to the left, Wraetha said, *where the mirror on his shelf sits. That is how he saw you.*

Well, anyway, he knew that I was the one Sorvo had chosen. He said Sorvo's real name, and I was worried if you had heard it, Jacey. He said that it was private, and that I didn't have to worry about him giving it away.

Yes, he has been particular about that, Wraetha said. *Even when I named my son, he refused to know it at first.*

Anyhow, it was like he knew what I was thinking. He told me his name: Yuriel. And then he said, *'In case you were wondering, I approve of Sorvo's choice. You will do this world good, and you will make us here at Amatol proud.'* And then he said he'd see me soon. He knew I was running out of energy, and he broke the image.

You are right, Honoras said. *He was able to read your mind. It is one of his Gifts. He also has a close connection to you, since he is my mother's Bonded.*

Oh. I'm tired; can I go to sleep now?

Jacey smiled, and the two dragons chuckled. *I suppose,* Honoras said. Wearily I laid down by his side, folding in my wings.

Before I could close my eyes, Wraetha said, *Liz, you have done well today.*

Aye, Honoras said. *We're all proud of you.* I looked to Jacey; he nodded. I smiled, and then closed my eyes as Honoras lowered his wing over me. Honoras told me the next morning that before he could peek his head in to tell me goodnight, I was asleep.

===

Ilian started in his sleep, jerking violently. Shaelynn snapped awake as well, sitting up quickly. She looked around wildly, but there was only Ilian near. She lowered the fist-sized rock she had been levitating in the air.

"Your reflexes are quick," Ilian said appreciatively. "You are ready. And just in time, too. I just had another vision . . . The battle is tomorrow. Come; we must tell the others." He helped push her to her feet with his muzzle, and Shaelynn quickly gathered her things in disbelief: the battle was tomorrow? Was she really ready?

Ilian read her mind as he always did. "Worry of nothing," he said. "I have trained you as best as I can. You will do fine." She gulped, not trusting herself to say anything. Unsteadily she got on his back.

"Make sure you don't slip," Ilian warned her. "We'll be going fast." When she was ready he crouched on his hind legs, and then sprang forward at a gallop. He was right; she did have to cling to his neck, for one, to stay on, and two, to keep his mane from whipping her face. The wind they created threatened to tear her bow and quiver off her back, but they held.

They quickly approached Tayna and Geoff's camp. As soon as the great number of tents was in view, someone had alerted them to their presence and a crowd had gathered at the edge of camp.

"Stay with me. We'll go inside Tayna and Geoff's tent and speak with them. When most of the crowd has left, you may go and see your friends. I do not want to attract Zathos's attention too soon."

"All right." He galloped straight up to the centaur and elf. They held the tent flaps open for them as they entered, smiling at the pair. Shaelynn had to lay forward over Ilian's neck to pass under the flaps, and he told her to dismount as soon as they were in.

"Right," Tayna said, trying to start conversation. "Do you have any news?"

"Yes. I had a vision this morning. The battle is tomorrow."

"What? We have one day to move all these people into position?"

"Correct. But I have an idea. I think I may have briefly seen it in the vision. You know that Liz is *Fravid-Sorva,* and there is another pair traveling with her and her dragon. I thought that the people could fight first off, but we remain in position. When the people get weary, we appear in the battle to help. It will strengthen them when they need it, and it will surprise Zathos's army."

"It sounds interesting. What are the positions you saw in the vision?"

"There will be three sections. One centered in front of the castle, and two flanking the center. But if Shaelynn and I were to aid the west flank, the other dragon and her rider the east flank, and Liz and Sorvo the center, it will do much good."

"It might work," Geoff mused from the back. There was a slight commotion outside, and then the tent flaps opened. Dasriel and Riman came in. They smiled at Shaelynn and Ilian and listened as he told them of his plans.

"I like it," Riman said.

"Aye, it's good, but we must be careful," Dasriel said. "If we time it wrong, it could be our downfall. If you come too early, you will use your energy too quickly. If you come too late—well, that's too late for everyone. That is obvious. But what will you do in the meantime?"

"We can aid those in the back. Shaelynn has learned some magic, and I believe I have trained her well. Liz has also found new abilities."

"You've learned magic?" Dasriel asked, turning to Shaelynn. Everyone else looked interested as well. Shaelynn nodded. For a brief demonstration, she bent down and placed her hand on the ground. She let her mind travel into the hard-packed earth, and quickly found its spirit. She entered it, and with her eyes open could see the ground begin to glow. Now was the hard part. She had done it right yesterday, but it was something she had done on impulse.

Shaelynn concentrated hard on every tiny speck of dust in the ground and willed it to move. Just next to her hand, a column of dirt and sand swirled upward. She let it curl around a couple of times and held it there for a moment, and then let it collapse back into the ground. It looked as if there had been no change in the dirt. She stood back up to see everyone's shocked faces.

"You learned to do that in four days?" Geoff asked in disbelief. Shaelynn nodded.

"Do you know how advanced that is?" Dasriel asked. Shaelynn did not answer, so she went on, "It can take ten years for a sorcerer or sorceress to build their skills up to accomplish that. And then it takes another year or more of practice and trial and error for them to simply do what you just did."

Shaelynn had to lean on Ilian to support herself. In four days, she had perfected something it took other people ten years to try, eleven or twelve to accomplish. There was no way she had really done it, but then she had just demonstrated it.

"Can you do it?" she asked Dasriel. Dasriel shook her head.

"I can feel for the spirit, but it doesn't glow like it does for you. I've never even heard of it glowing like that."

"I have," Tayna said quietly. Everyone looked to her and she went on, "My nanny used to tell me stories about it. It was a prophecy made by an elf a long time ago. Everyone thought he was crazy when he said it, but the legend goes on. Anyway, he said that the one who makes the spirits glow at the touch of the mind will redeem the land someday . . . . And that the one who does will put an end to it." Everyone stared at Shaelynn now, except for Ilian.

"I knew of it as well. There is an old fortuneteller that unicorns go to, to help find their Guide. She told me, 'For as she trains for the battle, she will become stronger, more powerful than any we have known. Spirits will alight at the touch of her mind, and nearly anything will do her bidding. She is destined to save Partaenia from corruption, from the evil that has taken over. Watch over her, Ilian, Unicorn of the Far West, In the Lands Unknown, for her life depends on you.' She never told me the last part you said, Tayna."

"Well, like I said, everyone thought the elf was mad, and legends can get twisted. Who knows?" She shrugged her shoulders, and the feeling in the tent became relaxed again.

"Shaelynn, you can go and see your friends now. They're still there, and most everyone else has left. I will be out in a moment." She nodded, and walked out of the tent. She thought about listening in on them, but decided against it. Whatever they were talking about, Ilian would tell her later.

Najee and his gang were still there, gathered in a small circle. Outside their group was Agathla, and Marl and Shamar. She smiled at them, and they all crowded her. She gave hugs to everyone in turn, but saved Agathla for last.

"So, you are a Guide now, eh?" she asked her. "I would never have thought of it. One of my apprentices now leads a unicorn." Agathla smiled at her, and they hugged each other tightly.

"It is good to see all of you," she told them.

"It's good to see you, too," Najee said. "Good luck in the battle. We all know you'll make us proud."

"Thanks." Marl came up to her now, Shamar in tow.

"Tell me, how is Liz?"

"She had a few rough spots, but she is fine. She is *Fravid-Sorva,* and she's training with her dragon now. There is another dragon that came out of hiding, with her rider, and they will fight in the battle as well."

"That is good to hear. The dragons are back, and they're on our side." He smiled, and clapped her on the back, and they walked back to their tents.

"Shaelynn, we must go," Ilian called. Dasriel and Riman were headed back to their tents, and Tayna and Geoff were standing outside with him. She waved goodbye to Najee, Supai, and Dush, and then got on his back once more.

He took off once more, headed south, where the forest was. It quickly came into view, and they saw the two dragons wheeling in the sky. They were flying in circles, rising up and down around each other, and then they corkscrewed through the air. Sorvo separated himself from the other one and flew a loop at about a mile and a half in the air. It made Shaelynn sick just watching it. She didn't know how Liz could stand it. She could see her on Sorvo's back now, wearing a cloak.

Chapter 17

WE WERE EXERCISING IN THE air, and I was flying on my own. Wraetha was supposed to fly up while Honoras and I circled each other, but she stopped in the middle of it, making Honoras and I pull up to avoid hitting her.

What is it? Honoras asked a little irritably. The day was hot, and he didn't want to fly right now, but Wraetha had insisted on it.

Shaelynn and Ilian are coming, fast. Liz, you wanted to keep your wings a surprise?

Yeah.

Go and get Jacey's cloak. It should be in his pack. But keep yourself, and your wings especially, hidden. Hurry.

I asked the bracelet for transparency, but flew down to the clearing even before it gave it to me. I landed and ran to his pack, going through it. Jacey's cloak was toward the top. I pulled it out and put it on, and then asked the bracelet to make it transparent as well. Again, before it did what I wanted, I was already flying.

I told Honoras to stay still for a moment while I got on him. When I was in the saddle I turned normal again, but kept my wings transparent underneath the cloak, just in case. By now we could all see Ilian's white figure racing across the plain, with Shaelynn crouched over his neck. Wraetha gave instructions for a flight pattern to make a show for them, and we started right away. Listening for Shaelynn's thoughts, I could hear that the twists and turns we were making were making her sick. I smiled and told Honoras.

She said she doesn't know how I can do it, I said, laughing. I looked down, and could see them approaching. They were almost to the edge of the trees now.

Let's go ahead and land, I suggested. *That way when they get there, you guys' wings are already closed and there'll be more room.*

Do it, Wraetha said. She flew down first, gliding in tight circles. She landed in the clearing and quickly brought her wings in to her sides. Honoras followed.

Tell Shaelynn where we're going and direct her to us, Honoras said.

Without answering him I focused on her, and said, *Shaelynn, can you hear me?*

What? Yeah.

We're gonna land in a clearing we found. Keep your mind open, and I'll direct you two.

All right.

Okay, go straight in. You're there. All right, turn west-southwest. Good. Straight on. I mentally kept track of them, by reading their thoughts on what they were seeing. They did good until Ilian jumped a log and turned away from us. *No, head west now. There. Can you see us?* I jumped up and down, waving my arms. I could hear Jacey sigh. I turned and scowled at him, and he grinned.

Yeah, we see you. Stop shooting looks at Jacey. I could see them now, and shot her the same look I had given Jacey. She smiled. Ilian stepped into the clearing, and somehow it seemed to brighten.

I hadn't really remembered what he had looked like, except that he was really white. And he was: he was pure white, whiter than anything I'd ever seen. He seemed to be illuminated from the inside. His mane and tail were the same white with bits of yellow or red, and they were really long and wavy. He reminded me of an Andalucian.

His horn was the most noticeable part of him, other than his whiteness. It was a silvery golden color, three inches thick at the base, and two and a half feet long. Its tip was glowing too. He nodded at me, and greeted the two dragons and Jacey.

Shaelynn got off him and ran to me. We hugged tightly, and then stepped back from each other. It had been hard for me to keep her from noticing my wings as she nearly crushed me. "So," she said, "what all did you learn?"

"Well, I guess being *Fravid-Sorva* gives me two abilities. One is a surprise; I'll save it for just before the battle. The other, is this." I stopped talking and stared at her, listening to her thoughts. She was bursting to tell me something, but it was hidden. Other thoughts were running through her mind, too. I cocked my head.

"You and Ilian stopped at the camp?" I asked. Her eyes widened.

"How did you know that?" she asked.

"And you talked of a battle plan?" I asked.

"How did you-? What's your ability? Can you read minds?"

"Kind of, but I learned to do that from Sorvo. No, I have another Gift. Watch this." I had seen a fox sitting on a log at the edge of the clearing. It was mesmerized by the unicorn. 'Red-furred one, please come here,' I told it. 'Stand by me for a moment. I and my friends will not harm you.' Shaelynn's eyes widened at my fox yips and barks. I thought they were going to pop out of her head when she saw the fox come trotting into the clearing. He sat down by my feet, gazing up at Ilian.

'Sing a song for us, if you will be so kind,' I said to it. It looked at me, and then sang much like wolves or coyotes do. Strangely, it wasn't just high-pitched yips, although it's all that Shaelynn or Ilian would have heard. I knew the fox was singing about the unicorn that had come to the forest and his rider, and how much he loved having them here. After a minute or so he was done, and he looked at me. 'Thank you, little one. Be on your way.' He tweeted his own thanks, and flew away.

"She has the Gift of communication with animals," Ilian said. I nodded. Shaelynn smiled.

"That is so cool!" she said excitedly.

"Yeah. And the bracelet will let me do stuff too. Watch." I asked it for transparency again, and in a moment Shaelynn was groping for my disappeared body. She found my shoulder, but I reached out with my hand and tickled her neck.

"Liz! Don't do that!" she squealed, jumping back. I laughed and turned normal again.

"You'll never guess what I found out I can do," she said excitedly. Then she stopped. "You didn't hear it in my thoughts, did you?"

"No, but I'm about to."

"Wait! Don't. Okay. I learned how to do magic!" Now it was my turn to gawk. She lifted four stones and had them do circles around her head like she was an atom or something. Then she stopped them and said, "Now you watch." She held on to one of the larger-than-fist-sized rocks. She stared intently at it, and it began to glow. It started faintly somewhere in the middle, but then it grew until the whole rock was illuminated. She looked up at me and smiled. She set the rock down, and it stopped glowing.

"That's what happens when I touch the rock's spirit," she said.

Interesting, Wraetha said, still staring at the rock. Then she turned to Ilian and said, *We saw you coming in a hurry. What has brought you here?*

"The battle is tomorrow." Everyone froze. Only Shaelynn didn't seem surprised. Ilian went on, "I had a vision this morning, and it showed me that the battle is tomorrow. Zathos will move his army out of his castle then, and we will meet him. It will happen just before dawn. Now, the vision gave me some information of how he will set up his army. He will have three sections to cover a wider area: a center section, and two flanking it. We will have our army the same way. But, I was thinking of something we ourselves could do.

"Since there are three of us, with our riders," he gestured with his head, "we can divide ourselves over the three sections. We could help from the back for a little while and let the people fight, and when they get weary we join them, lifting their spirits. We will help them take control of Zathos's army, and then to secure the castle. And, bring about his downfall."

I like it, Honoras said, *as long as we are doing enough to not make us feel guilty of being lazy.*

Yes, Wraetha said. *I do not like the feeling of staying back while others do the work. What did you have in mind of us doing?*

"Well, Liz and Shaelynn have learned some new skills, and they could help by putting them to use in whatever ways they can. And you three could help in whatever ways are needed on foot. If you are to secure the castle and kill Zathos, you will need to conserve your energy as much as possible." Ilian looked to Shaelynn when he said this. Some thought went between them, but I couldn't catch it. It was too fast, and they kept it too concealed. Even after this I couldn't find it. I listened to Ilian's plan once more.

"Liz, you can communicate from quite a distance, can you not?"

"I haven't tried it, but I'm sure I can. I can hear animals from quite a ways away. I haven't tried talking to them, though."

"If you can, then, see if you can disable Zathos's cavalry or any other animals he may use." I nodded. He turned to Honoras. "If she needs help, you may have to lend her some of your strength, but not too much. And if any of Zathos's army reaches where we are, we can all fight on foot. But if his beasts can fly, you may have to do so as well."

Were you able to see what kind of an army he has? Honoras asked.

"A little, but not very much. You know that he will have his black phoenixes and latharks. I have seen some of a cavalry, but beyond that I could not tell." Honoras nodded thoughtfully.

If he has a cavalry, then he will have the rest of his human army on foot, Wraetha remarked.

"Yes. I did not see an army on foot, but you are right. He is sure to have one. I'm not sure from where I saw the vision, but I could see some of our own people, just toward the bottom. He had his beasts first, then the cavalry. After that he must have his troops. It was beyond my sight, but they must be there. What else does he have to fight for him?" Silence rang after this question. They did not know if he had anything else. I thought for a moment, and then spoke.

"Where will Zathos be? And Avernus?" Ilian thought for a moment.

"Avernus might be at the back, directing the troops. Zathos is sure to be at the castle, perhaps on a turret or something, where he can see and influence the battle. He is powerful enough to do so, and Avernus is powerful enough as well, so he may be at the castle with Zathos, I am not sure. We will have to see. Either way, he can still have a great affect on the battle."

Ilian turned to me now. "Liz, you should know that we have a cavalry as well, about one hundred men strong. Marl has given his horses, and others are going to ride theirs. Shamar will be leading them, following Marl's directions. I think that this is where you can help the most before the rest of us move in. There are a few of the horses that have been trained for small combat, but otherwise they will not know what is going on. I need you to talk to them so that their riders will have no problems. Fighting should be their only concern." I nodded. He went on, "Use your second Gift if you need to, just don't overdo it." I nodded again, briefly wondering if he really knew what my second Gift was. Shaelynn looked a little confused, but didn't push the subject.

"Now," Ilian said, speaking to all of us, "Tayna and Geoff are already starting to move the people forward, and are dividing them into three sections as planned. Our cavalry will be the front of the center section, better to benefit you, Liz, and to fight Zathos's cavalry, which he will have stationed in the center as well." Now he turned to the two dragons to address them, loud enough for all of us to hear.

All of us can use mind speech, and Shaelynn is still shaky, so she can speak through me. We should keep a connection open at all times, to inform each other of the army's movements if we need to act together should a situation arise. He came back to speaking aloud while Shaelynn got on his back, responding to the smallest of thoughts, flickers of feeling that held everything she needed to know in it. Hmm . . . . interesting.

"If you have things you still need to cover before the battle," Ilian said, talking to Wraetha, "do them today. Shaelynn and I will follow the camp. Just make sure you are there and ready for the battle by dawn tomorrow." With a final nod to everyone, he left, trotting through the forest before he broke into a run at the edge of the trees.

Well Elizabeth, I want you to try something, Honoras said. *Ilian said for you to help the horses in our cavalry, and you could use your wings if you needed to. But, let's see from how far away you can talk to them.*

All right.

Find the black, and ask him what they are doing at the camp now. We'll see if he can hear you and if he will respond.

I'll try. I closed my eyes, and called up an image of the camp. Just as Ilian had said, they were all on the move. The black had five kids piled on his back, and the rest of them were walking close to him. Avinret was riding on his head between his ears. He seemed a bit irritated, but happy to carry the children. I was about to talk to him, but thought, Should I speak aloud, or direct it to his thoughts? The latter would definitely work, but I wondered if he could hear me if I spoke aloud. Just to see, I called to him. His head whipped around, his ears working like mad.

Good, Elizabeth. Honoras was speaking quietly in my mind while I held the image. *Now, I want you to ask him who his rider is for the battle, if he knows. Comfort him if he's a bit skittish, and then break the image.* I nodded for him to see, my eyes still closed.

Taking a breath, I asked the black, 'Do you know who will ride you in the coming battle?' His head whipped around again, looking for me. He whinnied back his answer, but it made the children start.

'Battle? My rider? We horses do not know of battles, and we cannot choose who rides us. But one of the children will ride me. The small one. He can shoot, and he can ride. I was chosen for him.' I guessed he was talking about Dush.

'Are you ready?' I asked him.

'What? Yes of course. I follow my rider's commands, and he knows what he is doing, so I am not concerned in the least. He will guide me well. Who is speaking to me?'

'I am Liz, the one they rescued from the castle. I am Bonded to the green dragon.'

'Ah, yes. Congratulations on your Gift.' This statement caught me off guard. He knew about Gifts? I said nothing, though. He spoke first. 'I can see the castle over the hill, I think. We are nearly there, and we will stop to make camp soon. I must go.' With that, he turned his head forward again and devoted his attention to the children riding him, who were starting to work with the reins once more.

I broke the image and opened my eyes. Honoras was looking at me intently, having listened in on the conversation between me and the black. Wraetha and Jacey were looking at me expectantly.

"He said one of the smaller children, probably Dush, was going to ride him. He said horses didn't know of battles, but he wasn't concerned at all. He said Dush knows what he's doing and he's confident Dush will guide him through it. He wanted to know who was talking to him, and I told him who I was. He said he could see something like the castle ahead of where they were, and the camp was starting to slow down."

Good, Wraetha said. *Well, whatever we need to work on, we can do it in the air. Pack up quickly, you two, and we'll be off.* Jacey and I set about doing as she said, gathering our things and putting them in our packs. It didn't take too long; Jacey kept his things together, and I didn't have very much to scatter around. We shared the rest of my dried meat while the dragons went off hunting for all of us. I was looking at my map, thinking about how far Shaelynn and I had come, when Honoras and Wraetha came back. Honoras was walking on three legs, carrying the leftover dried meat of a deer. I put some in my pack, and Jacey put the rest in his.

Are you going to fly on your own? Honoras asked as Wraetha leaped up into the air, clearing the trees before she had to beat her wings even once.

Sure, for a while. As soon as we get in sight of the camp, I'll get on your back.

Will you fly by me, then?

Sure. He seemed pleased at this and let me take off first. As always, I was surprised at my new strength. My wingbeats were powerful, steady, and they let me fly fast at an almost leisurely pace. Honoras flew comfortably beside me, happiness radiating from him. We flew side by side for some time, enjoying each other's company. Wraetha and Jacey were just ahead of us.

Liz, I can see the camp now, Wraetha said after a while. I sighed and flew above Honoras, dropping into the saddle and carefully folding my wings under Jacey's cloak. I asked the bracelet to make them transparent once more, and looked ahead. The camp was below us now, and everyone's faces were turned toward us. We flew on past the camp, then wheeled in a half circle and glided down to the ground, walking the hundred feet toward the end of the camp.

The camp was busy. Everyone was moving around doing something. Tayna was going from tent to tent, and Geoff was talking to some people in front of his and Tayna's tent. He lifted a hand while he talked to let us know he had seen us, and then dismissed the small group of people he had been talking to. He turned toward us with a smile.

"It's good to see you all here. Liz, do you feel ready?" He sounded concerned. I got off Honoras, jumping down and landing with a flourish.

"Of course," I lied. Inside, my stomach was doing flip-flops. I gave him a smile I hoped looked genuine.

"Well?" He held out his hands, expecting something. "What are your Gifts?"

'I can communicate with any kind of animal,' I told him in the centaur language. His eyes widened. 'And I can hear their thoughts as well. Right now you're half-thinking about weapons for everyone.' His eyes somehow got even wider.

"Well, that's useful," he remarked. We all laughed. "And? What's your other one?"

"I want to keep that a surprise for tomorrow. Or, at least until everyone's here. Where's Shaelynn and Ilian?"

"Somewhere around camp. Call them, and you can show us." I looked to Honoras to see if he approved.

It's your choice. I'm all for it. If you reveal it tonight, it can help with our plans tomorrow.

All right. I'll do it, then. Expanding my mind, I found everyone I wanted to see my wings tonight. I sent out my message to all of them: *Come to Tayna and Geoff's tent. I have something to show you.* I let them know it was me, and felt them coming.

Dasriel, Riman, and Tayna were there in an instant. I was glad to see her again and gave her a hug, being careful about my new strength. She still noticed it, however, and smiled at me.

"I suppose you'll show us all in a moment?" she asked. I nodded. There were footsteps behind the tent, and three children came racing around the side of it. Najee, Supai, and Dush slid to a halt, kicking up some dust as they did. They smiled sheepishly, and went straight to throwing their arms around my middle. All three squeezed tight, taking my breath out of me.

Shaelynn and Ilian appeared just then, and I smiled at her. She shook her head as the three pulled themselves off me. Just then Marl, Shamar, and Agathla came from the throng of people that had followed Ilian here. Avinret came bounding up behind them and jumped on Honoras's head, hugging one of his horns.

"Uh, let's go inside," Geoff suggested at the sight of the people that had gathered around in expectation. "Go ahead, I'll give them something to do." He let us go inside while he walked out toward the people. His thoughts told me he would give them his job of looking for extra weapons and such. Smiling, I went inside.

It was a bit crowded in the tent with everyone inside, even as large as it was. After Geoff came in it was even more crowded, but there was still enough room for me to spread my wings open. I waited until Honoras and Wraetha both had an eye in front of the flap to watch the goings-on to release the transparency on my wings. Even under the cloak, I could tell that Tayna and Geoff had seen them. Their eyes widened.

I took the cloak off, and amid everyone's gasps, stretched my wings out in the length of the tent. Agathla covered her mouth with her hand, and Marl and Shamar looked awed, as did the three children.

"Can you really fly with them?" Dush asked.

"Yeah. And they've made me stronger, faster. I can fight as good as Jacey now."

"What?" Geoff asked this question, shocked. "As good as Jacey? That's amazing!" Tayna looked like she agreed with Geoff. So did everyone else, except for those from Barda. They seemed confused, but Marl didn't.

"I want to see it," Marl said quietly. Everyone turned to him. "I've seen him fight, and I want to see if what you're saying is true."

"Where have you seen me fight?" Jacey asked.

"I'll tell you after you two fight. Now, let me see." He even backed up against the wall of the tent to give them some room. Everyone else did the same.

Jacey, you have the wooden staves in your pack, Wraetha said. He nodded and silently got them out, tossing one to me. As soon as it was in the air, he attacked. I flew to catch it, staying low for speed. I caught it left-handed and parried his blow, then switched to my right hand to fight back. I saw Geoff smile; he had taught me to fight with both hands.

Jacey parried my thrust and came back at me, using every bit of his talent. I didn't have to struggle with him, but I was having to work to get on top. We went on for a long time, neither besting the other for long.

Finally, Jacey caught on to one of my feints and attacked before I could finish it and held his sword to my side. I stopped in shock; it was the same exact place where Karbab had run me through. His stave was sitting right on top of the scar. He held it there for a moment, and then he released it and we backed away from each other, sweaty and breathing hard. My heart was pounding. Jacey would not look at me.

"Well, old man?" Jacey addressed Marl. His voice was different, very unlike him. It sounded vaguely familiar. "Where have you seen me fight?" The sound of his voice sent chills of warning cascading down my spine.

"I saw you fight Liz in Barda. You're Karbab." My knees became weak and I nearly collapsed. I felt my heart skip a couple of beats. It couldn't be. No-.

"Very good, Marl. I did fight her, and I would have killed her had her dragon not come for her." Now, I did collapse, my knees buckling underneath me. At the same time, Honoras's talon appeared through the flap and flipped the tent up, tearing its stakes from the ground. His other talon came in and wrapped itself around Jacey. One of his claws was at his throat.

You are the spy, Honoras snarled. *Tell us everything.*

"Do you honestly think that I came all this way as a simple spy?" Jacey laughed. Now that my wave of shock had somewhat passed, I could see similarities I had never noticed. His laugh, his build, the way he held himself. Only his face had changed; I couldn't believe he had fooled me.

"What do you mean?" Tayna asked. She and Dasriel were already moving in between Jacey and I.

"I killed the real Jacey in Mechem after I tracked the girl and her friend on their horse. I took on Jacey's form and deceived even you, Wraetha. I am a sorcerer, you fools!" he shouted, and a ball of energy exploded from him, throwing everything back, tossing even Honoras and Wraetha away as if they were mere sticks. And yet, I didn't move. Tayna and Dasriel were in front of me, blocking his magic. They had their own field of energy in front of them, and it had blocked Jacey's blow. Everyone else, though, had been thrown back at least thirty feet. Tents had been blown over, and anyone near had been flung back as well.

"Do you two think you can stop me?" Jacey asked, and he flung a hand out. A bolt of lightning curved around their shield, aimed for me, but Dasriel's hand was faster than his. She waved it out, creating another wall of their shield. Tayna swiftly did the same.

I had panicked, and had let down all my defenses. Everyone's thoughts had come flooding into my mind, Jacey's strongest of all: 'I must kill her. I am on Zathos's orders. She must die; she cannot ruin his plans.'

Tayna, Dasriel, he's going for me! He's on Zathos's orders, he doesn't care about anyone else! I yelled in their minds. If they heard me, they gave no sign of it. Jacey attacked again; their shield held, though it wavered.

I heard hoof beats behind me and turned. Ilian was racing to us, Shaelynn on his back. He leaped over me and ran to the shield as Shaelynn jumped off his back, landing next to me. Ilian touched his horn to the shield. It flared blue, and grew to create a bubble around us. A flicker of a thought flew from Ilian to Shaelynn. Immediately she pushed her hands to the ground, and a glowing rock wall grew in front of us, curving slightly, just enough to cover us.

Though I could see nothing of the fight in front of us, I could hear it. Jacey was yelling tauntingly at Ilian and the two sorceresses, who were grunting with the effort of keeping Jacey's power away from me.

"Liz, fly!" Ilian yelled, catching my attention. I hesitated; Shaelynn looked up, her face strained with the effort of holding the rock wall. "Go!" she urged. I nodded, and launched myself from the ground. At the same time a hole in the shield appeared, and I flew through it. Looking down, I could see Dasriel with her arms out, her energy force wrapped around Jacey and keeping Jacey's attention away from me.

Shaelynn had collapsed her wall and had crushed the rock into a ball, the size of a boulder. Bracing herself, she let it fly at the shield. It broke for a moment, and hurtled at Jacey. I thought for a moment that it would finish him, but through his magic he caught it, circled it around his head, and made it slingshot back to Shaelynn. Instead of dodging like I thought she might, like I would have done, she held her arms out, her feet planted. The boulder, going twice as fast than she had sent it, hit her shield and exploded. In an instant she had wrapped her shield around it and prevented the fragments from hitting the other three.

Elizabeth, look to Jacey! Honoras was yelling at me. I brought my attention to him. Dasriel's energy that had been wrapped around him had broken, and he had just flung his arm out, toward me. Another lightning bolt raced to me. I had only a split second's thought, but managed to whip myself sideways and barely avoid it. A feather on my wingtip had been singed.

I had another second's thought before another came racing for me. As I turned sideways again, the bolt forked and followed me. Instinct made my wings fold in, and I dropped like a rock. It was enough that the bolt ran out of energy and disappeared. Hurriedly, I asked the bracelet for transparency. It immediately gave it to me, and Jacey's face became troubled.

"You cannot hide from me forever!" he screamed. In the meantime I was watching everyone else. While Jacey's attention had been on either me or on the shield, Geoff and half the camp had circled the fight, weapons at the ready. Wraetha and Honoras were high above, watching carefully. Honoras was searching for me.

Jacey's hand shot out suddenly, his movement unchecked by anyone. Another bolt of lightning raced from it, but it sped toward Honoras instead of in my general direction. The bolt wrapped itself around his neck like a horrible collar, the rope in Jacey's hand. At the same time, electricity raced through Honoras. I felt it as well and curled into a ball of pain, but I still held the transparency.

"Save yourself and your dragon! Reveal yourself!" Jacey yelled. After another moment, I couldn't stand it any longer, and let the transparency fall. As soon as I came into sight again, another bolt of lightning had wrapped itself around me, holding down my arms as well as my wings. As I dropped from straight above him, Jacey pulled out his sword and held it at arm's length. I barely registered this; the electricity had intensified greatly. I wasn't sure what would kill me: the lightning, or the sword.

About halfway down the pain increased again, and I couldn't hold myself in a ball anymore. I arched my back, throwing my head back and releasing my scream. Just as I expected to die, the lightning and the pain disappeared and something caught me before I crashed to the ground. I was barely conscious, only half-realizing what was going on around me, but I saw it.

Honoras and I were on the ground, having been caught my either Tayna or Dasriel, who had given up on Jacey to catch us. At the same time, Geoff and many others had attacked Jacey with their weapons. Jacey, or Karbab, whoever he was, was lying on the ground in his own blood, dead. His eyes stared blankly at the sky.

Tayna and Dasriel had gone to Honoras, and Wraetha had landed close to him. Ilian was standing over me, and Shaelynn was blocking my view of anything. I didn't remember seeing them come. I could hear my heartbeat pounding in my ears, all over in my head. It was going fast, very fast. But it was slowing. It was going too slow now. My vision clouded, and all I saw was black, but amid it, Ilian's form bending over me, touching his horn to me, right over my chest. Then, nothing.

==

Shaelynn held Liz's hand, watching her to see what Jacey had done to her. Ilian looked at her, shooting her a quick thought: *Help. Horn.* She nodded, understanding. She watched Liz's face, which had gone slack, but she was still alive. Her eyes were unfocused, her mouth moving silently. Ilian had just started to bend his head down when she stilled. Her eyes stared blankly at the ground, and her grip on Shaelynn's hand loosened.

"No!" Shaelynn screamed. She looked to Ilian, but in response he plunged his horn straight through Liz's heart. Shaelynn stared in shock as he collapsed next to her, pulling his horn out in the process. It was dripping Liz's blood, but Shaelynn could see that the very tip had been broken off. The point of light that had been there was gone.

Shaking her head, she looked to Liz again. Her body twitched a little, and then her chest raised again as she took in a deep, shuddering breath. She took two more deep breaths, and then her breathing steadied as if she were sleeping. But Ilian was not moving. Letting go of Liz's hand, she twisted to hover over Ilian, barely breathing.

"No, no, no, . . ." she moaned. Tears leaked from her eyes and fell on his shining coat. Then, his eyes opened and his lungs filled with air once more. He sat up, resting on his knees. He looked her over, and then watched Liz.

"She lives," he muttered. Shaelynn nodded, not saying anything. Ilian looked at her once more. "I'm sorry. I meant only to touch her with my horn, but then her heart quit beating. I didn't even think—I wasn't even sure if it would work. I've heard of other unicorns doing it before, but I didn't—I wasn't sure— . . ."

"It worked Ilian," Shaelynn whispered. She could see a change in him: he was unsteady, unsure of himself. He was scared. "What happened?" she asked.

"I gave her that part of me that sees everything, that can see the certain future, the essence of unicorns. Pure life. It is sacred to us, and dealt with carefully. But if she had been dead for another moment, Sorvo would have died as well, and any hope of replenishing the land would have been lost. All of this would have been for nothing."

"So, what happens to her now?"

"She has my gift. Right now, scenes of everything that is happening now and what will happen soon is going through her mind, even if she's unconscious. She'll learn to sort it out and control it, and learn to use it to her advantage."

"That's why you've changed? You can't see all that anymore?"

"Correct. I'm nervous without it. But I'll be fine, thanks to you. Your tears saved me."

"What do you mean?"

"I would have died. The life I gave her would have been replaced by her dead one had you not cared for me. Your feelings awakened it. I was wanted, and so I live." They both remained silent for a moment, their attention on the dragon lying still on the ground not far away.

Geoff, Tayna, Dasriel, Riman, and others were crowded around him. His belly moved up and down with his breath, but other than that he gave no signs of life. He, too, was unconscious, but seemed fine.

Wraetha was on the ground some distance away, huddled alone on the plain, staring off into space. Shaelynn went to her, leaving Ilian to watch Sorvo and Liz. Wraetha gave no acknowledgement of her presence, except for a small twitch of her head. Shaelynn barely caught it, and she realized how far she had come. Before she came to Partaenia she had never really noticed subtle body language like that.

Wraetha turned her head around slowly, snapping Shaelynn out of her reverie. Shaelynn looked into her eyes; they were full of sorrow and hurt.

He was my closest friend, other than my Bonded. I knew him since he was a child. He grew up with us. He knew our ways, he—he must have told Zathos—her voice broke as she realized this, and tears leaked from her eyes. She shook her head violently, and then turned it away again. Unsure, Shaelynn simply put a hand on her massive foreleg.

Wraetha immediately started sobbing mentally, moaning words until Shaelynn could make them out. *I've killed our whole race—Zathos knows where we live—I raised him, and the betrayer killed him—all my fault-*

No, Wraetha, Shaelynn said firmly, walking around to stand in front of her. *Quit telling yourself that. It was not your fault that he was murdered, even with his skills he could never hope to outmatch a sorcerer. Karbab chose his own path, and look where it's gotten him. Jacey's death has been avenged. Now, straighten up, and see to your son.*

Hon—. . . Sorvo! she breathed, shock on her face again. She looked to the mass of people behind them and turned to Shaelynn again. *What happened? The lightning was enough to kill Liz. Why aren't they both dead?* She seemed distracted as she asked the last question, as if she were thinking of something else. *Did Ilian?*—Wraetha asked, hoping Shaelynn understood her.

Shaelynn nodded. She spoke aloud now, saying, "He meant to heal her with a touch of his horn, but she died before he could. He couldn't wait another moment before they both passed, he said, so he stabbed her through the heart with his horn and broke the tip off in it. He gave her-"

His life, Wraetha finished quietly. *And what of Ilian? He's not dead, is he?*

"No. I cried over him, and he said my feelings for him saved him. He knew he was wanted, and so he came back."

Yes, emotions are powerful, in humans the most. Did you know that? That is one of the things that sets humans apart. They can intensely feel great emotion, and the complexity and strength of those feelings and emotions are the main reasons we choose humans for companions. It is why, under even the worst of circumstances, your race survives.

"Oh. I didn't know that." Wraetha nodded her thanks, and slowly ambled over to her son. Everyone parted to give her room. Shaelynn looked away just as she settled herself in front of his unconscious body.

Her eyes traveled first to Jacey's body. All the swords had been removed from him by their disgusted owners, but all the arrows were left in him, making him look like a human pincushion. A traitor human pincushion, in her opinion. Walking past him, she spat on his body and kicked dust on him, as had everyone else. It hurt to know that he had helped her, and yet he had been a traitor. She wondered when he had killed the real Jacey and how much he had given away to Zathos.

The path of travel she had taken had led her straight back to Liz and Ilian, both of them sleeping. Exhausted from her efforts to protect Liz, she sank down next to Ilian and curled up next to him. Dasriel caught her eye just before she closed it and smiled at her. Shaelynn got her message: *I'm proud of you. You did well.* Shaelynn smiled back and fell asleep.

==

Liz's unconscious mind, the only part of her that realized she was dead, registered a faint pain in her lifeless body, in her heart. Something had stabbed her. It withdrew, but not before it left something behind, in her heart. Her body came to life once more.

Pictures, snapshots, almost, flew threw that part of her mind. Zathos—Ilian, collapsing next to her—Honoras, on the ground—Shaelynn, crying over Ilian—Zathos again, too fast—Geoff, standing over Jacey's body—Zathos once more. This time the pictures stopped, and she could see him clearly in his small throne room. He was raging, sending bursts of magical energy at anything that would break. He needed Jacey, and he had been killed, and he had failed. He had not killed the one that would defeat him. The one who would save the land. The one that would restore the magical world to the modern one. But only Liz's unconscious mind took this all in, among many other things, and she remembered none of it.

Chapter 18

ONORAS WOKE, AND IT WAS dark. His body ached, and his heart was racing, but he could not get his brain to focus. Finally, the fog that was in it cleared, and he realized he was sitting up in the dark, in the middle of the night. He wondered what time it was. For that matter, he wondered what day it was, and anything else he had missed.

Looking around, he saw his mother asleep on the ground next to him. Not too far from him, in the middle of a large deserted circle, was Jacey's body. He looked like a monster at first to Honoras, and then he realized that the arrows that had killed Jacey were still in him. Their owners were too disgusted to save them.

He moved his line of sight to anywhere but the traitor, trying not to think of what had happened. His eyes fell on the milky white form of Ilian. Shaelynn was asleep next to him, curled up on his shoulder. Something was missing, though. His eyes fell on Elizabeth, and his heart jumped severely.

Honoras almost fainted: the front of Elizabeth's shirt was covered in blood, all over her chest. There was an evident puncture wound, straight to her heart. He almost panicked, until he thought about it. He was alive; she couldn't be dead, or he would be too. Just to make sure, he looked down at where he had been lying. There was no body there. He wasn't a ghost. But how-

And then it clicked: Ilian had saved her. Honoras had heard of it before, but he had never seen it done. That was why the point of light at the tip of Ilian's horn was gone. It was in Elizabeth's heart, and it had given her life. Relieved, he settled himself down on the ground again. He wanted her to rest by him, but he knew how delicate she could be right now and didn't want to do anything wrong. Besides, his mother had wanted to sleep near him. He closed his eyes once more.

The next morning Tayna and Geoff were the first up. Silently they looked at one another and got up to wake the rest of the camp. The day was here; everyone must be ready. Tayna walked to the three injured ones while Geoff went to the people. She knelt down by Dasriel, who had fallen asleep on the ground shortly after she and Tayna had used their magic to help save Sorvo. Tayna lightly touched her mind, and all was well. She was only sleeping. She touched her shoulder and she instantly woke.

"It is time?" Dasriel asked quietly. Tayna nodded, and she got up to wake the others as well, joining Geoff in waking the people. Tayna next went and woke Wraetha, who woke Sorvo. He seemed all right, if not a little shaken up. Shaelynn seemed the same way as well. When Tayna gently shook her shoulder she snapped awake, two stones already levitated at eye level.

"Shh," Tayna said, putting a hand up to help calm her. "All is well. Wake Ilian and I will see to Liz. Make sure he is all right before you wake him, though." Shaelynn nodded and turned herself around to face Ilian. She closed her eyes for a moment. As she opened them and nudged Ilian to wake him, Tayna turned toward Liz.

She wanted to be the one to make sure she was all right, as she was the most advanced one in magic and Liz had been hurt the worst. Looking her over, she found her sleeping well. This was good. Lightly touching her mind, she felt the unicorn's gift had already taken affect. But Liz herself seemed all right. Tayna whispered her name, and she slowly came to.

===

My body was just starting to wake, my mind a blur from the pictures and visions flashing in my mind. Someone whispered my name. I wasn't sure if it was real. It was whispered again, more persistently. I willed my eyelids to open; they felt like bricks over my eyes. Tayna was kneeling over me, smiling a little. From the pictures in my head, I knew already that everyone else was up, and I was the one she was worried about more than anyone else.

I realized belatedly that today was the day—the battle against Zathos. Smiling at Tayna as she rose to wake anyone else, I sent a thought to Honoras: *Come here, please.*

You must really have been out to ask me politely like that, he joked as he walked to me.

Just help me up, I said. He slid a talon underneath me and lifted me up, holding both talons around me until he was sure I could stand on my own.

Don't look down too quickly, he started, *but you need another shirt, I think.* As he said this, I looked down. Of course. I freaked out.

"What?—What . . . . no, no. No—"

Calm down, you're fine, Honoras started gently. I interrupted.

"I'm fine?! My shirt is soaked—with, with my—my . . . . blood!" I shrieked, attracting the attention of anyone within a hundred feet. Quickly Honoras curled up around me to hide me from their view, holding me against his side. I fought him, though it hurt, in an odd way. Like I wasn't used to moving.

"What. Happened. To. Me?" I asked through my teeth to keep myself from shaking, taking a breath at every pause.

You died, he said simply. My mouth flopped soundlessly. Honoras made good use of my silence and went on, *The lightning that Jacey held us with attacked our bodies. Geoff and everyone else killed him before it could kill us. Well, before they thought it could kill us. His life gone, we fell from where we were, and either Tayna or Dasriel caught us with their energy. You remember this. Ilian and Shaelynn went to you while Tayna and Dasriel went to me, I think. I do not remember—my mother has just told me. Anyhow, we were both unconscious. But you died. The electricity of the lightning was too much. Before Ilian could help, your heart gave out.*

Why aren't you dead then? If I die, you die too, right?

Yes, but there is a moment before the other dies from the one. It is before the soul has left the body. After that, the other dies, and there is no saving either one. But before that could happen, Ilian helped in the only way he possibly could—he plunged his horn through your heart and left the tip of it in there. It was his life he gave you. In doing that he should have died. His life would have been replaced by yours, and it was, but Shaelynn saved him. I'm not sure how—something about emotions. You'll have to ask her.

I nodded to let him know I understood. He waited until he was sure

I was calm before he snaked his head around. Reading his thoughts, I knew what was happening. The flashing pictures helped too.

He saw Shaelynn first, so he asked her to get a shirt, either from her pack, wherever it was, or if she could find mine. She understood the reason and left quickly. Ilian was standing, still a little shaky. He asked how I was doing, and Honoras told him that I had accepted what had happened.

Shaelynn came back and handed my pack to Honoras, who took it gently in his teeth. His head came around again to face me, and he dropped it on his leg in front of me. He opened a wing and closed it around me, to give me privacy. He kept his head in to watch me if I needed help. And I did—I couldn't pull the bloody shirt off without the hole in my chest twingeing painfully. Also, he held the clean shirt over my head so I could slip it on with my arms up. I didn't feel ashamed in the least. In fact, I was grateful.

Don't try and walk—get in my talon. If you move too much, that might start bleeding again. I did as asked, leaning back into his talon before he lifted me up in it. He didn't want to disturb anyone with the wind from his wings, so he hobbled on three legs to Tayna's tent while Shaelynn and Ilian followed. Apparently trying to heal my wound required a lot of caution, and Ilian had to be there to give instructions.

Tayna was already there. I knew she was. The pictures flashing through my head were driving me crazy, but they were useful. I could see Zathos's movements at this time, and at the same time, everything that was going on in camp or anywhere else. I knew Geoff was now sectioning everyone off as planned, and weapons were being handed out. Riman was helping with the weapons, as were Najee and his gang. Dasriel was in the tent with us. Marl was with the cavalry, and so was Shamar. Agathla was with the archers, in the back of the left section. Avinret was riding in between the black's ears, and Dush was on his back, looking scared. Marl went to him and said something; it sounded like whispers in my head, almost unable to hear, but I picked up bits and pieces. Dush seemed comforted, and a little calmer. In response, the black stood more alert. Gratefully, Dush leaned down to rub his shoulder. I smiled.

"Liz?" Tayna asked me. I had been staring off into space, smiling. I snapped to attention and laughed a little.

"Sorry. Sometimes the visions butt in and I can't help but see them."

"You will learn to control them," Ilian said. I nodded. Already I could tell I was: whenever I needed to concentrate on something else, like now, they were mere blurs in my mind's eye.

"All right," Tayna started, bringing everyone's attentions to her, "we need to patch you up, Liz. Ilian, how do we do it?"

"What I did left a piece of my horn in her heart. It cannot be closed in there, for it has feeling and cannot feel trapped. The wound must stay open in some way."

"Can we stop the bleeding, at least? Close off the exposed veins?"

"No. My horn is pure, and it has already started to heal the walls of the wound. That is why she has not bled to death already. It will stop bleeding soon. But nothing can get into the wound. As I said, my horn is pure, and that pureness is keeping her alive by keeping the wound healed. If anything gets in, it breaks the magic, I suppose you could call it, and anything that was holding the blood back will be gone. You must find a way to keep anything from getting in."

"Can I close the skin a little and leave only a portion of the size of the hole there? That will lessen the chance of something getting in."

"Yes. But be sure not to close it completely. When you have done that, I would suggest you wrap it, but be sure to change the dressings daily."

"All right, it sounds good. Liz, lay down there on my blankets. Can you relax a little?"

"Not really," I admitted. I was getting nervous over the whole thing.

I can help, Honoras said. *Dragon lullabies work for her all the time. Is it all right if she sleeps?*

"Yes, that would be best. Just be sure not to put us to sleep as well."

Aye. Don't worry; Elizabeth, just listen to my thoughts, okay?

Call me Liz, I reminded him playfully. Honoras chuckled and sang the lullaby in his head, trying not to hum or sing it aloud. As I listened, everything else was blocked out, and even the pictures eased down a lot. Soon I was asleep, but awake, in a way. I knew what was going on, but it didn't matter. It was just a blur to me.

My eyes were open, but they were just slits, as if they wanted to close but didn't at the same time. I saw Tayna and Dasriel stand side by side over me. At the same time, they held their hands out over me, and they began to glow. I was mesmerized by it. The awake part of me was laughing at myself while the asleep part didn't care. It was a weird mix. I could faintly hear Honoras laughing at me. I was irritated, but it didn't matter.

Something funny was happening to my chest. It tickled a little; no, it hurt now. It stopped. Ilian was talking; couldn't understand him. Started again, funny feeling . . .

Wake up, gliad. Wake up. We are done. Honoras was speaking softly in my head. Go away.

Elizabeth, wake up. More persistent. No.

Elizabeth. Something pushed me. What? I blearily opened my eyes. Honoras's head was staring at mine. My brain finally woke up.

Did it work? I sat up quickly, but he pushed me back down again. Slowly this time, I rose. He seemed satisfied and let me stay up.

Yes. We did as Ilian said, and you are better. Just be careful for now.

What went wrong? Something went wrong . . . I don't remember. I was delirious.

You were funny.

And you laughed at me, brat. What went wrong?

Tayna and Dasriel put their magic too far down and it almost broke Ilian's magic. They backed off, he explained it to them again, and they closed up the hole a little. On the surface, at least. Your dressings have been put on, and Ilian said to be careful with your movements.

Wait. When is the battle?

It has begun. We are fighting now.

What?!

Karbab changed our plans; everyone has left already. You and Shaelynn are our second biggest concern, so they went on without us. We are to catch up now.

How far from here are they? I stood up quickly, my wings out. He looked at me sternly, and I slowed my movements.

Not far. Those in the back are just outside. But the frontlines are a good way ahead.

Why aren't we out there then?

I was waiting on you. Do you feel all right?
I'm fine. You sound like my mother. Let's go. He quickly pulled his head out of the tent to let me out. My pack had been brought in, and my weapons as well. I quickly put on the armor given to me by the elves in Zaniel, but left the arm guards as I couldn't get them on alone. I pulled my quiver and my bow over my head, putting the extra arrows from the elves into it. I strapped their sword to my waist, wondering if they had come yet. I scanned the pictures flashing like mad through my head. Yes; they were in the back with the archers. They were doing well. Shaelynn and Ilian appeared with the cavalry, who were near the front but still out of the worst of the battle. They were fine.

Impatient, I blocked out the pictures and walked quickly outside. Honoras was waiting and put me up on his back without a word. He did not take to the air, but walked quickly to the throng of people gathered just fifty feet from the tent. We were on a small knoll, and from the top of it we could see the battle below.

It was amazing and horrible at the same time. I realized the vast number of people we had gathered, and the equal amount of beasts that fought for Zathos. In addition to his beasts, he had his own small cavalry and many foot soldiers. The three sections were blurred together as one mass of fighting bodies. Black phoenixes were in the air over the thick of the battle, dropping enormous stones and such on our men. Screams and wails of pain echoed up to even here. In the distance, the castle loomed on top of its rock mountain with steep cliffs. I knew Zathos was there, watching the battle gleefully. Avernus was in the back, directing the king's troops.

Elizabeth, check on all of our horses. Remember the plan, Honoras told me. Without answering I flung out my mind to the horses in our cavalry. A lot of them were skittish, but most were faithfully obeying their riders. I calmed the scared ones, and encouraged them all. They continued on bravely. I kept an eye on them, watching the battle at the same time. Things were going well, but not as well as we would have wanted. We were outnumbered, not by much, but just enough to tell. And Zathos knew this.

I left our cavalry alone for a while and sabotaged Zathos's instead. I scared his horses, though some of them were hard to shake. They had been trained well for battle, and were difficult to break. But break they did. They reared or bolted, taking down Zathos's cavalry from the inside. In under fifteen minutes, his cavalry had been crushed. The battle was turning around. And Zathos was angry.

He didn't know who had taken out his cavalry, but he needed to take out his anger on someone. Obviously, he turned on us. A wicked, massive bolt of lightning exploded from the castle, forking into a hundred smaller bolts. In an instant they had found their targets and killed them all. A hundred of our men were gone. The status quo had changed once more.

It was a good effort, Honoras put in, choosing his tone carefully. I wasn't paying attention, really. The lightning had gone right over our horses, and our cavalry was about to go the same way as Zathos's. Quickly I calmed the horses once more. But something was wrong. One of the horses was riderless, and was panicking. I opened my wings.

I had left my mind open to Honoras, and he had read my thoughts. *No. You won't go. Stay here.*

Watch me. Before he could do anything I had turned transparent and had launched myself off his back. One panicked horse could take out our cavalry. I couldn't calm him from where I had been, so I'd go to him.

On my way a black phoenix had been flying over our army, looking for the best spot to drop a round mass of burning brambles. Drawing my sword, I ran it through and let it drop with its ball of fire back over on Zathos's side. Wheeling back to our side, I quickly found the riderless horse. I landed on its back and turned visible at once, folding my wings in and grabbing the reins in one hand.

'I'm here,' I told him in horse, gripping my sword tightly and taking my place in the battle. 'Just keep us in formation and I'll take care of the rest.' Immediately he got back into his place. In between opponents, Shamar and I glanced at each other for a moment. He nodded to me, and then turned back to a new challenger. I did the same.

Things were not going well. I could not concentrate on so many things at once. I was fighting, keeping the horses calm, sorting through the pictures in my mind to see how the battle was going, and trying to keep my emotions in check while Honoras yelled at me to come back. The battle was not going well for us. Zathos's enslaved races included werewolves, basilisks, vampires, and such on the ground while griffins, latharks, and black phoenixes were in the air. All of them had been turned evil by him, and they were too much for our men. The battle was starting to play into his hands. We were losing, badly.

Many more of our horses were riderless, but others of our men had followed my example and had gotten on their backs. Hoping someone would do the same for my horse, I turned transparent and took flight. The horse started to panic once more, but someone quickly took my place. This was better. Now I could really focus.

Our men were falling, quickly. They were getting weary. Tayna must give us the signal, soon. Hoping she would, I flew back to Honoras, taking out as many flying enemies as was possible for me. My chest was starting to hurt.

I turned visible once I was close enough to him. He looked extremely worried until I appeared, and then he looked extremely irritated. *That was a dumb idea,* he told me angrily. I said nothing as I landed on the ground. Ignoring him, I focused on an idea I had had in the air. If I could get into the horse's heads, why not any of Zathos's creatures? I decided on a griffin. Finding one, I mind-spoke to it. But as soon as it heard my voice, trying to turn its attitude around, it blocked me out. It was like a machine; it didn't think, just went on with its instructions. I couldn't get past its defenses, nor any of the other creatures. It was like they had no minds. Which, considering Zathos's power, they probably didn't, at least not enough of one to think for themselves.

Finally, Tayna gave the order to us. Honoras lifted me to the saddle, and we immediately took flight. Wraetha and Shaelynn and Ilian were supposed to see us and finally take action as well. They did; Wraetha took flight at the right flank, and Ilian and Shaelynn plunged deeper into the battle on the left flank, going right up to the frontline. Honoras breathed fire on Zathos's front ranks, wiping out a lot of them. But every time we did, we were in range of their archers and had to quickly pull out. In turn, I fired my arrows upon them. Once we were blindsided by four latharks, but I killed one that went for me while Honoras took care of the rest. With all the sudden movements he made in the air fighting them, I was grateful for Wraetha's training.

I shot an arrow into the last lathark's throat and Honoras and I watched it fall for a moment, crushing one or two of Zathos's men. Like zombies, the rest were unfazed and stepped over their comrades' bodies and kept on fighting. Looking around quickly, I saw that our plan had worked. Seeing us in the air, everyone else's spirits had been lifted and they were fighting harder, better. The status quo was changing again, in our favor.

Honoras and I fought hard for a long time. Sometimes he would let me fly on my own, until he felt the twinge from my chest that signaled I had had enough, and then he would make me come back and sit in the saddle. But while I was in the air, both he and I could take on Zathos's flying creatures. Latharks I left to Honoras, but I could handle black phoenixes by myself and it took me a while on the griffins, but I got them all the same. The latharks kept Honoras busy, and so I feared for my life when an exceptionally large griffin swiped my arm, cutting it deeply, and then took another swipe at my head, but I barely missed it.

It was a good flyer, and could maneuver around me quite well. At the same time, it was a good fighter, and only my sword skills put me on top. Still, I grappled with it for some few minutes, trying to get Honoras to help me.

He's stronger than me, I need help!

Get him yourself, I'm busy enough—he grunted audibly, loud enough from a few hundred feet that I could hear him. A lathark had bit into one of his legs. His head dived down and he ripped it off of him by its neck. The force broke it, and the lathark hung limp in his teeth. He threw it with his head, taking out another lathark that was coming. Both fell into the mass of people below. Distracted, I almost got my head ripped off by the griffin. Like a bear, it had swung one of its hind lion's paws at my head, and would have batted it off had I not dropped quickly enough.

It reacted quickly, sinking down to my level. It launched itself forward, grabbing me with all four of its legs, digging claws into my skin. Its eagle head dived for my exposed throat. I wrenched my sword arm from its grasp and plunged it into its neck, stopping it immediately. But when it dropped, I did too. I almost couldn't break its vice-like grip on me. Fifty feet from the ground, I tore myself from it and back-winged to catch myself.

In the process I had shredded the backs of my arms and legs, which were stinging painfully in addition to all of Honoras's wounds. He sank his claws into one last lathark and let it fall before he turned his attention to me.

See, I knew you could do it. Now get back in the saddle. You're hurting.

I'm fine.

You won't be, not if you don't get on my back. Now. Scowling, I flew to him and landed in the saddle. As soon as I was in he dived, flinging open his wings at the last moment and gliding over Zathos's troops, breathing fire upon them. But they had been ready for us. The ones at the edge of his flames were ready, and at once they threw their spears at us.

His armor deflected most of them, and they bounced off harmlessly. I thought that all of them had missed until Honoras grunted and skipped a wingbeat, crashing into our ranks. People scattered, but regrouped when they saw Zathos's men rushing to attack us. They protected us from them. Pain was throbbing in my upper left leg. A spear protruded from just below Honoras's flank.

Hang on, and brace yourself, he warned me as he turned his body to inspect it. Then, he suddenly grabbed it and in the same motion pulled the spear out. The whole spearhead had been imbedded in his leg; now that he had pulled it out, it was dripping his blood. More of it oozed from the wound. My leg was searing with his pain. *It's deep, but I'll live,* he mumbled, standing with some pain.

Thank you all, he said to the people around us that were keeping Zathos's men at bay. Keeping his wings closed for the tight space, he leaped up into the air before he opened them to carry us up once more. *Not so low next time, I think,* he said lightly, trying to be sarcastic. But I could tell he had been scared, for himself and for me.

We fought for some time again, but our efforts weren't as energetic. The spear wound in Honoras's leg pained him, and he was losing blood, slowly but surely. Finally, we had to touch down at the back of the battle so Tayna could heal it. While we were on the ground, I scanned the flashing pictures. Everyone on our side was tiring while Zathos's army was getting stronger, the taste of victory driving them on. Soon we would lose.

Chapter 19

ZATHOS WAS SMILING FROM HIS place on one of his castle turrets. It had no walls on it and it went out from the castle the furthest, the better for his view. I could see him in every other picture that flashed through my mind. But then his smile faded. His eyes were looking far off in the distance. His face became pale.

An instant burst of pictures exploded in my head, flashing a million miles an hour, but I could still make them all out: dragons, centaurs, more people, elves, unicorns, red and brown phoenixes, hippogriffs, dwarves, and sorcerers and sorceresses. They were coming, from all directions, from all places. They were coming to help.

Thousands upon thousands of them came, those that could fly coming first, carrying passengers, and the faster runners coming on foot, but still keeping pace with the flyers. It was the dragons that I noticed most, as did Honoras, who seemed to be in shock.

The whole battle miraculously froze as everyone turned to see the newcomers. Zathos's army became fearful for the first time. They turned to flee, but Zathos's voice boomed over the silent battlefield: "FIGHT THEM YOU FOOLS! FIGHT!" Reluctantly they remained in position, though every one of them was quivering in fear.

A great cry of joy rose from our army before they turned back to the fight that had picked up again. Meanwhile, the newcomers had arrived. For the first time I noticed three groups of dragons: a small group of no more than ten from the south, most likely those that had been in hiding; a slightly bigger group than the first that must have been from Amatol; and a last, enormous group that had come from the north. It was unbelievable.

Wraetha had flown over from the right flank and had landed quite heavily close to us, as if she wasn't focused on what she was doing. Three dragons landed in front of us while the rest of them joined ranks and flew over the battle; there were bursts of fire over Zathos's army of every color imaginable.

The three dragons were fully grown, and two of them had riders, one of them carrying an extra person, whom I recognized as Yuriel, Wraetha's Bonded. He got off of a deep purple dragon, whose Rider was a woman who seemed no older than thirty. She dismounted as soon as Yuriel was out of the way, nimbly leaping down on to the ground.

A golden brown dragon was to my left. He was riderless, and was one of the few that had been in hiding all this time. The last dragon, one of a silvery gray color, was to my right. His rider was an elf, I could tell. He easily dismounted, and with a nod to his dragon, walked to me.

"You are Liz, new to Partaenia and youngest of the *Sorva di Fravid?*" he asked me. I nodded solemnly. He smiled. "It is good to meet you at last. You have been what we all were hoping for." He swept his hand in a wide half-circle, indicating everyone. And—he knelt in a bow in front of me. The three dragons did the same, as well as the other two riders. I was shocked.

"Liz, do you know who I am?" The elf asked. I shook my head. He smiled a little shyly, and then stood up straight. "I am Myritius, one of the first three *Sorva di Fravid*. I was the first elf to be Bonded to a dragon." My eyes widened.

"That can't be true—you defeated the evil force—that was thousands of years ago-"

"Sorvo has taught you, then," he said, smiling and looking at Honoras. Honoras, who had dipped his head in respect to Myritius, now lifted it to smile back.

She has learned much from me, but mostly she has done it by herself.

"A humble answer from a dragon I have heard to be quite the opposite." They smiled at each other again. Myritius turned to me once more. "There is someone else you should meet then, if you don't believe me." He looked to the woman rider and she came forward.

"Take a guess at who I am," she said with a smile. It was a bit annoying, especially after I couldn't give an answer. "I am the woman Anna, last Bonded to flee Partaenia. They nearly killed me driving me out, and my dragon and I fled to Amatol. Other dragons were there with their riders, and we started our own community, waiting for the day you would come." My jaw had dropped, and now I felt like I couldn't pick it back up again. Thankfully, Honoras did it for me.

Enough jabbering, he said, though I could tell he was trying to keep his joyful emotions inside him. *We can talk later. We have the battle to worry about now.*

The battle is over; our ranks have finished it, Anna's dragon pointed out.

No. There is something else that must be done. This time, it was Wraetha that spoke.

Everyone turned to her, but Myritius' dragon explained. *Zathos and Avernus are still powerful. If we have any hope of winning, they must be defeated.* Now, everyone was looking at me. I was irritated again.

"I know. I have to get rid of them."

No, both of us do, remember? Honoras said, his great yellow eye looking me over, inside and out. *You are ready.*

"Well then, get going," Myritius said, waving his arms at me to get on Honoras's back. There was something else he had meant to say, but I couldn't hear any more of it in his thoughts; he was keeping them hidden well. Now that I thought of it, I hadn't seen any flashing pictures since the last explosion of them when our help had come. I called on them, and they came back at full speed.

The battle was going well. Most of Zathos's army was dead, and our army was pulling back to let the dragons finish it. Our men were cheering. But then they stopped, and a vision became clear from the blurry mess.

Shaelynn and Ilian had disappeared when the help had come, and they had gone up the trail to the castle. Now they were at the top, and Ilian stopped to let Shaelynn off. Zathos was waiting at the top of the wall-less turret, a hungry expression on his face.

I could hear him sneering down at her, "You wish to fight me, weak human? You think yourself strong enough?"

"I know I can defeat you, evil bastard," she shot back. She pressed her hands to the ground. It immediately glowed bright, that Zathos had to cover his eyes for a moment. Shaelynn took the chance to create a wave of earth that carried her to the top of the turret. Zathos was waiting, and struck out with his magic as soon as she had touched it. She blocked it, sending back a strike of her own.

"No," I breathed, as the vision faded. Ignoring the staring faces, I opened my wings and launched myself off from the ground, calling over my shoulder to Honoras in dragon, 'Zathos and Shaelynn are at the castle. They're dueling!'

Calling on all my speed, I flew like a bullet to the castle, over the top of the whole battlefield, turning myself transparent as I went. I flew straight through the ranks of dragons, not worrying about my altitude, as long as I reached Shaelynn as fast as possible. I had tunnel vision; all I saw was them. Nothing else mattered.

Acting on instinct, not even thinking, I drew my sword and made to run him through at full speed. A blast of his magic knocked Shaelynn to the ground, and in the same instant he turned and looked straight at me. Panicking, I pulled up and hung in the air like an idiot.

He smiled. "Ah, *Fravid-Sorva*, come to save your kin? No worry; she will be taken care of as soon as I kill you." Enraged, I flew forward again, sword arm outstretched. It was there, aimed at his chest-

He waved his hand carelessly, blocking the sword with his energy and knocking it out of my hands. Then his other hand shot out, and closed around my throat. Shocked, I let the transparency fall as his grip tightened.

"Your transparency doesn't work for me," he sneered as ropes protruded from his fingers and bound me tightly. When they were done, he released his hand from my throat and I could breathe once more.

Out of the corner of my eye, I saw movement: Shaelynn was getting up from whatever blow she had taken. At the same time, the dragons arrived, hovering in the air, unsure. "One move," Zathos said, kneeling to pick up my sword from the ground. Standing, he aimed it at my middle. "One move from any of you, and I kill her."

Like you didn't have plans on it, Honoras spat.

"Yes, dragon, that's right. I have been planning this from the beginning, and I see my plans have come through. You see, I brought them here. I saw that Liz would Bond with a dragon if she came here. And so, I brought her. She nearly ruined my plans, but I manipulated her so that she played right into my hands. And now, I have her."

Honoras snarled and made to dive for Zathos, but he held up a hand that stopped him. "Be careful, dragon. That might have been your last move. Another will certainly be. Now listen. I have a story to tell, and I want everyone to hear it before they die." He said this mockingly, as if we were mere children. It made my blood boil, as well as everyone else's, I could tell.

"You see, this *Fravid-Sorva* here," he made the ropes tighten on me, so that I squirmed for breath, "escaped my spy. Three times. No matter. But then, she escaped me. And I still had no information of the whereabouts of the dragons. So, I planned a battle. I knew it would bring her to me, as well as the rest of the dragons." As he said this, he looked around at the dragons hovering in the air. They glared back.

While he was distracted, a stone had come flying at him. Not expecting it, it hit him full in the back of the head, so that his magic faltered and the ropes disappeared and released me. He fell to his knees, dazed. From behind him, Shaelynn said satisfactorily, "Yet you didn't plan on Ilian finding me. I'm the one that will defeat you!" She made to launch another stone at his head, but before she could Zathos had made two quick movements. The first was when he rose to his feet from the ground, the second a jabbing motion with his hand. A purple streak raced for Shaelynn but she waved a shield in front of her that blocked it. The two set in on each other, spells flying back and forth.

One of Shaelynn's spells missed Zathos and went flying to me. Intending to sidestep it, I stepped off the tower without realizing it. I was falling, but my wings snapped open to catch me. Angry, I made to fly back up and fight with Shaelynn, but a pair of talons closed around me, narrowly missing cutting my wings. The green scales told me it was Honoras. He was holding me, hovering below the tower, so that I couldn't see what was going on between Shaelynn and Zathos.

Honoras, let me go! I have to help her!

No. She was right. She is the one that is supposed to defeat him. It is an old prophecy, but I never told you.

Why? I was screaming in his head now. *Why didn't you tell me, I could have stopped her, fought him myself-*

That is why. You would be overprotective, and you would interfere.

No I-

Stop. And listen to me. I quieted, watching the flashes of light from the top of the tower. It was the only part of the fight that I could see.

Honoras went on carefully, *If she can defeat Zathos, the result will be a force so powerful that it will destroy this world. Shaelynn told you a long time ago that for Partaenia, it is the year 9999. This is the end of our time.*

What? No, it can't-

But it is. Now, listen. The power that Zathos has is more than any normal being, even a sorcerer, can hold. Even Avernus can only dream of that power. When it is released, it will bring about the destruction of this land. It will also create a rift in time. You and Shaelynn must enter it to go back to your world. I, or anyone else, cannot go.

No. I'll stay here then, if you can't come.

What, and be killed?

We will die together. And anyways, if you stay you'll die, and I'll be killed too, right?

No. Your time has little magic left, not enough to sustain even a relationship between Guide and Follower. That is why no mythical creatures exist. Once you are there, our Bond will exist no more, as well as the one between Shaelynn and Ilian. All you'll have is memories. If Shaelynn wins, Zathos will die in something like a supernova. The center of it will be the rift. I will fly you and Shaelynn into it, and you will return home. No arguments, all right?

Okay. I felt defeated. All of this, for nothing. I'll lose Honoras, Shaelynn will lose Ilian, and the rest of the world will never know this place existed. I almost felt like crying, but not now. Now, I hoped that Shaelynn would win, somehow.

I watched the flashes of light intently, hoping to be able to tell what was going on. But then, the pictures came back; I had been blocking them. I watched them instead of the tower. Shaelynn was on the ground, Zathos over her. She struck him, powerfully. He blocked it, but some of the magic seeped through his counter spell and it knocked him backwards.

They went back and forth like this, until they were both heaving for breath and using less of their energy in the spells. Finally, Shaelynn struck him with a spell that threw him backwards. I thought she had won until he leaped up and made the same jabbing motion he had used before that sent a streak of purple magic at her. It lifted her off the ground, spinning her in the air and taking her back to the edge of the wall on the other side.

She didn't move, and I feared he had killed her. Honoras, seeing the vision through my head, groaned. Zathos walked to her proudly, almost strutting, his hands folded behind his back. Suddenly, my sword flew to her hand from the ground and she plunged it through his heart, so that the tip protruded from his back. At the same time, some form of magic raced up the sword through her hands. Zathos's form wavered, and fell. An older man slumped to the ground, his hair light blonde instead of black, his brown eyes replaced by misty gray ones. His frame became smaller, and a wiry man lay on the ground, gasping for breath. Shaelynn's spell had broken Zathos's spell on himself. He had become Markus again.

She stood over him, disbelieving. I could hear what went on between them. Markus spoke quickly in between breaths, which were obviously paining him. I was surprised he was still alive.

He said to her, "Do it. I know you can. Destroy me, before he takes over once more. Do it now, while I am good."

Hesitating, she looked at him uncertainly. His hand grabbed hers and he pulled her down next to him. Closing her eyes, she placed her hands on him. His body began to glow, and it became brighter and brighter. I knew what she was doing.

As her mind mingled with his spirit, his body began to shine so bright that she had to turn her head away. At the same time, I could see the light from the tower. It seemed as if the sun were sitting there on top of it. Then, she took on his spirit, and his body seemed to explode and dissolve at the same time. Just as Honoras had explained, a ring of light flew out from his body. A ball of spinning matter was forming over the two of them. I guessed this was the rift. Immediately, Honoras launched himself forward.

Grab her wrists! he said as he glided over her. The ball was spinning faster now, and it was glowing white hot. More rings of light were reverberating from it. Shaelynn, barely awake, reached up to me. I grabbed her wrists, but almost let go when we jerked her skyward. The pull was instant, and I thought it would rip my arms from their sockets.

Honoras, talking to both of us, said, *I'm going to slingshot you toward the rift. As long as you fall into it, you'll be safe.* Just after he had said this, the talons holding me swung downward, and with a tremendous force, went forward again and let go of us. We flew for the ball of matter, hurtling toward it. Looking back, I saw Honoras watching me with a sad face. Shaelynn at the same time saw Ilian. Then, we hit the ball and sort of sank into it like a pool of gel. It was cool, like water. We saw the ball spinning around us, and then a huge ring of white light exploded from it, and Partaenia was no more as we raced through time.

Our world flew by us. Shaelynn and I couldn't help but watch as the world was destroyed, leaving no trace of any life. Water filled it, and then sank back down. Creatures appeared, then the dinosaurs. They disappeared, and man came. They grew, and learned. They lived with the environment, and spread out over the world. Finally, Shaelynn and I couldn't watch, and instead we held each other close, our faces buried in each other's shoulders.

Then, the matter around us disappeared, and the spinning stopped. Looking up, I saw that we were sitting on Shaelynn's bed, just as we were six and a half months ago when we left. But it was morning now. It seemed as if only a night had gone by. Dumbstruck, we went through the motions of getting dressed, as we would have before we went to Partaenia. As soon as we had hidden the clothes we had worn there, Caden knocked and opened the door at the same time. He smiled at us, and we gave our best smiles back.

We didn't talk of Partaenia for a while. We told no one, and kept it to ourselves. But we still noticed the differences in each other. I had lost the bracelet, as well as my two Gifts and Ilian's flashing pictures. I even checked my chest, and there was no hole through my heart. I wasn't even sure if the tip of his horn was still in there, or how I was still alive. As for Shaelynn, she had lost her magic. Honoras had been right: there wasn't enough here to sustain out talents.

Partaenia had changed us as well. Both Shaelynn and I felt lost without Honoras or Ilian, but Shaelynn was worse off than me. I was getting better, but she seemed to be going downhill. Honoras told me that the bond between unicorn and human was like lovers. They couldn't be without the other for long.

But finally, after three months of pretending to be fine, we had to meet each other upstairs after church. Shaelynn was the one that gave out first, bursting out with tears and blubbering on my shoulder. I held her, knowing how she felt. Finally, she was done, as was I. We sat down on one of the couches, and she told me what had happened on the tower before Partaenia was destroyed.

Zathos was created when Markus performed a spell wrong, trying to gain more power. The other person took him over, and he was trapped inside himself while Zathos took hold of Partaenia. But he learned that he could influence certain things that Zathos did, if he did it right.

So Markus, using some of that power briefly, foresaw one of us from us from the future destroying Zathos and setting him free. So, to get Zathos to send us there, he told him that we were going to destroy him, but if he brought us there he could destroy us first.

Originally, he had his eyes on me. It was really Shaelynn, and she came on accident. I was supposed to read the spell by myself, not with her. So through Zathos, Markus brought me to Partaenia, to kill Zathos. But once Markus saw Shaelynn fighting Zathos, he knew it was her and started to weaken Zathos from inside him. That was how she had won.

When Shaelynn took on Markus' spirit, she knew all of this as if it were one of her memories, she said. But it was only of Markus, so I think she was safe from being taken over by Zathos.

There was something else, she said, that Markus knew was going to happen, but he was keeping it hidden from her, somehow. Every time she tried to get it, she got a feeling that she would know in time.

When she was done talking, and we told each other everything we knew about our time in Partaenia. It was past lunch, and so we left to our homes. Once more we forgot Partaenia for a while.

Shaelynn was at one of the malls in Albuquerque with her family, walking from store to store, bored and depressed as usual. Her mom, Teri, stopped at a clothes rack outside a department store, talking about the shirts, but she was talking to herself because Shaelynn wasn't listening. The feeling of sadness and depression had suddenly lifted. Looking around wildly, she saw a tall man her age walking straight to her. He had dark blonde hair that fell over his eyes, and stunning blue eyes. His smile was perfect, as was everything else about him.

"Hey there," he said, stopping just in front of her, "Shaelynn, redeemer of the magical world."

"Ilian!" She threw her arms around him, and for the first time, kissed him. It was electrifying. They pulled apart, and she asked breathlessly, "How did you get here?"

"Like I said, you saved us. The magical world can exist now, in the same world as this one. We are in hiding for now, but you and I will help."

"But— .... How are you human?"

"I chose to be. Once I have found a Guide and we have completed what we were supposed to, I can become human to suit you. If we have a child, that will be the next unicorn, and the cycle continues. It is how we are."

"Shaelynn, who is this?" Teri had come over. Ilian bowed to her slightly, smiling.

"Mom," Shaelynn said, looking from Ilian to her, "This is Ilian. He's a new boyfriend; I met him a while ago, and he's finally back from a long trip." Shaelynn's mom smiled and shook his hand.

"It's nice to meet you, Ilian. I'm glad you came back, because this is the happiest she's been in months." He smiled, and she went back to shopping while they enjoyed each other's company.

At the same time, the flashing pictures appeared again, and I saw what happened. I was camping in the mountains, and it was a good thing I was alone, because the pictures suddenly burst into my head and they nearly knocked me over.

I was on my usual morning walk that I take when I go camping, and I couldn't believe it when I heard wingbeats. Instantly the forest around me awoke with thoughts and actions, and my wings sprouted from my back. They were cramped underneath my sweater, so I took it off and spread them out. Above me, the wingbeats grew louder and any animals in the area fled. A mass of shimmering green scales landed heavily in front of me. I smiled.

Honoras!

It is good to see you, my gliad.

How-

Remember the spell on the bracelet? It was like instructions for you. When you two did what it said, it brought you home and destroyed the time difference. The two worlds have been united! We live and thrive here now.

Honoras? I asked carefully. He noted my change of tone and gestured for me to speak. *Would you like to go flying?* I asked with a grin. He smiled happily and launched himself into the air, and I was right on his tail. The wind in my feathers and the weightlessness of flying brought it all back, and I closed my eyes as I did a loop in the air. Honoras laughed, and I opened my eyes.

Wraetha and Yuriel were waiting, both of them smiling. Far across the endless mountains, other dragons were flying through the air. I saw Myritius on his silver-gray dragon, as well as Anna on her purple dragon. They beckoned and we went to them, flying and diving and twisting gracefully in the air. Finally, I felt at home and happy, flying with the dragons.